ELECTION
2064

Scott McDermott

For Jenny,
who makes me
want to be
my best me

2060 Presidential Election Results

Ticket	League	Votes	Electoral College
Acton Granger[*] *(no running mate)*	Reformation League	54,297,115	**272**
Elijah Schroeder[**] John McNamara	Conservative League	46,222,867	**204**
Christopher Wilson Emily Shapiro	Freedom League	37,665,158	**134**
Aiden Ellis Juan-Manuel Ramirez	Progressive League	31,127,955	**22**
Brandon Thomas Christine Young	Values League	5,549,126	**3**
Amber Townsend Shadid Rabazz	Urban League	2,743,568	**3**
Adam Villanueva Rebekkah Sloan	Social League	1,645,639	**-**
Other	Misc.	901,138	**-**

[*] Elected President [**] Selected Vice President

Scott McDermott

PROLOGUE

April 14, 2063

Loop. Around. Under. Through.

The knitting needles flashed in her hands, throwing off metallic jangles with every stitch. The only other sounds in the room came from the regular pings of the heart monitor and the less steady *whoosh* of the respirator pump. Her husband's chest rose and fell as the oxygen fed into him.

Loop. Around. Under. Through.

The blanket was coming along slowly. When she was really humming, she could do forty rows an hour. Right now she was barely managing half that, but it kept her hands steady and her mind occupied.

A cough seized him. She dropped a needle and took his hand, feeling the convulsions through his limp fingers. She massaged his palm, reflexively checking his pulse as it settled back to normal resting.

"Bear," she whispered. "Come back to me."

But he remained unresponsive. The monitor resumed its pinging drumbeat, the PanoScreen on the far wall dimming its glow. Another screen cocooned around his chest, projecting his vitals in a softly luminescent holo. She stroked his hair and leaned in, brushing a kiss on his temple for what felt like the millionth time.

Her Bear looked smaller already, as if the hospital bed was swallowing him at the edges, but he was still a giant of a man. She let out a quiet sigh, picked up her dropped needle, and resumed working. He might already have plenty of blankets, they draped over his body in cascading layers – but she felt he needed this one to truly be warm. Because it came from her.

Loop. Around. Under. Through.

My husband might die at any moment, and all I can do is tie a bunch of knots.

As her fingers maneuvered the yarn, turning it around and back again – repeating, repeating – she felt the repeating of their lives. All of this was unnervingly similar to the time she met this sleeping giant, three decades ago. It felt like yesterday, in that she could still picture every detail of his face when she first laid eyes on it, and twenty lifetimes ago, in how that face had aged. But governing will do that.

And the circumstances between now and then, though mirrored in setting, had their differences. Then, the hospital didn't block off an entire floor for this single patient.

No, then he was just a kid who'd run into some hard luck (though, considering what could have been, he was lucky indeed). Another casualty of conflict, bouncing around the convoluted bureaucracy of the VA before finding his way to the Long-Term Recovery Ward. She almost forgot what war he'd been wounded in.

But she remembered that day, clear as noontime sun. She even recalled the thoughts going through her mind, as if she could pluck them like grapes from a vine – the first thought being, *How could someone that immense ever get wounded?*

And how he'd smiled at her from his hospital bed, sipping groggily out of a milk carton. "Ma'am, I got shot in the ass," he said, as if to answer her thought. A morphine drip may have slurred his speech, but it put him in a breezy mood. "You gonna fix me?"

Her second thought was, *Handsome, probably, when not doped up.*

"Fortunately," she responded, "the backside is an alright place to take a bullet, considering. My guess is, whoever shot you couldn't reach your head. Is the army growing soldiers in labs now, or are they breeding you with grizzly bears?"

He gave a mock bear's roar, clawing the air – then began to laugh, a gurgle of spittle escaping his mouth. Her toes inched toward him, as if she was drawn in by his gravity – a stray comet, chancing upon a star, finding orbit.

"I'm just a little larger than most," he said. "Growing up, everyone was telling me to play football."

"Maybe if you had, you wouldn't have taken a bullet in the butt."

"Ain't that the truth. I coulda been a contendah!" It was a truly terrible Brando, but he flashed that cocky smile like a reflex as he pulled another swig from his milk straw. *So he likes old movies*, she thought. *Maybe there's some depth to all that mass.*

"Doctor, um, what do I call you?"

Her thoughts became disconnected; relay runners dropping the baton. *Did I forget to say my name? Did I forget my name?*

"Oh...well, I'm Dr. Harper." His smile never wavered, even if the morphine rendered it askew. It was the smile that sank her, right then, and she offered a proposition rarely extended a new patient: "But you can call me Susannah."

Feeling awkward for putting that out there, she pulled back. "Or just, you know, Doctor," she said. "Doctor Susannah might work, too, I suppose."

Now she was floundering. What was happening to her? *Professional, professional*, she thought, trying to calm butterflies she never knew she had.

He held out his hand. It was coarse and heavy like a cinderblock, but warm. "Corporal Granger. You can call me Acton. You can remember that because if there's a problem, I'll *act on* it."

Something foreign escaped her. *Did I just giggle?* She hadn't giggled since junior high. "You know that's horrible, right? You should never use that line on a woman ever again."

Neither of them realized it at this point, but he wouldn't have to.

"Yeah, probably," he said. "But I bet now you'll remember my name." Susannah realized that her hand was still in his and yanked it away, too quickly. "Well, Doctor Susannah," he said, looking up from his own fingers, "I'd say it's a pleasure to meet you, but I have a feeling that before we're done here I'm not going to like you very much."

And he was right about that, for a while.

It didn't take her long to see why football wasn't an option – or any other sport, for that matter. He got around easily enough for someone his size, especially with shrapnel ringing down his left gluteus and iliotibial tract, but in the rehab room he was an oaf. All that muscle, and so little coordination.

The first few weeks were hard. They called each other every name in the book, and a few that weren't.

She wondered now, looking to pinpoint the moment those grueling, combative rehab sessions became something more – and beyond that, when he told her he loved her, that he needed her to push him the rest of his days, or he'd be worthless – whether both their lives would be in very different places if he'd been born with just a little more coordination and picked up a football like everyone in his hometown expected.

Would they have met? Unlikely, unless you placed heavy bets on fate and fairytales. Would he have accomplished all he'd done without her? She doubted it, and though that felt self-important, it was probably true. Sometimes a star needed something to shine on to feel whole.

Susannah always assumed that if he'd had a shred of athleticism to match his bulk, maybe he would've retired from a nice, short career as an offensive lineman and gone back home to marry his high school sweetheart. But she had no idea that the goofy-grinned army man had bigger dreams. And he kept those dreams hidden for some time, as was his nature, until he trusted her enough to pick out a ring and offer his name.

He finally came clean on their honeymoon, as they slurped umbrella drinks poolside in Key West. It took a half-dozen Rum Runners to spill it. And it all sounded innocent enough – he wanted to try his hand at local politics, as a State Representative. In North Dakota, the races weren't especially competitive, and a seat had opened where he thought just about anyone could win.

Susannah didn't know it at the time, but the rest of their lives hinged on her response. *Of course*, she'd said, without hesitation. *It's perfect for you.* And he'd smiled again, the smile that she came to live for (turned out, it wasn't the morphine that made it crooked, it was just *like that*).

All right, I'm gonna do it! he said. And that was it – they'd flicked over the first domino of Acton Granger's political career. On and up he went, from one elected office to the next, toppling each new domino with a mixture of opportunism, fortune, and a loving wife's unique blend of encouragement and sacrifice.

Now, three decades later, here they were. They'd reached the end of the chain and toppled the biggest domino of them all, but some unknown force had exacted its price. Was it worth it, if his life was to be cut short like this?

Susannah's brain spun wildly. All the *what-ifs* swarmed like bees in her mind. Where would *her* life be, if in another strand of history she never crossed paths with this man? Was it even worth pondering?

She checked the time – dawn approached, and with it the doctors and nurses and aides and minders and hangers-on would sweep back into another whirlwind of a day.

Adding to the whirlwind – at eleven sharp, the Acting President was scheduled to visit, and Susannah didn't even know where to begin with *that*. The media had deemed the nation to be in crisis, and it appeared they were finally right about something.

She went back to her needlework, practiced hands resuming repetitive motion. She tried to empty her thoughts, to find her center. As her mind settled, her heart continued chugging – the rhythm of *willhemakeitwillhemakeit* pulsing in each beat, and it would not quiet, no matter her meditations.

Acton Granger was her beloved, and though she shared that love with all the millions that adored and revered the 54th President of the United States, she was the only one that shared his name.

She'd had two days and nights to absorb the shock of what had befallen her husband and brought them to this hospital room, but a new feeling brewed inside her. After the sorrow, the worry, the hope, the anger, and the fear, what came now was need, a need for answers. And it was a feeling no amount of knitting could quiet.

Loop. Around...
Who?
Why?

Scott McDermott

Book One

Getting In and Falling Out

October 9, 2062-April 14, 2063

CHAPTER ONE

"You may have noticed that I come to this distinguished convention without nominating a vice president. I am sure most in this League would prefer that I not take this step; they'd prefer I find someone of like mind and like beliefs and deem them my running mate and my successor. But this country is a house divided – with a divide so vast that no single League can bridge it by itself. With that in mind, should I prevail in this election, in the tradition of Washington and Adams, I promise the second-highest office to whomever my chief opponent may be. Only then might we become a nation united once again."
  - Acton Granger, acceptance speech for the 2060 Reformation League nomination – July 24, 2060

The motorcade wound through traffic in the suburban Chicago flatlands.

It was a smaller procession than Elijah Schroeder was used to – protocol required the vice president have a police escort of at least four marked vehicles and multiple advance teams, to seal off upcoming intersections and on-ramps – not to mention the Secret Service and intelligence details. But for this trip, he just had one unmarked SUV in front and behind him, and he scrapped the limo for a less conspicuous (if no less armored) passenger van.

Feels good to get away, he thought.

In fact, it had been years since Elijah had ridden in a vehicle that actually shared a road with anyone not in his escort. He'd left his handheld pano back with Cassidy, and felt an acute anxiety without the do-everything device on his person, but busied himself observing other vehicles and their occupants through heavily tinted glass. As he watched, curiosity budding, he tried to recall the last time a stranger within a few feet of him hadn't been pre-occupied, above anything else, with being in the presence of a national political figure.

Truth was, he reveled in this opportunity to observe natural human behavior. It was like scratching a voyeuristic tickle he forgot he had.

Before the Second Civil War, most cars on the road operated without human drivers. Known as Autonomous Vehicles (or AVs), they'd become almost universal, until an enterprising member of the Underground discovered that an AV made for a useful remote bomb. The government hastily passed an AV Prohibition, pulling all but human-ops off the road. As the war faded into history, the Granger administration scrapped the ban as their first executive order and AVs were making a comeback.

The vice president entertained himself by watching the new automateds integrate with the remaining human-ops. When he used to make his living as a professor of economics, Elijah would actively monitor episodes in human interaction to understand basic motivational behavior. He'd sit outside a coffee shop, for instance, watching who would hold the door open for others versus who would not. What was economics if not the study of altruism, people weighing the common good against their own wants and needs?

Most would find observing such routines implacably dull, to be sure, about as exciting as staring into a fishbowl. But Elijah remembered an old saying from one of his professors – in mathematics you might solve for y, but in economics you solved for *why*.

There are two types of people in the world – those who use a turn signal, and those who don't.

The left lane opened up ahead. Elijah saw this as an altruism at work – for the middle lane vehicles in front of them, traffic in the left lane would now be faster, thus worth the inherent risk of occupying it. This might even hold if more than one vehicle went for the faster lane. Sure enough, two cars pushed hard into the open lane, but one had cut the other off. The two jockeyed for position, swerving this way and that – but in doing so, they lost speed, and one almost veered into the motorcade.

The irony, Elijah considered as the motorcade passed them by, was that if one car had let the other take the left lane and stayed in the middle, both lanes would've moved faster. AVs didn't have this problem.

Exiting onto Route 14, the motorcade transitioned from a stacked multi-level highway to a flat road, dotted with industrial parks and the occasional neighborhood. A string of trees framed the road on both sides, their leaves altered by the season to a menagerie of fall colors.

Elijah looked behind him, and through miles of film and haze he could still make out the skyline of downtown Chicago. For the most part, it still consisted of vacant skyscrapers with crumbling edifices. The Second Civil War – Civ-2, as it was widely known – had been hard on Chicago, but he saw signs of encouragement.

Six, no, seven construction cranes, he counted, their perpendicular silhouettes rising in the distance. *It's a start.*

The motorcade took another turn, this time onto a driveway and through a security gate that opened at their proximity. They coursed down a winding stream of asphalt that plunged into a thicket of trees, their leafy branches brushing the sides of Elijah's van. The foliage was so thick the sun only peeked through in spots, blinking on and off like a strobe. Disoriented, Elijah turned his eyes ahead.

Eventually the forest-tunnel opened into a small, nearly-vacant parking lot, dwarfed by an enormous building just beyond, hundreds of yards in width.

The caravan filed into a roundabout at the building's entrance as a man and a woman awaited them, next to a non-descript sign that read **Endure Technologies**. Elijah drummed his fingers on his thigh as the van parked. The driver came around to open the door, now assuming the role of the vice president's protecting agent. Though the sky was cloudless with rain in the forecast, the agent held an umbrella over Elijah's head as he disembarked.

Can't be too careful, Elijah thought. *Goddamn drones everywhere.*

Buttoning his coat, the vice president walked over to meet his welcome party. Yannik Vogel was tall and slender like Elijah himself, wearing a crisp black suit with a red bowtie. His face exhibited pronounced European features and though he had just celebrated his hundredth birthday, he appeared more like a man of some indeterminate middle age. As Elijah appraised Vogel closely, he could discern the handiwork of multiple reconstructive operations, a vibrant exterior stretched over something more ancient on the inside. Elijah noticed Vogel wore tinted enhancement glasses, the new ones with a two-mile range, probably to keep tabs on his motorcade as it approached.

The woman was just an inch or two shorter, her hair tucked in a ballerina bun so tight her forehead looked pained. Unlike Vogel, someone Elijah recognized instantly (but had never met in person), the woman was unknown to him. She appeared slightly younger than Elijah's mid-forties, and no surgical procedures appeared to fudge her age. Though a lab coat concealed her figure, Elijah would've recognized through a potato sack the flattering shape underneath. She seemed to catch his gaze and adjusted her sunglasses uncomfortably, clutching at a PanoPad.

Vogel rushed up to take Elijah's hand. "Mr. Vice President." His voice contained enough of a Germanic accent that his syllables ran together – *Meesterveizprezheedent*, pronounced in one long word.

"Thank you, Mr. Vogel. Great to finally meet you in person."

Vogel removed his enhancement glasses, revealing startlingly white-blue eyes – wagon wheels with icicles for spokes, sparkling like diamonds in his skull. "Welcome to Endure," he said. "We appreciate your efforts to be here."

"It's not every day I pull out my tracking chip and go off the grid. The chip is safe with my wife – Cassidy went straight from the airport to the fundraiser, just as you recommended."

"We value your...discretion." Vogel occasionally paused in his speech as he searched for the proper English. "As I said in earlier...communications, I prefer our mutual friend not know we are meeting, at least at this time. I promise, we will make this visit brief so you can return to your duties." Vogel turned to the woman in the lab coat. "My companion is Dr. Meijer, our head of research. She will answer any of your questions."

"A pleasure," Elijah said. Dr. Meijer nodded in his direction, but held on to her PanoPad without offering a hand.

Elijah glanced at Vogel, as if to ask, *She's ok?* The German only offered a tight-lipped smile in return, then clapped his hands. "Well! Let us get right to it. Mr. Vice President, if you would follow us inside."

Elijah's protection agent handed over his umbrella and stepped forward silently.

"If you'll humor us," Elijah said, "he'll want to go in first and check the place out."

"Of course," Vogel said, opening the door. "We will be walking through the lobby, and then you may scout the rest as we proceed."

The agent walked through and disappeared for some minutes before reemerging with a nod. He took Elijah's umbrella and folded it away, then held the door.

Elijah stepped through the threshold into the building. He saw Dr. Meijer pull down her sunglasses, revealing the same diamond eyes as Vogel, white-blue irises that were nearly blinding.

"Oh," Elijah said, "Are the two of you related? I didn't realize."

"Dr. Meijer is my granddaughter, yes. Ours is a family business."

"That's quite a gene. Does it run through the whole family?"

"It is referred to as Waardenburg Syndrome, but we do not consider it some kind of...illness. It is genetic, as you say – the white part around the eye turns blue and the pupils become very bright. It is quite rare, but every Vogel is born with it, as far back as anyone can remember. My wife used to joke how easy it was to find our children in a crowd, and it always made for interesting family photos."

Elijah chuckled. "I'm sure."

They stood in a foyer as ornately decorated as the building's exterior was plain. A crystal chandelier dominated the space overhead, enormous but delicate. It refracted light and color in all directions, spilling millions of fractals onto the manicured arboretum (complete with hybrid orchids and other engineered botanicals), and highlighting the lavish modern art pieces that lined walls of grained marble. Elijah caught a glimpse of something darting around his feet before he realized the floor was transparent, exotic fish streaming underneath.

"An in-ground aquarium?" Elijah mused. "Business is good."

"These have been prosperous years of late," Vogel admitted. "But most of the...glitz and glamour is confined to this space. Our visitors typically remain in the lobby area, but as an honored guest, you get to see the whole dog and pony show."

Vogel took the lead, transforming into a tour guide. He gestured toward an area opposite the garden, a few lush chairs retreating into a dim hallway. "Some conference rooms and offices off that way, nothing exciting. Everything else is through here."

He walked them through the arboretum, complete with flittering rare butterflies, and past an empty reception desk. A door stood embedded in the wall, fitted so neatly that Elijah barely noticed it. His protective agent stepped forward a second time to scout ahead, this time returning in just seconds. He affirmed the environment ahead was safe and they stepped into a hallway, walking past the faint hum of a server room before arriving at another door.

This door was of brushed steel and appeared monstrously heavy, as if to a bank vault. Upon their approach, a robotic arm emerged above where the knob might be, holding what looked like a foam sponge between two pincers.

Vogel pulled the sponge out and bit into it, making an impression with his teeth. He handed it back to the robot arm, which retracted back into the door.

After a positive buzz of identity confirmation, the door slid open. Elijah's agent stepped forward.

Vogel coughed nervously. "Ahem, I would actually rather not have someone in there unsupervised. I assure you, nothing in there is dangerous, you have my word."

The agent didn't take his eyes off Vogel, but spoke to Elijah. "Sir, I strongly caution against entering the premises without my checking them in advance."

"It's all right, this man is President Granger's Sponsor. If you worked with the president during the campaign, you should know him well."

Vogel interjected, "I would like to say I am the president's friend first, Sponsor second."

"Either way," Elijah reassured, "I'm sure whatever's beyond that door doesn't pose any harm." The agent protested, but in these situations the protectee had the final say, if they insisted forcefully enough. Elijah patted his guardian on the arm as he filed past.

Once through the door, he found himself on a catwalk overlooking a sunken floor. The catwalk branched out every forty feet or so, forming an elevated lattice pattern throughout, the occasional staircase spanning down to the bottom. On the floor, rows upon rows of steel cylinders stood like miniature grain silos, each about two feet in diameter and eight feet tall. They numbered in the thousands – no wonder this building looked so enormous on the outside! At about eye level, each cylinder featured a translucent window the size of a PanoPad, a pulsating light flashing from within – red, then blue, then white – all in unison.

"Holy smokes," Elijah said. "What is all this?"

Vogel offered a polite smile that looked strained on his reconstructed features. He led the vice president down a staircase and to the first cluster of cylinders, arranged in a ten-by-ten grid. Above this grouping hung a placard from the ceiling: *Females, 19-21, Caucasian*. Similar placards hovered over neighboring clusters, with labels like *Males, 36-40, Hispanic*; *Females, 61-65, African-American.* And so on.

Elijah couldn't help himself – he leaned in for a peek through the window of the nearest silo and touched the surface. "Why isn't it cold?" he asked.

"We do not freeze them," Vogel said, but he left it at that.

Elijah peered in further, looking for the light source inside – a PanoScreen, positioned a few inches in front of the face.

"That is Amber," Vogel said. "She appreciates a clever advertising jingle, enjoys Christmas movies, and has a...soft spot for anything with cats. Sad to say, in this last election you had very little chance with her."

"College females weren't my best demographic. Except maybe econ majors."

Dr. Meijer stepped forward. "Grandfather, you know we shouldn't linger down here."

"Of course. We don't want to disturb anyone's sequencing. Elijah, follow us, please."

After a tour around the catwalk and a look at the data center, Vogel, Dr. Meijer, and Elijah sat in a conference room with the agent begrudgingly waiting outside – after he'd been allowed to case the room first.

Vogel rattled at some controls and the room's four walls went full pano as he cycled through environments. "Which would you prefer: *Spring Meadow, Caribbean Cabana*? Something else?"

"Anything is fine."

"Oh! You'll like this one. *Coney Island*. Feels like home, no?" A boardwalk spanned the wall to Elijah's left, with Coney Island's famous amusement-park landscape beyond it. It felt like being there, so much that he could almost smell the cotton candy. The resolution was astounding. To his right was the beach, the water of New York's Lower Bay spilling out to the ocean, reflecting a sun-brightened sky.

Vogel stood up and poured himself an espresso. "Now that you have seen our little facility, some history. Many decades ago, before your long period of civil...unrest, Endure Technologies was created for persons suffering from the bovine flu. Those infected looked to preserve their bodies in a cryogenic state until a cure could be found. As the flu became an epidemic, Endure's owners were overwhelmed by the demand. They became victims of their own success – the maintenance cost for each cryogenic unit was...extensive. They were losing millions of dollars a day. Then the war began, and a new problem – many of Endure's subjects lost their next of kin, so their bills were no longer being paid. The company faced bankruptcy and the unfortunate...consequence of being forced to release these subjects. But the flu still had no cure, and that meant a death sentence for anyone in here."

Vogel sat back down, sipping his espresso. "What an opportunity! When I was much...younger, I looked far and wide for a facility like this for my research. Thousands of people, from all walks of life and every state in the union – except for maybe a couple of the newer ones. This," he gestured back beyond the security door, which now happened to be the Coney Island Wonder Wheel, "is now the best neuromarketing research facility in all the world."

"And what is neuromarketing, exactly?" Since seeing the silos, Elijah found it hard to contain his brimming interest, but Vogel apparently wanted to walk him through every detail.

"I will get to that in a moment, but know this. Surveys, focus groups, polling – all of it is useless. In those studies, there is bias. You cannot get around it. The waking mind...interferes. Whenever you see something and decide whether you like that something or not, noise gets in the way. Whether you think your spouse or friends will also like it, whether you had a good experience with something similar, perhaps even what you had for breakfast or the last song you listened to. And there is always that voice in the back of your mind telling you how you *should* feel. All of those factors influence your decision, and it makes a mess. What we do is turn off the noise. To register accurate opinions, we remove the conscious mind and focus on cognitive reactions at their most basic."

As Dr. Meijer tapped away at her PanoPad, Vogel smiled and resumed his history. "So, I purchased this facility and moved it in a new direction – not just preserving these...specimens until they might be cured, but utilizing them while we have them, applying their shared knowledge and testing their reactions to stimuli. I also got rid of all those expensive cryogenics as you mentioned – we found another way. This gave birth to neuromarketing. And what a success it has been! We test messaging, branding, product placement. Businesses consult us to know what drives a person to prefer one type of soda, toothpaste, vehicle, what have you."

"So, like a subconscious focus group?"

"Precisely! Then, a short time ago, a new phase. It

was...accidental, if I am being honest. We had no intention of getting involved in electoral politics until someone approached us, working for a relatively unknown presidential candidate from North Dakota. I met this candidate, and I decided to become his Sponsor. And we put the full weight of what Endure can do behind him."

Schroeder remembered hearing whispers during the campaign, that Granger had some sort of technological ace in the hole, but his sources were never close to sniffing it out. Though sponsorships were not required to be publicly disclosed, Vogel was not shy with his support, but how his business operated and how it assisted the campaign were both guarded secrets.

Even now, after touring the building and hearing Vogel's initial summary, he still wasn't sure what went on here.

Elijah hoped the German was getting to the point, but after only knowing the man for an hour he sensed a penchant for theatrics. Vogel was still winding up, the pitch was yet to come. "Our subjects may have been confined in isolation for thirty years, but with our special incubation, their brains never age. We discovered that for the best response data, they needed to eat – not food, but a diet of information. We keep their PanoScreens active around the clock to keep them abreast of national events. Tastes can shift depending on the cultural mood. For instance, as the war ended, there was a...seismic change, a yearning for unity above all else."

That appeared to be Dr. Meijer's cue. She set her PanoPad on the conference room table and pulled at its corners, stretching it wide and flat. The vistas of Coney Island dimmed around them. Meijer used a nimble set of hand gestures and vocal commands to activate a holo display, hovering above the stretched pano. The holo showed a diagram of the human brain, divided into quadrants. Some statistics and other figures flashed below the diagram that Elijah could not decipher.

"This is a file for one of our subjects," Vogel said. "He is a forty-three-year-old pipefitter from... South Alassippi, it's called now? Let's call him Mark. The file is from May of 2060."

Elijah thought backward to the campaign season. May would've been toward the end of the primaries, two months before the conventions. With their League nominations wrapped up, the remaining candidates would be plotting their strategies for winning a general election. Granger had won the Reformation nomination easily, while Elijah's campaign had slogged through a bruising primary to limp away as the nominee of the Conservative League.

Next to the brain diagram, a video appeared – one of Granger's old campaign ads. Candidate Granger loomed large in the foreground, surrounded by a dense forest of elm trees in his native Dakota environment. Meijer dragged a thumb across the timeline, fast-forwarding the ad. The brain diagram flashed different shades of color as the video moved forward, mostly confined to the area marked *Frontal Lobe*. Meijer zoomed in on that area, magnified enough that it resembled a maze of clotted spider webs.

She pointed to some of the starker colors. "Sequences are monitored using a blue-red spectrum, which show whether the different processing centers react positively or negatively."

Vogel interjected, "It shows us if they like what they see."

Dr. Meijer pushed the Play button, and the ad moved in real time along with the neurological readouts. "At this point in time, our pipefitter's brain is reacting to the test ad. We can show hundreds of ads with various differences to find the most effective. This version performed rather well – you can see how the blue starts to overtake the red as Mark connects emotionally to Granger's inspirational message."

Elijah thought he recognized the ad – the future president was either flaunting his salt-of-the-earth background or his service in the Yemeni War. Mark's frontal lobe reacted with splotches of blue in several places.

"Each highlighted area," Dr. Meijer pointed out, "is a connection to different qualities – trust, strength, and so forth. In this frame, Mark is connecting with the sense of unity and family that Granger made his central campaign themes. With your Civil War recently ended, these themes did very well. To measure this precisely, we compare Mark's responses to the overall group."

Interesting, Elijah thought, *but nothing earth-shattering so far.* Still, he felt Vogel had more to show.

The German smiled, as if reading his thoughts. "Still with us so far? Good. At regular intervals, we will run a test – a...snap poll, if you will. We show our subjects an image of each candidate and quantify the responses for the different qualities we measure. Because there's no noise, our predictive models for determining who will win an election are precisely accurate."

Polling had been the bane of every politician since the first democratic election, its methodology and accuracy the source of endless debate. But there had to be more.

"Can you play the ad one more time?" Elijah asked. Meijer

obliged, and Granger was again touting his roots. Elijah pointed to another quadrant at the back of the pipefitter's brain, marked *Occipital Lobe*, where shades of green were forming. "What's that there?"

Vogel jumped forward animatedly, the science clearly exciting him. "Ah! They told me how smart you are! This part of the brain controls vision, but it is also where ideas...originate. Where new thoughts are formed. Which is why this particular subject, and this particular ad, were so exciting." He turned to Dr. Meijer, who met her grandfather with a look of, *If you'll let me continue?*

Vogel sat back down.

Dr. Meijer pointed to some highlighted areas within the occipital lobe. "As I was getting to, opposite the frontal lobe, where you react to something, here you're acting on that reaction. At this moment, our subject is doing precisely that."

As Granger was going on about his uplifting backstory – war wounds healed by his wife's love, and how he would heal America's wounds the same way, or something dopey like that – the pipefitter's occipital lobe became a lit Christmas tree of green. Vogel was practically jumping up and down.

"The...brighter shades you see, the bigger the idea – you know, light bulb! Ding!"

Dr. Meijer ignored her grandfather's animations, something she'd probably been doing her entire life. "When we see something as vivid as this, it can be exciting. Observe – if you zoom in here, you can see the different areas have different shades of green – an emerald hue here, a mint color there. They are very specific and important. If we hit play again, slowing it down to just microseconds, we can take these different color patterns and approximate them."

Elijah thought Vogel might explode, but he wanted to make sure he grasped what Meijer was saying. "Approximate them? Into what?"

"Well, phonics, basically."

"Phonics? Like parts of words?"

"Yes!" Vogel exclaimed, jumping around and clapping him on the back. "String the phonics together and you can form words, even sentences!"

"That's – wait a minute, you can translate his thoughts into sentences? Are you saying you can read his mind?"

Vogel looked like a kindergarten teacher about to award a gold star, but Meijer was more subdued. "These moments of inspiration can be mapped with enough specificity that yes; we can approximate it into language. I wouldn't say translate, not yet. Each brain palette is slightly different; there is much trial and error. This is one decipherable sample out of millions."

She zoomed in on the occipital lobe and slowed the playback further, slow enough that Granger looked almost fully still. "You see this splash of cucumber?" She touched it on the holo and text appeared.

Phonic designate: /ie/

"There are vowel phonics and consonant phonics, you may remember. This one, *ie*, is a vowel phonic, like in *tie* or *lie*. Taken by itself, it stands for the word *I*, like *I want this* or *I like that*, which is the beginning of most thoughts, really."

The playback inched forward, nanosecond by nanosecond, and a splurge of darker green appeared above and to the left of the fading cucumber shade. Meijer touched it.

Phonic designate: /w/

"Our first consonant phonic," Meijer said. "And then another two phonics right after it, here and here, a vowel and another consonant." She pointed to an olive area and a teal.

Phonic designate: /i/

Phonic designate: /sh/

"I wish?" Elijah asked.

Vogel beamed. "We have seen this pattern often enough to approximate it with relative...confidence."

Vogel signaled to Meijer to speed things along. She hurried through the rest of the playback, tapping out phonics until they appeared in a string.

/ie/ /w/ /i/ /sh/ /h/ /ee/ /d/ /p/ /i/ /c/ /a/ /c/ /u/ /n/ /s/ /er/ /v/ /u/ /t/ /i/ /v/

Elijah puzzled it out. "I wish he'd pick a conservative?"

Vogel clapped him on the back. "This is before the conventions, mind you, when the running mate...speculation is at its peak. Mark clearly likes our candidate, but something holds him back. We assumed Mark's wish meant he wanted Granger to pick a more conservative Reformer, someone to balance the Reformation League ticket. We showed him everyone we could think of, but no one stuck – Granger still did not have Mark's vote. Dismayed, we started to look...elsewhere. Candidates from other Leagues. The one that finally pulled Mark over the line was this handsome man."

Meijer tapped her PanoPad and Elijah saw a picture of himself on the holo.

He stared at the image, trying to piece his thoughts together. "But Granger didn't say at his convention that he would pick me. He said he would pick whoever came in second."

"Well, we could not just go out there and say it! As his opponent, you would have said no thank you. But you were the choice. And given our polling data, we knew it would be you. Yes, it was a...gamble, that the electorate would associate a vote for Granger as one that essentially included you on the ticket. The media likes to make a game of polls, this person is gaining, this one is crashing – but people do not change their minds. They might pretend they do, but they lie – to pollsters, to friends, and to themselves." He pointed to brain on the holo. "But! Just to be sure, we run another scenario." He nodded again to Dr. Meijer, who keyed in more commands.

"Same person, same ad," Vogel said. "Now, we add your image while it's playing. And boom!"

The frontal lobe was almost blinding with light. Mark the pipefitter's brain was as vibrant as Vogel's body, the seams of the German's refashioned skin stretching in the light.

"We were curious about these results at first," Vogel said. "We compared Mark's readings with other subjects across a variety of...demographics. Then we pulled back to the whole group, the collective subconscious of all our subjects. We call this the Hive Mind. And the Hive Mind confirmed what our friend Mark saw – although you and Mr. Granger were two very different people, agreeing on almost nothing when it came to...issues, you were his perfect compliment. Granger conveyed strength, confidence, trust. These are classic Alpha Male qualities. Yourself, seen as intelligent, kind, sympathetic. You made the perfect beta." Vogel had clasped his two hands together, shaking them demonstrably. "The synergy of the two was tremendous."

Just how am I so sympathetic? Elijah wondered for a moment, then let it pass.

"I'm the beta to his alpha," he said. "Isn't that humbling. Mr. Vogel, did you bring me here to humiliate me?"

"No," Vogel said. "I assume you accepted my invitation because you had a question – *why did I lose?* Maybe that explains much of it. But I asked you here to tell you this. Since you have been vice president, we have seen some...changes."

"Yeah, my approval rating has fallen twenty points."

21

Vogel shook his head and tittered, as if humored by Elijah's lack of faith. "Actually, our responses show that as the president...governs, taking slings and arrows from all sides, you are gaining in some of those alpha qualities."

"Really?" Elijah was never good at sarcasm, but he hoped it came through here. "When I lost, the conservatives all turned on me. They thought I blew a winnable election – I guess it's nice to hear you tell me that I never had much of a chance. And that was *before* I accepted Granger's offer. Once I took it, they turned on me all over again."

"Based on our findings, we knew who would win this election very early on. And the next election, we will know as well, perhaps...earlier. Our science improves every day. But we are getting ahead of ourselves."

Elijah kept thinking backward, putting the pieces together. "I remember Granger's convention speech so well; it was like a kick in the chest. A brilliant maneuver. He invoked George Washington and John Adams – Washington won the presidency and Adams came in second out of a crowded field, which back then made him vice president. I guess at that point, I knew we were fucked."

Vogel's accent thickened the softer he spoke. "It made Granger the...front-runner almost overnight. As we had expected."

"And the rest of us scrapped at his heels for second place. But you knew how that would turn out, too."

Instead of responding, Vogel pointed to the brain diagram on the holo.

Elijah remembered the first days after losing the election – a dark, dejected time of self-immolation. He ran a good campaign with good ideas, or so he'd thought. Elections can hinge on thousands of factors, most of them out of your control, but at the end of the day it comes down to how many people believed in you.

A question popped into his mind. "How did you know I would take the job? I've never been hooked up to your machines."

Vogel shrugged. "Ah, our biggest gamble of all! You are correct, we did not know if you would or would not. But Granger trusted you to do it. He thought you might appreciate the...history it invoked, and that you would appreciate the symbol of unity."

"But all his talk of unity was a lie. A tactic to win."

Vogel jumped at the accusation. "Win, yes! But you must win to govern! And what a team you make. He inspires, you perspire. Can you not say that it works?"

Elijah sighed. Now he was looking for his words, even with English his native language. "It's been...bumpy."

He reflected on the night of the election and the painful concession call. The new President-Elect had been as gracious and kind as could be. *I made a promise to the country that sort of involves you,* he'd said to Elijah. *Help me keep it.*

Elijah made no promises then, merely saying he'd think about it. And think he did, when he wasn't feeling despondent. A week later, Granger called again, offering to discuss his offer in person. Elijah reluctantly invited him to his summer cottage in the Hamptons. Granger had looked even bigger to him then, barely fitting through the doorway, casting a shadow as wide as the living room. Elijah was prepared to turn him down, to say it would never work, but eventually he bought into the man's earnestness and the ebullience of his character. *This won't go over well with our factions of loyalists,* Granger told him. *The war remains fresh in so many minds. But I have your back, so long as you have mine.*

The last thing the president told him: *On the plus side, making history sure is fun.*

With that, Elijah accepted and the two rivals set about forming a government. And after two years of fits and missteps, setbacks and struggles, that nation was beginning to shake off the rust, an old locomotive churning out steam.

Elijah considered his original question. "So why *am* I here?"

Vogel looked at Dr. Meijer and nodded. She turned off the holo and the lights came back up.

"Such intelligent questions," Vogel complimented. "Granger was the first and only candidate we have sponsored. He won't be the last."

Schroeder studied Vogel as he twiddled his bow tie. The German tried to smile and look relaxed, but there was tension behind it – whether it was from the anti-aging treatments, his angled features, or something more, he wasn't sure. "I do not much care for politics," Vogel admitted. "I did not become Granger's Sponsor for any...partisan reason. I am not concerned with his policy to re-introduce immigration or his position on paying for reconstruction costs – nor yours, for that matter. I am a businessman concerned for my business. This company has made great strides, poised to make more. In time, we will need to sponsor another candidate. I am assuming you will again seek the presidency when the opportunity arises?"

"Honestly, I don't think I have it in me."

Vogel gave him a look as if to say, *My data tells me differently.* Perhaps he was right – Elijah's mind did ponder the future, even as it still litigated the past.

"Campaigning wears on your soul," Elijah insisted. "Maybe in '68, when Granger's second term is up. I'd have to think the president's re-election is a lock."

Vogel only said, "Possibly, but we have no way of knowing without knowing the candidates."

"It's still a few months before anyone jumps in, but I expect some will begin making noise after the midterms."

"A lot of time between now and then, to be sure."

"Well, I wouldn't dare run against him. If he asks me to stay on, I would. Right now, I'm a man without a caucus. Approval in the twenties, pilloried from all sides. Conservatives no longer trust me, if they ever did. And though it can be painful working under Granger's bleeding heart, I'm no Benedict Arnold. Like you said, against all odds, it does sort of work."

"As we knew it would," Vogel said with a smile, pointing behind him. "But they say in politics, circumstances are forever changing."

"Not according to your polling. But if they do, feel free to invite me back. Maybe by then I'll understand all this." There was catharsis to this trip, he supposed. He'd been comparing himself to Granger for years, during the campaign and after, now that he worked for him. Trying to find where he failed and the president succeeded. Knowing the cause of it, however jarring, brought some peace. The alpha to his beta, and all this technology. He wondered if he could have won with Vogel as his Sponsor – what a weapon this was!

"Tell me, what did Granger say the first time you showed him this facility?"

A flash of disappointment crossed Vogel's face, and he hid it with an air of wistfulness. "If he had ever accepted my invitation, I could tell you."

"He's never been here?"

"We have worked very closely with his...aides. Mr. Ricketts, mainly. The president, not as much."

You and I have that in common, Elijah thought. He checked the time, well beyond his scheduled appearance at the fundraiser. "I should be going."

"Ah!" Vogel exclaimed. "But there's one more thing to show you.

Dr. Meijer, may I borrow your handheld pano device please?"

Vogel's granddaughter fished in her coat pocket and handed it over. The lights went down one more time.

CHAPTER TWO

"I don't care what the nursery rhyme says, anything that falls down broken can always be put together again. That's the beauty of our Constitution."
  - Acton Granger, debate excerpt – October 17, 2060

For Tess Larkin, her father's study was the most beautiful place in the world.

Her love began with the skylights – three of them, angled and wide, inviting broad bands of sunlight into the room. During the day, the light would journey from one side to the other, passing over the scores of books – *actual books!* – that lined the shelves, as if to highlight each of them for a period. Fiction novels, biographies, poetry collections, and classics populated the stacks, along with her recent contributions of legal dictionaries and briefing books. And there was her special corner, reserved for her romance collection when the occasional indulgence was required. Tess felt more at home here than in her own apartment, or anywhere else. She felt a sense of vigor, of enlightenment, as if the collective wisdom within all these storied pages hung in the air, waiting to be inhaled. This was why she never missed a chance to come by on Sundays.

Stuffing herself in her favorite leather lounger (quite possibly the most comfortable chair in the world), amidst piles of paperbacks and hardcovers, Tess looked up from her book and watched her father, seated at his desk a few feet away and attending to a soup bowl. *Funny, he never lets me eat in here*, she thought. Tess pretended to read as she noticed the spoon quaking within his fingers, spilling its contents back into the bowl. He put the spoon down resignedly and attended to the surface pano embedded in his desk.

How many Sundays will I have left with him?

"Everything all right, Daddy? Chowder too salty?"

Richard Larkin replied without looking up. "You're thirty now, Tess. You can call me Dad, Papa, whatever. Just something, *anything* other than Daddy."

Tess tried again, with feeling. "Dearest Patriarch, how is the homemade bowl of clam chowder that I slaved over for you?"

He sighed but not without a subtle smile. "Dad will do," he said, returning focus to his pano without commenting on the soup. Tess noticed the bowl was still nearly full. *Must be stone cold by now*, she thought. *Does he notice?*

She went back into her book (Leonora, the constable's daughter, longed for Sergio, the pirate captain – but he'd rejected her for the high seas), as she kept one eye on her father. He struggled with the pano – his fingers, so nimble and sure when he picked up his guitar, lingered lost in the air. He dropped his hands to his lap, defeated.

"Tessa, help," he said quietly.

"What's the matter?" she asked, trying to sound chipper and nonchalant. She set down her book and took the few steps over in a *no-big-deal* pace.

"I'm trying to get to the news and this dang thing won't let me."

She reached around from behind and cradled his wrists. "Ok, not a problem. Just wave this hand to the right to open your favorite sites, like that. Now point to the site you want. ABCBS News is the third link down; I think you like that one? Good – now, to cycle through stories just move this finger, like you're flicking something. There you go."

"Thank you, I've got it now."

"Here to help," she said, still chipper. A fleeting memory jumped at her – her ninth birthday, the first time her dad had bought a pano and showed her how to use it. He hadn't been as patient, Tess remembered.

After a few more pages into Leonora's yearning tale, she saw him struggling again. "If you're looking for the crossword, just draw the letter C in the air."

"Ah." Richard followed her instruction. Soon he was working his daily puzzle, locked in, forefingers in a confident dance as he spelled out the various clues. Some skills, like reflexes, never dwindled.

He asked casually, without looking over, "Honey, where's Bruin?"

"The cat?" She tried to find a positive way to say it, but if he'd forgotten that Bruin had been gone for years that was more devastating than a difficulty in handling a soup spoon and trouble with pano controls. She fought the recurrent urge to take him by the shoulders and shake him, as if she could jostle the memories back. Maybe he'd remember burying Bruin in the yard, or that he still placed fresh gravel over his resting place each year.

"Oh, Daddy..."

But Richard broke out in a sheepish grin, waving his hand as if to say *Eh, I was just fuckin with you.*

"Dad, don't ever – Jesus, don't *ever* do that again." Now she wanted to shake him for a different reason. Tears welled in her eyes.

His smile vanished. "Oh, look...I'm sorry, sweetheart. You're right. It's just, I need to keep a sense of humor about some things." When she didn't look at him, all he could say was, "Please don't cry like that."

"I'm serious. I won't come over anymore."

They both knew she was lying. "You love it here, and you know it," Richard said.

She could not deny it, but every time he forgot something, her heart broke a little more. Pretending to forget was somehow worse.

Tess picked up her PanoPad – time to let Leonora's pirate-pining go for a while, and check in on work.

Some minutes later, after a completed crossword – and probably the quote acrostic, by now – her father piped up again. "Any men in your life I should know about?"

Tess rolled her eyes his way, making sure he registered her derision.

"Whoa," he said with a laugh, "sorry for caring. What's got you so busy that I won't meet my first grandchild in the foreseeable future?"

"Do you have to bring this up every time?" She squirmed with obvious unease, though the question didn't really bother her as much anymore – anytime he was engaged and lively, even at her expense, was fine by her. As for her dating and any potential reproduction, she had a valid excuse – there simply was no time, not on Speaker Cunningham's watch.

She held up her PanoPad. "If you must know, right now I'm reading through some White House petitions."

"But you don't work for the White House, Tessa," her father said, then paused. "Right?"

"Right, I work for the Speaker of the House. But part of being an Assistant Policy Director is finding new ideas. I check out these petitions from time to time and see if there's anything we can run with. This is one of the few places where anyone in the country can propose a new law, or push to strike down an existing one. And if a petition gets enough signatures, the White House has to craft an official response – no matter what."

"How does the Speaker feel about you combing through sites devoted to the Executive Branch? And...what's his name again?"

"Cunningham. He'd hit the roof of the Capitol Building if he knew about it, actually."

"Careful, Tessa. I hope you're not putting your career in jeopardy."

"I don't think it's quite that dire. Most of these petitions are pretty self-serving and small, but some are worth a read."

"Pardon my second cousin? Legalize whatever drug I just got busted with?"

She smiled. He hadn't been this animated in weeks. Tess referred to these moments as Lucid Time, those fleeting periods when her father was himself again – inquisitive, to the point of combative. His thirst for knowledge was an urgent one.

"Some petitions can be more off-the-wall. Here's one: 'Require the president to appear in Major League Baseball's Home Run Derby.' It has over five thousand signatures. He's big, but I heard Granger had two left feet when it came to sports. Oh, they want him to appear mainly so he'd be tested for PEDs beforehand. I guess that's clever. Another one you'd like: 'Issue a statement demanding the restoration of Milo Georgino's *Snark!* account, revoked unfairly by social media fascists who take bomb threats too seriously.' Eight thousand signatures for that one."

"Democracy in action," Richard Larkin declared.

Tess scrolled down her pano, looking for more examples while he was still engaged, a narrow window that could close at any moment. "Oh, you'll like this one: 'Introduce an amendment to the Constitution, one that nullifies the Constitution.'"

"Ambitious, that one."

"Whoever wrote this must be a first-year law student," she observed, and started reading. "'Herewith, on the occasion of the two-hundred-and-seventy-sixth year of its creation, we the people request proposal and passage of a Constitutional Amendment, and that this Amendment shall strike down the constraints of those who may lord over us, so that Natural Law and not our so-called elected representatives shall govern this nation.'"

"Natural Law, I think they're on to something – I've always thought the trees should be in charge, myself."

"I don't think that's what they mean. There's more, if you want to hear it?"

His face changed. "That's ok. You get back to what you were doing." In a flash, he'd gone back to a distant stare – as if someone pushed a reset button and he was still booting up.

More like powering down, Tess thought.

Richard Larkin returned to his cold soup, listlessly stirring his spoon.

"I guess it's not entirely crazy," Tess said. "The Amendment thing, I mean." But he was lost again, Lucid Time another runaway memory.

Tess thumbed through other petitions. A handful stood out as halfway plausible. A proposal for a New Orleans Dam Project. A request to further incentivize Automated Vehicles. A demand to prosecute the company that manufactured faulty pano battery casings.

But her mind kept going back to the Amendment petition. Apart from whatever Natural Law implied, was it really so crazy? Tess knew as well as anyone how ridiculous the system had become – Speaker Cunningham and his petty, backbiting politics a prime example. The original Constitution had created a beacon of freedom in its beginning, but all Tess knew was a nation torn apart by infighting and civil war. Had the country become broken enough that it required questioning its sacred foundation?

She didn't realize that her father, in an aftershock of lucidity, detected her inner tensions. "You're biting your nails again, Tess. Onto something?"

"I don't know. Just wondering if I could convince my boss that America's most hallowed document could use a rewrite."

"I think I've told you the only way to convince anyone of anything." She blinked, at a loss. The disappointment in his tone was cutting. "Get them to think it was their idea in the first place!"

It was amazing how he could seem completely disconnected one moment and then drop a bomb of wisdom the next. *Always with the grand pronouncements*, Tess thought, smirking. Was it his condition or, if her mother was still around, would she say this was how he'd always been – seemingly aloof, only to come in with perfect advice when it was most needed?

"But Theresa," Richard Larkin said (and he only used her given name when it was Something Really Important), "if you're even thinking about a do-over for America's Constitution, it would probably be easier to rewrite the Bible – or the Koran, for that matter. My brain might be slipping, but you're the one off your rocker."

If he was being honest, he was more than slipping. *Daddy, we need to talk about selling the house.* She wanted to say it so badly, it threatened to erupt from her at any time – but she couldn't quite get there, not yet. Some things couldn't be unsaid. And it could be the one thing her father might never forget.

The truth was, there would never be a good time to bring it up.

Another part of it, probably, was selfishness. Did she just want everything to stay the same, if only to keep her weekly visits? Undoubtedly. These Sunday afternoons were her only rest stop from a life moving a thousand miles an hour. Cunningham was a more demanding boss than she'd ever imagined – which was amazing, since Congress accomplished so little.

Still, the house had to be sold, and soon – a glance at her father's quivering soup spoon confirmed it.

Just not today. If he was in the mood for argument, she'd keep it to politics. "I'm just tired of all the hacks in this town," Tess said. "They pretend they're all chosen disciples of the Founding Fathers, as if George Washington whispered some secret code through the centuries that only they can hear. Nothing ages perfectly. We have challenges that our founders never imagined. How does an eighteenth-century document apply to the post-information age?"

Her father adopted the slightly-chiding air that Tess remembered so well growing up. "Tessa, that's what amendments are for, what legal precedents are for. The damn thing wasn't written on a stone tablet. I did send you to law school, didn't I?"

"Yes, but look how divided everything is. Do you really think we'll ever pass another amendment again? Two-thirds of the states and Congress? They wouldn't be able to pass a law saying the sky is blue."

"It does look a little gray today."

"Not helping. You turn on the PanoNets, all you hear about is someone saying the other guy is crapping on the Constitution, only to cover that they're wiping their own ass with it. Accusations and finger-pointing, all day every day, while our problems mount and mount. We can't do anything as a nation anymore. And that's not what our founding document wanted – it was meant for us to work it out so we can solve the big things." She sighed. "I'm just tired of something so brilliant, so blessed, used as a weapon."

"It's politics, Tessa. Everything's a weapon."

She looked up at the skylights. The sun's straight yellow rays broke through the cloud cover, blinding her face in radiance. She closed her eyes, mind churning. "Maybe what we need..."

And then it hit her.

CHAPTER THREE

"The effort to 'Stack the Senate' began in earnest in the late two-thousand-twenties. Under the Constitution, a state is assigned House Representatives based on its population, but receives two senators regardless. Red states with overwhelming margins in their legislatures opted to divide themselves, adding two loyal senators for each new state they created, hoping to forever hold a filibuster-proof Senate Majority. Some states split into two relatively equal parts, such as East and West Kentucky. Others were more ambitious, becoming three separate entities – as Utah divided into Salt Lake, Wasatch, and Brigham. Not to be outdone, Texas divided itself into fifths – Mountain Texas, Border Texas, Coastal Texas, Central Texas, and the most Texan state of them all, Greater Texas."

- from A History of the Five Texases, Francisco Aguilar, published 2057

"**M**r. Richardson? The governor will see you now."

About damn time. Jamie grabbed his knapsack and jumped out of the waiting room sofa. A head rush turned his world inky-black for several disorienting moments.

"Mr. Richardson? Are you all right?"

Jamie blinked until his bearings returned. "I'm good, lead the way." He followed the assistant down the hall toward the governor's office, trying to steer his eyes from her backside's ample contours. *For a white girl, not bad – must be the food down here.*

Before reaching the office, the assistant turned abruptly to the right, reaching instead toward a side door leading out the building. She opened it for Jamie and they stepped onto an expansive lawn, a sandstone path meandering amongst the fescue.

At the path's end, Governor Shelby Monroe bounced in the grass with a fleet of tiny dogs – corgis, by the look of them.

The governor stood shorter than Jamie expected, her burnt-orange pencil dress reaching near her ankles. Famous for her fashion choices (or infamous, depending on whom you asked), today's selection was no less bold – the dress bore a pleated front, studded with oversized white buttons, and her signature tassels hung from the shoulders. The string of pearls around her neck almost exactly matched her white-to-silver hair, which reminded Jamie of a swirled bulb of cotton candy glossed with metallic spray paint.

Governor Monroe looked comfortable in the height of the afternoon, fanning herself intermittently as she ran back and forth amongst the dogs – sometimes chasing, sometimes being chased. As Jamie approached, he could hear the governor lecturing her pups in rapid monologue.

"Faster, Reagan! Lincoln, look at me! Don't bite your sister, try to keep up! Good boy!". The corgis were falling all over each other on stubby legs, their bottom-heavy torsos flattening the grass in wide swaths.

The assistant stopped Jamie a few feet in before the governor – *Don't interfere.*

In time, Governor Monroe stopped her frolicking and turned to face them. If she was at all embarrassed at being observed by a stranger prancing around with her pets, it didn't show.

Instead, she pulled a handkerchief from a dress pocket and dabbed her forehead. "Whew, it's a hot one! Maybe those global warming dorks were on to something." She smiled ironically as she tucked the kerchief back.

"Afternoon, Ma'am," the assistant said.

The governor cocked her head. "Trixie, you don't have to call me ma'am, I've told you that a million times. Who's that behind you?"

"This is Jamie Richardson, the...what is it, videographer?"

The governor looked at Jamie with an expression of surprise he instantly recognized. *This is why I don't put pictures of myself on my work*, he thought.

But she recovered just as quickly, as any decent politician might, and her natural enthusiasm returned. She bounded over a corgi toward him. "Oh, silly me, of course! Jamie, hi!"

"Governor, it's a pleasure to finally meet you." Jamie reached out formally to shake her hand, and she took it with an enthusiastic jolt, sizing him up as she did so.

"Call me Shelby," Governor Monroe said, breaking her grip and turning in one motion. "Walk with me! Come, come!"

Does she think I'll obey commands like one of her dogs? Jamie wondered, but by then she was heading back down the pathway. And damned if he didn't hustle up to join her. Behind them, Trixie gathered up leashes.

When he caught up, Shelby put a hand on Jamie's shoulder, a gesture that startled him. "I hope your flight was ok?"

"Fine. There was an overnight layover in Houston."

"On your way from California? Those shitbrained airlines will never make sense, even after we lifted the interstate travel restrictions." Jamie shrugged. He'd wanted to spend a night in Houston if only to see the Deportation Resistance Museum, so it was no big thing. "We'll cover your expenses, of course," she said with a wink. "I know they pack those planes like sardines now, but once we get a Sponsor, we'll be flying all over these United States, and in style! Ever been to Greater Texas?"

The governor shifted gears so often, Jamie found it difficult to keep up. "This is my first time in any of the Texases, Greater or, uh, not-so-great."

"Ha! Well, you picked the right one to pop your cherry on. Whatcha think so far?"

"Everyone's got a pistol on their hip."

"Safest place you'll ever be," the governor proclaimed, as if by reflex. "Let's go inside, hot as the devil's fireplace out here."

The governor led the way to her office. Textured adobe walls were adorned with oversized landscape paintings – depicting horsemen, cattle, and horsemen herding cattle. Jamie saw trinkets and knickknacks everywhere – ancient pistols on the bookcases, decorative mini-boots on the shelves, a massive longhorn affixed to the wall.

Is this a governor's office or the gift shop at the Alamo?

Shelby took her place behind a mahogany desk draped in cowhide. Above her, the Greater Texas flag – a large star in the middle, with four smaller stars at the corners – overlapped ceremoniously with the Texas Lone Star version from decades before.

"Need a drink?"

Jamie sank into the leather of a low-slung chair before the governor's desk. "I'm all right, but thank you."

Shelby Monroe shook her head with a smile – *You'll not refuse my generosity here, mister* – and stabbed her desktop pano with a stout index finger. "Trixie, bring water. Yes, from the spring. You're my favorite!"

Trixie was in the office with a water tray within half a moment, setting it down and disappearing just as quickly. Jamie took a gracious sip. He couldn't remember the last time he'd been offered fresh spring water, a luxury in California and probably even more so here.

Monroe watched him carefully as he drank, her face like a mother saying, *I know what's best for you, don't forget that.* Jamie nodded in appreciation as he set down his empty glass.

"So!" she exclaimed, slapping her palms on the desk. "Welcome aboard. You're my first campaign hire, which is very exciting for me. Would you like to show me your equipment?"

Jamie was glad he'd just swallowed his water – else he might've choked on it. "My equipment? Oh, right." He dipped into his knapsack and pulled out his video instruments, carefully laying them out on the desk. Each camera was the size of a pencil eraser. "I mainly shoot with these. They're the new PZ330 PanoLenses, they work well for both tight and long shots. Versatile and reliable."

"I see," the governor said, picking up one of the floating drone cameras and examining it like a jeweler. "Are they quieter than the PZ220's?"

"Why...yes they are," he said, startled at her knowledge. "The stabilizers are just a tinge wider so they don't flutter as much. That's what made all the noise."

Shelby nodded. "My husband and I used to take those old 220's out on hunting trips. They'd wobble and scare away the ducks."

Jamie went back to the knapsack and pulled out his gloves, intricate wiring woven into the fabric of the palms, funneling into padded fingertips. "Like the 220s, they're controlled with these, using what's called Gesture Mode – well, I guess I don't have to tell you what that is. I've done some custom programming to these. They can do a lot more than the standard models. They have a better range than the 220s, about seventy-five yards, depending on how many are in the air at once. But the closer I am to a subject, the easier they are to control."

"How about for holo vids?"

"That's more intrusive. I would need four cameras, hovering around you in each quadrant."

"Can't you do it with three?"

"I could, but the edges get distorted."

"Hmmm." She set the drone down, looking to Jamie for more.

"Right...there's also a Pincam that you can wear, I would embed it to the flag pin on your lapel. It's good for first-person, point-of view shots, like when you're in front of a big crowd. It has a fish-eye lens, and can take stills."

She scrutinized the Pincam, barely a dot as it lay on her fingertip. She looked pleased.

"So...is there anything you want to know about me?" Jamie asked.

She looked at him with a wry smirk. "All in good time," she said. "But you're still hired, if that's what you're getting at. I saw what you did for Governor Reynolds and it just about knocked me to the floor. You turned that poor old stiff into a compelling candidate, and somehow or another Utah's reddest state elected a Progressive. If that ain't remarkable, I don't know what is."

He laughed. "Wasn't easy."

Shelby leaned forward, sizing him up once again. "Now, I know I'm no Progressive, the good lord is kind. I don't know what your politics are, but I'm assuming you're a professional and that won't get in the way of things."

"Just here to do a job, ma'am. That's to tell your story to the people, best as I can."

"Good to hear," she said, leaning forward. "Let's be honest for a sec. Some of my colleagues in the Freedom League are going to look at your, uh, complexion and maybe have a hard time with it. It's been a few years since the war, but hell, some folks are still broken up about the first one and that was two hundred years ago. You all right with that?"

"Of course, ma'am."

"I know the Freedom League has some ways to go on social issues. Between ourselves, that's part of what this campaign will be about. Your skin don't matter to me, darling. Black, blue, yellow, don't care. No matter where we go, you'll be fine if you stick close."

Jamie wasn't exactly sure of that. The Governor's quick register of surprise when she saw him spoke volumes – *Not a lot of my people down here.* He wondered if she would've called him out of the blue and flown him across the country if she'd known his urban roots. She didn't ask his background when she called, and Jamie certainly wasn't going to offer it up. This was work on a presidential campaign, a step up in his career. And the money had to be better.

If I need to follow around filming a rabble-rousin', gun-totin' Greater Texan crazy enough to think she can get to the White House, then so be it.

"When do you want me to start?" Jamie asked.

"We have a meeting in the conference room in twenty minutes."

Jamie flinched. "So...now?"

She flashed a broad, matronly smile. "We move pretty quick down here, Jamie, you'll catch on. It's a gathering of my closest advisors, and I'll want it recorded – we won't announce officially until the Spring, but my staff needs to prepare for what's coming. Maybe it will make a good opening scene in the first PanoVid? Or maybe it can just be a practice run – of course, you'll be the judge of all that. I know I promised you creative control when we spoke. You were quite insistent."

Governor Monroe's fingers flew around on her pano and she wrote a number in the air above the screen. "Here's your first payment and a retainer. Our first trip will be to Washington in February. That's for FACPAC – as I'm sure you've heard, I was asked to give the keynote address – and we'll have you fully accredited as a member of my team by then."

The pano in his jacket pocket vibrated favorably and emitted a loud *cha-ching!* as it notified him that a payment was received. If that wasn't enough, it followed up with a gangster voice emitting a familiar rap refrain – *Git dat paper son!* – a download that Jamie considered amusing at the time.

Shelby gave no sign of hearing it, holding her natural disposition of warm amusement. "Yes, absolutely," Jamie said, pushing through any awkwardness. He certainly didn't know what a FACPAC was, but didn't really care at this point – now that he was gainfully employed and able to pay his bills, the rest was just details.

"I hope you'll find that generous. When we have a Sponsor, it'll only go up from there." Shelby paged her assistant one more time, who appeared within the office so quickly it was like she'd been beamed in. "Trixie will have some forms for you to sign after the meeting, but for now you should probably start setting up. I'll be down in the conference room in, oh, fifteen minutes now. Better hurry."

Jamie stood. "I appreciate the opportunity, ma'am. I'll do my best work for you."

The governor clapped him on the back, her smile never breaking – wide and knowing. *Now that, mister, was never in doubt.*

"Bless your heart," she said. "Now go on and get ready!"

The conference room was draped with similar cattle-rustling paraphernalia to Shelby's office, reminding Jamie of a highway rest stop. He barely had time to get his rig into place before the governor's staff filed in. A thirty-something woman was first to enter, strutting in cowboy boots and wearing a plaid tea dress. She flashed a curious, hesitant smile Jamie's way before sitting.

Two more women followed – one in a yellow blouse and the other in a patterned frock with leggings – both with footwear identical to the first. The three of them exchanged breezy, familiar pleasantries and after those initial *Hellos* and *How-are-yous*, they started messaging each other on their panos, tittering excitedly.

Which was when they cast their collective eyes at Jamie. "Excuse me, sir?" Yellow Blouse raised her hand at him. "Do you know what this meeting is about?"

Jamie was checking his monitor, making sure the float-cams were synced with the sensors on his gloves. "I don't know much at all. Just got here, really. But I have the feeling if I said anything, the governor might shoot me."

The women all gave a nod of understanding, as if to confirm that was indeed a possible outcome.

Jamie tried to remember the governor's instructions from a minute ago. *I want a tight shot down the hall as I approach,* she'd said. *One cam can be of my profile, one filming from the back, and a third a medium three-quarters shot from next to the conference table.*

But as she'd pointed out herself, Jamie had complete creative control. Governor Monroe was a woman who knew what she wanted, and he was already wondering if that would be an issue. Governor Reynolds, his last client, had been hands off, treating him like an afterthought until he saw how many PanoViews his films were getting. But Reynolds never interfered; Monroe, he wasn't so sure about. Nevertheless, this being his first day on the job, he gave the governor a pass and set everything up how she wanted – with a few flourishes of his own.

Two more women entered – Trixie the Assistant and someone

that looked like her twin, only with slightly darker hair and more business-like clothing. They took the remaining two spots around the table.

This could be trouble, Jamie mused. It didn't help that all these women looked like models, dressed for some kind of rodeo runway. However, before he could further reflect on these potential distractions, a pair of quick claps rapped from the hallway, ringing out like pistol blasts. His cue.

Jamie crouched into position and tapped his gloves together. They came alive with a faint glow through the wiring and a slight vibration in the fingertips. His left index finger controlled Camera One – by extending the finger, the camera floated down the hall. He pushed the rest of the cams into position with the remaining fingers on his left hand, controlling their focus and range with the matching digits of his right.

"Ready!" Jamie called, then counted down from five. He checked the monitor one last time, displaying images from each cam.

The governor clapped once in acknowledgement.

"Record," he said aloud, and in response to his voice command, the feed was live. Camera One opened with a slow fade into focus, beginning on a detail from one of the hallway paintings – a sheepdog, shown leaping across a Texas plain, herding cattle into a pen at sunset while cowboys looked on approvingly.

Jamie twisted his hand to the left and the camera panned down the hall, switching to a longer focus. It picked up the governor as she strode into view, staring straight ahead, walking like a prosecutor into a courtroom. Jamie pulled in the other cameras to form a triangle around her as she entered the conference room.

The five women around the table stood and greeted her with spirited applause. *Maybe they know more than they were letting on*, he thought.

The governor took a deep breath and clasped her hands together, beaming appreciatively at the adulation of her staff.

"Afternoon, Boot Squad!" she exclaimed. Jamie panned around the table to capture the atmosphere. Each staffer knocked on the table in response and leaned forward, breathless. The governor went into her speech, her voice gathering strength like a dust storm. "Ladies, we've been through a helluva lot over the years to get where we are. We went from rich, to poor, through war, and then took our first step to the City Council. After many wonderful years, we took another step to the Mayor's desk, and though that town was dry as a powder house, we turned it into Greater Texas's biggest water supplier. That allowed us to take yet another step, to this here Governor's Mansion, and we've been kicking ass for the state ever since. Now, we are at a crossroads. I've thought long and hard about this, as you know. I want you to be the first to know that it's time to take one more step, the biggest step, the granddaddy of them all. We're going to run for President of the United States!"

She'd barely gotten the words out before the staff – er, Boot Squad, as the governor deemed them – erupted in cheers and applause. Jamie worked his gloves to catch every hug and hand-squeeze before turning the cameras back to the governor. The atmosphere was heavy with the weight of this momentous announcement, but light in their relaxed behaviors. They all looked like riverboat gamblers playing with house money. It took a full minute before Shelby spoke again, bristling with pride.

"There are exactly seven hundred and fifty days until Election Day. I want you to go home tonight, kiss your boyfriends and husbands, spend as much time as you can with your kids, and then tell them you will see them in seven hundred and fifty-one. Because holy hell do we have our work cut out for us."

The seated women exchanged glances, bemused but not at all surprised at the governor's candor.

"This is the last time I will ever say this," the governor declared, and she snapped her fingers at Jamie to emphasize, *This'd better not be in the final cut.* "President Granger may look like an oversized, clumsy gorilla, but he's smarter than he looks. He'll probably be the most difficult incumbent to topple in the last fifty years. The good news is, we can be smart, too. A lot of big names might sit this one out. And with a half-dozen Leagues making a bid, it might only take a quarter of the vote to win this thing. Shelby Monroe can get that in her sleep!" They laughed raucously, one of them chipping in a *Hell yeah!* for good measure.

"Believe it or not, ladies, our mission is bigger than the presidency." She snapped at Jamie again – *Okay, this you'll want to get.* "The Freedom League has become plundered by doomsayers and profiteers. They've stopped trying to win elections, instead clinging to old battles already lost. They're looking backward, resigning themselves to extinction – all sizzle, no steak. Worse, some are pledging allegiance to the Conservatives, who still think we're their sheep. It's time we stuck a hot poker in the eyes of these posers." Shelby started pacing side to side, her hands gathering passion. Jamie moved quickly to keep the cameras out of her way. "Here's how we do it. They say freedom is the ability to live without fear, and I for one believe there are still too many scared people in this country. Freedom is not a regional issue. Small government is not some niche cause. If we practice what we preach, we will reap what we sow, and we will gain a following. It's time the Freedom League had a candidate with some friggin' balls, and despite what some suggest, it usually takes a woman to provide them!"

The room erupted so loudly Jamie was surprised the doors remained on their hinges. *A half-dozen women sure can make a lot of noise.* Shelby Monroe, not at all winded, breathed a slow inhale. "Besides the courage of our convictions and all that, we have another weapon in this fight. Everybody, meet Jamie Richardson. He's going to be my shadow for the next two years, filming our campaign. Everything that happens on the trail, from public events to candid moments with you gals backstage, goes on tape. Get used to him. Fortunately, he's easy on the eyes. The way he moves those cameras around, it looks like he's doing tai chi or something. Just adorable. If you saw the PanoSeries he did for Arnold Reynolds, he almost single-handedly got that bleeding-heart, ultraliberal gasbag elected in the capital of the Mormon church, of all places. Imagine what he can do for us!"

The governor turned to Jamie and gestured toward her staff. "Mr. Richardson, my daughters and I welcome you into our family."

Daughters? All of them? But as he regarded each one again, he could see it, though they must have gotten their father's height gene. *Well how do you do.*

"Trixie, you've met," the governor said, pointing them out. "That's Tammy, she's our Communications Director. Tawny, the brunette, is my Chief of Staff." In truth, she was only slightly less blond than the others – all had tresses of sun-soaked straw. "Tracy over there does the polling, and Trudy is my speechwriter."

The Boot Squad – also apparently known as the Monroe daughters – waved warmly, their collective resemblance to the governor now obvious: the curl of their mouths, light-gold skin, and expressive brown eyes. And of course, they all had matching footwear.

Jamie lifted his arm and waved back in response, just before remembering some vitally important bits of information: his four cameras were still filming, still floating around the room, and still in Gesture Mode. They swung sideways in one wild, sweeping lurch,

Camera Two knocking Trixie in the head.

"Ow!"

"Shit! Sorry!"

The governor looked his way. "Better tighten up, Jamie," she said. "You're one of us now."

CHAPTER FOUR

Audience member: *Do you prefer the old two-party system, or what we have now?*

Governor Granger: *Are you asking me whether I prefer half the country hate me no matter what I do, compared to three-quarters of it?*

Audience: *(Laughter)*

Governor Granger: *Seriously, though, I think the two-party structure was like trench warfare, where one side advances a few feet, the other side retreats a few feet, and then you get up the next morning where the opposite happens, and the cycle repeats itself in an endless loop. Over time, that exacerbated some fundamental problems, first being that as a country you never really get anywhere. The other problem is when you're stuck in a trench you sure learn to hate the other guy in that faraway trench. Eventually, you see them as something less than human.*

Today, the fog of war is lifted and we're back on an open field – and if we want to get anything done, we're forced to form alliances, to reach out to other Leagues. None of us can form a majority by ourselves – we're all minorities now, would you think of that! But if I want to make some headway on the environment, I might call up the Progressive League. If I need help shoring up our national defense, I might call on the Freedom League. I would certainly meet with the Urban League to discuss rebuilding our cities and infrastructure. The Conservative League – well, I'm not sure what I'd do with them yet, but I'll think of something. The fellow leading their primary now, Governor Schroeder, we might be able to find

common ground. I hope I didn't just kill his campaign.
Audience: *(Laughter)*
- Acton Granger town hall meeting in Claremont, New Hampshire
– January 15, 2060

When Elijah Schroeder returned home from Chicago, they were already stringing up the holiday lights.

In the middle of October?

It seemed both the holiday and campaign seasons started earlier with each cycle. But sure enough, as the motorcade (a full contingent this time) approached the front gate of the US Naval Observatory, volunteers were busy transforming it into a winter wonderland.

At the heart of the US Naval Observatory, One Observatory Circle had been the traditional residence of the vice president for almost a century. Just two miles from the White House – though this was, in essence, also a *white house* – it had its own charms, an old plantation residence affixed with neo-classical trimmings. Originally built for the Naval Observatory's superintendent, much had been added once it transitioned to the home of the nation's second-ranking official, but it remained relatively modest. Contrasting the white exterior was a sloping gray roof, tilted at a high slant, with black shutters framing an abundance of windows. A porch bordered the right side, its many-spindled railing wrapped around the home's niftiest feature, a tower running up the corner. On the inside, the tower's round rooms served as the dining room on the first floor and Nolan's bedroom on the second. Along the porch, pairs of white columns dripped from the eave every ten feet or so, the narrow spaces between them popular nesting sites for pigeons escaping the hubbub of downtown.

Apart from the house, the rest of the Observatory maintained its official functions as the Navy's national science center. A set of atomic clocks kept the official time of the United States. The Office of Astrometry measured the precise orientation of the earth and other bodies in the solar system, and the telescope (though now a relic, its vantage dulled by neighboring city lights) was still popular for private tours.

Schroeder rode in his assigned vehicle, a state limousine called Freedom Two. Weighing five tons, and with an armored body eight-inches thick, it was capable of withstanding plasma grenades. The interior felt cramped even when he sat in the back alone.

He was not alone on this trip, however. Whenever his wife rode with him, Schroeder was forced to sit uncomfortably close to her, so much that they joked the Secret Service was conspiring to have them conceive another child. It was a welcome intimacy on most occasions, but this was not one of those times. Over the last two days, Elijah had noticed a tangible silence in Cassidy, her stoic reserve turning into a cold shoulder as they scrunched together, hip to hip. Every turn that forced his weight into her only reinforced her lack of forthcoming.

Or, it occurred to him, probably several hours too late, *was it something I started, that she's reciprocating?* It was a difficult question in any marriage when games were played.

He watched her from the corner of his eye. She sat fully straight, a posture she'd perfected over the years, eyes set forward in a plain expression, punctuated by a hint of wistfulness.

She caught him staring, frowned in his direction, and looked out the window.

She wants to know where I disappeared to, he realized. *But beyond that, she wants me to open up to her, to spill my secrets unprompted, and relieve her of the burden of having to ask.*

Cassidy Schroeder had nursed a healthy competitiveness all her life. She was willful and proud, already a talented litigator when they met and on a partnership track at a prominent firm. At the time, Elijah was a yet-to-be-tenured Associate Professor at NYU. Cassidy awakened the ambition in him, becoming its driver. She pushed him to take risks he never saw himself taking, among them convincing him to leave his cushy faculty job to run for the New York State Legislature.

Once in his first elected office, his political aspirations took off. The Conservative League was always keen on credible numbers men with convincing smiles, and his career trajectory quickly trumped Cassidy's. If she harbored any misgivings, she never said, but as the demands of being the wife of a national figure grew, she was forced to quit her job and become a full-time campaign surrogate. She became a tremendous asset, and when she wasn't trudging along with him on the trail, she would hang back in Long Island while he shuttled back and forth to Washington. She found fulfillment in tending to their three children during his time in Congress, and supported him earnestly. But as his stature grew beyond anything they ever expected, she began to wither in his shadow. When he returned to New York to run for governor – and won – they had a good few years, but suddenly she withdrew and never came all the way back, holding hands with only the fingertips. Most times, Elijah never quite knew where he stood with her.

As the limo passed through the gate and into the driveway, she let out a long sigh, as if fully deflating, and turned to face him. "All right, hotshot, last chance."

"Sorry?"

"We're not officially home until we walk through the front door. So technically, we're still on our trip. I'm giving you the opportunity to come clean before it's over. Where did you go?"

"It was state business, Cassidy. I told you that." Another strain on their marriage – as he trafficked deeper in national secrets, he was forced to withhold more of himself, though the secrets of Endure Technologies were more personal.

"Bullshit," Cassidy said. Her eyes blinked rapidly – a tell of her level of annoyance if there ever was one. "I had your pano in my purse. I let you stick me with your embedded tracker, traipsing around your donor friends with that thing in my skin for hours. That was un-fucking-comfortable, but I wore it because you promised to tell me why, and your exact words were *before we got home*." She pointed to the approaching residence, now a hundred yards away.

"I...I learned things. Unexpected things," Elijah said. "I can't right now, not until I sort it out." Her piercing stare, just inches from his face, drew a small concession. "I'm sorry."

She continued glaring at him as the limo came to a stop, her gaze probing and pointed, as if trying to pull the thoughts out from behind his eyes.

Yannik Vogel might be able to help you with that, Elijah thought. *Maybe I'd know my own thoughts better if I plugged myself into one of his silos.*

An agent opened Freedom Two's door. Cassidy filed out with a cursory, "See you inside," and swept toward the house, not looking back. How she loved to storm away from him! When he was governor and they'd come home from a fundraiser or charity event, Cass always made sure she was the first one in the door. She'd hightail it from the limo, in an almost comic sprint, anxious to greet the kids. It was a passive-aggressive gesture not lost on him. *She had to let me know they're more hers than mine*, he thought. *That because she's Around, she wins the game of Who They Loved More.*

As he exited the limo, he wondered if anything had changed.

* * *

Some hours later, following a quick dinner alone and a bit of work in the home office, Elijah decided it was time to check in with the children. He knocked on Ellie's bedroom door, paused a moment, and pushed it open.

Inside, Ellie Schroeder turned around in her desk chair and beamed over at her dad. "I knew it was you!" she giggled. Elijah stepped over a holo emitter by the door and smiled back.

Ellie was well younger than her siblings, what you might call an unexpected arrival. Cassidy, a mother who didn't always understand the difference between an insult and compliment, used to call her My Favorite Mistake.

"Hey there, Bubbles," Elijah said, using his own preferred nickname. "Can I hang out for a bit?"

"Of course! You can help me with some math stuff."

"They give you homework in kindergarten?"

"It's just some coin problems. I can do it but it's boring."

Elijah adopted a look of mock puzzlement. "Coins? What are those?" He scratched his chin exaggeratedly.

His daughter slapped him playfully on the thigh. "Oh, come on, *you know...*" She searched for the words. "They're those things that jingle in your pockets that you buy stuff with."

"I didn't know we still used coins anymore." Truth be told, he'd been advocating for shutting down the U.S. Mint for years, the production costs long outweighing the value of the currency they produced. But to do so would inflame the copper industry, so the Granger administration kept throwing money away, spending fifty cents to make quarters.

"Mom always says you're good with money stuff. Don't let me down."

"Whoa, pressure's on!" *So Cassidy does pay me the occasional compliment when I'm away.* "All right, whatcha got?"

Ellie pulled up to her desk and Elijah took a seat on the bed next to her, casually pushing aside some toys. She brought up her desktop holo. "Okay, here," his daughter said, gesturing for him to come closer. "It's all set up for you."

Elijah couldn't help but laugh, she was always roping him in to do her homework. *A crafty one*, he thought, *just like her mom.* "How about we do it together?"

When Ellie tossed out a frown that eerily resembled the one he'd seen from Cassidy in the limo, he said, "I don't think your teacher had that in mind."

"Oh, all right," Ellie pouted, her mischief thwarted.

"What's the first problem?" Elijah slid back to the corner of the bed, so he could see over her shoulder and not be in the way. The holo showed an animation on the desk, coins coming together in neat stacks before flying around again. Something that looked like a cartoon grizzly bear danced around the stacks, juggling more coins with his four arms.

"That's Mookie the Coin Monster," Ellie said. "You have to feed him the right amount. In the first problem he's asking for twenty-five cents." She plunged her hand into the holo, reaching for a quarter from the stack of coins with her forefingers. The image responded to her touch, the likeness of the quarter rendering inside her grasp as she brought it over and dropped the coin in Mookie's mouth. The Coin Monster chewed on his treat quizzically before breaking into a broad smile, the holo dinging a correct answer. Mookie did a celebratory jig around the desktop lamp.

"You're pretty good at this."

"That was an easy one! They get harder. Now he wants forty cents."

"Greedy Mookie." Elijah watched her think it over briefly, placing her finger on her mouth and look at the ceiling, again just like her mother. Then she drag-and-dropped a quarter and three nickels, the holo again responding in congratulations, this time with Mookie popping confetti-filled balloons.

Ellie had Mookie up to asking for $5.90 before she got stumped. Elijah pointed out the five-dollar coin floating by itself over the edge of the desk.

"Oh, I forgot they made those now!" Before feeding it to Mookie, she pulled it close. "Daddy, who's on that one?"

"That's Abraham Lincoln, our sixteenth president. He used to be on the penny, but they stopped making those before you were born."

"What's a penny?"

"It means one cent."

"Oh. What could that buy?"

"Not much. It used to be worth something, but over time money loses value due to something called inflation, and there's the consumer pricing index which..." He trailed off after realizing he'd lost her.

"Do they put all the presidents on money? You could be president someday, right?"

Schroeder felt a swift kick in his abdomen that only a child's innocence could provide. *Thanks, kid.* "I don't think they'll make any new coins for a while, most people use biometric payments now." He poked at her playfully. "But maybe if I was president, I'd make a new coin just for you."

She pulled back, giggling. "You can do that?"

"Sure I could. Even though I'm just the vice president now, I could even ask the president for you, if you're really good."

"I'll be good! I'll be good! Wait, you're the vice president?"

"Yes, silly, that's why we're in Washington now."

"Oh, right. You know, my friend Marco said in class that most companies have lots of vice presidents. He said America should too. Do we have just one?"

"Yes, sweetheart, there's only me."

She scratched her chin, perplexed. "Well, I'm sure you do as good a job as twenty other vice presidents would!"

"Bubbles, I can't wait till you can vote. Give daddy a kiss. Let's do a couple more problems, then get you ready for bed."

After feeding Mookie more coins and reading Ellie to sleep, it was a little before nine when he knocked on Charlotte's door.

Charlotte Schroeder was not yet a teenager, but had long discovered her teenage angst. When they told her Ellie was coming into the world, Charlotte was none-too-pleased that her status changed from Younger Child to Middle Child – and her irritation never dissipated, becoming resigned withdrawal. Elijah and Cassidy had been left with an ever-growing mystification in how to connect with her.

From behind the door there came a half-hearted, "Yes?"

Elijah poked his head in. "Hey, Charlie," he said. Charlotte didn't turn, instead her face pressed close to the makeup mirror that her parents had argued over buying for her last birthday. It was on full magnification as she practiced applying a new eyelash hue, her blinking eyes the size of saucers in the reflection.

"If you keep looking at yourself through a microscope, you'll forget how beautiful you are."

"I know what I look like. Boys are already trying to look down my shirt at school."

Elijah took a hesitant step forward, brushing past the holo inside the door. "Boys aren't too discriminatory," he said. "When I was a boy your age, I tried to look down every girl's shirt."

He got her head to turn slightly that time – it was with a look of startled disgust, but still. "Gross, Dad," she said, and went back to makeup practice.

"Why don't you put that away for a minute? I want to talk to you. What are you working on in school?"

"Just the usual."

"Anything I can help you with?"

"Well...it's not economics."

Elijah and Cassidy had spent many nights debating the best strategies for getting your tween-age daughter to respect you, but those lessons were far away now. The frustration of being shut out by someone he loved so completely drained any clever retort.

So all he said was, "Show me anyway."

Charlotte finally turned fully around and assessed his resolve for a long second. When he didn't appear to waver, she acquiesced with a simple "Fine," and waved him in.

Elijah weaved through the debris of clothes and books that were strewn about the floor – biting his tongue about the mess the whole way, reminding himself that an adolescent's bedroom is supposed to be a shitheap. He sat at the foot of her bed, careful not to disturb anything.

Her desktop holo was active, displaying the planets of the solar system. It was a fancier model than Ellie's, with a wider image range, floating planets orbiting the sun in a looping time-lapse.

Charlotte fidgeted at the controls and the solar system expanded, covering half the room.

"Astronomy?" Elijah asked. Charlotte looked at him like it was the most obvious thing in the solar system.

"We're studying Mars, the Asteroid Belt, and Jupiter this week."

"Neat." He put his hand through the holo. The image wavered as his fingers waded in and out.

"Actually," she said, "we did have a question come up at school – how come China was able to send people to Mars and we weren't?"

"Well, China never intended to bring those people back. They decided a one-way mission was worth it, and I guess they found volunteers that agreed, but it was very sad when they died. But the president and I have had some long discussions about a Mars mission, actually."

"The president? What did he say?"

"Well...he would like to do it. It's incredibly expensive to get people there, but many more times that to bring them back. Maybe the Chinese had a different calculus when it comes to human life."

"But what if someone volunteered to stay there, and said it was ok? Or if they were super-old anyway?"

"Well, the president says there's no price on a person's life. I agree with him on that."

"But in Civ-2 thirty million people have died. Thirty million, and for what? What's another two lives to reach another planet?"

"It's not that simple, honey. It's not the American Way."

"What is the American Way? Kill each other over petty squabbles?"

What is she always rebelling against? he wondered, realizing he'd been asking himself this question for years. *Is it me, or something bigger?*

"Those days are over, sweetie. That's in the past."

"Is it?"

"Ah..." Elijah wasn't about to get into an extended argument about the country's penchant for civil wars so he changed the subject, walking over to her window. Across the yard, the bubble of the Observatory Telescope was framed in a full moon's beneficent halo. "Have you ever used the telescope over there to see Mars in person?"

She shook her head. "What telescope?"

"It might be old, but it can still be useful sometimes. You know, like your father."

He got a chuckle out of her that she tried to keep him from seeing. *Too late, I got you*, he thought. *There's my Charlie.*

"How about I take you sometime? Seeing actual stars in person might give some perspective."

She met him with hesitance, but was considering it.

"Come on, it'll just be you and me. We could shut the whole place down for a private tour, and then get sushi delivered." Charlotte had found a love of sushi on a state visit to Japan when Elijah was governor. When in doubt, a little bribery never hurt – that was Econ 101.

"Yeah...Ok. That sounds kind of fun."

"Awesome," he said, with a slight hesitation. *Did kids still say awesome?* She didn't roll her eyes, so maybe. *Better quit while I'm ahead.*

"Goodnight, Charlie. Study hard, but give me a kiss first. I love you."

. * * *

Now that he'd reached some measure of connection with Charlotte – however fleeting it may be – he went to Nolan's door and banged loudly.

No answer, so he knocked again. After another moment of waiting, Elijah pushed the door open a couple inches.

He was met with the deafening sound of gunfire.

This is exactly what I needed, Elijah thought. *What's he playing this time,* Orion's Minions *or* Civil Strife?

When he didn't see any alien hordes or space battles, he confirmed the latter.

He ducked into the room and was instantly riddled with a string of virtual bullets through his chest, but they passed through him unencumbered. He looked at his feet, making sure he avoided the holo. Nolan crouched by the bed, facing away from him and spraying ammunition in the opposite direction, having more success in ducking the return fire than his father. *Doesn't count if I'm not activated yet,* Elijah thought.

Once he got close to his son, he still had to shout in his ear. "HEY! PAUSE!"

Nolan whirled around with his holo rifle up, before realizing his dad wasn't an enemy combatant. "Oh, sorry," he said, triggering a controller slung on his hip. The game stopped and silence engulfed the room.

"They did a good job with the soundproofing," said Elijah. "I couldn't hear you at all outside. Your mother will be pleased."

Nolan shrugged. "Pretty cool I guess. What's up?"

"Just saying hey. Dad stuff. Do your homework?"

"Had a little bit of history. It's done."

"How's Allie?"

"She's good. She wishes I had a car so, you know, we could go on a proper date."

"She wishes? Or you do?"

"Hey, she did mention it at school the other day," Nolan said defensively. Though Elijah's son had always been popular, Allie was his first real girlfriend, and their relationship was in those initial, self-conscious stages.

"You know the deal on that one."

"Yeah, mom made it pretty clear. But I still don't get why we can't even go out together in a state car."

"I'm not allowed to ride in an AV either, if it makes you feel any better." Because they ran on operating systems that could potentially be hacked, the Secret Service had banned the use of AVs for protectees and their family members. "But don't worry, I have some agents that would love to chaperone. They're excellent company."

"What about Dwight?"

Dwight D'Amato had been Elijah's longtime body man when he was governor. "Dwight hasn't been around in a while," he said softly.

When Nolan didn't say anything, instead looking at the floor and absently fingering his holo rifle, Elijah clapped his hands to pick up the mood.

"All right, enough catching up. Plug me in."

Nolan smiled. "How much time you got?"

"Your mother is a little ticked at me, so let's say half an hour."

Nolan pulled up the game menu and selected *Add Player*. The holo scanner took a quick measure of Elijah's figure and body mass before coating him in virtual soldier's fatigues, complete with patches of body armor and other high-tech gear.

"What level are you on?"

"Frisco." Nolan pointed to the Golden Gate, crumbling in the distance by the bedroom window.

"Wow, you got pretty far."

"You're gone a lot. We could do other levels – New Orleans, or Houston? The bridge battle in New York was cool–"

"No, not that one," Elijah said, body seizing. "San Fran is fine. What's our weaponry?"

"I've got an extra AR-95 you can use."

"That'll do."

Nolan tapped up his inventory and tossed the simulated rifle to his father. "Do you want me to restart the level?"

"Nah, let's frag!"

"Nerd." Making sure his father acknowledged his eye-roll, Nolan keyed the start button and the room again became a war zone.

Elijah took stock of his surroundings. He and Nolan were members of the Majority Coalition during the last year of Civ-2. The San Francisco level would be recreating the Majority's assault on the Underground's West Coast headquarters. If Schroeder remembered his history, the Majority came in by sea from across the bay in Vallejo, amassing forces overnight on the far side of Alcatraz Island. Just before sunrise, two hundred assault boats made for Fisherman's Wharf on the north coast. They established a foothold at the Wharf after incurring heavy losses, and those remaining charged inland to take back the city.

Elijah saw that Nolan had already gotten through some of the heaviest fighting on the wharf and made it a few blocks to the southeast. He'd done well – most of their squad was still alive and his health and armor were nearly full. *Maybe we should've let him enlist a year early*, Elijah thought.

A handful of enemies came out from under cover behind some overturned trolley cars. After Elijah took one down and Nolan dispatched three others, father and son jogged in place together, moving the game map forward. They trucked down Columbus Avenue, bearing straight for the Financial District.

They crossed an intersection, low-slung apartment buildings lining both sides of the street. A few Underground forces emerged from the rooftops, raining fire from above. Nolan took the left side, clearing one roof with an inferno grenade, leveling the entire building. Elijah took the right, picking off troops with a high-caliber rifle. After the area was clear, they jogged in place again, moving further south toward Bay Street.

They ran into a barricade and were forced into a detour to the east, away from the rubble of Chinatown. Two walking tanks clambered down the façade of a shelled-out office building – halfway down, they sprang off the bricks in a reverse swan dive, blasting rockets as they dropped to the road in front of them.

"Take cover! Go for the claws!" Elijah shouted, but Nolan was way ahead of his father, already firing his grenade launcher. After dispatching both tanks with a few precision plasma grenades, they pushed forward into a clearing, where they encountered heavy sniper fire. Elijah lost his leg armor and took some health damage. He squatted down to apply his healing balm while Nolan blasted away at the sniper nests. The shooting let up once they moved along Bay Street, but they hit another barricade at Stockton Street and were forced further to the south.

A block later, they found themselves looking at a narrow lane on a sharp uphill slope, tall buildings in all directions. Strategically speaking, it was a horrible position to be in.

All the barricades they'd come across started to make sense – the Underground was controlling their movements, herding them into an ambush.

A voice barked out from behind – "COMPANY, HALT!" Father and son, along with the other digital members of the squad, stopped and turned as the Sarge came forward.

The Sarge was their platoon commander throughout the game, briefing them before each mission stage and interrupting at key points to offer strategic advice. "Take heed," he said, pointing ahead. "The elevation works against you. You're going to need to get up Telegraph Hill as quickly as possible. You'll come to a park where there's little cover, but you need to take out that tower in the middle. There are some fallen trees you can advance behind when you get there. Now let's move out!"

It was only then that Elijah noticed it. The sea-foam eyes. The chiseled jawline that gave way to softened cheekbones. And the most telling feature, the sheer size of the man.

The Sarge was almost an exact likeness of President Granger.

Was Vogel behind this? he wondered, but after learning what the German was capable of, he thought he knew the answer. *I'm sure the game developers asked for a fortune.* Civil Strife was the latest in the series, and like the other entries – *Civil Conflict, Civil Clash,* and *Civil Engagement,* among others – it was a smash hit, far out-grossing any movie release. He tried to think which episode came out right before the election, was it the one where the Sarge led an air battalion through the Rockies?

The game-version of the president had harder features – a more protruding nose, a steelier gaze – but the resemblance was undeniable. There were even some flannel patterns on the Sarge's uniform, mimicking the president's go-to casual wear.

No wonder he crushed me with the younger male demographic, Elijah thought. Anyone who played *Civil Strife* regularly knew that the Sarge was the best damn commander the world had ever known, his awesomeness surely projected in young minds onto a presidential candidate who happened to look just like him.

"Nolan, pause it!"

His eldest again froze the game. "What is it, Dad? The ambush is the best part."

"Who does that remind you of?"

"I don't know. Patton?"

"Look harder."

"Actually, he kind of looks like The Preacher from the *Vampire Coven* games."

Elijah supposed that wasn't surprising. *If he's in one game series, he's probably in a dozen.* Come to think of it, he also resembled Orion in *Orion's Minions.* "Don't you think that looks like the president?"

"Huh?" Nolan looked at his dad, something not computing with him. "Which one?"

Isn't it obvious? Elijah was about to respond as the bedroom door swung open and three agents filed in.

"Sir, sorry to interrupt," the lead agent said to Elijah, "but we're on lockdown."

"Again? What is it this time?"

"A foreign object came over the fence. Might just be an errant drone, but we need time to confirm. Until then, you'll have to come with us."

Elijah looked over to Nolan, throwing up his hands. "Sorry bud, to be continued."

Nolan shrugged. "Hey Dad, I didn't know you had so many friends," he quipped. "Tomorrow night, maybe." He saved their progress with a tap and turned the console off.

Elijah turned back to his protection team. "All right, let's go," he said. The other two agents took their positions, one in front and one behind. The lead agent stayed back to collect the rest of the family.

Elijah leaned forward and tucked his head, clasping his hands behind his ears as he'd been taught. The agent behind him pushed a forearm into his back to bend him further, and they moved out of the room as a unit, down the stairwell and toward the bunker.

As if history were repeating itself, Elijah was once again in an armored, cramped space with his wife. It was after midnight, but the grounds had yet to be cleared, so they were 'asked' to spend the night in the bunker. It was dark except for the tea lights recessed in the ceiling, and quiet enough that he could hear his own breathing.

Cassidy rolled over, seeing he was awake. "Last, *last* chance?" she offered. Her tone was warmer this time – perhaps this latest safety scare, however common it was becoming, had reminded her how she felt about him. Or she'd had some wine.

He turned on his side to face her, and they met nose-to-nose.

"How did you get the embedded chip out?" she asked.

"It's not deep. If you stick a placeholder that's roughly the same size the skin doesn't heal over it, and you can just slide it back in." He pulled down his pajama top to show her the scab on his collarbone, but it was too dark to really make out.

"I don't think Granger would be happy to know you're going off the grid."

"I think he would be less happy to know that Vogel insisted on it."

"Vogel? The president's Sponsor?"

Elijah nodded.

"What were you doing with him?"

"He invited me to his headquarters. Endure Technologies...some amazing stuff over there. Let's just say I found out why I lost. And...maybe, how I might win if there's a next time."

"A next time? I sincerely hope for your sake that your next words were, 'I won't begin discussing that without talking with my wife first.' You know what that did to us."

"It was a grueling campaign. But it got us here."

"Yes, in this wonderful, amazing steel box. How far underground are we right now, a hundred feet? Two hundred? Super fun. Well, I suppose I should be glad we're locked away in a bunker, if that's what it takes for you to talk to your wife." Her tone was sharp as ever, but she smiled and her body relaxed next to his. "I hope you also told Mr. Vogel that running would be one of the dumbest moves you could make. This experiment that Granger had in mind, you and him together, it's actually starting to pay off. The country is warming to peace."

Elijah marveled at his wife – every now and then, she was downright optimistic. But she wasn't wrong – his own popularity might be down, but something was stirring in the country. Brawn and brain, a former army man from North Dakota and a math nerd from New York, made an impressive team.

Every alpha needs a beta, as Vogel had said.

And since they hailed from rival Leagues, when they worked together they could have that rarest of political commodities: a mandate.

"When I took this job," Elijah said, "I knew I'd have to hold my tongue a hell of a lot. But I didn't realize quite how hard that would be."

"Just in public. You can vent to me whenever you want."

"I'm holding you to that."

"More importantly, I've seen you change. You were so goddamn glum after the election, it was as depressed as I've ever seen you. Except for...well. I was just worried that this time you wouldn't come back. But you swallowed your pride when you went to work. I'm really proud of you for that, maybe even more so than if we'd won."

He'd never heard her say that before, and didn't know how to respond.

Fortunately, she decided not to wait for an answer, instead looking around the room. "Do you think there are any PanoCams embedded in these walls? Is someone watching us down here?"

"I'm sure of it," he said.

She kissed him anyway, and before he knew it she was on top of him.

CHAPTER FIVE

"Voters don't want to elect a president. They want to anoint a savior."
  - Victory in 2048, Freedom League strategy memo

Jordan Cromwell looked to the stars.

It was well before dawn, an hour before his usual early wakeup, but he found it difficult to contain his excitement. Today was a big day.

He often consulted the stars on nights like these. As a child, whenever his mother had deemed his behavior poor – and she found almost every excuse to do so – she sent him to his room and locked him in. Left to his own devices, with no television or smartphone (this was before the invention of the pano, which rendered both devices obsolete), he would lay on his bed and stare through the room's single skylight, his only window to the world.

The room was often dead quiet, and he would be free to contemplate the stars, the heavens, and everything in between. Most children would find this mind-numbing to the point of psychosis, but Jordan grew to relish spending his formative years in solitary confinement. He'd lie awake, looking upward as celestial bodies crawled past, night after night. He even created charts and made up his own constellations. He would often imagine pointing them out to a stranger. *There's Megatron, and to the east, Darth Vader – that little triangle is the front of his mask, see?*

Jordan didn't remember exactly when he first heard the Voice, but it was shortly after his fifth birthday. Per usual, he'd been on his bed, watching a particularly clear night sky play out above him.

See that bright star? That's the tip of Boba Fett's antenna.

And shockingly, something answered him, in a voice deep within his mind.

That's Polaris, said the Voice.

At five years old, Jordan had yet to pick up an astronomy book – he was born slow, as his mother never failed to remind him, so most books he read were still the size of construction paper, with at most two sentences per page.

For most children that age, memories grew shrouded over time, fleeting. But this night he would never forget, as if each moment was preserved in amber.

How did I just know that? he remembered thinking.

Polaris is also called the North Star, said the Voice. *It's over four hundred light years away.*

At first, the Voice came to him occasionally. But it *knew things,* not just about Polaris. It helped Jordan with his schoolwork – explaining big words, walking him through math problems, providing answers on tough tests. More importantly, it taught him how to behave, how to act around adults, and how to get people to like him. Or, if they didn't like him, to at least respect him.

The Voice came from someplace *other*, in a way that he could not explain, but would never dare to ask – to do that, he thought, would risk losing it. It came from inside, even though it felt *beyond* somehow, but it didn't really matter. All Jordan knew was that he should pay attention.

And that his life had a purpose.

Jordan Cromwell began dressing up for school. He said *please* and *thank you* to all his teachers. He socialized with his schoolmates, to the extent that they considered him a trusted acquaintance. He ran for class president in Third Grade, and after Laura Ogilvy peed her pants in Show-and-Tell (through another little something the Voice had taught him), he won easily.

Jordan would be class president the rest of his academic career.

The Voice taught him how to turn every conversation into the means of achieving a goal. It taught him the little under-and-up trick that rescued his first sexual encounter from disaster and made it a triumph. It taught him how to put his stamp on the world around him, showed him what the force of his will could accomplish. It set him on a path, and he dared not deviate from it.

So when the Voice told him in his final year of Harvard Law to ask the meekly pretty Helen Sanders for a date, he did. And when it told him, some months later, to ask her to marry him, he did.

And when it told him to fish out an old ski mask from the attic, sneak up behind her late at night in a shopping mall parking lot, take a tire iron to her kneecap and then force himself upon her, he did. That had been harder – she'd almost wrested his mask off in the struggle (the Voice had commanded him to do five hundred push-ups every morning for as long as he could remember, and sometimes that came in handy, plus he had to remember not to do the under-and-up move), but it had worked, too. In his first real campaign, when Mrs. Cromwell told her harrowing story of assault and how her husband's love brought her back, voters – especially women voters – ate it up without bothering to chew.

The Voice told him that having daughters instead of sons would also help him connect better with women. That took some improvised chemistry and a little luck, but it worked.

In fact, everything the Voice told him to do worked. And that was how a loner kid with a barely-average IQ became the Freedom League's junior senator from East Kansas.

When Jordan came to Washington, the only thing the Voice hadn't told him was how achingly boring it all was. When he spent his early career working up to District Attorney, courtroom procedure could be dull as hell, but at least there were the occasional fireworks. You had the visceral pleasure of locking someone away, having the privilege to watch their faces drop when they lost their freedoms. In the Senate, it took an hour to get a meeting together, another hour to decide what the meeting was about, then the meeting itself lasted three hours. A set of procedural votes would take half a day. And if there was a committee hearing – the Voice had him join both Judiciary and Homeland Security – the entire workday was shot. And Jordan couldn't get things done by himself anymore, he was trapped by colleagues who loved nothing more than hearing their own voices rebound off the hallowed walls around the Senate floor.

He attempted to lay low during his freshman term, to learn the ropes and keep quiet. He accepted a few invites to the Sunday shows, and was always surprised when they introduced him with labels like *The brashest voice in Congress* or *The East Kansas firebrand*. He didn't remember ruffling so many feathers, he was just doing what the Voice instructed.

He was biding his time those first couple of years, waiting for the big move. And now, as far as the Voice was concerned, his time had come.

In his Inaugural Address, President Granger proposed something Jordan considered radical, even if the president had campaigned on it and won. Granger wanted to re-open the nation's borders and allow immigration to flow again. The Voice had been active that day, but when Granger went into his incomprehensible argument that allowing foreigners to trespass on the nation's sovereignty would be a good thing, it rattled in his head, louder than ever before.

This is your chance! The cross you have to bear! The Voice was so loud in his mind, Jordan half-turned to Helen to see if she'd heard it.

Bear that cross he would. But the first several months of the new president's term showed little progress on the immigration front. First, Granger spent an inordinate amount of time with his wishy-washy vice president crafting a set of giveaways and concessions that they sold as economic recovery. Once that piece of pork was fried, Granger then lifted the interstate travel restrictions and abolished regional tariffs. Cromwell had little interest in these issues, only doing a few interviews each week and holding minimal demonstrations outside the Capitol. Most of his colleagues in the Freedom League tried to fight these losing battles more directly within the walls of Congress, only to get steamrolled.

So Jordan waited until the immigration issue came to the fore. He sat back while Granger and that patsy Elijah Schroeder met with congressional leaders to formulate some broad goals. He remained idle while the Reformers and the Progressives and the Conservatives hammered out its finer points – as with any major legislation, it took several fits and starts just to get through committee. And he sat on his hands when the legislation nearly died there – it took leveraging the lone Urban League member, Senator Umberto, into a yay vote, buying him off with a new Chicago park that would get shot up and overrun by the homeless by summer. Congress was disgusting.

But Jordan's wait was over. Because today, the immigration bill was coming to the Senate floor.

It was finally his turn.

As one member in a hundred-and-fifty, it's difficult for a United States Senator to stand out from the pack, to *grab headlines*. You could be fiery and brash in your interviews to get attention, but for real coverage as a mover and shaker, you had to get results by flexing some legislative muscle. Really, there were only three ways: you could put a hold on an executive appointment; you could be the deciding vote on something (which was how Umberto got his shitty park); or, you could play the ultimate power card. The filibuster.

Jordan had only put holds on a few judges, so he wasn't making many waves there, and he probably wouldn't ever be the swing vote on anything. So when his moment came, the filibuster would be his weapon. He could still the hear what the Voice had told him during Granger's inaugural address.

This is your chance! The cross you have to bear!

It would all came down to his willpower and stamina. When the Senate votes on a bill, a simple majority rules. But before a bill reaches the Senate floor, it needs something called cloture, which requires a sixty percent vote (or super-majority) to pass. Why it took super-majority to permit voting on a bill, and a simple majority to actually pass it was anyone's guess, but rules were rules.

So it would be during the cloture vote that he would mount his filibuster, where that super-majority would have to break it. In today's Senate, getting such a coalition together could take days.

And all during that time, he'd have half the Legislative Branch of the United States Government all to himself. All eyes in Washington would be fixed in his direction.

As Jordan sat in his back yard pondering, the stars soldiered on across the heavens. Snake Eyes, his favorite made-up constellation, drifted toward the horizon. Night tilted toward dawn, and the atmosphere's color brightened from black to purple. He lowered his eyes, scanning his earthly surroundings. Dew formed on the ivy shrouding the shoddy back fence. Icy condensation filled the cracks of the patio pavers, the moisture burrowing and creating new cracks every day, which would soon bleed into the foundation.

This old house is becoming a shithole, he thought.

A light flickered on from the kitchen inside. Helen. He watched her silhouette float from one window to the next as she called for him, searching. It took her forever to realize the back porch door was ajar, but eventually her head poked out.

"Jordan, it's freezing out here! What are you doing?"

"Hello, sweetheart." He forced a smile. "I couldn't sleep. Thought I'd get some air. It's not that bad once you get used to it."

She stepped out into the cold, immediately shivering, clutching her robe at the shoulders. "I know you have a big day, but you're not going to talk for very long if you catch cold."

"I just wanted to sort my thoughts."

"You can't do that inside? Where it's warm?"

"Jesus, Hel—"

Go with her. The Voice popped into his mind like a bursting bubble.

"Hang on, one second," he said to Helen, standing up. He listened to the Voice again, then added, "And another thing – I love you."

She looked back at him before retreating inside. "Oh, darling, *I* love *you.*"

Once back in the house, with Helen making coffee (using milk, not cream, like he told her), Jordan checked the morning headlines on his pano, perusing through some of the friendlier press outlets to the Freedom League. There he was, a couple of links below the fold: *Filibuster Drama – Senator Readies Launch to Kill Immigration Bill.* In the article, it took two paragraphs to even mention his name.

You won't be below the fold after today, the Voice told him. *Not ever.*

"The chairman recognizes the senator from East Kansas."

Jordan rose from his seat and the typical murmur that percolated Senate proceedings fell into a stony silence. "Thank you, Mr. Chairman. I would like to submit a commentary, for the record, about this piece of legislation."

The chairman looked down on him from the Senate pulpit, grunting into the microphone. "Yes...so we've heard. Very well. The chairman yields the floor to the senator from East Kansas."

Cromwell reached into his bag and pulled out an oversized thermos of coffee. He would have to monitor his intake wisely, needing enough fuel to keep him speaking for hours – but not so much that he'd require a bathroom break. If he stopped at any time, the filibuster would end and he'd yield the floor back to the chairman, who could immediately call for cloture.

He hoped the dehydration tablets he'd taken earlier would sufficiently dry out his bladder, but silently reprimanded himself for not resorting to a catheter. That would have removed the possibility entirely. He didn't want to pull a Laura Ogilvy in Show-and-Tell.

The coffee wasn't his only fuel. Food wasn't permitted on the Senate floor, but some members stashed candy and other snacks in their desks, which would come in handy if he needed a rush of sugar to keep him going.

And as he approached the lectern, the plasma-gel inserts he had Helen sew into his shoes warmed his toes. Even sitting for a moment could end a filibuster, so foot comfort was paramount.

Jordan looked to his left as he walked forward. Other senators were standing up to file out, perhaps believing their time would be better spent elsewhere. *Fools.* He saw some in the leadership moving among them, whipping votes. It would take ninety to stop him. Jordan was sure that would happen eventually – and the bill would no doubt pass immediately after – but that's not what this was about.

Keep whipping, pissants, Cromwell thought. *In the meantime, I'll be streaming on every pano from coast to coast.*

Jordan strode with swagger as he reached the lectern that would serve as his defining moment, the Voice resounding like a choir of angels in the cathedral of his mind.

You've reached the brass ring! it exulted. *Now grab it!*

And grab it he would, but he needed some of that extra fuel first. He stopped in front of Eldrick Higgins, senior senator from Pennsylvania, whose desk was traditionally stuffed with Hershey's chocolates. Higgins could only bite his lip as Jordan dug his hand in and pulled out a few Kisses, unwrapping one and plopping it in his mouth.

Almond, nice. He reached down to deposit the wrapper in his pocket, but missed – the candy wrapper slipped out of his fingertips and fell onto the floor.

Jordan bent down on a knee to pick it up.

He heard a shout in his head: *No! Don't—*

Just as his knee made contact with the carpet, a hand shot up behind him.

"The chairman recognizes the senator from Pennsylvania."

"Mr. Chairman, I propose we move to a cloture vote."

"Motion considered," said the chairman. "Any seconds?"

"What? Wait!" Jordan protested, jumping back to his feet.

The chairman rapped his gavel. "The senator from East Kansas yielded his time when his knee made contact with the floor." He looked around the floor again. "Any seconds on cloture?"

"But I didn't sit! It's not the same!" Cromwell was gesticulating his arms wildly enough that the wrapper, still on the floor, flitted farther away.

Another gavel-rap, more strident this time, rang through the chamber. "Senator, I would be happy to bring in a football referee to explain the specific rules, but down is down."

Several voices from behind clamored, "Second!"

"The motion is seconded, moving to cloture. We'll schedule the cloture vote for three in the afternoon, and vote on the bill immediately after. With that, we are adjourned."

The chairman let out a happy whistle of relief and the gavel came down once more.

As he sulked down the long corridor back to his office, a parade of delivery drone 'copters passed over Senator Cromwell's head. He stopped and watched as they flew down the hall like aerial ants, marching through the door at the hall's conclusion to deposit their cargo. A moment later, each drone swung back into view, empty-handed, filing back towards him.

Jordan's moment had gone viral. Since viewers could pause and zoom in on the Senate floor's live PanoStream, the offending candy was easy enough to identify, and offerings of Kisses mockingly poured in. Looking at the 'copters, many candies were already unwrapped for his benefit.

Let's get this over with, he thought, and hurried forward. Charging through the door to his office lobby, he was nearly rammed by a 'copter as it was setting down a fresh basket of Kisses on an un-sturdy pile above his assistant's desk. Cromwell jumped backwards to avoid the drone, giving a startled shout that silenced the room.

The eyes of his dutiful staff, trying to corral the hordes of Kisses into manageable quantities, turned to him. Cromwell panned his eyes across theirs, their looks of despondent concern telling him everything he needed to know. When they flooded toward him with their empty consolations, he brushed them off. "I have a private meeting to attend to!" he erupted, and dodging mountains of candy he raced to his private office, locking the door behind him. Flopping messily into his desk chair, the senator sat back and shut his eyes, digging inside his mind to seek out the Voice.

There was no response.

He supposed he wasn't surprised. The only question was, had his Voice abandoned him forever? That shouldn't surprise him either – in his biggest moment, he'd failed spectacularly and now had to live down a national embarrassment.

Helen called, offering vague sympathies. He wasn't even in the mood to yell at her for calling him at work, instead hanging up wordlessly when she started to repeat herself.

In an act of self-flagellation, Jordan activated the screen

embedded in his desk and checked his office PanoMail, which was already exploding with interview requests from media members. Fucking vultures, they just wanted to pick at his political corpse.

He looked at his *Snark!* social media stream, and 'CandyCromwell' was the highest-trending buzzterm.

He turned to the news and he was indeed above the fold on every PanoSite's front page. Most had his travails as the main headline – must have been a slow news day – complete with looping animation of the wrapper floating downward and his feckless effort to retrieve it. The headlines clearly reveled in their own wordplay:

Failibuster – Candy Wrapper becomes Senator's Achilles Kneel

Senator Takes Knee during Filibuster, Gets Fili-busted

Chocolate Meltdown on the Senate Floor

And the most direct one, with a close-up image of the wrapper itself:

Kiss of Death for Politician

So that's all it took these days – in the span of a few seconds, his career was ruined. Everything he'd worked for his entire life collapsed when his knee did.

It began to dawn on him that, guided by a Voice that he never questioned or understood, he'd been gliding on autopilot, ever since he was a kid looking through a skylight. He'd never experienced a major challenge or setback since. No hardships, not even a minor failure.

As a result, he'd never had to cope with losing. And now, in this utter calamity, his mind was a wasteland, his ego scorched earth. He wasn't prepared for this.

It was all too much to bear.

Years ago, back when he was about to ask Helen to marry him, the Voice had instructed Jordan to seek her parents' blessing first. They invited him to dinner, Helen's mother roasting pheasants that Helen's father had bagged on a recent hunting trip. The Voice had prepped Jordan for this seismic encounter with detailed instructions, but it all left him the moment he set foot in their house. The pheasants were consumed in awkward silence.

It wasn't until dessert that Helen's father lowered his glasses to the tip of his aristocratic nose and said, "Jordan, did you perchance have a reason for joining us tonight by yourself? Might there be something that maybe you wanted to ask us?"

Before Jordan could muster a response, Helen's father dropped his spoon and said, "Come with me."

Jordan followed him into his study. He filled two lowballs with fingers of fine bourbon and handed one over.

"You seem a decent young man," he said, "even though it's like you're always waiting for someone to tell you what to say before you say it. My advice to you is be a little less cautious and speak your mind. If you're going to be a successful litigator and politician someday, you're going to need that off-the-cuff ability. Politics is all about gut – not about rehearsed, canned lines. Some people can be disarmed with a smile and a pithy witticism, but more often it takes what's in your heart. Especially when you're courting voters, am I right?"

Jordan nodded. They clinked glasses and Helen's father went to his desk. "If you want our blessing, you have it. In fact, my wife has a ring for you, the ring that her mom gave to her. I know law school has been expensive, so you may borrow it until you can afford one of you own. And I have a gift for you as well."

He reached into the bottom drawer of his desk and pulled out a lockbox. After pressing his thumb to the seal, he pulled open the lid.

"Since my little girl is going to live under your roof, I want her to be protected. Take this, keep her safe. It's been in our family for generations, but it still shoots and shoots well. Promise me you'll use it to protect my Helen, and you're welcome in our family."

He promised, and his future father-in-law handed him the revolver.

In his office, Jordan now reached into his own bottom desk drawer and retrieved that same lockbox. His own thumb now triggered open the lid. With a suddenly trembling hand, he pulled out the revolver and placed it on his desk. He didn't immediately notice that this reactivated the desktop pano, showing all his new mail messages.

He decided to call Helen back.

She answered his link immediately. "Hi sweetheart," she said, her voice colored with empathy. "I must have lost you earlier. Are you feeling any better?"

He ignored the question. A drip of water fell on his desk and he realized he was crying. "Listen, Helen," he said. "There is something you should know."

"What is it, honey?" Her words were rushed, nervous at his tone.

Jordan wasn't sure where to begin. He lifted the revolver. Had it always been so heavy?

"This is difficult to say..." he started, and could hear her trying to stifle the quickening of her breath.

"...Yes? I'm listening."

The gun in his hand, he glimpsed at the swell of new mail messages, almost closing the surface pano before something caught his eye. It was from a sender he did not recognize, a man named Landon Breaux, but it was the title that intrigued him.

Cromwell in 2064, it read.

Jordan set the revolver aside to tap open the message, remembering after a moment his wife was still linked.

"I haven't always been the best husband," he said to Helen. The message on his desktop opened to show the picture of him with the wrapper that all the PanoNets were running, minus one thing. The candy wrapper in the foreground was edited out. Instead it focused on Jordan – kneeling, hand outstretched, eyes wide.

He gestured to zoom on the image, at the look playing across his face while he reached forward. Without the wrapper, his face seemed to have a whole new meaning. He looked awestruck, but at peace, in the same moment. He looked like a man who had just seen the face of God.

A single paragraph sat below the image, but before Jordan scrolled down to read, he let go of something he'd held onto for a very long time. He found the words and began to speak to his wife. "Years ago, Helen, you went out one night to pick up a few things for your sister's birthday party. The night you were attacked. I don't think you ever knew this, but I followed you to the mall."

He absently fingered the revolver as he talked, the weight of his sin already beginning to ease. He began to read the message from Mr. Breaux, how the Voice had trained him to multi-task!

Senator Cromwell, Landon Breaux's message started, *Maybe you heard of me, maybe not. But I've been following you for a long time.*

"When you were inside shopping," he told Helen, "I waited for you in the parking lot."

What you did today, Breax's message continued, *is what my poker buddies might call a royal flush of fuckery. But to me, it was something else entirely – a sign.*

"Helen, if you remember, it was really goddamned cold that night, and holy hell if you weren't taking your time."

That picture of you kneeling shows me you're a penitent man. And penitence, my friend, is something I can appreciate. It's not important that your filibuster failed.

"I remember thinking about you while I was out there. Your face, your eyes. Your heart."

What's important is that you mounted one at all.

The other end of the pano had gone terribly silent. Jordan kept on with it, even though as he read he felt his voice growing more absent. "I remember thinking about how I'd sworn to your father that I would protect that heart."

I'm the CEO of a company called Monochromatic Industries. We used to be a government contractor, but since we went private, we're really poised for growth.

"I failed you in that. I failed him in that."

Our main goal is to protect the people with what we build. Personally, I fear for the safety of our great nation.

"And I failed because I was selfish. I listened to something—"

I'm sure that like a lot of your Senate colleagues, you have aspirations. To make that happen, you'll need a Sponsor.

Jordan suddenly stopped talking as he read the remainder of the message. It was just one more sentence, but by the end he forgot Helen was even still linked and waiting for him to continue. It took nearly a minute before her quavering voice came back on the line.

"You can go ahead, honey," Helen said. "You can tell me anything."

Jordan blinked when he heard her, then started talking very quickly. "What? Oh...well you see, I just wanted to say that, when I was waiting there, you know, because I'd followed you, you know...I wanted to bring you that jacket you'd forgotten, the brown one, because it was so damn cold. But what happened was, I decided to go home after a while, because I wasn't sure where you'd gone inside, and it wouldn't do much good to give you a coat when you were already leaving. And for a long time, you know, I felt responsible for your...because if I'd have stayed, you know, maybe I could've been there, and what happened, maybe, wouldn't have happened."

Silence. Then, "Oh, *honey*..." she said, awash with sympathy. "You've been living with that all this time?" He could hear her crying on the other end as he put the revolver back in its lockbox and clicked the lid shut. "Look, you know what that did to me. I broke into a million pieces that night. I was in a dark place for a long time, a *very* long time, for what I thought would be forever. But with your love, and your understanding, eventually I was reborn. And I've come to realize that I'm stronger for it."

As Helen kept talking, Jordan suddenly wished he had some of his father-in-law's bourbon. That was good shit!

"Sometimes," she went on, "things happen to you that are horrible, worse than you can imagine, but that's how it's meant to be. Because those bad things humble you. And over time, they strengthen you."

"You know," Jordan said, "you couldn't be more right. Thank you for that, and your forgiveness."

"I love you with my whole heart, Jordan."

"I'll be home a little late tonight, but, uh, maybe we can talk more then."

"I'll have dinner waiting."

Exhaling deeply as he hung up, Jordan read the last sentence from Landon Breaux's PanoMail again. His pulse quickened with every word.

Reach out to me, as I am fully prepared to sponsor your campaign in becoming the next President of the United States.

Somewhere inside Jordan Cromwell, a familiar echo returned.

It always works, said the Voice.

CHAPTER SIX

"I know some of you have argued, after decades of division and war, that we should we simply call ourselves 'The States of America'. Some have asked if there's anything united about us that's left. I am here to say there is, and there always will be."
  - Acton Granger, State of the Union Address – January 18, 2062

The House chamber was bedecked with all the trappings expected of a presidential visit.

Every balcony dripped bunting of red, white, and blue. Each member's chair had an armrest affixed with a miniature flag. Stars and stripes framed the aisles.

Patriotism was making a comeback.

A buzz simmered throughout the House floor. The president would have a lot to brag about in his third State of the Union. The economy was expanding at a steady clip, with job creation at solid margins. Even the former Underground districts were showing gains, though whether the administration's Reconstruction Initiatives inflated those gains was open to debate.

The Initiatives had been Elijah Schroeder's first test as the president's second-in-command. Due to Schroeder's background in economics, Granger had personally directed him to construct the policy for economic stimulus, get other Conservative League members on board, and shepherd its implementation.

That was not what happened.

After consulting everyone he could think of – fellow academics, think tanks and policy shops, and members from every League – Schroeder locked himself in a room and crafted legislation that he surmised could please everyone. President Granger praised it upon review, saying it was both daring and pragmatic.

Once it leaked to the public, everyone immediately shat on it.

The view from the right: The Initiatives were a deficit-busting, runaway expansion of government. Schroeder had become Granger's shill faster than anyone could have expected. If he hadn't switched his League affiliation by now, he should. The president had a hand up Elijah's ass and was using him as a ventriloquist's dummy.

The view from the left: Half the Initiatives were tax cuts – where were the investments? Was there nothing for education? Why would the president trust this signature policy to someone who opposed him, whose ideas had been defeated in the last election?

Two months after being sworn in, the vice president found himself in the vortex of a flushing toilet. He lost all his old friends without any new alliances to show for it. The ink was still wet on his political obituary, but it would dry up soon enough and cement his fecklessness as a two-time loser.

Then, during one of their weekly lunch meetings, Granger reiterated his promise. *I said I had your back, remember?* He stepped into the fray with the full force of the bully pulpit still in its honeymoon phase. The president supported his deputy, dismissing the rancor as outdated tactics of division that had taken the country toward war in the first place. Those same tactics would not fuel its reconstruction.

It still took a well-timed dip in the stock market to force all parties to the table, but the Initiatives passed mostly intact in a nail-biting vote.

The only problem for the vice president – though the policy had been his brainchild, the president received the acclaim for getting it through.

Now, though the Initiatives were unwinding, the country was beginning to find its feet. Elijah still worried that the economy had yet to reach escape velocity from the need for stimulus (as a Conservative, this was something he never thought he'd admit), but progress had been made, no doubt there. Beyond that, there was a larger progress, a sense the country was on the mend.

It was ironic, then, that as America began to stretch its legs, ready to stand again, partisanship returned in earnest to the Hill.

It had never gone away, as the fight over the Reconstruction Initiatives had shown. But elected leaders had grown careful after the war, speaking in muted and cautionary voices, trying to at least hinge to truth and fact. This was in stark contrast to the time before, when the country sank into a morass of dog whistles, gaslighting, and vile rumors. The underlying problem was money, and nobody fundraised off of being an adult.

It was an old adage – outrageousness got attention, and attention got money. Now that the country's economic engine was creating wealth to spread around, members realized all too quickly that grandstanding produced dividends.

After all, Sponsors looked for victories, not compromises.

Elijah Schroeder chewed on all this as he paced in the wings just outside the House chamber, awaiting his introduction. States of the Union always had a long procession of notaries, with the vice president being one of the first officials called, announced after ranking members of the Senate.

The Deputy Sergeant at Arms strode forward, bringing forth his booming voice to hush the masses. Even when he cleared his throat, it sounded like cannon fire.

"Mister Speaker," he roared, "the Vice President of the United States!"

A smattering of cheers and applause drizzled from the galleries as Elijah entered. He wore his politician's face, smiling and waving enthusiastically to no one in particular. It deeply conflicted with his mood.

Dozens of House members had lined the procession aisle. To attain such premium real estate, which included the opportunity for a face-to-face moment with the Cabinet and the Supreme Court, they had to arrive hours before everyone else. Of course, the real prize was a handshake with the president, especially when in full view of the PanoCams broadcasting to their districts. Some members even slept in the benches the night before.

Elijah did a quick face-check as he proceeded down the aisle – it was lined with mostly Reformers, several Progressives, the few elected Urbanists, and even a rogue Freedom Leaguer; all staking positions for a fleeting interaction with the leader of the free world.

The entire Conservative League, he noticed, had shied away from this ritual, massing together on the opposite side of the floor. *It's come to that*, Elijah thought. *Not even the pretense of feigned collaboration.*

The vice president made his way slowly, attending to each outstretched hand – and he shook them all, even when sensing limp energy in their grasps. None of these members had waited hours for him; these were not his people. He felt like the class nerd dragged to the party by the prom king, and only because the prom king had lost a bet.

Elijah ran out of hands to shake and stood listlessly for a moment at the center of the floor, which was dominated by the House rostrum. Elijah always felt the rostrum resembled a wood-stained wedding cake, with its rounded shape and multiple tiers. During regular House sessions, the bottom two tiers comprised of clerks, notaries, and other unelected parliamentary officials, with the top tier reserved for the Speaker. The seat assignments were different for the State of the Union – the president spoke from the second tier, with Elijah and Speaker of the House sitting directly behind him on the third. During the speech, the PanoCams would be on all three individuals; Elijah didn't realize how much he detested this until the president's first speech, when every tic in his body language was analyzed by an obsessive media. From then on, he tried to remain as stoic as possible.

In the nineteenth century, the rostrum had been made of marble, but was so heavy the Capitol's foundation bent under the weight. Following that, it was constructed of a fine walnut that had lasted upwards of two hundred years, laurel wreaths etched into the front panels with the words *Peace* and *Justice* ingrained alongside.

Elijah traced a finger on the rostrum's polished wood as he paced around it, climbing the back steps to its highest tier. The Speaker of the House awaited him.

A lifelong member of the Conservative League, Speaker Archibald Cunningham had been a congressional fixture for forty years. A Capitol meeting room and adjoining hallway were already officially named after him, but the Speaker's wing had been informally referred to as Archie's Lair since Elijah was in Congress. Though rumors of Cunningham's retirement always were rampant, Elijah knew only death would force away his gavel. The Speaker hailed from Pensacola, representing Florida's first district, and had a bigger hard-on for the military than anyone Elijah could think of. In his time as master of the House, Cunningham had forged a coalition of Conservative and Freedom League members that amounted to an overwhelming, unbreakable majority. He'd been able to juggle the multitude of competing interests with remarkable ease, and any threats were either quickly squelched or offered shots at a Governorship or Senate seat.

Cunningham was scratching his birdlike nose as Elijah reached the rostrum's top tier.

"Mr. Speaker, good to see you again."

"Elijah." Cunningham acknowledged him with a terse nod. The vice president knew Archie would profess he had precious little time left to dabble in formalities, but the indifferent greeting surely had purpose. With Archie Cunningham, even small-talk could turn into a verbal wrestling match, and he was always maneuvering for leverage. Some people never stopped debating.

Schroeder nestled into the plush leather of the vice president's chair. It didn't feel quite right – he wondered absently if Cunningham had ordered it lowered. The two men sat side by side, looking out at the congressional members milling about the floor as they awaited the rest of the procession.

"I haven't seen you since the midterms," Elijah said. "I hope you weren't too disappointed."

"The president might have made some modest gains, but we're still in the majority. The country will reject him in time."

"Come on, Archie, we both know that anytime a sitting president *gains* legislative seats, it's damned impressive. It's practically unprecedented."

Cunningham only offered a mild shrug. Elijah had come in a little hot; the Speaker's weapon of choice would be indifference, even as his words had teeth. "Now that he has a better chance at passing his agenda, people will see him for what he is. He'll overreach, they always do. Just look at the immigration bill. We gave him an inch and he tried to lasso the moon. There will be a reckoning in the next election. Immigration scares people, and scared people vote."

Elijah smiled in spite of his spiking heart rate. Few pushed his buttons so adroitly. "I thought you weren't one to operate on fear."

It was the Speaker's turn to smile, his wrinkled mouth split wide to reveal the glistening capped teeth of a professional statesman. "I'm not, unless the people have something to fear."

The murmur in the chamber rose audibly as movement surged in the wings. The president was in the building.

"I remember an old mentor of mine," Elijah said, "who once had wise words. He told me that to understand the pulse of my electorate, I shouldn't worry about the GDP, or my macro employment model, or other data that might consume a numbers-obsessed economist like myself. Keep it simple, he used to say. Count the number of construction cranes in the skyline of your district. If you see a couple, you're doing okay. A half-dozen or more, you'll get reelected. Now tell me, Mr. Speaker, how do you think that mentor of mine would respond if I told him in my trip to Chicago, I counted seven cranes?"

A trickle of pride penetrated the speaker's contemptuous demeanor. "Never forgot that, did you?" He patted his knee, thinking. "I suppose I should appreciate that you've retained one of my lessons. How I wish it were more. To counter your argument, I would remind you that a Conservative House has kept your president at bay, curbing his worst intentions, and allowing the people to grow instead of the government. We have succeeded as a check and balance, where his vice president has not."

"I'm not supposed to be his check and balance."

"You're not supposed to be his hostage, either." An edge had darkened the Speaker's voice. It disappeared just as quickly. "Sometimes, Elijah, to stand with someone, you have to stand against them."

"Is that what you're doing with me now?"

"My boy," Cunnigham chided, "I fought like hell for you in both the primaries and the general election. You were a son to me. When you lost, we lost."

That stung Elijah, and the Speaker well knew it. The worst part of losing any election was failing those who'd invested in it. Elijah Schroeder was by no means been a perfect candidate, but he'd run a strong, principled race, or so he thought. Now that he knew how Granger's technical operation was leaps and bounds ahead of his, with the neuro-sorcery of Endure Technologies behind it, Elijah felt his loss had less to do with his own shortcomings. Still, when ballots are cast and more are for the other guy, it's impossible not to take personally.

Elijah remembered another thing his old mentor used to say, during one of their many nights at the Capitol Club. *When you're losing, change the game.*

"My fight continues," Archie said. "I hope yours does as well."

The Sergeant at Arms strode forward, this time announcing the Supreme Court. All six were present, though some hobbled with their collective seven hundred years of age, and they proceeded down the aisle at a snail's pace to the front row.

"I've found it better to fight from within," Elijah said.

Cunningham scoffed, his vitriol tangible. "Please. You've thrown your lot in with these Reformers." He gestured to the left side of the House floor. "Reformers. Progressives. Two sides of the same coin. Why can't they just all call themselves liberals anymore? It used to be easier to keep track of 'em. Another example of how slippery they are, I suppose."

While Elijah offered no reaction, the Speaker continued. "The thing about liberals – they sink their claws in with promises of change, of puppy dogs and rainbows on a bright horizon. People can be suckers for handouts, or empty job titles where they don't really do anything."

Elijah knew exactly where this barb was trained, but had come with ammunition of his own. "Speaking of jobs, I heard there's been some turnover in your office."

"Yes, I had to fire one of my chief aides. She'd come aboard the term before last. She was my policy...well, something-or-other, can't remember exactly. But she was good, a data head not unlike yourself."

"Why'd you let her go? I thought you liked those types, to do the heavy lifting."

Cunningham dismissed this attack with a half-hearted sneer. He looked as if he'd end the conversation there, but couldn't help indulging for a moment in a juicy disclosure. With Cunningham, you never knew if he was sharing anecdotes with a friend or leaking information. "This aide comes to me with the nuttiest idea I've ever heard. She actually suggested – and get this – that we should hold a second Constitutional Convention to rewrite our founding document." Cunningham actually laughed at the notion, a scoffing titter escaping his nostrils. "She'd written a whole manifesto about it, too. Completely absurd. I don't know how the liberals got to her, or maybe she was one of them all along. Either way, it was a shame. I let her go before she finished the next sentence. Can't have those kind of ideas going around."

Another Constitutional Convention, Elijah thought. *You don't hear that proposed every day.* Elijah tried to bury the curiosity in his voice, asking casually, "What was her name again?"

"I never said her name. But it's Theresa...Larkin, if I recall. You should tell your buddy Granger about her, he'd love it. Maybe he planted her on my staff as a joke, who knows."

Theresa Larkin. He tucked the name away, changing the subject. "Any expectations on the speech tonight?"

Speaker Cunningham shrugged, perpetuating his contrived air of disinterest. "More of the same. A lot of moral shaming mixed with pie-in-the-sky optimism. His level of naiveté is the only thing that continues to surprise me. Why should I suppose any different?" He turned to Elijah, eyes narrowing. "And why would you ask? Expecting something special?"

"Well, I'm hopeful that we can finally make some progress on the tax front. Maybe you and I could find some room on that."

"Yes, that's right...didn't you have a big proposal that you expected to be shared tonight? Another plan to please everyone, like your Reconstruction Initiatives?"

Elijah stared back at his former mentor, giving away nothing. But on the inside, knots were forming.

"Sorry to say, your plan was left on the cutting room floor. Taxes only get a fleeting mention toward the end."

"How do you know that?" Elijah demanded. "You've seen the speech?"

Cunningham pointed to the back of the House chamber. "See the young page by the door over there? That's George. His parents have been generous supporters and asked me to find a position for him. He's been loading the text for the HoloPrompTer for almost a year now. He just has to make sure I get an advance copy of everything he puts in."

Look at him revel in this underhanded maneuvering, Elijah thought. *He's positively giddy.*

"You'll learn someday, Elijah, about liberals. What Granger just did with you and your tax plan is nothing new. Liberals smile at you and wave fifty cents in front of your face. Then they steal a dollar from your back pocket."

"Actually, it's understandable," Elijah countered, burying his disappointment from view. "You and I both know this speech is all about immigration."

"He got his bill. The Senate gave up the store after that joke of a filibuster. The Freedom League can't hold their peckers without us Conservatives. Bunch of imbeciles."

"If I recall, bills have to pass both chambers. What happened to yours?" Cunningham only rolled his eyes. Elijah had scored on this point – above all else, the Speaker took pride in his ability to corral his caucus.

Elijah pressed further, leaking a tidbit of his own. "The president is going to re-open Ellis Island in March, big ceremony. Will you be attending?"

The Speaker smiled derisively but offered no answer. "Will you?" was all he asked.

The two men left it there. Elijah looked around the floor, where House and Senate members were backslapping jovially, inquiring about each other's families – normal workplace chatter. It was nice to see this typically rancorous setting in a pleasant mood. Up in the domed ceiling, a ring of light framed a stained-glass eagle, taking flight. Or it was landing, Elijah could never tell.

The gallery was full now; all honored guests had made their seats. Susannah Granger, in a breathtaking gown of light pink, took her place in the first lady's balcony. She looked like a long-stemmed rose. The Sergeant at Arms announced the Cabinet, and they filed down the aisle to great applause.

All chatter then dissipated to a whisper, and finally there was no noise at all. The Sergeant at Arms took another step forward. Elijah could hear his inhale.

"Mr. Speaker, the President of the United States!"

It was always a marvelous moment. As the president strode in to the familiar rousing beats of *Hail to the Chief*, a tumultuous uproar greeted him like rolling thunder. The noise billowed off the walls, engulfing the room.

From Elijah's vantage, the president crossed in front of the oversized holo portrait of George Washington, protruding from the far wall of the left wing. Acton Granger waded through a sea of outstretched bodies, beaming at each representative as he traded handshakes and high-fives and fist bumps. He allowed some of the female members a peck on his cheek, gazing up sheepishly at Susannah with each one.

Elijah always thought the president's physical size was most apparent in a crowd. Some members standing on benches still barely reached his chin. Granger kept working down the aisle, making businesslike progress. He shared a look of respect with each Supreme Court Justice and a look of resolve with each member of the Joint Chiefs. Then he bounded up the steps of the rostrum, standing all at once directly in front of Elijah. Even though they were on different levels, the president stood eye to eye.

He shook Elijah's hand with his routine vice-grip, then the Speaker's. As was custom, the president offered printed copies of the speech to the two men. Elijah almost wanted to tell him not to worry about handing one to Cunningham, but demurred. Instead, he set down his copy and continued his applause as the president turned his back to him and addressed the nation.

The speech concluded, and Elijah had to admit it was a soaring, left-center argument for inclusive progress and a positive vision of an accountable government. He only had to tally how often Speaker Cunningham squirmed and bristled in his seat to gauge its effectiveness. As the president hammered his points, the visible delight from the left side of the aisle boiled to exultant fervor.

After a triumphant conclusion, the president again whirled around to face Elijah and shake his hand. This time, the handshake was different, more direct – Granger held Elijah's palm in his grasp for an extended moment, patting his shoulder with hefty solemnity. The president then reached into his coat pocket and handed him a slip of paper. With a final nod toward the stewing Speaker of the House, Granger descended from the rostrum.

Elijah sat down and waited for the president to work the congressional rope line, fielding praises from fellow Reformation Leaguers and the bulk of the Progressives. The members huddled around him with an eagerness so tangible, it was as if they wanted to swallow the air he breathed. Granger gave an inclusive speech, a reaching out, but his followers surely recognized the partisan thrusts within and basked in the canny context of his barbs.

Speaker Cunningham had retired without a word, likely to his chambers for a scotch and cigar with someone new to mentor, likely one whose loyalty he wouldn't someday have to question.

Minutes later, as all camps migrated to their respective corners to spin the speech for the PanoNets, the chamber was all but empty. Elijah had been booked for an interview with *ABCBS News*, but he found himself at a loss for what to say. Which side was he on, anyway?

He retreated further in his chair, pulled out the slip of paper the president gave him, and began to read.

Eli, I know you're disappointed. If the midterm results taught us anything, it's that the opposition Leagues will band together to fight us tooth and nail – though I can't figure out if it's in spite of, or because of all the progress we've made. I hate to say it, but we're back to the trenches for now. Learning from our setbacks on the Reconstruction Initiatives and this recent victory in immigration, the team felt it best to rally the Reformers and pull in the Progressives. Enthusiasm from our side will force those against us to piss lines in the sand. That way, when it comes to your tax plan, the Conservatives and Freedomists will already be backed in a corner. And that's when I'll call on you, to come in like a rising tide and lift all our boats, and forge a lasting compromise on this important issue. You're my ace in the hole, don't forget that. My mistake last time was leading with that card instead of waiting for the right time to play it, but we're getting smarter and playing the long game now.

Give my best to Cassidy, the four of us are long overdue for dinner again. – AG

Elijah folded the note carefully, tucked it in his jacket pocket, and went out to do his interview.

CHAPTER SEVEN

Governor Granger: *Hello, little lady! Do you have a question for me?*

Audience member: *Um, yes, Mister Governor sir. (Reads from card) Could you tell me the difference between a Reformer and a Purgressive?*

Governor Granger: *Kid, holy hell are you adorable. How old are you?*

Audience member: *I'm this many! (Holds up six fingers)*

Governor Granger: *Wow, that's a lot! That was a great question for someone your age. Ladies and gentlemen, I swear to God this girl isn't a plant.*

Audience: *(Laughter)*

Governor Granger: *What's your name?*

Audience member: Sarah Watkins.

Governor Granger: *You know, Sarah, sometimes I wonder about the difference myself. All I can say is we switched to this League system some years back, instead of what were called parties, not that a group of politicians is much of a party. There were only two of those parties but they kind of split apart because different groups within them had different ideas. And I guess they decided to call themselves Leagues because a lot of people are invested in the horse race of politics, thinking campaigns are just a game or a sport. You'll see more of that when we get to something called Debate Season, but that's for later.*

What I've said before, Sarah, to people all across the country, is that the League system is better than what we had, because there's more room for ideas and more need for consensus. Our differences with the Progressives aren't very wide, that's true, but we do have them.

I would best describe a Reformer as someone who wants to make big changes that hopefully help everyone live better lives, and a Progressive is someone who wants a lot of little changes that someday becomes big change. Now, if you were to ask me the differences between some of the other leagues – like the Conservatives and the Freedom League, for example, though they try to get along for strategic reasons – well, Sarah Watkins, I would probably be talking until you were this many. (Flashes ten fingers over and over)
- Acton Granger town hall meeting in Cedar Rapids, Iowa – June 22, 2059

FACPAC was bustling.

The Freedom and Conservatism Political Action Conference was an annual opportunity to spend a weekend casting indictments and invectives against the president and his liberal enablers. The conference drew supporters of right-wing politics like an electromagnet, and they descended on the District with unrivaled passion.

Per tradition, the event was held at a ritzy convention center on the Maryland side of the Anacostia River. The governor of Greater Texas, Shelby Monroe, waited just outside its main entrance, assessing her reflection in the tinted glass.

A sharp gust of wind came off the water, and the tassels on her royal blue ensemble fluttered violently. The governor widened her stance, leaning into the gale and giving a quick nod to her youngest daughter and assistant, Trixie.

"We all set in there? Jamie?" Trixie rapped a knuckle on the glass. She likely couldn't make out anything more than shadowy outlines through the tint.

From inside, Jamie Richardson put the finishing touches on his rig. He could see the governor struggling against the elements and getting impatient. *It's a good thing her hair is an immovable object,* he thought, as he knocked on the glass twice in response. Trixie relayed a thumbs up to her mom.

"Oh, thank goodness," Shelby said to Trixie, grinning in sarcasm. "I feel happy as a clam at high tide!" As the double doors swung open to welcome her, the governor stepped across the threshold and into the conference center, the wind at her back.

Jamie had his first camera floating in front of her at knee height, tilting upward, so she came in like Gulliver descending on Lilliput. In Gesture Mode, he curled an index finger to pull the shot wide, zooming out, as her five daughters fell in side-by-side behind her, boots clacking the linoleum floor in harmony. The six of them turned to saunter down the wide, curving concourse that ringed the inner assembly rooms.

Thirty feet above the floor, Jamie's second camera swept in for an aerial shot of the crowd responding to her entrance. People were everywhere, lingering around vendor booths that hawked holobuttons and animated placards with slogans like *Keep America American*, *GRANGER MUST GO*, and *Schroeder's a Traitor*. A holo booth allowed people to make PanoClips of themselves shaking hands with prominent League figures in digitally-constructed settings like the Oval Office and Senate floor.

All around them, the inside of the building's glass wall served as a long, continuous PanoScreen, ten stories high, broadcasting a highlight reel of accomplishments made by Conservatives and Freedomists alike.

As Camera Two held its broad, top-down angle, it captured every double-take as the governor and her familial entourage approached. A spontaneous rush of cheering erupted, along with several wolf whistles – whether in support of the governor's politics or approval of her contingent's attractiveness, Jamie wasn't sure. Nevertheless, the multitude dove toward Shelby and the rest of the Monroes, begging for a handshake, autograph, or PanoPic.

"Oh my heavens!" Governor Monroe exclaimed, giving out hugs as the throng encircled her. The aerial cam drifted toward her silently, tightening its zoom.

Once she'd greeted everyone within a stone's throw, the governor broke away. "Sorry, y'all," she shouted behind her, "but I have a meeting to get to!" They groaned momentarily before a parting round of applause and at least one *Give 'em hell!*

Trixie escorted the group down a side hallway to a private lift tube.

"Top floor," Monroe said, but nothing happened.

"Mom?" Trixie pointed to a panel next to the lift tube door.

"Oh, my access pass. Jamie had it. Jamie?"

"Right, my fault." Jamie pulled the lanyard from around his neck and handed over the governor's access pass, which Trixie waved in front of the lift tube sensor before absently handing it back.

"Top floor," the governor said again, and they were whisked

skyward.

When the lift tube opened at its destination, Jamie's third camera was waiting, picking them up as the Monroe team marched out in unison. The uppermost floor was packed with offices – mostly for League insiders and event coordinators, along with green rooms for the political talent. Stepping out from the lift tube, the floor was a labyrinth of corridors.

Jamie's first thought was, *Where's the reception team?*

Down one hallway, two men and a woman were talking hurriedly. One of the men finally turned and noticed the new group. He sidled up to greet them, tugging at his collar.

Something's very wrong. Jamie sensed that Monroe could see it too.

The man wore an electric blue suit with champagne-colored boat shoes, fingers bedecked with blocky gold jewelry. A blonde comb-over made a lazy effort to cover his sunburnt scalp. "Governor Monroe!" he said, forcing a toothy grin. "Welcome to FACPAC!"

With his Southern drawl, it sounded like *We'll come to fuck pack!* Jamie had no idea what that might mean, but it still sounded funny.

"Myron, good to see you. We do appreciate the invite."

"I must say, we didn't expect you until the afternoon."

"Oh, nonsense, my man has been setting up for hours if you didn't notice. Jamie, this is Myron Collins. He's the Commissioner of the Conservative League and he runs this event." Myron glanced at Jamie quizzically, a polite nod hardly masking his suspicion.

Shelby eyed the Commissioner. "What's the matter? Why are you sweating?"

"Well," Myron said, again fingering his collar. "There's been an issue with the schedule."

Monroe said nothing and stood still, waiting for him to elaborate.

"Um, well," he continued, "we were sort of forced to offer the keynote to someone else."

"Forced? By whom? Aren't you the one that puts this thing together?"

"We have a planning committee, but I chair it, yes."

Governor Monroe was suddenly very aware of Jamie's camera, which floated silently over Myron's back shoulder. She cast Jamie an annoyed side-eye and took a deep breath. "So, Myron, which of your Conservative League friends is important enough to take my spot? The vice president wouldn't be so nuts to show his face here, would he?"

"The committee opted for Jordan Cromwell, the senator from East Kansas."

Jamie checked the video playback on his wrist-mounted monitor. For the first time since he'd met her, the governor appeared at a loss for words. All she could do was stomp her feet at the frazzled organizer, and then she regained her voice. "Cromwell? *Candy Cromwell?* Are you fucking kidding me?"

Myron stepped back from her range and adjusted the cufflinks of his suit jacket. "Senator Cromwell has made it very clear that it wasn't some silly candy wrapper that caused him to kneel in the Capitol, it was a gesture of subservience before God. Apparently the secularists in the Senate simply could not handle this saintly man's public display of worship, so they tried to punish him with some lame parliamentary ploy. They may have been able to silence our friend on the Senate floor, but we will give him a voice here."

"Jiminy Christmas," Shelby said, bewildered. Then it dawned on her. "He's going to run for president, isn't he?" It was more statement than question. "He must have a Sponsor – who is he? How much did he give you?"

Myron took another half-step backward. "Mr. Breaux has always been a generous friend of FACPAC, but that's hardly the reason—"

"Oh, spare me. Breaux, was it? Never heard of him."

"We still have a speaking slot for you tomorrow afternoon," Myron said. "We also added you to one of our group panel discussions, where you'll be the main attraction." The governor remained unimpressed. "And you are, of course, in the straw poll."

That was at least some consolation. The straw poll was a conference tradition, where after the last speech was given, attendees voted for their choice for president. Whoever won was guaranteed front-runner attention from the media and a lasting interest from top Sponsors.

Shelby Monroe let out a long, low murmur of resignation. "What's the panel?"

Myron checked his organizer's pano. "Let's see...ah. *Uniting for a Cause: How Conservatives and Freedomists Will Take the Country Back Together.*"

Jamie's cameras caught a sparkle in the governor's eyes that Myron seemed to miss.

"Yeah, sure," Shelby said. "All I need is a microphone."

* * *

Back in the lift tube, the governor nudged Jamie. "We're obviously not using that footage," she said. "Be sure to erase it."

Jamie shook his head. He would entertain her notions of creative control, but deleting footage was sacrosanct. "I'm not here to shoot your best angles," he said. "I'm here to get every angle." She bristled, looking around at her team. They collectively shrugged, and to Jamie's surprise the governor didn't protest further. "Look," he continued, "no one wants to watch something whitewashed. They want human struggle. An underdog story is the best kind of story."

The lift tube slid open back on the main level. Trixie led the team again through the throng toward the Potomac Ballroom. The governor paused for more autographs and pictures, smiling as ever, but Jamie noticed the sharpness behind it, like a knob dialed up. Newfound purpose saturated in her eyes.

They mingled around the floor until Shelby had a moment with just about everyone. Above them, the giant PanoScreen switched off its live feed of the previous discussion panel and reverted to the taped loop of Conservative and Freedomist accomplishments. Jamie noted that the loop included a clip of a man on one knee, head bowed, on what looked like a floor of Congress, with someone angrily pounding a gavel in slow motion in the background. *That's good camera work*, he thought.

"Mom." Trixie brushed past a conference attendee dressed in colonial militia regalia – for a lot of these folks, the Revolution never ended – and took Shelby's hand. "We should get going."

"Very well," the governor chirped. The group made their way into a side ballroom.

"Wow, not even the main stage," one of the daughters moaned. Shelby pretended she didn't hear.

Inside the ballroom were dozens of rows of mostly empty chairs facing a mostly empty stage. A few signs encouraged heavy PanoPosts on *Snark!* and other social media.

For group panels, the stage was arranged with a line of plush sofa chairs, situated armrest to armrest, each with a tiny table in front. Mugs with the *FACPAC 2063* emblem rested on each table. A crew of gaffers moved about quickly during the intermission, checking the lighting and sound. Some in the back switched around a set of flags, positioning the Greater Texas sigil in prominent view.

Shelby took the lead and trotted onto the stage for a quick inspection. She tested the cushions of the sofa chairs, grimaced disapprovingly, and then went backstage. "I'll get swallowed up in that thing," she lamented, as a crew member fastened a microphone to her lapel. "All right, girls, time to prayer up."

The Boot Squad formed a circle. They joined hands and bowed their heads as the governor tried to squelch her foul mood with some words of divine invocation.

Jamie had gathered his cameras, checking their settings and signal strength. Her prayer concluded, the governor wandered over and placed a hand on his shoulder. Her annoyance and frustration had fallen away, replaced by a kind of possessed focus.

"If you're going to get every angle," she told him, "don't miss this one."

He nodded and went out to the floor to finish his configuration. His attention would be on audience reaction – and as intermission was winding down, a stream of people began to file in and find their seats.

The room was halfway full when the house lights came down. As a measure of the National Anthem blared through the speaker system, the voice of a faceless announcer cut in. "Ladies and gentlemen, please welcome your moderator. You know her, you love her – from the Conservative Channel's *Riley'd Up*, Riley Hastings!"

A woman Jamie assumed was Riley Hastings sprang into view as the lights popped off in a sequence better suited to a rock concert. Riley beamed a radiant, practiced smile as she waved to the audience like someone who'd never outgrown her pageant past. Jamie's first thought was that her wavy blond hair betrayed too many roots. She strutted up and down the stage in a skirt that appeared to strongly favor freedom over conservatism.

"Welcome, everyone!" Riley announced, doing her best to lift the energy in the room. "It's so great to be back at FACPAC with all of you! Today's panel is here to discuss something we talk about all the time on *Riley'd Up* – which incidentally is available to PanoStream anytime, anywhere. It's something we all need to be better at. But first, let's bring out our distinguished speakers. My first guest, from the Freedom Channel's own *Freedom Hour*, Michael Rothchild! Our second guest, hailing from South Alassippi's fifth district, Conservative League Congressman Michael Lamb! And finally, in a special treat, the distinguished Governor of Greater Texas, Shelby Monroe! Oh, it's so wonderful to have you all here!"

The two Michaels waved generously to the audience as they sank into their cushioned chairs. Shelby waited an extra beat before coming out and went straight to her sofa, eschewing the normal waving routine that Jamie had come to recognize – a blend of pointing over the crowd mixed with a victorious boxer's two-handed fist pump.

Jamie maneuvered his cameras around the floor, Shelby's voice fresh in his mind: *Don't miss this one.*

Riley Hastings paced the stage delicately. "As I mentioned earlier," she said, "and as any watcher of *Riley'd Up* can attest, today's topic is perhaps the most important of the weekend. It's about how we can come together, as Freedomists and Conservatives. This conference needs to be the beginning of something big. Did you all know that if our Leagues were combined in the last presidential election, we would've had over seventy million votes? Hello, landslide!"

The audience stood to cheer this hypothetical victory.

"Our divisions have hurt us for too long," Riley went on. "Michael Rothchild, let's start with you. What do you see as the advantages to getting the Freedom League and the Conservative League back together again?"

"Thanks for having me," Rothchild said. "The good news is this has started already. They say nothing unites like a common enemy, and in our case that's the president. We're seeing this in Congress as members realize that they can only stop him if our two Leagues vote as one."

"Quite right!" Riley assented. "Hopefully the passage of the immigration bill was the last straw. We have to stand together against this leftist, divisive, imperialist president! Congressman Lamb, is this what you're seeing on the front lines?"

"First of all, it's great to be here," Michael Lamb said. He immediately jumped into his canned remarks. "And what a crowd! Personally speaking, if we just remembered that God is the great unifier, those on our side of the aisle would speak with one voice, the voice of our Creator. I've spoken to Speaker Cunningham personally about this very thing."

Riley took a long, earnest nod. "Truer words have never been spoken – we need to listen to and speak with God's voice, indeed. And how about you, Governor Monroe? I must say again, it's such an honor to have you on our panel. I'd love to have you on my show sometime! What are your thoughts about Conservatives and Freedomists coming together?"

Here we go, thought Jamie, and though he had no idea what was coming next, he saw the governor coiling like a cobra. He gestured delicately, bringing his cameras in tighter.

Shelby shifted in her chair, mulling it over. Then she threw up her hands. "Well, Riley, I'm frankly at a loss here. I don't believe I was invited to the right panel, because frankly that's the last thing we should do."

Riley stopped her delicate pacing. "I'm sorry?"

Shelby turned to the audience. "Have we lost our collective memories? What the Conservatives mean by *coming together* is asking the Freedom League to shut their collective traps and follow along with whatever self-enriching establishment nonsense they deem fit to jam down our throats."

If Riley had been thrown off by Shelby's tack, she recovered quickly. "I am sure you would agree, governor, that in a democracy it's better to have more votes than the other side?"

"Sure, darling, I can count. I don't expect you to remember why the Freedom League was started in the first place – I'm guessing you didn't get your job based on your sense of history. You probably just swallowed the Kool-Aid just a smidge faster than the thousand other blondes that applied. If it was only Kool-Aid you were swallowing."

"My swallowing has nothing to do with—"

"Sweetheart, it has *everything* to do with it. You're here because you're a pretty package that can sell. This whole conference is built on selling. You're filling people's minds with what-ifs and coulda-beens, and while you do that, you're taking their money. These fine folks in the audience worked hard for their income, they don't deserve to spend a thousand dollars to get filled with your vapidity. Besides, if they paid close attention, they'd realize that what you're selling is nonsense. You're not *empowering* them; you're convincing them to give power to you! What are you offering in return, besides listing all the ways the president is screwing them? What would you do that's better?"

"Our philosophy is better," Michael Rothchild said, unbuttoning his suit jacket. "The Conservative philosophy helps anyone who works for it."

"I'm sure that looks great on a book jacket," Shelby retorted. "My daughters came with me today. You know what I told them growing up? If someone asks for your money, they're not working for their own. And they expect that you aren't working either, or else they'd have some respect for what you earned. It's no secret that Conservatives think the Freedom League is their ugly stepchild. They make fun of us from within their ivory towers, and then trot us out when they want to show how salt-of-the-earth they are. You are right, I was invited here, and you had some nice things to say about me in front of these nice people, but I'm just a puppet to the people who put these things together. They're just trying to pull my strings to give you a show, and then they'll go back to their towers, same as before. Only now, they'll remodel the ivory with gold."

Riley Hastings let out a long sigh directly into her microphone. "Your accusations would have more merit if FACPAC hadn't asked Jordan Cromwell to be its keynote speaker. He is the Freedom League's fastest rising star."

"Don't even get me started with him. He's a puppet that knows he's a puppet, which is worse. He does his little dance, feet moving so fast you don't look up and see the ones pulling the strings. That's not what the Freedom League is about. We're supposed to be the renegades, the independent thinkers. We go it alone. If you want to win, then you can follow us. But we only follow ourselves."

The ballroom had fallen into a confused silence. Riley offered a rebuttal. "So...you just expect everyone here to fall into your way of thinking? Is that freedom?"

"Poor girl, you miss the point entirely. They should fall into their own way of thinking, because that's in their interest. Politics has become the new religion. And look, religion is a wonderful, beautiful thing. It goes beyond our sense of self, to a greater humanity that connects us. But we have to acknowledge that for a very long time religion was a tool that powerful people used on the poor and uneducated, to keep them in line. And we have to ask ourselves if we'd rather sit in a church pew stuffing our savings in the donation basket or maybe, just maybe, we'd be better off trying to connect with God in our own personal way."

Jamie's cameras scanned the room, capturing blank faces and open mouths. It dawned on him that Governor Monroe was the smartest person in the room, by more than a little. Still, as he looked through the monitor at all those faces, he couldn't help but think Shelby was committing political suicide.

And she wasn't done. "And let's not forget, religion can motivate people to kill. Democracy should never do that. Who in here wants another Civ-2? The last time the Freedom League got doped into supporting your candidates, that's what happened. Thirty million lives lost! Look, I realize that when you break up with someone, there are many conflicting emotions. It's horrible at first, and you pine and ache and wail at what you lost – even if you know the relationship was destructive. But we have to remind ourselves why we left. It was to forge our own path, a better path."

Shelby was standing now, pacing the stage. "So to my Conservative friends, what has this conference done for you? Has it helped your family pay its bills, or your children go to school? I shook hands with Myron Collins an hour ago, have you seen what he's wearing? His suit alone could've put my daughters through college. People, casino owners don't get rich if the rest of us are winning!"

A slow creep of boos began to dot the audience, like the first leaks in a dam. If Shelby heard them, they only sharpened her. "Frankly, true freedom lovers have more in common with the Reformers – with the president – than they do with you. At least Granger sees what's really broken, and is trying to fix it, instead of charging people money to tell them how he *would* fix it. Elijah Schroeder saw that, saw the need to throw his lot in with him, and now you all hate the vice president, too. One of your own. I might disagree with what they're doing, but I recognize they're trying to solve a problem. The so-called Conservatives and their Freedom League lackeys – *they* are the problem."

Jamie didn't know if it was the mention of the president or the vice president that broke the silence, but the invectives that rained forth were loud and unkind. The audience turned into an unhinged mob, casting a deluge of curses upon Shelby Monroe.

The governor remained on the stage's forefront, standing tall.

"Shout me down if you must! But I'm the only one here actually with your interest in mind. I ask you, please – tonight, in a quieter moment, consider whether what I say isn't true. Reflect on the people in your life that are looking out for you, that are cheering you on, not basking in your cheers. Who came here to be heard, and who came to hear you."

A modicum of silence had returned to the room. "Thank you," was all the governor said, and turned away. She pulled off her lapel microphone and tossed it to a flinching Riley Hastings – when it hit the floor, a loud pop rang through the speakers. But Shelby was already out the door, her daughters scrambling to keep up.

"Well, you wanted an underdog."

Shelby nipped at the straw in her margarita. She and Jamie sat across each other at a kitschy resort bar. The Boot Squad had long since retired to call their spouses and children, perhaps to inform them the campaign had ended before it began.

Jamie could only offer a sympathetic smile. Three gin and tonics had loosened his nerves. "I thought it was amazing."

"Think they'll invite me back next year?"

The governor laughed, a wistful chuckle, but Jamie was more serious. "If you're winning primaries by then," he said, "they'll have to."

Shelby appeared to doubt this possibility. She took another pull of her margarita, long diluted by melted ice.

"Well, Myron was pretty clear about tomorrow. You know, some say campaigning is poetry and governing is prose. But the truth is, campaigns are done in black and white, and governing is gray. Those people don't understand gray. And they vote for nitwits in the primary, idiots who promise the world but are quickly revealed as idiots once they have an office. Then, when it comes to the general election – the vote that matters – the Conservatives have the only viable candidate. It hurts me that they force themselves into going against their own interests. Sadder still, they don't even realize it." She drummed her fingers restlessly on the table. "I guess it's kind of nice knowing I don't have to give a speech tomorrow. I don't get many vacations!" Her laugh was louder now, if no less wistful.

Jamie looked around the bar, which had mostly emptied out. A few stragglers played hologames in the corner, paying them no attention.

Suddenly, the governor leaned in over the table between them, setting down her elbows and tucking her fists under her chin. She examined Jamie with a new appreciation. "You're a quiet one, aren't you?"

"Not always," Jamie said, slightly uncomfortable. "I'm just better at expressing myself through my work."

"We can't all be the Chatty Cathy, I guess. But by now, you should know all about me – and what you didn't know already, you sure learned today! My turn."

Jamie squirmed and wished his drink was full. "Not much to tell. Grew up in a small town. Progressive area, still diverse. My parents split during the war."

"I'm sorry to hear that."

"Dad was pro-Majority, in that he just wanted the violence to end. He was white, maybe I never told you that." Shelby's note of surprise answered that for him. "Mom supported the Underground, supported it *hard*. She left to fight when I was twelve. Never saw her again." He lost himself, staring off at nothing in particular.

Shelby sat back, saying nothing, letting him speak.

"That was half my lifetime ago. Feels longer, but also like yesterday, you know? I dunno, a lot of people went through worse. I ended up going to school – a good school for someone like me, learning computer science, but then there was the Education Hiatus, when the war got really bad. The Hiatus only lasted a couple months, but I didn't see the point in going back after."

"Just an awful time," Shelby conceded softly. "On all sides."

"Governor, can I ask you something?"

"You know you can."

"You had no idea I was black – or half-black – when you hired me, did you?"

"Does it matter? It didn't to me."

"I was just curious. Some folks looked pretty shocked when I showed up at your mansion."

"They're mostly good people. It takes time. The war divided us, but the war's over. Divisions should end when wars do, but it doesn't work that way. Still, you be careful. Not everyone knows you—"

Jamie had a habit of tuning people out whenever they stressed caution. He was still thinking about his mother, leaving in the dead of night, sacrificing all she loved to join a hopeless cause. The governor would have liked her.

As Shelby talked, Jamie subtly reached into his knapsack and palmed one of his cameras. He set it on the table while she wasn't looking, making sure it had a decent angle. Instead of answering her questions, it was time to ask a few.

"You know, Governor, you said I should know everything there is to know about you by now, but that's not the case. Turns out, I did about as much research on you that you did on me – I thought it might cloud my impressions."

The governor chuckled gamely. "That so? All right, ask away."

"What was your husband like?"

"Benjamin? A selfless man. Grossly outnumbered – he had no idea what to do with all us girls, bless his heart, but never complained. He worked all the time to keep us afloat. Then he struck it big – oil made a comeback at the beginning of the war, you might remember, but then the bottom fell out. He took it pretty hard, leveraged debt up to his eyeballs, and then his heart gave out."

"How old were the girls when that happened?"

"Teenagers, most of them. A handful, all of them. Each in their different way – you'll see when you get to know them. But they turned out better than we could've imagined."

"Why do you want to be president?"

The shift in his questioning threw her for a moment (the margaritas might be at fault in this), but she adjusted ably. "I would remind you that I'm not a candidate yet. But it's something I think about, usually at night. Maybe that's what happens when you sleep alone. Frankly, I wished more people asked that of a candidate – why can you do the job better than the other guy, or gal? It's amazing how many can't answer. For me, like most things I guess, it's simple. I want to teach people to help themselves."

Jamie followed up with more questions, and her responses, if just a little boozy, were direct and honest. This openness, the dropped guard, was his focal point. He felt more drawn in as she went on, laying bare her dreams and her fears, both for her family and the world at large.

They talked until the bar closed, then parted with a friendly goodbye. Jamie checked to make sure his camera hadn't run out of power and rushed up to his room to work through the night.

The sun shone brightly the next morning, the last day of FACPAC. Jamie's main entrance pass still worked, and he was one of the first ones in. He wandered around the main hallway, pretending to look for souvenirs in the maze of vendor booths, but checked his pano every few feet. He could detect the wireless signal that fed the giant PanoScreen, but where was it coming from?

Not surprisingly, he discovered the source came from well above the convention floor. *Must be up around those offices*, he thought.

Fortunately, he still had the governor's pass. He found a lift tube and used it to access the top floor. Since Shelby had decided to fly back early, he wouldn't have much time if he wanted to catch his ride.

The hallways weren't as empty as he hoped, but he had his rig with him. If he pretended to set up a camera as he did yesterday, no one would interfere. A few personnel might give him an extra glance, but he was used to that by now.

Jamie swept the halls with a practiced nonchalance, tracing the signal power through his pano until he found what he was looking for.

Several hours later, Jamie boarded the governor's plane and slunk down the aisle, nearly tripping over a loose corgi (Jackson or Thatcher, he wasn't sure). He passed Shelby's office – the door was thankfully closed – and since he didn't see the girls, he figured they were all in together for their regular Squad meeting.

Which was just as well. He found a seat in the back row and pulled out his pano. After keying in a few commands, he turned the device off and tucked it back in his pocket. He closed his eyes and silently counted the seconds.

As it turned out, there weren't many to count – they were still idling on the runway when the office door was thrown open.

"JAAAAMIE!" Shelby's head jutted out sideways from the doorframe, locking immediately on him, no matter how low he slunk in his chair.

Jamie attempted to look puzzled, innocent. He expected a shocked response at first, but not outrage. "Yes, ma'am?"

"Don't call me ma'am. Get over here! Inside! *Now!*"

He shuffled up the aisle like a death row inmate on his final march. The Monroe girls passed by in atypical silence, avoiding eye contact. Trixie closed the office door behind her, shutting Jamie in with the governor.

"Put your ass in that chair," the governor said, pointing. Jamie vaguely recalled an incident when his mother had said the same thing, back when he'd gotten in a fight in third grade. "I just got off the line with Myron Collins. Any idea why?"

Jamie gave a single nod. No sense playing coy.

"I thought you might. As you can imagine, Myron is very upset. Apparently, a video has been playing on every PanoScreen in the building for the last ten minutes, and they can't get it off."

Jamie kept his head down, speaking to the floor. "I can take it down if you want me to."

"What's the video?"

"It's the first episode of your PanoSeries. It's, well, everything that happened this weekend. Meeting people on the floor. Your conversation with Myron. The discussion panel. Our conversation last night."

"Last night? Jesus, you were filming that?" She paced around the cramped office, boots stomping audibly on the shallow carpet. After a few laps, anger gave way to curiosity and she sat down. "How'd you do it?"

"I put a camera on the table while we were talking."

"Not that. How did you get the video to play on all those screens?"

"Oh, sorry. I took your pass, but I erased all the records where it was logged. Each time it's scanned, like for the lift tube, the record exports to a log file. I just had to find each log file in the security database—"

"Actually, don't tell me! Fuck!" She couldn't seem to decide whether to sit or stand. She stood up again and walked around her desk. "Computer science, you said. Guess you paid attention in those classes. So then what, you hacked the feed?"

"Yes, I can control it with my pano. Every screen in the building."

The governor whistled. "They have cameras everywhere around there, you know – oh, you did something about those, too? Wow. Well. Jamie, listen to me. None of that really matters. Look at yourself. You have to know something. With that crowd, some people's eyes were fixed on you, whether they would admit to that or not. They'll figure it out sooner than later."

A part of him knew that, of course. He felt suspicious castings on his skin the moment he set foot in the building. But he spent a lifetime trying to block that out, and sometimes it even worked.

I have to believe they see me as I see me, he thought. The alternative was a lot more painful.

"I'm sorry," he said finally.

"I'll call Myron back. I can tell him it was just a silly stunt. Then you can take it down." Her eyes flashed to the door, dismissing him. As he turned away, she said, "But take your time doing it."

Jamie exhaled, reaching for the door.

"One other thing, Jamie. Actually, sit back down. In politics, there are always a million variables from each day to the next. Poll numbers go up, they go down – most of the time, you have no idea why. Could be some new economic report, could be a speech you gave, or a law you signed – if you did all that between one poll and the next, you can't tell what's pushing you up and what's putting you down. It's not very often you get a chance at a controlled experiment, to know the direct effect of a cause. I know it pissed everybody off at the time, but I wanted people to be thinking about what I said at the discussion panel going into the straw poll. It's going to be a crowded field and we have to stick out somehow. We're going to define our turf and stick out in this election, but first I need to know if that turf is solid. It will tell us whether we have a viable strategy moving forward."

Jamie nodded.

"We have something the other campaigns don't. Know what that is?"

Jamie shook his head.

"A message. It's not one that people want to hear at first, but they need to. And we will live or die by that message, but we will never stop preaching it. Got it? Glad you understand. Now – tell me more about the video."

"I wanted to show people why you are who you are. So they see you as I do."

"Then don't apologize. But if you have another crazy idea like that, you see me first."

Shelby walked back around her desk and plunked back into her governor's chair. "All right, that's enough berating. Let me make this call. Once you take it down, bring in your pano and get the girls, we'll have a little viewing party."

He did as she asked. After watching the episode, the Boot Squad was stunned into silence. But they were smiling.

"Every angle," the governor said.

"Yes, ma'am."

At some point over South Arkansas, results from the FACPAC straw poll came through. Governor Monroe came in second, losing to Senator Cromwell by three points. No Conservatives cracked the top four.

CHAPTER EIGHT

"As a nation, we need to look backward and ask where we went wrong. How did the greatest country on earth get to this place of strife and division and war? Those are good questions, worthy questions, but we must also look forward and ask what's within ourselves to turn wrong into right."
- Acton Granger, speech to the Coastal Florida National Guard – March 12, 2062

Tess Larkin was crushing her interview.

She'd been rehearsing for the last two weeks, focusing on how to transcend the usual talking points and make a sincere connection. She practiced demonstrative, sharp gestures when trying to reinforce her arguments and open-handed, inviting ones when turning anecdotal. She had to be both cold and warm, and able to switch between those attitudes without betraying any stress.

To successfully interview for a politician, I have to act like one.

She bristled at the irony, for a politician she was not. She had the policies down cold, no problem there. Tess was every wonk's wet dream. The problem wasn't the knowledge as much as her demonstration of it. She was well aware of her abrasive, dismissive nature – what her father deemed in her younger years the *I-know-its.*

Tessa, he would say, *you'll know things better than anyone, and they'll resent you for it. So try not to hold it over their heads.*

For both father and daughter, that was easier said than done.

Tess would argue she simply followed his example, and that anything incorrect was worth correcting.

Everything she'd learned, a lifetime of learning, came from him. But now, in the twilight of his lifetime, she had to watch him fade away, his fighter's intellect losing round after round. After moving back in with her father last month, she'd gotten a front row seat, to watch him toil against an impossible opponent. She was happy to play the corner-man; to tell him he wasn't fighting alone. But the worst part was, his spirit was losing as much as his mind. *It's hopeless, Tessa – why bother?*

On top of all that, her lack of employment was giving her cabin fever. In her old job, her every opinion mattered, her every decision had consequence; she felt like a cog in the wheel of the world. Now, she was a full-time caretaker, her father's sole companion as he diminished.

Before Speaker Cunningham unceremoniously fired her, she'd been the best policy advisor he ever had. But the *I-know-its* had reared their ugly heads, and Cunningham had no appetite for unconventional thought. He was a knife-fighter, not a visionary – so any talk of refurbishing the pillars of American democracy fell on unwilling ears, and she found herself toting her belongings in a cardboard box.

But that was in the past. Today, she could put all that behind her. She no longer advised the country's third-most powerful person, but she could leverage that experience into a new life on the other side of the Hill.

So now she sat, deep in the bowels of the Russell Building, the Senate's main office complex. She kept her back rigid in perfect posture but her arms loose and free-wheeling, and mashed every interview question served her way screaming back over the net.

Earlier, riding the MetroLoop to the Capitol, she remembered her father's words: *The only way you convince anyone of anything is to get them to think it was their idea.* She didn't want someone to hire her, she wanted them to think they couldn't live without her.

Senator Barbra Duncan was the second-ranking member of the Senate Appropriations Committee (and a card-carrying Conservative like Speaker Cunningham), but Tess was betting the similarities ended there. When she'd called, the senator asked Tess for a face-to-face interview immediately, something Tess found curious – policy and advisory personnel met with a Chief of Staff initially, or someone even below that. But Tess took it as a positive sign of the senator's serious interest, which only heightened the intensity of her interview preparation.

And that preparation was paying off. Duncan was a serious player, known to hang around the smoke rooms of Washington's most exclusive clubs, indulging in a cigarillo and a flavored martini after long legislative sessions. Her hair was reddish-orange, like a simmering ember, with streaks of silver running from the roots to the tips. *Most politicians would dye those out,* Tess mused, *but Barbra Duncan doesn't have to.*

As the interview began, the senator took an informal perch on one end of a sectional sofa and Tess settled into an ornate wooden chair. A delicate coffee table lay between them, a paperweight of the Capitol Dome pinning down some document folders.

Tess flashed her best inviting smile, which she'd practiced until her mouth was sore the previous night.

Duncan played it nice at the open with an abundance of pleasantries and small talk, with a natural warmth Tess could only dream of adopting. Her voice was like a fingernail raking over the teeth of a comb, gravelly from the cigarillos, yet soothing. Then, before Tess could realize, the senator moved to business. The interview didn't feature questions in the exact sense of the word – Duncan merely orated for a few minutes before stopping suddenly, waiting for Tess to pick up on her thought. It was as if the senator was better suited to a larger audience feeding off her perspective and eloquence, rather than the back-and-forth of an actual interview. Her monologue opened with a grandstanding statement about the lasting damage the liberal strands of the Reconstruction Initiatives had done to the economy. Tess tried to beam genuinely as if her dithering pronouncements were the greatest insights she'd ever heard, waiting patiently for her to get to the flipping point. As she moved into a denunciation of the larger ethos of the Reformation League, she then waxed mournfully on the denigration of free enterprise. This was where she paused, looking on Tess to restore her faith.

Since Speaker Cunningham had obsessed over the Reconstruction Initiatives to the umpteenth degree, fighting the vice president over every clause and condition, Tess was intimately familiar with them. She wisely omitted her admiration of some of the genius that Schroeder had integrated to the bill – such as tax credits for crowdsourced infrastructure projects – but proffered that as the Initiatives wound down, the free market's invisible hand would naturally take over. She concluded her point by walking through the financials systematically, recalling exact figures and projections from the Congressional Budget Office's latest restatement.

Tess could sense Duncan was studying her responses carefully, but aside from that the woman was a blank slate. She assumed the senator would appreciate a good sparring partner, someone she could work with into the night, perhaps intermingling deep legislative policy dives with some old-fashioned girl talk. Tess swam in the possibilities – *maybe we share a weakness for romance novels!* What a difference this new life could be, compared to her job before, where Speaker Cunningham had a reflexive aversion to anything personal.

Tess crossed her legs to punctuate the conclusion of her answer. Duncan smiled enigmatically before launching into another monologue, waxing at great length on the campaign sponsorship structure and arguing that Sponsors needn't be disclosed to a prying electorate. Then she stopped, practically midsentence. Tess picked her up, citing the two legal decisions from the last decade that saw no reason to compel such disclosure. She didn't mention her elemental disdain for these decisions, nor detail the dangerous precedents they'd set, but did allow that candidates with sponsorship transparency tended to connect better with a distrusting public.

So asked, so deftly answered.

The senator's third question, which turned out to be her last, was in a rather different vein – and not just because it was an actual question.

"Can you tell me a little bit about your master plan to destroy the Constitution?"

Tess recoiled as if punched, but tried to maintain the warmth in her smile. "Sorry?"

Duncan stood from her perch in the sofa. The silver in her hair flashed in the light. "I don't typically mingle with House members, they have their side of Capitol Hill and I have mine. But I ran into Archie Cunningham after the State of the Union and he was just dying to tell everyone about this advisor of his. He wouldn't shut up about you. Frankly, I wanted to meet you in person, if only to make sure the man wasn't pulling my leg."

"I have no intention of destroying anything. I don't know where he got that."

Senator Duncan sighed and reached into a pocket of her pantsuit.

"Ms. Larkin, I've kept a copy of the Constitution on my person for the better part of two decades. I know every word – forwards, backwards, sideways, upside-down. Now, if you think the Bible comes from a divine source as I do, then this document is the greatest composition in history authored by human hand. So when Archie Cunningham tells me he had a policy advisor who thought she could do better – well, I thought, *I have to meet this girl.* I expected wings, or a halo, so I'm a little disappointed."

"I don't know what the Speaker told you, ma'am, but that is far from what I proposed."

"Either way, you're out your damn mind. How can you work for the Conservative League if you aren't a Conservative? I asked you two questions – red meat that any faithful League member would pounce on – and you toss up figures and court cases with the passion of a doorjamb."

"I was speaking in policy, not agenda."

"My dear, you can't have one without the other."

A sudden spasm coursed through Tess's body, like a rubber band snapping. She wanted to grab the paperweight on the coffee table and throw it out the window – but her body tensed up, fighting any movement. The only thing she could manage was uncrossing and then re-crossing her legs, and then she didn't know what to do with her hands. She straightened her back even further, and Duncan looked at her, puzzled.

"You're an odd little bird, aren't you?" the senator asked.

Perhaps the only reason Tess didn't completely explode was the horrifying realization that her past exploits had spread through Washington like a viral PanoVid, and any further misadventures were likely to circulate just as quickly.

Don't be anyone's punchline, Tess thought – as Duncan looked on, smirking.

Finally, after an interminable silence, she found her footing and stood. As she pushed for the door, Tess decided to take one parting shot.

"Fuck you very much for your time, Senator Duncan. I'm sure your constituents appreciate that this is what you do with it."

"Nice meeting you, Ms. Larkin. Best of luck with your mission."

You won't cry, you won't, Tess promised herself in the lift tube, and immediately broke that promise when she exited the Russell

Building. She found a bench and let her emotions run their course, shooing away any concerned passersby with a flippant backhand. Eventually the tears abated and she collected herself, recalling one more Richard Larkin pearl of wisdom.

Don't let anyone see you struggle, Tessa. Always keep your chin up and your shoulders back.

She stood up and breathed a long inhale, then started walking. But as she scuttled down First Street toward the Capitol South MetroLoop, her eyes remained downcast.

Chin up, shoulders back.

She tilted up her head, fixing her eyes forward, and straightened her torso. As if by miracle, there was a tangible elevation in her humor.

She looked around the Hill – there really was nothing like this place in all the world. As the sun crested over the marble frieze of the Supreme Court building to her left, it bathed the elongated dome of the Capitol in a yellow glow. Tiers of scaffolding still bordered much of the building, and a construction crane stretched over the North Wing – a completed restoration after the damage inflicted during the war was another year away – but the structure was never not beautiful. Neither was what it stood for, the Statue of Freedom at the dome's tip punctuating the sky.

Tess wondered if she'd ever be back – to work on the Hill again, to see the restoration finally finished, to be part of something that mattered. But she had to face the truth that she'd likely lost the privilege of working here forever, landing on some hidden black list fostered by Speaker Cunningham and his many cohorts.

Chin up, shoulders back.

Her pano started buzzing as she passed the Library of Congress. It wasn't a link she recognized, but she answered anyway – she'd put some feelers out on possible caretakers for her father.

"Good morning, Ms. Larkin? Hold one moment for the Vice President of the United States—"

"Oh, for chrissakes. I don't know who this is, but I've had enough of games!" She closed the link with a flourish. There had been plenty of embarrassment for one day.

Pano still in hand, Tess decided to check in on her father. Their devices permanently linked, she could see where he was at all times. *Still at home, good.* Remembering to keep her chin raised, her shoulders back, she descended into the underground MetroLoop.

* * *

But he wasn't home. She called his name as she came inside, first expectant of a response and then longing for one. She darted through the rooms of the house and her heart dropped when she saw his pano on the desk in his study.

Ohshit, she thought, words blurred in panic. *Ohshitshitshit.*

She checked the back yard. No sign of him, but the gate was still locked.

Her pano buzzed again. She thumbed the answer button without looking at the link.

"Dad, that you? Where the hell—"

"Ms. Larkin, please hold for the Vice—"

"Seriously, fuck off!"

She thrust the pano in her coat pocket and rushed out the front door.

Fortunately, he hadn't made it far. After a few heart-bursting minutes, she spotted the back of his head bobbing amicably down Calvert Street. It wasn't on his old walking route, but it was close.

She hesitated a moment to let her pulse normalize. Then she came up behind him.

"Dad! *Dad!*"

He cocked his head at first, as if he wasn't sure her voice was real. Then he turned around. "Oh, hiya Tess. What's the matter? You're not wearing any shoes!"

"Took them off a few blocks back," she panted. "Heels aren't easy to run in. But that's beside the point. What the hell are you doing out?"

"I was trying to find the garage. You know, with the pattern on the door? I was looking for my gardening shears. Then, well...I guess I decided I'd go on a walk."

Tess paused, still breathless. They didn't have a garage. "Pattern? What, the woodgrain? That was our old house in Brookline. Remember?" She touched his upper arm, careful not to let him go. "How long have you been outside?"

He thought it over, gears spinning but not connecting. "I'm not really sure," he said finally.

"Dad, you got lost. Do you understand?"

He looked around, searching for a recognizable landmark. Though it wasn't his usual route, he'd still been on this street a thousand times over the years. "Lost? Guess I am," he confessed.

"Listen to me. You can't do this anymore, ok? If you want to walk, I'm more than happy to go with you. Looks like I'll have lots of free time, actually. Otherwise, you can't leave the house by yourself. It's dangerous out here. I know it sucks and I'm sorry."

She expected him to protest – to put up a fight, to say she was making something out of nothing. But could see behind his shy, embarrassed smile a concrete, entrenched fear, and with it an acknowledgment: he had no idea where he was or how he got here, and the realization must be terrifying.

"Sorry, Tessa," he finally said.

She put her arms around him and squeezed. "I know, Daddy. You're all right." She pulled back and stroked his hair. "I'm gonna get you one of those tracking chips, ok? I can't lose you again."

She saw tears brimming in his eyes, and he looked away as she noticed, but he nodded.

Her pano hummed again. Another unfamiliar link, but she clicked on it. Maybe chewing someone out would make her feel better.

"Whoever you are, I'm sure you're just thrilled with your own hilarity, but this is *not the time*."

"Theresa Larkin? Don't hang up." It was a familiar voice, just not one she'd ever heard in person.

"Okay..."

"Apparently, you're difficult to get a hold of. My assistant said you thought she was pulling some kind of prank, so I thought I'd try you myself."

She panicked for the second time that day. "That...really was her? I mean you? Oh, *ohmygod*. Mr. Vice President, I'm so sorry. Today's been...um, not great."

He chuckled. "Believe it or not, I get hung up on more often than you'd think."

She was afraid to ask why he was calling, so she remained quiet.

"Look," he said, "I heard you had some interesting ideas and I was wondering if you could meet for lunch sometime."

"Sometime?"

"Well, sometime...as in now? I can have a car pick you up in five minutes. It'll just take you to the Observatory."

"Five minutes?" She calculated how far she was from home, added it to the time it would take to look halfway decent again. God, she was a sweaty mess. "How about fifteen? I, uh, just worked out."

A short pause. "Fifteen would be fine."

"One more thing. Can I bring my dad?"

The vehicle arrived exactly as scheduled and whisked them westward to the Naval Observatory. It was a short ride – about a dozen blocks to Massachusetts Avenue, and then a few more through Embassy Row – that had the advantage of not giving Tess enough time to overanalyze what had just happened.

Still, her mind raced faster than their AV, which wound through traffic with startling efficiency. Her father seemed to be enjoying himself – it was his first trip in an Automated and he kept asking why there wasn't a steering wheel. "Where is it taking us?" he asked.

"The vice president's house," she replied.

"Really? Who's that now, Truman?" He gave her a wicked grin. Lucid Time, and his sense of humor, still made the occasional appearance. But Tess would bet anything his joke was just a cover; he really had no idea who the vice president was.

They pulled into Observatory Circle as a chilly rain began to fall. Tess admired the house through fine streams of water drifting down her window. The mansion looked like a relic from another time, but the rain gave the window shutters a reflective sheen.

Tess was surprised to see Elijah Schroeder waiting for them in person, standing at the edge of the porch with his wife.

Elijah even clambered down the steps toward them with an oversized umbrella, while Cassidy Schroeder hung back. The rain intensified as Tess climbed out with her father, and they hustled toward the house at the vice president's side. Once out of the weather the pleasantries began.

"So glad you could make it on such short notice," Elijah began. "This is my wife, Cassidy."

"Pleased to meet you, Mrs. Schroeder," Tess said. "My father and I admire you very much."

"That's very kind, Theresa. Mr. Larkin, I'd be happy to give you a tour."

Richard Larkin looked to Tess. "Go with her?" he asked, nodding at the second lady.

"Yes, Daddy. She'll show you around. I'm sure there's a library somewhere."

"And it's enormous," Mrs. Schroeder said.

Richard smiled as broadly as ever – he would feel at home around books, no matter where he was.

Mrs. Schroeder took the umbrella in one hand and Tess's father in the other, leading him across the lawn toward the Observatory Annex.

As Tess entered the house, Richard called back, "I thought I told you never to call me *Daddy!*"

Lunch was a pickled salmon salad with parmesan crisps and pomegranate seeds, but that wasn't the best part.

"Have all the water you like," Elijah told her. "There's a reservoir out back."

It was crisp and clean, even compared to the Congressional Cafeteria.

Tess, feeling nearly drunk from the water, admitted, "This is actually my second interview today."

"Interview? Is that what this is?" Elijah smiled, adjusting his glasses. "In a way, I guess. Just curious, what was the other one?"

"Duncan, Western Michigan."

"Barb? She can't say hello without giving a floor speech."

"I got that sense." Tess watched the vice president closely as he tended to his meal, nodding to the housekeeping staff and referring to them by name. They looked relaxed around him. It was a stark contrast to the sanctimonious politicians she was used to being around, blind to anyone below their level – whether they be foodservice help or policy advisors.

Elijah Schroeder was also blatantly attractive in person – in a Clark Kent, handsome-but-overselling-the-nerd-part way. But he seemed much more natural than he came across on the PanoNets. Tess was careful to push any indecent thoughts from her mind.

The vice president reached over with a pitcher and refilled her water glass. "So you're probably asking why you're here," he said.

"It occurred to me once or twice."

"Well, look, I'm sure you know this, but you used to work for my old boss."

"I was afraid of this. So Cunningham told you, too?"

"Relax – can I call you Tess?"

She nodded, dumbly.

"When Archie mentioned your name, it sounded familiar. Turns out, I'd read one of your policy proposals – on eggplant subsidies. Sometimes I get stuck with the less glamorous bits of executive governance. But it was remarkable how you framed your case, I was moved."

Tess tried to contain her shock – she wasn't so surprised that the Vice President of the United States had read that proposal as she was that anyone had. "A vital source of vitamin K," she heard herself saying.

Elijah laughed. "Yes, an essential vegetable."

"Officially it's a fruit, but..." Tess stopped, kicking herself. Sometimes the I-know-its couldn't help themselves.

Elijah laughed harder, a pleasant melody in his amusement. "All the same. But eggplants aren't why you're here, Tess. Something's been stirring inside me. Maybe it's from being around all these Reformers these past couple years, but we need some big ideas. Something that makes us better as a people, makes this country whole again. When the Speaker told me he what you proposed, I thought it was an idea so big that it warranted exploration. I know it got you fired, but he's a little more set in his ways than I am."

Tess tried not to snort at the understatement.

Elijah pulled his chair closer. "Tell you what – if this is an interview, I'll ask you a question. Put yourself in a primitive society. You've got four loaves of bread, but you have to feed five people. Imagine that you can't split the loaves, cut them in half or anything. It's a whole loaf, or it's nothing. What do you do?"

"No matter what, someone doesn't get a loaf?"

"Could be one person, could be all but one person – if you give one person all the loaves. You'd be creating a dictatorship, then – but yes, assume at least one person would be without any bread."

"I guess I have some questions of my own, then."

"Thought you might."

"Are they, relatively speaking, the same people? Age, gender, ability?"

"Assume they're a microcosm of a larger society. So, no – some are more productive, but they might also take more to feed."

"Then I could give the bread to the four most deserving..."

"Not sure how that would be determined, but all right."

"...Or the four hardest working..."

"Darwinism, natural selection? Most would call it a cruel system, though humans are the only species that doesn't fully abide by it. Do you think defying natural order makes us more naïve than our animal friends, or more evolved?"

"...Or I could give the bread to the four hungriest, and leave the strongest one to find some other means."

"Hewing towards socialism?" He was teasing her now.

Tess squinted. There had to be something else. "Can I exchange the bread, trade it for something more divisible?"

Elijah smiled at her, slapping the table. "Ah, you've discovered the barter system! You're thinking like an economist – better be careful. If you're going to work for me, keep this problem in your mind. You can see with each answer you lay the foundation for a different kind of society. And isn't that what a constitution is designed to do? So, that brings us back to your big idea. Can you tell me what you had in mind?"

"Well..." she demurred, her morning's confidence shaken.

"This isn't a trick. It's not like we hang people for treason anymore. At least, I hope not."

"You don't sound so sure! But all right, I'll lay it out for you. How much time do you have?"

"The afternoon is pretty clear. Cass can keep your father entertained, take him to the telescope. There's some pretty cool science stuff in the Annex."

"He'd love that – the science stuff, I mean. As long as he's supervised."

"If you're still here by dinner, maybe Nolan will want to play hologames with him, or Ellie will braid his hair."

Wait, what? Tess dropped her fork, clanging noisily on the salad plate. Was that some kind of joke?

Elijah seemed not to pick up on her momentary confusion. "How long has he...been like that?"

"The dementia? It was early onset, but it only really took hold in the last few months. Or maybe it was years ago, and I've just been in denial. He'd wandered off when you called. It scared the living daylights out of me."

"Cassidy's grandfather had something similar, though later in life. If you should need one, I know a top-rate facility that's affordable. We used it back when I was a lowly House member."

"We're not there yet, but that's very kind, thank you."

"Offer's on the table. Anyway, first things first – this is for you." He slid a pano across the table. "This is how we'll communicate, keep it on you at all times, don't tell a soul, et cetera et cetera. If I can convince the president to give this idea a chance – I'll be honest, it's a longshot – I'll officially add you to the payroll, so you can get benefits and all that. You'll be compensated as a contractor for now, but until then, I need you to keep a lid on this. You can't tell anyone you're working for me, not yet."

"I'm not known for leaks. Even if Speaker Cunningham trashes me about everything else, he'd back me up on that. And you don't have to worry about my father, he'll forget he was ever here by midnight."

He nodded, having assumed as much. "Second, that's a secure pano – no open links – but you can't be too careful. It's best you and I never mention the word 'constitution'. We're not there yet, anyway. That being said, we can call it the Convention Project. If anything does get out about this, for whatever reason, that would be better for both of us."

"Convention Project, got it."

The vice president took the last bite of his salad and set down his silver. "All right," he said, "tell me what you've got in mind."

CHAPTER NINE

"Over many generations, the divided halves of this country led each other to the edge of a cliff. From this precipice, they stared into an abyss called war. It was inevitable, then, that when one side jumped, the other was all too quick to follow."
  - Acton Granger, speech at Yankee Stadium Memorial – August 5, 2060

The ferryboat churned through New York's Upper Bay.

It didn't have far to travel – the trip from Manhattan's Battery Park to Ellis Island was only a couple miles. It was a windy morning, with a fine, misty rain that kept one's skin in a perpetual tickle. The sun had dwindled into memory, buried behind clouds the first two weeks of March.

But it was a beautiful, bright day to Benjamin Allen. As he stood on the ferryboat's prow, his eyes drilled through the fog at the vista ahead. Standing across the bay was the magnificent Lady Liberty herself, her statue looking resolute as always, flaming torch hoisted high.

Liberty Island was not their destination, however. In the middle of the bay, the ferry slowed and pivoted ceremoniously toward Liberty's little sister, Ellis.

Built up in the late nineteenth century, Ellis Island became known as a beacon of opportunity for American immigrants from across the globe. At its peak, the immigration center processed ten thousand souls each day, including future American icons Bob Hope and Cary Grant. Ellis Island was America's primary immigrant hub until the 1950s, as the majority of prospective citizens began arriving by plane instead of boat. The island stood idle for a time, until becoming a museum in the late twentieth century, but interest eventually waned and Ellis faded into obscurity.

Until now. With the passage of his immigration bill, President Granger had decided to reintroduce Ellis Island as a national symbol, making it the first immigration center for the country's newly open borders. A savvy politician recognizing an opportunity, the president had decided to make a national event of it, with all the pomp and circumstance befitting the monumental occasion.

"Beg your pardon sir, a cocktail for you?" Ben Allen looked down to his left and saw a hand outstretched with a highball of gin fizz, his favorite. He turned to face its server with mock incredulity.

"This boat ride is barely twenty minutes long, how'd you find that?"

Dylan Tomlin only responded with a teasing smile. He handed over the highball and squeezed in next to Ben on the railing, a tight fit amidst the crowd of other passengers. Dylan was quite a bit larger than Ben, but he managed to fit in wherever he went, and he could always find a drink.

The two of them watched in silence as the ferry drew closer to land. Ellis Island was largely manmade, built up on excavated soil from New York's first subway tunnels. The island's layout was in a basic rectangle with a docking area cutting a narrow vertical through most of the middle, so it resembled a squatted *U*-shape.

The two sides of the U were distinctive, Ben remembered, having toured the island as a child almost sixty years ago. When it was operational, Ellis's right side held the Main Building, a limestone behemoth that resembled an old train station. It warehoused incoming migrants as they were processed, which included a medical exam and often took several hours. Just beyond the Main Building stood another large structure used for storing baggage and valuables. A courtyard lay to that building's side, open to views of both Manhattan and the incoming ferry.

Ellis's left side had always been closed to the public, containing a private hospital and assorted administration buildings. Ben remembered a bridge connecting the island to Jersey City on the opposite side, but the bridge had long been taken by water. He wondered if it would be rebuilt now that the island was open again –

the latest studies were indicating that sea levels had finally begun to recede. *There's a positive to the world running out of oil,* Ben thought.

"They've really cleaned up the place," Dylan observed, as the island came into view. He was right – after the museum had closed, Ellis had gone to seed, its buildings crumbling under their own heft. Most of the island's thirty acres eroded, but it had been re-dredged and ringed with levees that Ben hoped might also shield them from a frigid breeze.

The closer they got, the better it looked. The reconstructed Main Building shone even through fog, the fresh glass in the windows looking like tiny beacons. A small, triangular jetty stretched out toward them from the island's right side, a single flagpole hoisting the seventy-five-starred American flag, rippling favorably.

Dylan tucked his hand in the crook of Ben's elbow, giving it a squeeze of nervous anticipation. *After all this time,* Ben thought, *we're a country of new beginnings again.*

Now that he could see over the levees and into the courtyard, the setup for the ceremony became clear. Opposite sets of bleachers faced each other, with a wide procession aisle running between them. A stage had been erected at the aisle's end with some VIP seating and a backdrop of flags and banners.

"This is incredible," Dylan breathed.

"I'm just happy we got an invite."

"Don't give me that. You've championed this cause for a generation. I may be the only one that knows it, but none of this would be happening without you."

"I'm just a rich guy in a backwater state that's seen lots of residents either die off or move south. We need people, wherever they come from."

"Maine isn't backwater," Dylan protested.

"Maine is the definition of backwater. That's what makes it so wonderful. But there's a difference between backwater and desolate, and that's what we're becoming."

Dylan's pride may have clouded his outlook, but Ben knew his husband agreed, deep down. "All the same," Dylan said, "But look who changed all that. I couldn't be prouder of you for this. After all, who was asking for an open border before you? Who forced the issue by only sponsoring candidates that supported it? The president's seal is on that podium, but this is your party. Drink your drink."

Ben was happy to oblige, taking a long pull of the gin fizz. He looked back at Dylan, who was typically dressed to the nines and in full fashionista mode. Even his raincoat stood out, a grooving purple and all straps and flaps, looking like he belonged on some kind of Galactic Council. Somehow, it fit him.

In so many ways, Dylan was Ben's opposite – brash where he was quiet, impulsive where he was methodical – and in most of their two decades together that had worked just fine. Ben had spent so many years dialed into his work, he considered Dylan the spritely relief to his dullard self, the colorful contrast in his grey palate.

But in the year since his retirement, Ben was spending considerably more time at home, and the colorful contrast was now full up in the foreground, constantly needling for attention. Ben had to admit that thoughts of moving on crept in, something he would've figured to be the last thing to ever occur to him.

Lately, however, there was some restraint in Dylan's whirling dervish. He'd become newly capable of muting his eccentricities when needed. Ben had no desire to see his companion lose any part of what made him special, but appreciated that his specialness could be controlled. As a result, they'd been clicking better than they had in years.

Today, however, Dylan's fashion choices appeared to defy that recent restraint. Ben couldn't withhold his opinion any longer.

"Care to explain that coat?"

"You like it?"

"I didn't say that," Ben said, with a whiff of amusement. "The president's going to be here, you know."

Dylan mock-pouted in protest. "Don't be surprised if he points me out during his speech. Look, this is what happens when you let me go to Fashion Week. Check this out." He raised a sleeve as the misty drizzle intensified. Ben puzzled at what he was seeing. Raindrops were gathering a few millimeters above the coat's material before pushing sideways around it, as if repelled by a force field.

Ben brushed the sleeve with his fingers. "Huh. It's completely dry."

"Amazing, right? It's made of something called caliphan – I have no idea how it works, but it's the new rage. Rumor is the government invented it. No doubt, this is the finest raincoat ever made. It never gets wet, even in a hurricane!"

"It's a neat material, but do they make anything out of it that looks normal? A lot of those flaps seem impractical."

Another look of protest was shot Ben's way. "You can convert it a bunch of different ways. I'm not sure how that works yet. But I'll get you one before we head back."

"Why buy one, when you can get two at twice the price?"

"Now you're learning how to govern. What do you think, hood up or hood down?"

"Down. Your hair would hold up better in a hurricane than the coat."

The ferry crept closer to land and slowed to prepare for docking. A few men hustled about on shore, readying ropes and a disembarking ramp. Ben's view of the courtyard was now fully clear, a holo of the presidential seal rotating slowly in front of the podium on the stage. He found himself fixating on it.

"You still think about running, don't you?"

Ben scoffed. "This old queen, president?"

"You've broken barriers before, what's another one?"

"I don't think the country's ready for a president and his First Husband."

Dylan feigned grievance. "They would love me!"

They sure would, Ben thought, *until they saw your White House decorating budget.*

"Besides," Dylan continued, "you've sponsored so many candidates, no one would notice that you're sponsoring yourself. I think it would set a good example, for a Sponsor to put their mouth where their money is. And the country could use someone with your genius."

The ferryboat eased into docking and the engines went full stop. Ben and Dylan moved to exit with the rest of the passengers. They stepped down the ramp and followed the stream of people toward the courtyard.

As they reached the bleachers, an event official approached, giving Dylan a brief smile before turning to Ben.

"Mr. Allen," she said.

"Yes?"

"I'm from President Granger's advance team. The president has requested that you appear on stage with him along with other distinguished guests during the ceremony."

Ben felt an urgent tug at his sleeve. "Just a moment," he said to the official before turning to Dylan. She nodded politely.

Dylan pulled Ben back a step, keeping his whisper out of earshot. "You know what this means, right?"

"You can handle a couple hours without me. I'll just be a few feet away."

"No, don't you see what he's doing?"

"Who?"

"Granger, that's who. He's pulling you close. He *sees you as a threat.*"

Ben scoffed. "Really, I'm glad you think so highly of me, but that's probably the last thing on his mind. I'm just a guy with deep pockets that maybe the president would be interested in dipping into. Aside from you, no one's even considered me a possible candidate, let alone felt threatened by me." *Plus, I get a better view of history.*

The official leaned toward them. "And you're Mr. Tomlin, I assume? We also have a special arrangement for you in the front row."

Dylan tried not to beam, but this clearly pleased him. "Well then," he said. "Hanging out with Big Shot over here has its perks."

"You're just now realizing that?" Ben teased.

The official brought out her pano, gesturing to forward their new credentials. She frowned and tried again.

"Here, allow me." Ben took hold of the pano and used the same technique, encircling each virtual pass with a forefinger and flicking it first at Dylan and then toward himself. He handed the pano back to the official, who walked away and smiled in dubious thanks before returning to her post.

"She actually was doing it right. The new release has trouble registering smaller hands."

"Don't go crazy," Dylan said. "You're retired, remember?"

"If there's one thing I hate, it's a buggy interface. That shouldn't happen with a major release."

"It's not your problem anymore. Look where we are. Besides, you have bigger dreams, remember? And today, one is coming true."

They kissed goodbye briefly, and Ben turned to the stage entrance. He spun back after a few steps. "You know, you're right," he said to Dylan. "Maybe tomorrow, we can talk about that other dream."

Dylan smiled his *gotcha* grin, turning away with a bounce in his step.

It was coming upon noon and the president was late. Ben passed some time trading small talk with the dignitaries on the stage –

mostly ambassadors and members of Congress. He seemed to be the only one from the private sector. A few empty seats remained for those in the Cabinet traveling with Granger.

As conversation stalled, Ben retreated into his thoughts as his eyes settled on the rotating presidential seal a dozen yards away. Could Dylan have been right, that the president invited him only because he thought he was a threat? If so, was it a mistake to come? Ben wouldn't have missed this occasion for the world, but he did check to see if he'd be in the background shot during the president's remarks, and even shimmied his chair a few inches to the left, as if that would make a difference.

Two years into office, Acton Granger was already a historic figure, racking up legislative wins and presiding over a resuscitated economy. How could Ben Allen beat someone like that, given that the country only knew him as a tech magnate? When the president first announced his campaign, he was dubbed the *North Dakota No-Name* – an unknown from another backwater state. He'd worn his anonymity like a badge of honor, saying it kept him free-wheeling and loose, until suddenly he was the front-runner. Could Ben do the same, if he ran? Did the *Maine Mogul* have the same panache?

As for strategy, funding would of course not be an issue, but his appeal might be. He was an old computer geek and not exactly a natural politician. Most Progressives would sit this one out, given the president's popularity. That meant a limited primary. He had deep ties to the Progressive League, sponsoring many of their campaigns, but would they see him as viable given that he'd never run for anything himself? And if by some miracle he won the nomination – what about the general election, what chance would he have?

Progressives ran strong in the Northeast – where there were almost two hundred electoral votes, if you included all three Pennsylvanias. The president would own the Midwest, the Conservatives and the Freedom League would fight over the South, and the West Coast might be up for grabs. The calculus was tricky, but if he could hold his home turf and spend heavily in the coastal states, it was possible.

New York might be the biggest challenge. Elijah Schroeder, as a native Long Islander, might complicate things if he chose to stay on as vice president, but no one could say if that would happen. It was one thing to govern with someone in a different League, it was another to campaign with them. Granger might consider him a drag on the ticket and cut him loose. If he stayed on, Schroeder could turn away progressive-minded Reformers who looked for a less compromising option.

Which best explained why the vice president wasn't here today, even though Ellis Island was his back yard. Granger had been wise to give Schroeder some distance on this issue – especially since most Conservatives adopted, at best, a wait-and-see position.

The other question on Ben's mind – why run? It couldn't be just about breaking barriers. He would have to play down his sexuality to all but his most ardent supporters. Dylan would get frustrated by that, always quick to wrap himself in a rainbow flag. His husband also wouldn't understand the effort involved. No more sunset walks, thermoses of gin fizzes in hand, down to the shore. He'd be un-retiring and then some.

Then there was the money. He made so much on the pano there was an almost limitless supply of it, but a presidential campaign was tens of billions of dollars, nothing to sniff at. To justify the investment, he would need a cause – and without his realizing, the president had just outflanked him on immigration. He would apparently need to fine-tune his political instincts as well.

But what cause? What could he champion that might launch him into a contender?

The sound of approaching aircraft snapped him out of his reverie, and Marine One seemed to appear all at once against the backdrop of the Manhattan skyline. The quadcopter was a beautiful bird, sleek and stealthy, its four horizontal rotors dancing across the mist. It was flanked by a pair of hoverjets, and they flew past the island at a distance, with all eyes watching their arcing path. Marine One settled down regally on the other side of the island, behind the old hospital. Once it touched down, the hoverjets vaulted upwards into the cloud cover, the only hint of their presence now a low hum.

Music began to play from pano speakers around the stage, lending the scene a campaign event vibe. Those wandering around in the bleachers took their seats and waited. After a couple of upbeat pop songs, the familiar notes of *Hail to the Chief* rang out, and Ben closed his eyes, just briefly, his imagination taking hold. *I could get used to hearing that*, he thought.

Acton Granger soared onto the stage, throwing his massive arms out in a figurative embrace of the crowd. Many politicians now mimicked the president's greeting, in various degrees of failure – you had to have arms that long for someone in the back row to think you could reach them.

Granger took to the podium, speaking without notes. He effortlessly ticked off the names of those who'd joined with him in this common cause of furthering the interests of diversity and strength, tossing out quick anecdotes for each. When he got to Ben Allen, his tone turned personal, heavy on admiration with even a tinge of awe. How courageous this tech pioneer and philanthropist had been for all these years, when most everyone had turned against this cause in fear.

In the front row of the audience, Dylan was smiling and probably thinking, *Told you so.*

And now, the fruit of Ben's labors sped towards them. A cigarette boat streaked toward the island, hovering smoothly over the chop. At the boat's aft, with hands on hips and a foot propped up casually on the side railing, stood the man who would be America's first immigrant in two decades, looking like Washington crossing the Delaware.

He was a man that Ben knew well. About three years after the war broke out in earnest, Ben had felt a twinge in his ear, then a nagging, dull thrum. Turned out, some of the microfusion batteries in the second-generation pano had a faulty casing, leaking radiation. Pano-related cancer exploded into a firestorm – big enough to warrant a media-coined nickname, the Pancer Crisis. As someone who was glued to multiple devices in work and in life, Ben was a prime target. Dylan had always told him his addiction to his little magical device would be his undoing, and he'd been right.

"I have Pancer," Ben told Dylan, once he'd heard the news after ordering MRIs for everyone in his company. "Stage four." He remembered how Dylan, who didn't always keep up with current events, reacted with a fit of laughter.

When that subsided, all Dylan could ask was, "What the fuck is Pancer?" But he grew more serious as Ben relayed each grim detail. He helped Ben scour every medical journal they could find, no matter where it came from, until happening upon a theoretical procedure detailed by a prodigious Osaka neurosurgeon by the name of Hijori Nakomuri. They liquidated most of Ben's fledgling fortune at the time and flew to Japan for the procedure.

Months of recovery followed – multiple tumors in Ben's brain had been cored out and replaced with stem cells, which took time to develop. He never would have survived without Nakomuri, but he wouldn't have lived without Dylan Tomlin either. He drove Ben crazy back then, too, but was at his side during those agonizing few months when Ben didn't know if all his cognitive and motor functions would return. For the most part, they did – Ben still had some episodes now and then (Dylan called them Space Cases), as if someone had tripped over his power cord before hastily plugging it back in. But on the whole, his brain had grown nimbler and more agile with the younger, fresher stem cells at the helm.

Now, so many years later, Nakomuri wanted to bring his talents to the United States. With no small amount of lobbying (and promises for future sponsorships), Ben Allen had secured for his old doctor the honor around which this Open Borders ceremony revolved. Other boats bearing other passengers would follow, but Nakomuri was to be the first. And once admitted into the country, he was coming to Maine – Ben had gotten the surgeon a residency at the Portland Medical Center, which would immediately jump twenty spots in the national rankings with his tenure. There were still thousands of Pancer patients stateside who had been stuck in the country once the war broke out, though many had long since died.

Nakomuri's boat docked opposite the ferry and the foreign neurosurgeon set foot on American soil, greeted with buoyant eruption. The doctor waved and smiled awkwardly, unused to such public fawning outside of medical circles.

Taking it all in, Ben didn't know which he enjoyed more – the scene itself or watching it play out on Dylan's face in the front row. He looked back at Ben, shedding visible tears. Ben fought back the urge to hop down from the stage and watch it all unfold at his husband's side.

Any doubts he ever harbored about leaving Dylan, his heart answered them in that moment. He loved him. He loved him. He loved him.

Nakomuri took the long walk around the courtyard, along a red carpet that took him between the sets of bleachers and up to the stage. There, the president waited, ready to ask the Japanese doctor the famous set of twenty-nine questions that once greeted every American immigrant when Ellis Island was open.

What is your name?

How old are you?

Are you able to read and write?

What is the Constitution?

And so on.

Once completed, America would have a new ingredient in its

melting pot.

Nakomuri paused his approach while the president formally introduced him. The applause reached a crescendo, and Hijori bowed and blew kisses to all quadrants of the audience. Ben brushed back his own tears, overwhelmed by the spectacle. The stagecraft was simply better than anything he could dream. He dismissed his half-baked idea of running for the presidency, as if he had any prayer against the giant in front of him, the man who had just fulfilled Ben's most ardent aspiration. He only felt an enormous surge of pride, in his country, in humanity, and in his own part in this magnificent day, pride so swelling he worried his flesh might not hold it in, that he might explode and shower all these dignitaries with his gratified innards.

In the blink of an eye, it all splintered into chaos.

From his periphery, Ben saw a faint blue flash from halfway up one of the waterfront skyscrapers in the Manhattan skyline. Just as quickly, Hijori Nakomuri, famed regenerative neurosurgeon and soon-to-be first immigrant, spilled forward onto the carpet as that same pulse of light flickered through his skull. His legs and arms twitched in the throes of instant death. A wisp of smoke exhaled from the hole in his head, liquefied brain matter gargling out, forming ragged clumps in the doctor's hair.

The crowd reeled from celebration to horror, then shifted into panic as other light-flashes followed, peppering the bleachers indiscriminately in deadly spurts. It was a weapon Ben had never seen before, seemingly harmless bolts of light carving through anything they touched, even the ground.

A larger flash blinked from the skyscraper across the bay – red this time, like a muzzle blast – and Ben could see a pinpoint growing larger as it trailed toward them.

Someone fired a missile at us, he thought. *We're all dead.*

But Ellis wasn't the missile's target. Instead, the javelin-shaped projectile screamed past overhead, as it made for Liberty Island and the statue bearing its name. Breaking the sound barrier, the missile left a shuddering boom in its wake, and anyone who hadn't taken cover was thrown to the ground.

A focused sphere of bright green light detonated in the Statue of Liberty's upraised forearm, just below the base of the torch. At first, nothing happened. The crowd, pausing to bear witness even amidst raining death, initially gasped a breathless sigh of relief. Someone next to Ben questioned if it was a dud.

Slender fissures started to appear around Lady Liberty's wrist like infected veins, rippling into seams and cracks as acid ate its way through the oxidized copper of the statue's patina. The structural framework inside the arm began to liquefy, dissolved by ravenous chemical reactions. The statue's hand – and the torch it grasped – wavered on its dissipating base, slipping downward. It tipped forward hesitantly, tottering, then pitched into open air, tumbling hundreds of feet to the ground below. It landed on its side, half bouncing and half breaking apart, spinning out wildly upon impact. The sound of it rang across the bay like a terrible church bell, delayed slightly by the distance between the two islands, as if it took an extended moment to confirm the horror of the sight.

"Great God Almighty." Ben Allen didn't know if the words came from his lips or someone else's. *Even during the worst of Civ-2,* he thought, *no one touched the Statue.*

Cries of anguish spilled out across Ellis Island, as a disbelieving audience absorbed what it was witnessing. Then, remembering their danger, they tumbled toward the ferryboats in a tsunami.

In front of Ben, a blanket of agents had fallen upon the president in a protective ring. They activated the Hamster Ball, an insta-flatable shelter sphere, furiously pushing Granger inside it as if trying to stuff a newborn back in the womb. No sooner had the president been enclosed that a beam struck the bubble in a glancing blow, turned away by the Hamster Ball's reflective outer layer. Four agents gathered at one side, pushing hard in poetic unison, and the sphere rolled forward. Plunging off the stage, it picked up speed and barreled toward the quadcopter on the other side of the island.

In the sky above, the two escorting hoverjets dropped back into view from the cloud cover. They hurtled toward Manhattan and the source of the carnage, scanning for targets. But with the Statue of Liberty an amputee, America's first immigrant murdered, and the president spinning away like an oversized marble, the perpetrators must have decided their work complete and the shooting stopped.

The jets listed aimlessly in the wind and rain, either unable to find something to shoot at or unwilling to take the shot. The offenders had chosen their vantage deliberately, a densely populated structure where collateral damage from retaliatory fire would be enormous.

The hoverjets returned and lingered over Ellis Island at a low, deafening altitude. Beyond the hospital, Marine One blasted off, nestling between its escorts, and the three aircraft darted away at impossible speed, fading to hazy specks over open water.

Ben realized in all the madness he'd barely moved. The dispersant crowd was streaming aboard the ferry, their shouts and screams moving with them, leaving an unearthly silence after such monumental noise.

Dylan!

His eyes moved back and forth with frantic urgency, looking for his love. He did not take long to find. Before the stage were dozens of scattered bodies, some shot, some trampled. A few were still twitching, others writhed in soft moans, but most had gone still. Enshrouding one, in the first row of risers, was a coat of purple caliphan with the hood down, rebuffing both rain and blood as its excess of flaps rippled in the wind.

CHAPTER TEN

"The Second Civil War was borne from lies. If my election refutes just one of those lies, it's this: those who called themselves the Majority, weren't."
- Acton Granger, Inaugural Address – January 20, 2061

Jordan Cromwell allowed Helen a kiss goodbye, walked down the block, and stepped into the waiting airpod.

He didn't tell his wife where he was going, of course, only that it was official Senate business. She'd swallowed it easily enough.

The 'pod was a top-of-the-line model, reassuring in that it shed light on the depth of his Sponsor's resources. A ramp lowered from the belly of the fuselage, molding into steps as he drew near. Jordan entered the empty craft and bolted himself in.

A voice came across the comm. "Morning, Senator."

It was the first time Jordan heard Landon Breaux speak, a low rumble peppered with a Cajun accent's cheerful mischief.

"Good morning, Mr. Breaux. I look forward to seeing you."

"I'll have you down here in no time." With Breaux operating the controls remotely, the airpod lifted into the air. Jordan absently wondered how much money it took to get one of these sanctioned through the FAA's restrictive policies.

Once the aircraft was a thousand feet up, its carbon fiber frame became nearly transparent and Jordan had a panoramic view of both earth and sky. His stomach lurched at the sense of floating in nothingness and he nearly doubled over from nausea.

"Sorry 'bout that," Breaux said. "Might've turned that on a little quickly. Focus on the reflectors in the wings if you start feeling queasy."

"I should be fine."

"All right, see ya soon."

The 'pod started to hum as Landon keyed the thrusters, and Jordan was on his way.

An hour later, the gulf coast teemed with life below him.

The freshman senator was unused to such vibrant ecology. Back in Kansas, the earth was flat and plain. Washington was all concrete jungle, save for a few scattered parks. Here, as he stared through the clear bottom of the airpod, the land heaved beneath him as if a sentient being.

Everything below was brilliant green or brilliant blue, clusters of vegetation and swamp blotting the landscape in an irregular patchwork. Landon's voice taught him how to use the magnification controls, amplifying his view. Jordan turned them all the way up and at three thousand feet he felt he could pluck the leaves from every tree he passed over. It was dizzying, but incredible.

The airpod was tight quarters, its fuselage little wider than a coffin. Jordan's head bumped the canopy even when he flipped his seat facedown. It would feel claustrophobic if the 'pod didn't look halfway invisible – if anything, the craft was like an extension of Jordan himself, if he'd sprouted wings and could reach near-Mach speeds.

Landon's voice rumbled again over the comm, continuing the near-constant narration that had run through Jordan's voyage. One thing Jordan had learned about Landon Breaux on this flight – he liked to talk.

"And on your left," Breaux was saying, like a docent at a museum, "you'll be passing by good ol' Mobile, South Alassippi – largest port in the gulf."

Jordan watched passively as the flight console responded to his tour guide's remote, the 'pod tilting toward the city so its passenger could appreciate Mobile's splendor. Jordan was not entirely impressed with this view – the prize of Largest Port in The Gulf was not what it used to be. Instead, he tried to block out Landon's grumbling drawl and tune in another voice, *the* Voice, but it continued its stubborn streak of silence. It had been a week since he'd felt that reassuring tickle in the back of his mind, and Cromwell feared the growing gaps in contact were widening.

The airpod pitched over the water at the Gulf of Mexico's edge. Cromwell watched lackadaisical waves tuck themselves in quietly over the sand as his flight continued west of Mobile.

On the comm, Landon went on for a few minutes about the varieties of sea life still edible in the gulf – "Farther south you go, the pinker the shrimp get!" – as Jordan contemplated his weekend itinerary. He needed his Sponsor's resources like a gulf fisherman apparently needed those pink shrimp, but that made this trip no less dreadful. Jordan might hail from the Midwest, but he was no hillbilly – he was a Harvard man. The idea of jaunting through the bayou turned his stomach more than flying in a transparent airpod.

But it would only be a weekend – candidate and Sponsor would get to know each other, maybe they'd shoot a rifle or two, and Jordan would leave after making a handful of empty promises. After that, he'd have all the campaign cash he could fathom.

Jordan had done his research since he first saw Landon's name cross his pano, seconds before he was to confess his heinous offences upon his wife and blow his brains out. Breaux certainly had the makings of a Sponsor, gaining vast fortune as a defense contractor. He was a scientist first, from what Jordan read, and an entrepreneur second, a pioneer of weapons technology that kept the nation safe.

There the records stopped. Breaux's company, Monochromatic Industries, cut ties with its government benefactors and went dark.

Jordan tried accessing the classified details of Breaux's dealings with the Pentagon, but he didn't serve on any Armed Services committees, so his requests were denied. He'd asked around among his Senate colleagues and been rebuked. His inner Voice was also of no help. Landon Breaux was cloaked in mystery.

That hadn't stopped him from throwing money Jordan's way, however. Usually there was a delicate ritual between a candidate and their Sponsor, a dance of negotiated positions, staff approvals, and campaign strategy, that took months if not years. Getting the firm commitment of a Sponsor was a Holy Grail in politics, and they almost always wanted a seat at the table before the first payment was tendered. Not so with Breaux – he doled out funds without asking if they were needed. Taking one look at the airpod, Jordan knew he was good for it.

Up ahead, the edges of a chalky skyline sharpened through the haze. "My blessed city," Landon said. "May her sacrifices not have been in vain."

Jordan stretched forward to observe New Orleans in the distance. In the nation's early years, the Crescent City had been a strategic lynchpin at the heart of its fiercest wars. It was no different with Civ-2. During what history considered the Second Civil's darkest moments, the Underground and their Minority sympathizers controlled the city's lower wards, and with it the critical shipping lanes from the Mississippi River to the gulf. The Majority made a tactical calculation and ordered a bombardment to take out the protective levees in and around New Orleans proper. The resulting floods made quick work of the insurgency, but the city was lost. Anything under two stories disappeared beneath the expanded river, now an unbridled lake, a new sister to Pontchartrain in the north.

The airpod slowed into a descent as the city drew near. Jordan turned off the magnifiers and flipped his seat back to an upright position. The rooftops of the French Quarter barely broke the water's surface, appearing as planks of floating plywood from above. Breaux piloted the airpod around the St. Louis Cathedral in what used to be Jackson Square, its three spires dripping moss like candlewax. The Sponsor remained uncharacteristically silent as he navigated the craft toward downtown.

As the city's taller buildings came into focus, what once were prominent banks and swanky hotels rose out of Lake New Orleans, cocoons of concrete with steel skeletons. They bobbed in the water like bath toys in an oversized tub, specks of lichen blotching their surfaces in moldy pockmarks. Untamed vegetation sprouted everywhere, in odd places at odd angles. Flocks of geese and herons and cormorants swapped rooftops as if in a gang war, taking and ceding territory.

And just like that, he was past it. The 'pod turned due south, plunging deeper into the bayou. The patches of green within the swamp grew greener, more lustrous.

"I look forward to having you in my home," cracked Landon's voice, and the comm went silent. The 'pod found a clearing of steady earth, hovered momentarily, and then sank into it. The belly of the fuselage spilled open at an angle and slid Jordan gently to the ground.

Standing up with a brush-off, he surveyed the area. The grass stood a foot tall in most places. Live oak trees, no doubt hundreds of years old, bent over like hoary giants with hunched shoulders. Crows flitted about their limbs, squawking loudly at Jordan's presence.

Jordan was asked to come alone, normally his favorite way to travel (or do anything, for that matter), but now his aloneness felt...lonely. Vulnerable. He was a small man in a foreign, busy environment. He looked forward to returning to Washington, a feeling he was not accustomed to.

After absorbing his surroundings, Jordan spotted a path leading east, partially obscured by outsized ferns. He started forward, the muddy terrain seeping freshwater around his loafers with every footfall.

The path wound beneath a canopy of weeping willow trees, Jordan ducking between their dangled tendrils. He came upon a grassy clearing. Scraps of vehicles littered the landscape like a junkyard – an old hydro-engine here, a boat frame there, rusted heaps on stacks of brick. On the far side, squeezed amongst a bank of live oaks, stood a dilapidated cabin no bigger than a doublewide trailer. The house (and Jordan had a hard time calling it that) barely propped up a roof of discolored slat that sagged at the corners. The rest of the cabin fared no better – the wood looked chewed, the railings were missing half their spindles, and the lone window was boarded up. It looked as if the swamp might swallow it at any moment.

It was hardly a home befitting one of the country's richest men. But as Jordan came within a hundred yards, he saw Landon Breaux out front, perched on an old oil drum and spooling a fly-fishing line. The airpod's remote control lay on a plastic crate next to him, emitting a faint holo, next to a tobacco pouch and a mason jar of unidentifiable reddish liquid.

Seeing Jordan, Landon brought his hands to his mouth and called out, "Well hello there, fella!" He waved the senator over hurriedly – *Come on now, haven't got the time for you to sit and stare.* Jordan quickened his pace, treading softly across the wetlands.

Jordan silently rehearsed his introduction as he approached. The closer he got, the more trinkets, widgets, and contraptions were in his path, littering the yard like landmines.

"You made it," Landon said, not getting up. "Gotcha here in ninety minutes, like I said. Grab a spot, will ya?"

Jordan extended his hand. "Mr. Breaux, so wonderful to meet you in person."

Landon Breaux fixed him with a narrow gaze. He looked astonishingly unlike his two-trillion-dollar worth and more like a bumpkin you might spy rocking on their porch, watching traffic and chomping through a hayseed. A goiter swelled in his throat and gave him a decidedly toad-like appearance. The only part of him that looked refined were his glasses, perched dangerously far down his nose as he spooled his line, probably fitted with enhancement lenses. *How long has he been watching?* Jordan wondered, suddenly self-conscious of his movements once he'd left the airpod. Breaux's eyes were perceptive and quick behind those glasses, darting from Jordan to the rustlings of nature around them.

No, there was nothing hayseed about his eyes at all.

"Don't worry about formalities here, son. They don't mean much in the swamp."

Jordan continued with his prepared remarks, undeterred. "I appreciate you inviting me here. This is such a magnificent place—"

"It's a dump. But I like it that way." Breaux stood up, shaking out his legs. "Come on inside. I got plans for you."

The Sponsor lumbered up the eroding porch steps and led the way in. It was not a dump on the inside, not quite. Antique furnishings clashed with modern gadgetry and equipment, hoardings of what Jordan's mother might call doo-dads. Though they looked nondescript at first glance, there was an intricacy and artisanship apparent in their workings.

Against the closest wall were stacks of plastic bricks, piled floor to ceiling. Next to that, a row of micro3D printers worked steadily, each no bigger than an infant's shoebox, carving smooth curvatures into bricks within. The opposite wall was a full PanoScreen, tuned to a half-dozen channels at once, broadcasting busy images. And next to that...well, was an armada, weapons of every sort – rifles, pistols, automatics, old and new.

"Ruger LC9," Jordan said, pointing to one.

"You know guns?"

"Some guns." *I might've swallowed a bullet from one of those if it weren't for you.*

In front of the weapons cache sat a workbench, strewn with components of other weapons broken apart – barrels, grips, stocks, and springs, compiled into neat little mounds. Mixed among the components were other elements Jordan didn't recognize – tiny lenses and mirrors, cylindrical molds of plastic that looked like pen casings. Some of these disparate materials were fashioned together into what looked like miniature flashlights.

"You'll want one of these," said Landon, handing him a device. "Just don't push any buttons. Let's get you suited up."

Clad in waders, a camo pullover, and with the little flashlight-thing in his pocket, Jordan fell back into his bucket seat as the fanboat revved up, wind pummeling his face. Landon had warned him to strap in, but the boat was quicker than he'd imagined, tearing across the water like a skipping stone.

"Hope you're ready for some fun!" Landon called. The boat's three large fans at the back were arranged in a V, and once they kicked in fully they were deafening. Around the sides of the boat, several smaller fans pointed downward to provide lift.

The tallest trees poked about ten feet above the swamp, allowing a view for miles in every direction. The only sign of civilization was a string of power lines on the horizon, marching away in the distance.

Mark those well, said the Voice in its familiar tickle. It had returned without warning, ringing clearly in the back of Jordan's mind even amidst the boat's clamor. He instantly felt a surge of comfort, as if enveloped in a warm blanket, even if he had no clue what the Voice was getting at.

Breaux cornered the boat deeper into the swamp at breakneck speed. In his mouth was a thick cigar – unlit, he just chewed on the end. Over the thrum of the fans, he shouted for Jordan to look out for gators. "Dozens of 'em out here, shout when you spot one and I'll get us up close!"

Jordan nodded absently, checking if the Voice would offer anything further. *Mark those well* – what did it mean? The powerlines had diminished to a blurred, shallow line behind them.

"Whoa now!" Breaux cut the fans and they idled forward through thick black water. "Over to your left. Six-footer, I reckon."

Jordan looked. A snout barely broke the water's surface, the gator's scaly eyes regarding them suspiciously.

"How do you know how big it is?" Jordan asked.

"See how from the nose to the eyes, it's about six inches? That's smack-dab how many feet they are. The gators around here finished hibernatin' only last week, so they're still a bit sluggish. They just lay out among the water hyacinths and let the sun charge up their batteries. Then they'll cool off with a swim, and they repeat the process all day long. Not a bad way to live. This is all private land, so they have plenty of room to do what they need to."

Breaux grabbed a long pike and leapt to the front of the boat. He stuck the pike into the water to pull the boat toward the reptile. The gator's snout slowly backed away, eyes narrowing. "Come on up, Jordan! And bring those marshmallows."

Jordan pulled out a plastic bag from under his feet and tried to hand it over. "Nah, you go ahead, toss a couple in," Landon said, mischief in his voice. "See what happens."

Jordan obliged, lobbing a couple marshmallows near the snout. "Gators love them marshmallows," Landon said. "I wish I loved anything that much." Sure enough, the gator's mouth arched open wide and it pushed forward, gobbling the fluffy treats eagerly. It moved toward the boat with an expectant grimace. Jordan took a half step backward.

"This here's Lola," Breaux said, leaning dangerously forward to get a close look. "She's about ten years old. Go on, give her a few more."

Jordan plopped a few marshmallows in the water and they disappeared just as quickly. Lola was showing some energy now, her body rising from the surface, tail swaying in wide swaths, practically wagging like a puppy's. The gator's mouth clamped down on each marshmallow with frightening finality.

"Hungry son of a bitch," Jordan said.

"Food's getting scarce. These hyacinths are invasive plants, they choke everything else off." Breaux poked at the leafy plants floating in the water, densely thick and seemingly everywhere. He turned the pike on Lola, jabbing playfully. She was now inches from the boat's edge. "All right, girl, see you later."

Lola obligingly slinked away, and Landon vaulted back into his captain's chair. "Let's find some more, shall we?" He powered up the fans and Jordan was thrown to his seat, clutching the marshmallow bag.

They toured around other rivulets of the swamp. Whenever he slowed the boat, Landon resumed the same chatty narrative offered during Jordan's airpod ride. The senator had grown tired of this endless monologue, tuning it out until he heard the Voice once again.

Listen well, said the Voice. Jordan refocused his attention.

Landon was discussing the Indian tribes that used to inhabit the area. "Back before any of us white folks came through, these lands belonged to the Choctaw. Most tribes had many long traditions – some were lost, some persist." Breaux spat a wad of chewed cigar out of the fanboat. "One thing I admired about the Choctaw was that manhood was earned. You didn't just become a man because you turned a certain age or had curly-hairs growing in certain places. No, you had to prove yourself, pass a test. A rite of passage."

Next to the boat, a rustling began within a glossy batch of hyacinths. A rodent's sniffing nose sprouted from the leaves, darting back and forth, inhaling feverishly. It seized on a scent and came forward, revealing the rest of its face. To Jordan, it looked like an oversized gerbil, with thick porcupine quills for whiskers. The creature assessed the boat as it lifted itself on hind legs, still sniffing.

"That's just a nutria," Breaux said. "Big river rat. Don't worry, they're friendly. Where there's one, there's thousands – unlike the gators, they hang together."

Breaux pulled out a miniature flashlight device like the one he'd given Jordan. In one dazzlingly smooth motion, he aimed it at the nutria and pushed a button with his thumb. A bluish pulse of light sprang from one end of the cylinder and hit just above the animal's left eye, carving out an instant pinhole. The rodent fell back with a whimper and sank in the flora.

"Whelp, there's my dinner," Breaux said. "They're actually quite tasty if you cook 'em slow enough. Make a helluva gumbo." He grabbed a fishing net and leaned out to retrieve the body.

Jordan was speechless. "What just happened?" he finally could ask.

"New prototype." Landon flashed a grin. "The older versions were rifles – big suckers, weighed a ton. Good range, though. Donated some of those. This here's the handheld model. I finally figured out how to make the quark emitter pocketsize. It's got a slider, here, where you can make the beam wider or narrower, depending on the distance you want."

"What does it do?"

"You just saw what it does. You were watching when I zapped that critter, weren't you?"

"Yes, but...how?"

"Oh, I'll show you exactly how. When you get back, you'll really see it in action." Breaux cast his eyes about the swamp. "This is as good a spot as any, I suppose." He used the pike to pull them into a patch of land forged by the roots of two low-slung cypress trees. "You'll need your gear and your weapon. Prolly wise if you left the marshmallows."

Jordan turned to his host, confused. The Sponsor gestured at the makeshift island. "This is your stop," he said.

"My stop? For what?"

"Your rite of passage."

"Rite of – wait, *you're leaving me here?*"

"You seem like a nice fella, if a little aloof in person. But before I further invest in your campaign, I need to know some things first." He chewed on the butt of his cigar and spat again. "The world is full of harsh environments. They're all the same, really, and you survive in each living by the same rules. I need to know that you can survive out here. That you can be like the Choctaw."

"I am a United States Senator!" Jordan fought the impulse to rush at Breaux, push him over the side, and take the fanboat for himself. He recalled how quickly Breaux had just brandished his flashlight weapon and reconsidered.

Jordan mulled his options. Most of them resulted in a quick death, it seemed.

Relax.

The Voice steadied him with a single word, its soothing articulation oscillating down his spine. Jordan looked again at Breaux, but this time without petulance or protest. He took a step toward the edge of the boat.

Breaux clapped his hands together, a new thread of respect in his voice. "Got big plans for you, like I said. Prove yourself worthy by making it out here and I'll give you everything you want. All it'll take is one night out here."

Jordan would normally be pissing his pants at the thought of spending the night among scores of hungry gators, but the Voice's presence soothed his fears. "Well, if you say so," Jordan said, and tossed his pack of belongings onto land.

"My man," Breaux said, clapping Jordan on the back as he disembarked. "Now, she'll be dark soon. You could either hole up here for the night or try an' get somewhere else, but the gators are nocturnal, and like I said, food's been scarce. But I got faith in you. See you on the other side!"

The fans spun to life and rushed the boat away, leaving the senator from East Kansas to fend for his life in the swamp.

Jordan should have been wracked with panic, but instead felt only a soothing calm.

You've got this, the Voice whispered. He had no choice but believe it.

* * *

Shortly after noon the next day, the senator from East Kansas walked up to Breaux's cabin for the second time, feeling quite different from the first.

He was dripping wet, for starters – the swamp fell away from him as if he were molting.

But the differences went beyond that. As his feet squished across the muddy knoll of Breaux's front yard, the oozing earth was a part of him now. The bayou had seeped into his veins like swamp blood.

Jordan spotted Landon Breaux sitting on the same oil drum in front of his cabin. The Sponsor was whittling a shaft of basswood, his thumb maneuvering a carving knife with incredible dexterity. Beneath the blade, an alligator snout had begun to take shape, each scale delicately notched.

Landon looked up, adjusting his glasses. "Faster than I'd reckoned," he said, the low rumbles of his voice betraying surprise and appreciation. "I was hoping to have this finished for you."

"It's beautiful."

Breaux set down his tools and stood. He put an arm around Jordan's shoulder, ignoring the slop still dripping from his poncho.

"Come in," the Sponsor said. "Something you need to see."

Jordan followed him into the house. It had been extensively cleaned up, the scattered doo-dads and other scraps all swept away. The workbench in the corner was the only furniture to speak of.

The six-panel PanoScreen was in full holo mode, tuned to but one channel now, its image occupying the entire room and thus basically the whole interior of the house. The holo showed the floating torso of a breathless news anchor. "We're going to show this to you one more time," she was saying. "Again, this footage is from a bystander at the scene when the attack unfolded."

The holo switched to a crowd of people standing on bleachers, taken from what appeared to be a handheld PanoCam. Jordan heard a voice he recognized and instinctively flinched with repulsion. The shot tilted to the right to show a stage with a podium. Sure enough, President Granger was speaking, the Statue of Liberty as his backdrop.

"The Open Borders Ceremony?" Jordan looked over to Landon, still standing in the doorway. "That was this morning. What happened?"

Breaux said nothing but his nod suggested that Jordan would find out soon enough.

The holo tilted back left to show a man walking down an aisle between sets of bleachers, waving like a celebrity on a red carpet. *"The attack began just as Hideo Nakomuri, the nation's first immigrant in over twenty years, was being introduced. We warn our viewers again – this is graphic content."*

A bolt of blue light flashed across the holo and Nakomuri fell. Gasps and screaming followed. The image shook wildly as the carrier of the pano started running, while more bolts lit up the room. People were falling to the left and to the right, ribbons of flesh as their remnants.

Jordan reached into his pocket and took out the flashlight device. "Those are your weapons," he said to Landon.

The Sponsor gave a solemn nod. "Weaponized Light is the new equalizer in the fight for America's freedom."

On the holo, the camera tilted upward, showing a missile streak past. People shouted and ducked down. *"Here again is the strike on Lady Liberty,"* the news anchor said. The shot switched to an aerial view of the statue from above Liberty Island, probably coming from a news drone. It zoomed in tight on the Statue's forearm and a green torrent of light filled Breaux's cabin as the projectile hit. As the light dimmed, cracks appeared in the statue's shell, smoldering chemicals chewing away the oxidized metal.

"That's the work of an Eraser," Landon said, pride lining his voice. "It can melt a tank with six inches of armor."

The shot pulled back to show the full Statue of Liberty, now eight feet tall and directly in front of Jordan, so close he could see the rivets within her robe. The torch wobbled and dropped in slow motion. It bounced lifelessly on the floor and settled at his feet.

"Jesus Christ," he gasped. Reflexively, he knelt to pick it up before remembering it was just a hologram, broadcast from a thousand miles away.

The holo switched back to the bystander cam on Ellis Island. As it jostled amidst the carnage, a large sphere rolled past at high speed, surrounded by men with guns.

"The president?" Jordan asked.

"Whisked away in that bubble thing. Never seen one of those before."

You wouldn't have, Jordan thought. Just as they'd concoct an antidote to any developed biological weapon, the government would create their own defense for Landon's weapons, and in secret.

"But no matter," Breaux went on, "Granger wasn't the target.

Better to have him running for the hills, anyhow. He'll get condemned for this even if he'd tried to stay. But the migrant was the mark. Maybe this Nakomuri was a fine fellow, but that's not the point. The thousands, the millions that follow him – they are the problem. You think there won't be bad seeds in there? People that want to destroy our country, destroy our way of life, and we just invite them in? I say no. This is a cancer. And when you go after a cancer, you eliminate every cell. It ain't fair, but it's how it has to be. If you let a cancer come back, it comes back *meaner*."

Breaux clicked off the holo and the room went dead. "Sadly, I've seen it all before. America is a fragile thing. I'm sad to admit it – sometimes you love something too much to see it for what it is. Land of the free, home of the brave? Not anymore. We're weak. There was a time, back when, that America's power kept the world in check. We were the righteous balance to the rest of their ilk. Then we softened. What were we thinking – that if we let just anyone in, the benevolence of our freedoms would wash over them, as if there was something in the water? Fools. Hatred isn't something you just give up, not their kind of hatred."

Breaux went over to his workbench and started applying spot-solder to join a string of lenses. "What was done had to be done – someone's gotta put a foot down. Sacrifices must be made, like New Orleans in the war. But we won't lose our resolve, not this time. After today, the fearful will show how weak this country really is, shaming it with their hysterics. Remember this Jordan – reality is the construct of the bold, and we will create a reality where there's only one plausible solution for America's future. For as long as it takes."

Jordan stared at the weapon in his hand. So small, so light, so deadly! "Until what?" he asked.

"You run for president, and you win."

CHAPTER ELEVEN

"We may have had our differences on the campaign trail, but I promise you this. Elijah Schroeder is an honest man, a decent man. When I am president, he will be my first council, my most private confidante, and America's best shot at unity. And should anything happen to me, he would make a fine successor."

- Acton Granger, general election victory speech – November 2, 2060

"What's the number?"

Elijah looked around the Situation Room. There was enough brass around the table to rival the Boston Pops. Some of the generals were beamed-in holos, but they were so lifelike Elijah had trouble discerning them from the real ones. They all huddled tightly over the long, stained-oak table, their creased uniforms weighted down by medals and distinctions.

One of the generals pulled the figures. "Thirty-seven, sir. Almost a hundred injuries, mostly from trampling."

Thirty-seven dead. "Goddamn. Anyone we know?"

"Nakomuri, of course. A cabinet undersecretary, some State Department staff. Most were invited guests or loved ones."

A horrific tragedy to be sure, but Elijah couldn't stop thinking all the ways it could have been so much worse. There were a thousand people on that tiny island, a barrel of fish if there ever was one. Whoever these terrorists were, they seemed more bent on making a statement than inflicting mass casualties. Unless this was just their opening salvo. "What else do we know?"

The first response came not from a general or security liaison, but from the White House Chief of Staff, Brian Ricketts. Because of the overwhelming military and intelligence presence, Ricketts had been relegated to a seat in the back corner, usually reserved for aides. He did not appear happy about it. "Did anyone say when the president will be back online?" he asked.

The Chair of the Joint Chiefs, Rachel Saks, pointed to the latest communiques on one of the many wall panos. "He's still undisclosed, somewhere over the Atlantic. A storm offshore is causing interference in his tracking chip. He could be back any minute, but tough to ballpark."

"But we know he's safe?" Ricketts again, half out of his seat.

"Yes, we've got him on radar and the vitals from the tracking chip are normal, though understandably elevated. When the aircraft scrambled, there was no choice but to go through the weather. Given the weapons the terrorists used and their range, they had to get the president out over water as fast as possible."

Elijah shifted in his chair at the head of the table, occupying for now the president's seat. The chair had been modified to fit Granger's outsized dimensions – wider armrests, a deeper recess for his extended legs, a taller back. Rather than lower the chair so the president's thighs might tuck underneath it, the Sit-Room table had been lifted several inches. Elijah felt like a child at Thanksgiving, errantly invited to eat with the adults.

He sat as tall as he could, trying to ignore how ridiculous he felt. He placed his elbows on the table and felt the stretch in the back of his dress shirt.

Two of the PanoScreens showed slow-motion playback from Ellis Island's closed circuit feed. Even slowed down, the flashing bolts of baby blue light spitting through the crowd were terrifying, cutting people down like paper scraps.

Elijah had never seen weapons like that, even in *Civil Strife*. "Can someone tell me what these things are?"

The brass all looked at one another, as if they shared a secret and no one wanted to be the first to spill it. The Joint Chiefs Chair swallowed. "They appear to come from a project called Weaponized Light. The project was pursued in earnest by the Defense Department during the last administration, but President Granger scrubbed it when he came into office. We terminated the standing agreement with the contracting company. Our best guess is after we ended the program, they continued to pursue the technology."

"This came from us?"

The chairwoman shrugged.

Eli scanned the room for the FBI Director and found Carter Pitts seated behind a general. "What company? Carter, why didn't we keep an eye on them?"

"Well, that's complicated, sir. Legally, we're very limited."

"Why is that?"

Ricketts, White House Chief of Staff, chirped up again, this time standing up all the way. "Come on Eli, don't you know? These weapons manufacturers get a pass in Congress. How much did they give the Conservatives in the midterms? The Freedom League? How much did they give to your campaign?"

"I was sponsored by a group of hedge fund managers, you know that."

"Of course you were. And where did all their money come from?"

Elijah ignored him and eventually Ricketts sat down. "Tell me about the company," he said to the table.

Rachel Saks checked her PanoPad. "Monochromatic Industries, owned by a man named Landon Breaux. It does appear he's an active Sponsor."

Ricketts harrumphed triumphantly in the background.

"We need to talk to Mr. Breaux," Elijah said.

Carter Pitts spoke up tentatively. "We can try, sir, but as you know any licensed company making weapons is exempt from litigation or prosecution caused by someone using their products to break the law. A bill, passed earlier this century, took that off the table."

"When we terminated the contract, why didn't we take the license away?"

Ricketts snorted loudly. The Joint Chiefs Chair shrugged. "That was a decision left to Congress," she said.

"Well, find him and see if he'll cooperate. Let's get back to the weapons themselves. Weaponized Light, you called it? Can someone tell me how it works?"

Rachel stood. "I'm not a scientist, sir, but I'll do my best." She activated the holo writer from her PanoPad and started to draw in empty space. "Light is basically a visible electromagnetic wave that travels along a beam." She drew two parallel lines with a squiggly line between them. "You have regular light, which is polychromatic, meaning it has several different frequencies." She drew more squiggles before gesturing to erase them. "Another kind of light, focused from a single source, has just one frequency. Thus, where Monochromatic Industries gets its name. The Weaponized Light program looked for a way to harness and enhance this frequency by adding matter to it." She redrew the single squiggle and added dots along it. "If you can add tiny bits of mass – in this case, a few billion subatomic particles, using what's called a quark emitter – and plug them in along the wave property, then the light itself can penetrate almost any surface."

"By giving the light just the little bit of weight, you make it deadly."

"Correct. When their contract was terminated, Monochromatic had yet to develop the ability to set the beam to focus at a specific distance. The project was still in the early stages. To state the obvious, it would appear that's changed."

"We took the shackles off them," Elijah mused. Firing the company certainly freed them from all kinds of government regulations. He looked back at Rachel. "You said the weapons could penetrate almost any surface. I noticed one of the beams bounced off the President's Hamster Ball."

"Yes, the Secret Service upgraded it with reflective carbon fiber a few months ago, just in case."

"So, we knew this was a threat?" Dress shirt be damned, Elijah pushed his elbows up on the table forcefully. He wondered if the ensuing fabric rip was audible.

"We knew it was a technology with a lot of promise that might find its way to adoption."

"Jesus. And they shoot just like a regular firearm?"

"There are differences. It's a beam weapon so there's no physical projectile, at least nothing that weighs more than a nanogram. No projectile means there's nothing to trace. Ammunition is unlimited and the range is very high. They also don't make noise when fired."

Elijah tried to quantify all the ways these features made for an incredibly dangerous weapon. He couldn't. "That's the worst of it?" he asked, trying not to sound despondent.

"We also asked the contractor to make them as light as they could, to not weigh down our troops. They're made almost entirely out of plastic, no metal."

Elijah put his face in his hands. "All right, back to this contractor and Mr. Breaux. They were designing a new weapon for us, and we fired them. But they decided to finish what they started, because here we are. Are they selling them in the PanoShop, or how did anyone get a hold of them?"

"We don't know yet, sir. We're assuming they were stolen."

"Why assume anything? Carter, the FBI needs to find that out. If you need any congressional approvals, I can lean on the Conservatives that will still take my calls, and we'll make sure whatever resources you require are expedited. You'll get a blank check on this one."

From the back of the room, Brian Ricketts snorted. Elijah remembered hearing the Chief of Staff was Granger's loudest voice against following through with the campaign promise to appoint him vice president. If he could describe the Chief of Staff in three words, they would be *total, partisan*, and *hack*. But Granger somehow found Ricketts an effective manager, and valuable when it came to keeping the West Wing staff in lockstep with the president's strategy.

I wonder if he's the one that decided to fire this weapons company and then ignore them for two years. Archie Cunningham would have a field day when he got wind of this. It was like telling Oppenheimer to go fuck himself the day before he finished the Bomb.

Elijah looked around the table and saw only Granger's men. At the beginning of Civ-2, several rogue battalions splintered from the military at large, some of them whole regiments, defecting to protect the Minority. This became the what was known as the Underground. At war's end, some of the career commanders folded back into the government, but generals were politicized now, on par with Sponsors, their support (and the men in their command, if it came to it) a necessary asset for any campaign. When Granger came to prominence, his Purple Heart was a key that unlocked their endorsements, further propelling his candidacy – an outcome, Elijah had to assume, that Yannik Vogel and Endure Technologies had surely anticipated.

The men around this table showed deference and respect toward Elijah, no question. They were professionals, raised by the chain of command – meaning the vice president, sitting in the president's chair, was afforded the same courtesy as the man he stood in for. But a cursory look at each general's face showed their hearts weren't in it; they were going through the motions, sharing perfunctory intel, biding time until the president returned. Granger had walked two tours of duty in their shoes, taken a bullet for his country. These people would die for him.

And while Granger's ass was getting shot at in Yemen's desert bluffs, Elijah was studying International Trade Policy at NYU.

The vice president shifted uneasily in the president's massive chair. "What about the missile?" he asked.

The brass looked at each other, not sure who he was addressing. Finally, someone spoke up. "That weapon was a common one, sir. Called an Eraser, it's used to disable armored vehicles. It's shoulder-mounted, fires an eighteen-inch projectile, and compact enough to fold into a suitcase. The whole rig weighs maybe ten pounds."

"A projectile was fired. Can we collect any physical evidence from that?" Elijah knew he was reaching, and he got the sense that every question he asked revealed the shallowness of his grasp on military matters.

"Not particularly, sir. Different versions of the weapon have delivered different chemical payloads over the years, but it's designed to break down compounds to their basest elements, which makes it impossible to trace. The technology is still classified, and we don't want foreign entities learning from it."

"Foreign entities? How about domestic? But you're saying the weapons used were chosen for a specific reason, to leave no trace behind. So, this was a professional attack." Elijah could feel the scrutiny in the room as everyone else watched him puzzle out the obvious.

"Undoubtedly, sir. Military precision."

Aside from Elijah's tapping his thumb on an armrest, silence pervaded the Situation Room. Slowly in unison, heads turned toward the head of the table, waiting for a question, an order, anything.

"All right, what about the jets?" Elijah asked. "Did they see anything when they flew to the source of the attack?"

That got people moving. A general swiveled to his assistant in the corner. "Captain Jones, bring up the feed from HJ-Alpha."

The captain tapped her PanoPad. "Actually, the Alpha was scanning a different building from where we believe the attack came from."

"Fine, the Beta then."

"Yes, sir."

An alpha and a beta, Elijah thought, his mind drifting back to how Vogel had contrasted the president's persona to his own. *There's irony at work here.*

The different wall panos switched to the second hoverjet's belly cam in one enormous shot, 3D infrared with impossibly high definition. It aimed down at the island a few thousand feet below, panning in a regular pattern as it monitored the scene. Human figures came through in green outlines with an orange glow within, signifying their body heat. The lone figure of Nakomuri walked slowly between the hundreds standing still around him. The top-down view of the hoverjet captured just his head and shoulders, like a wide green oval punctuated by a circle in the middle. The figure stopped and the circle tipped forward – Nakomuri bowing. Then a flash blinked on the screen, pale yellow in the infrared. Nakomuri's oval stretched thin as he fell over, the orange glow already dampening.

The attack commenced in earnest, and the camera from the hoverjet darted about as if a toddler had seized the controls. The view shifted from the mess of the island and turned horizontally toward the skyscrapers of Manhattan, which in infrared looked like columns filled with thousands of tiny orange blobs – New York's busy residents going about their business. The bursts of Weaponized Light still looked the same yellow, but as the bolts streaked under the plane Elijah swore he could see the tiny wave-particles buzzing within them, though that had to be impossible with his naked eye.

The skyscrapers grew very large very quickly as the hoverjets sped towards the source of the attack, but the shooting stopped just as they reached within a hundred yards.

The skyscraper went from a hive of frenetic activity to a kind of static paralysis, as people froze in reaction to two military jets floating just outside their windows, weapons trained. But in the foreground, near the top floor, two human figures were moving, their infrared outlines blurred by motion. They looked to be replacing a windowpane, then packing up supplies before breaking out in a run. Half a second later, they were descending flights of stairs, several at a time. Unfortunately, others in the building recovered from their stasis and started running down with them. Whoever the moving figures were, they were lost in overlapping imagery.

"Stop it there," Elijah said. The general nodded to the captain, and the screen paused.

"Could we have taken a shot?" Ricketts asked.

"The pilot hadn't pinpointed the shooters yet," Saks responded. "Thousands of people in that building."

Finally, someone else asked a dumbass question, Elijah thought.

"So, just two men," Elijah said, thinking out loud. He'd expected a whole squad. "One to shoot into the crowd, one to fire the rocket at the statue."

"Surprisingly, only two, yes," a general concurred. Other men were nodding.

Elijah felt a softening in the leather cushion of his chair. The longer he sat in it, the more it contoured to his body. "Back it up to when the jets first get close, and zoom in on their faces," he said. The general nodded to Captain Jones. Through the infrared, they could see small but visible outlines around both men's eyes. "Enhancement glasses," Elijah said. "They could see for miles. And they could've been filming the whole thing. Zoom in a little further?"

The faces now took up most of the screen.

"What did this look like on normal camera settings?" Ricketts asked.

"The building is just blue mirror glass, sir. No visibility inside."

"They got the pane up before we could see them?"

"Afraid so, sir."

Elijah focused on the gray outline of the glasses. With the infrared, you could only see the negative of them against the background of orange faces.

"Those look like the new XTRs, don't they? With the wider lenses?"

He was met with blank stares, but Elijah felt a warm thrum in his brain, knowing he was onto something. These were tough men, soldiers all, capable of things Elijah couldn't dream of – but he was an analyst at heart, and a damn perceptive one.

"Those are still pretty rare, yes?"

Carter Pitts said, "They are."

"Can we go through all purchases of those nationwide, focusing on whoever bought two or more at once?"

There were murmurs of agreement. Elijah always felt a warmth in his skull when his brain was really clicking, this time it spread through his body. The leather in the president's chair felt supple as it melded into him.

"And back to those weapons," he said. "They might be untraceable if they've been stolen, but what about the holes in the ground? You said there's no projectile, but particles are introduced to the light, what kind of particles? Is there any way to recover what they were, and trace where they may have come from?"

The generals looked at each other. For a second, Elijah thought he'd posed another dumbass question and lost all momentum, but they began nodding.

"To be honest, sir, we hadn't thought of that. The particles might be the smallest form of matter, but as a rule of physics matter can't be destroyed completely, so there might be something to there. We'll get on it right away."

Maybe this chair wasn't so big after all. "All right, everyone, we have a playbook for these types of emergencies. Let's execute. We'll meet again in two hours."

Elijah stood. The generals stood with him.

From the back, Ricketts was checking his pano and decided to get the last word. "The president's back online and coming back to the White House. He'll touch down within the hour. I'll brief him, but instead of two hours we'll need to reconvene immediately after."

"Fine." Elijah saw no need to argue. He hurried out of the Sit-Room, anxious to get upstairs.

He found her in the Solarium, knitting.

The White House Solarium was first conceived as a rooftop camping area during the Taft administration, providing the first family a cool place to sleep during the summer – before the days of centralized air conditioning, the residence was sweltering even at night. The area was built up into what Grace Coolidge called the Sky Parlor before officially being labeled the Solarium later in the 1920s. The room was where Franklin Roosevelt took lunch to break from meetings about the Great Depression and the Great War, and where Reagan rested after he'd been wounded by a would-be assassin's bullet. It was an escape for those burdened by the presidency, as well as their loved ones.

The Solarium had so many windows, it was like a long PanoScreen of the sky. Sunlight coated the carpet with an intense warmth. Ferns and flowers grew everywhere, mingling with casual furnishings. Elijah always thought it resembled a beachy greenhouse, and such a contrast from the formal spaces downstairs.

Susannah Granger sat on the edge of a couch cushion, fingers working inattentively at a pair of knitting needles while she stared into a small pano perched on the coffee table. The events of Ellis Island played out for the thousandth time on its screen.

Susannah did not seem to notice him come in. He coughed subtly before saying, "Hey, Sue."

She jumped as if struck by lightning. "Oh! Eli. Didn't see you there." She nodded at the pano. "This is all so awful."

"I know. I'm sorry to disturb you. I'm glad to hear the president's all right."

"I was just able to talk to him. Calm as could be. Nothing seems to shake that man."

"Mind if I sit a moment? I know he'll be back soon."

"Of course. I'll barely see a whiff of him I'm sure."

"How are the kids?"

"They'll be fine. How—how's Cassidy?"

"Worried about me."

"I can relate." Susannah set aside her knitting. "Nervous habit," she said. "I remember when I was still practicing medicine, whenever there was a crisis I could usually make things better by using my hands. Set a bone, bandage something up, apply a stent. Now, things are literally out of my hands, all the time. Somehow, I still need to use them, if only to keep them busy."

"I'm sure once the president sees you, he'll feel worlds better and gain a new focus on his job. He feeds off you. That's not nothing."

"The funny thing is I don't even know what I'm making anymore. It was going to be a scarf, then maybe a sweater. But it's too big, now, even for him! I think I might turn it into a blanket."

"I like the colors."

"The red feels inappropriate right now, doesn't it?" Susannah stood up, stretching wobbly legs. She walked toward the bay windows, her figure ignited by the sun. Even in her agitated state, she was just so goddamn beautiful. Elijah forced his eyes toward his feet.

"We've got weapons that can cut people to pieces with the push of a button," she said. "Do you think we're born insane, or does the world make us this way?"

Elijah's mind drifted toward his children. He wanted nothing more than to see them in their bedrooms tonight.

"I'm sorry for the spot you're in," Susannah said. "You don't know how grateful he is for you. There isn't one in a hundred from the Conservative League that would've stuck by him as you have. Or one in a thousand. I know you feel squeezed and alone."

"Your husband has always been gracious."

"In times like this, it takes a lot to hold back the *I told you so's*. Everyone is just going crazy on the PanoNets. All their hindsight is just so damn amazing – they're falling over each other patting themselves on the back. If you're always saying something bad will happen, you're going to be right eventually. A broken clock doesn't congratulate itself the two minutes a day it's right, but these assholes sure do."

Elijah reached over to the blanket, assessing its texture with his thumb and forefinger.

"Did anyone bring up the pledge?" Susannah asked.

He snorted. "Thankfully, no." When he'd first agreed to the role of vice president, someone – Ricketts, more than likely – leaked out that Granger wanted Elijah to sign a pledge, promising that if anything happened to the president, Elijah would respect the will of the voters and let another Reform League member take the job. The leakers hoped Elijah would take this condition as an insult and rebuke the president's offer. Instead, he called Granger, and was not surprised to learn the president-elect had yet to hear of it. "My job can't go halfway," Elijah told Granger then, and he said the same thing to his wife now.

"That wasn't Acton's idea, Eli. But you know that. And I know how you felt about the immigration policy – too much too soon. But you've never said a word in public to contradict him about this or anything else, and that's everything to us."

Elijah nodded in appreciation, but something else crept in his mind. There was something he'd wanted to ask her ever since he'd met with Yannik Vogel, all those months ago – *what do you know about Endure Technologies?* Did she know the real reason why Elijah was chosen, that it was simply to guarantee her husband's victory? But this wasn't the time. He knew Susannah was the president's confidante, but he also knew that in these circles, many secrets were held from your spouse. Cassidy would attest to this.

Does Susannah know about Vogel's project with the panos?

Instead of asking, he joined the first lady by the window. Beyond the South Lawn and the Ellipse stood the Washington Monument, its dusky shadow stretching down Constitution Avenue. A crowd had gathered around it – mostly to mourn, though a few anti-immigration demonstrators waved taunting banners. Elijah could almost hear their chants in the distance.

"I admire you, Elijah – for the flack you take for us," Susannah continued. "During the campaign, we tried to respect your situation with your family. It's funny how only now, during a tragedy like this one, do I begin to comprehend all you've gone through."

"It's fine, Sue. Your husband ran a good campaign. He stayed out of the mud." Of course, now Elijah knew why – Granger didn't want to kneecap his beta.

He stood close enough to Susannah that wafts of her perfume tingled his nose. Before Vogel had ever told him he was the beta to the president's alpha, Elijah had known he wanted what the alpha had. To taste what it tasted. He remembered that moment, over two years ago now, they shared in the most un-romantic of places, a freight elevator in the bowels of the Los Angeles AllenCo Center. It was during the *United America* tour, when the president was rolling out his newly-minted vice president from coast to coast.

He knew, both then and now, just how wildly inappropriate and stupid it was, but he wanted to taste it again. It was only a fleeting second in a dingy elevator, but he needed it. He put a hand around her hip and leaned forward.

This time, she slipped away.

"Eli, that won't happen again."

"Of course. You're right. I'm sorry."

He'd kissed her back in Los Angeles, just once. He'd expected a push, a slap, a scream, but he couldn't help himself. And for a moment back in the freight elevator, she'd pulled him in, her lips responsive, her body inviting.

They hadn't spoken of it since.

Mookie the Coin Monster was hungry. Ellie Schroeder fed him dutifully, working through her counting problems.

I really should upgrade this software, Elijah thought. *Nolan gets a new game every couple of months.* He wondered if Mookie would resemble President Granger in the newest release.

"Something the matter, daddy?"

"Tough day at work, Bubbles. What's the next amount?"

Charlotte was a little less ornery than usual, which was good. They talked about a boy she'd been spending time with at school, but she swore up and down it didn't mean she liked him. They talked about the person she admired most (her mom) and her biggest fear (her dad getting hurt).

They talked about life. And a little bit about death. But only a little bit.

She even let him kiss her forehead goodnight, which he did so carefully, his lips only brushing her at the edges.

"Do we have any games where we're not shooting people?"

"I dunno, Dad. You get the games."

So they shot people, running in place around the war-torn streets of Chicago in *Civil Strife's* final level. The two of them were really rolling, covering each other's backs as they cleared through Millennium Park and starting working up Michigan Avenue.

Nolan paused the game.

"Hey Dad, I've been thinking. After high school, I think I want to join the military."

Elijah started to choke up, emotionally volatile after the day's events. He swallowed. "Nothing would've made me prouder, son. You sure are a hell of a shot."

They played some more, about to the reach the last Underground Boss inside Tribune Tower. The bedroom door opened – *Another fence breach?* Elijah wasn't sure he could spend another night in the bunker.

Instead of a swarm of agents, Cassidy stood in the doorframe. She was trembling.

Elijah had seen that look before. Stomach sinking, he turned to his son. "Nolan, hit pause."

Cassidy took a hesitant but determined step forward. "No, Eli, turn it off."

"Nolan, stop the game." Elijah said it knowing this was not what his wife meant, either.

Cassidy took another step inside the room. "Are you gonna make me do it?" Her Brooklyn accent came through when she was most upset. She folded her arms across her chest, and her right foot began tapping at the floor as if she were syncopating a bass drum.

"Baby, please don't. Not tonight."

She set her gaze at him, imploring him to comply. When he didn't, her hands balled into fists and she stepped over to the room's holo generator.

"Cass," he begged. "Please."

"How do I—" She struggled with the controls, banging the side of the device in frustration and swearing. For a moment, she looked like she might unplug it from the wall. But she took a breath, found the proper button, and pressed it with conviction.

Nolan flickered once, twice, and vanished.

"Five years!" Cassidy screamed. "He's gone, Eli! I can't let you do this anymore – you have to face reality!"

Cassidy Schroeder wheeled around and rushed out of the room, as if it was the last place she ever wanted to be. He could hear her stifled sobs grow louder as she retreated down the hallway.

Her voice called back, "And I'm turning off the others!"

Elijah realized he was standing in the pantomimed posture of holding his holo rifle and numbly dropped his arms to his sides. He stared at the empty space where his son had been, his feet shuffling backwards blindly until he felt the wall at his back. He collapsed to the floor and stayed there.

CHAPTER TWELVE

"Don't call us Freedomists, Freedomers, or heaven forbid, Freedom Leaguers. Call us the Free."
- Shelby Monroe, Greater Texas Governor's Ball – January 17, 2062

"Okay Jamie, fire another one at me."

Jamie Richardson shifted uneasily on the toilet seat. The only sitting options in the master bath of the Governor's Mansion consisted of the bathtub's edge, the toilet seat, or the floor. He regretted his decision immediately. It was one of the newer ergonomic models which kept pinching his tuxedo pants, and he had to keep reminding his left hand not to hover over the bidet sensor.

He scrolled through a list on his pano and read aloud in his best hardpan Texas drawl, which was admittedly terrible. "Governor, how do we keep this country safe from domestic terrorism?"

Shelby Monroe set aside her eye pencil and regarded herself in the mirror, blinking repeatedly. "Actually, I might have a microphone, so..." She picked up the eye pencil again, holding it to her chin, then jumped into her talking points. "I'm glad you asked, because I have a plan. The weapons used in the Ellis Island Massacre are unlike anything we've seen. We must find where they come from and stop them from getting into the wrong hands – just imagine if they showed up in our cities! As that is contained, we need to go after the perpetrators of this horrific act with every vestige of power that this country can muster. The president's shown an alarming weakness—"

Shelby shook her head, cursing. "Sorry, let me start over." *The president* has *shown*, she mouthed, over and over, trying to rid herself of contractions. She double-tapped the mirror to zoom closer on her face and applied extra foundation to her cheeks, going through her response again.

Afterward, she said, "Jamie, you need to ask a really tough follow-up. Call me on any bullshit. If I say something like 'the president dove into this Open Borders policy too rashly,' you should interrupt with something like, 'are you saying the president asked for this to happen?' Be as insufferable as you can. Where we're going, insufferable is on the menu."

Jamie took note, but this was hardly his forte. "Wouldn't Tammy or Trudy be better to practice with?"

"Are you kidding? They take twice as long to get ready as I do."

The governor shook out of her robe as she left the bathroom and hung it on the door. Jamie's discomfort multiplied. He kept his eyes on the pano, though the governor seemed not the least bit self-conscious reviewing her talking points in the nude. She came back a minute later in her undergarments – which featured a significant amount of architectural reinforcements designed to cinch, lift, and push.

Shelby returned to her eye pencil. "Grab my dress, will you? It's the black one with the sparkles, laid out on the bed."

Jamie went into the bedroom and carefully lifted the dress out of a garment bag. It was a tasteful ball gown with minimal tasseling, but in full light he thought the sparkles might blind someone in another county. He helped the governor balance herself as she stepped into it, making a few adjustments and tucks as she pulled it up. "Not bad," she said. "Zip me?"

His fingers, masterful at subtle movements when manipulating his cameras, weren't built for such a tiny zipper. The governor hummed to herself patiently through his struggle. Eventually he managed.

I feel way too good about not fucking that up, he thought.

Shelby studied her figure in the reflection, turning to this angle and that. "Whatcha think, with a jacket or without?"

Jamie swallowed. There was an unseasonable chill this night, though he wasn't sure how much that mattered, if at all. "With?"

She put the jacket on, took it off, put it on again, her eyes narrow and discerning. "Good call. Now, let's go get ourselves a Sponsor."

* * *

The seven members of the Monroe campaign – Jamie, Shelby, and the five-sibling Boot Squad – snaked through downtown Dallas in a provided limousine.

"Nice ride," Jamie observed.

"It's fine," the governor said. "But I prefer my pickup."

Jamie was learning to discern Shelby's true feelings from her political persona's – though close, she wasn't *quite* as homespun as she let on. He arched an eyebrow at her as if to ask, *Really, though?*

Shelby offered a coy smile in response, roughly translating to, *All right, you got me that time.* She played at the control pad that operated the Mr. Cocktail, moving about its robotic arms that could mix and serve drinks on demand.

The buildings around them grew taller and the lights brightened as they wound deeper into the heart of the city. They passed through Dealey Plaza and turned toward the banking district.

Jamie surveyed the limo's other occupants. The governor's daughters all looked ready for the Academy Awards, fully coiffed in floor-length gowns that had to be astoundingly uncomfortable. Or, Jamie considered, did they just look uncomfortable when he glanced in their direction?

Once the campaign would begin in earnest, a platoon of advisors, minders, and other professional help would surely be added to the group. Jamie was just the first outsider of many, and the girls seemed to know that. They remained friendly, but cautious – as if they'd bound themselves in a protective cocoon around their mother. It wasn't overt, but their wariness at how close he'd become with Shelby wasn't subtle, either.

He had his work cut out to gain their graces. It didn't help that they happened to all look alike, and he harbored a nascent fear that he'd slip and call one of them the wrong name. They only needed an excuse to turn malicious, it seemed. He'd have to find a way to get to know them and earn their trust.

Tammy, the Communications Director, was the eldest. She wore gaudy earrings and liked to whistle to herself whenever she found things too quiet. Tawny, as the governor's Chief of Staff, was the boss of the group, not suffering any nonsense – she'd inherited her mother's finely-tuned bullshit detector. Tracy was the pollster, which made sense because she constantly asked questions and was adept at seeing patterns in random responses. Trudy, the speechwriter, was the introvert in the family – which was to say she wasn't *completely* outgoing. Jamie liked her the most, recognizing the kindred spirit of a fellow artist. He found himself observing whenever she'd slink off to the background, her face blank with a dreamy gaze as she sought to compose her mother's words.

The four of them – all except for Trixie, whose role as an assistant was to focus her attentions on the governor's every need – constantly attended to their panos, whether sending out press releases, memos, poll questions, or just plain gossip. They also took a hell of a lot of PanoPics. Often, they'd just message each other, back and forth in an endless group chat, sharing all the things they didn't want to say aloud – a running conversation put on hold when there was work to do, and instantly resumed when work was done. Trudy liked to tape gag interviews with the others, occasions where she'd break out of her shell. *Tammy, how would you describe the governor's position on breakfast cereal? Which is more representative of the Freedom League – Snap, Crackle, or Pop?*

Jamie noticed that these sessions typically involved extensive bouts of giggling, and though he knew full well he wasn't a female and not in the Monroe family, he hoped at some point they'd allow him in on their jokes. However, the fun they had didn't mean they neglected their roles. He was impressed by the work ethic, intelligence, and drive in each of them. They made a formidable team, and since they were family, no backbiting or disloyalty would rankle this campaign.

"A toast," Tawny said, as she took a champagne flute from Mr. Cocktail and raised it. "To mom's campaign. May it overflow with generous contributions." The girls clinked their glasses and hollered gleefully.

"We can only hope," Shelby said. "Just three weeks until we announce, though I still don't know where that'll be. Could be a stadium, could be a barn. Guess it depends on what goes down tonight, right ladies?"

A honky-tonk anthem played on the radio and one of the Monroe sisters cranked the volume. Another flipped on the mirror ball holo. The girls sang along with the lyrics and moved in unison, performing a line dance in their seats, the stomps from their high heels as thunderous as any boot. Shelby joined in, clapping in all the right places.

Is this a presidential campaign or a bachelorette party? Jamie marveled.

The limousine settled in front of a blue-mirrored skyscraper. Shelby motioned for everyone to file out. "Remember girls, be nice to everybody. But the flashier the hat, the less money they have."

As the lift tube elevated them to the penthouse, the air was quiet except for Tammy's soft whistling. Jamie adjusted the pincam in his bowtie, going over the governor's instructions in his mind.

You can film, but you can't look like you're filming – at least, not until my speech. These types would rather stay behind the curtain.

The lift tube dinged open. Two men awaited them, the first supporting a drink tray of six delicate glasses filled with yellow-green cocktails. The second man had his own drink in hand, lifting it as he greeted them.

"Ladies, welcome back to the Greater Texas Petroleum Club." He was long and elastic in a refined tuxedo, with bright eyes and professional good cheer. He looked as if he'd been drinking for a while, but accustomed to that situation and able to pull it off.

"Hello, Jack." Shelby stepped forward and gave him a friendly peck on the cheek. "Girls, you remember Jack Skelton?" Maybe they did or they didn't, but they all nodded eagerly and shook his hand.

Jack turned back to the governor. "Shelby, so delighted for you to join us this evening. We've got Texas Martinis at the ready for all of you."

The man with the tray handed out glasses to everyone but Jamie.

"Two's the limit," Shelby said quietly to her daughters. "Get flirty, not drunk."

Jack offered a quick toast and they brought their glasses in. Jamie, with nothing better to do, stepped back and took a couple stills with the pincam by tapping his thumb and forefinger together inside his pocket.

Toast concluded, the Monroes sipped and nodded their appreciation. "Damn, Jack, that's delicious," Shelby said. "Okay girls, go socialize. Those of you with rings, try not to draw attention to them. Remember the hat rule!"

The Monroe sisters skipped off into the Petroleum Club. Jack Skelton stepped back to get a full view of the governor, looking like a cattle rancher appraising new livestock. "That's quite a dress. You look absolutely stunning."

"Thanks. After all these years, I'm finally used to stuffing my bits into one of these things. When are you going to change the name of this place?"

"Sometimes we're bound by our traditions. Besides, the Water Club doesn't have the same panache."

Shelby turned to Jamie, pressing a hand in the small of his back to inch him forward. "Jack, this is Jamie Richardson. He's the famous filmmaker who's been working with my campaign. Jamie, Jack is not only the proprietor of this beautiful establishment, but an old friend."

If Jamie was famous, it was news to him, but Jack smiled and held out his hand, impressed. "Filmmaker, eh? That must have been your work that got everyone so fired up at FACPAC."

"Jack, you don't know the half of it," Shelby said. "Shall we?"

"Of course," Jack Skelton said, and made a debonair flourish of taking her arm in his. "Lots of people I'd like you to meet. They're all members, so you know their wallets are heavy and their taste is unparalleled."

Jack escorted the governor like a wedding usher, Jamie following behind. As they stepped through a set of expansive double doors, the interior of the club smoldered in its own extravagance. Mahogany paneling lined the walls, the finely-etched wood imparting gravitas, while the ceiling teemed with chandeliers of elegant crystal. To their right, a set of glass cabinets displayed a collection of rare minerals, each of them magnificent specimens of geology. The floor doubled as its own PanoScreen, displaying a slowly-rotating animation of the universe's swirling stars beneath them – an effect that looked amazing but confused the hell out of Jamie's feet. He noticed, not without appreciation, that the governor's dress matched the floor perfectly, sparkles and stars complimenting one another like symbiotic organisms. It was impossible to distinguish where the universe ended and she began.

About two dozen men sauntered about the club, coalescing around each of the Monroe sisters in small clusters. As Shelby had predicted, almost all of them wore Stetson hats ranging in size and flare, along with bolo ties and blazers made from animal hides. Most of them carried guts like oil drums. As Jack and the governor stepped in, one broke off and approached them.

The man shook Jack's hand, and the club owner turned to Shelby. "Governor Monroe, you may remember Nathan Moore, President and CEO of Moore Resources."

"Of course," Shelby said. "If I recall, the last time we met you were supporting my Conservative opponent in the governor's race."

Nathan Moore laughed uncomfortably. "Guilty as charged, I'm afraid. But you sure beat the pants off of him, didn't you?"

Jack Skelton stepped away, nodding at each of them with a look of, *I'll just let you two work it out.* Jamie stepped back as well, keeping them in frame while pretending to inspect the grand piano.

"That was quite a weekend at FACPAC," Nathan Moore said. "I was there when your little tape started playing. Nice recovery. I talked to our friend Myron Collins afterward, he told me how much you'd won him over. He was so pleased to help set that up."

Shelby almost choked on her martini. "Help set it up? Is that what he said?"

"Yes, he told me that when you couldn't do the keynote he suggested you put together something else instead. He wouldn't shut up about how amazingly it all went. You might be viable yet."

"Interesting. I'll be sure to thank him." Shelby took another sip to hide a wry smile. "Remind me, just what is it that you have Moore Resources of, exactly?" Shelby was tapping her wedding ring on the stem of her martini glass, a habit Jamie had come to recognize as a harbinger of her displeasure.

"We used to provide energy sources mostly – natural gas, oil – but now we're into water distribution."

"A lucrative industry these days."

"Half of success is timing."

"What's the market price for a barrel of water lately, about five hundred?"

"A little higher, but that's about right."

"What would it take to get that down a notch or two?"

"Well, ma'am, as you know, this drought's lasted a decade and the price is determined by the market. Supply and demand."

"Certainly."

"With the whole business at Ellis Island, prices have spiked across the board."

"I didn't know the Statue of Liberty was connected to the water supply. Did she double as a storage silo?"

Moore decided to change the subject. "Now, Governor, I'm not a member of the Conservative League, though I typically support them. I tried not to take offense with some of the more colorful things you said at FACPAC, but I hardly think Myron Collins or anyone else is looking to fleece the people."

Shelby grabbed a shrimp from a passing hors d'oeuvres tray. "They're not charging five hundred a barrel for our most precious resource, I can tell you that."

"Look, my friends here and I are looking for a way to support you. Maybe not all – hell, some of them came just to air their grievances or ask for a favor. I see promise in you, the way you connect with the folks 'round here. It surprised the hell out of me that you won, but then it kind of made sense when I thought about it. And that was a fine video at FACPAC, it really was. I doubt, though, that a little Texas wit will be enough to get you into the White House."

"That's precisely why I'm here, Mr. Moore. I need a little Texas money, too." She bit the shrimp and realized there was nowhere to put the tail.

The waterman rubbed the brim of his Stetson between his thumb and forefinger. "You may have heard I'm nearing retirement and grooming my eldest to run the business one day." Shelby shook her head but smiled politely. "Anyway, I tell him there's a difference between strategy and tactics. You use tactics to get attention in the short term, you use strategy to succeed in the long."

"Sound advice."

"If I were to consider sponsoring your campaign, I need to know there's a sound strategy for victory. I need to know there's depth. I need to know that you'll be more than a cartoon."

"A cartoon?" Shelby laughed at the slight, giving Moore a playful rap on the arm. "I didn't know a cartoon could raise five daughters in the middle of a war, put them all through college after their father died, and go from fetching coffee to governing the greatest state in the union. Since you're one of my constituents, though, I do appreciate your opinion – tell me, if I told you to kiss my ass, do you think that's a strategy or a tactic?"

The governor handed Moore the shrimp tail and moved on before he could respond. Jamie decided it was time to check in on the girls.

They were faring little better, from the bits of conversation that he heard. One potential donor, to Trixie: "Does your mom have any national security chops to speak of? Boy, these coquettes are delicious."

Another, to Tawny: "If I were leaning toward the Freedom League, I'd probably support Cromwell. I heard he might have a Sponsor and he's already prepared to announce next week. Supposedly his terror platform has real teeth."

Discouraged, Jamie circled the room more quickly, looking for anyone with a drink tray. More snippets of conversation followed him.

"—not sure she'd be strong enough to withstand—"

"—don't see how she'd get support from the generals she needs—"

"—her campaign shouldn't just be a family operation—"

"—the betting markets have her under ten percent to win the primary—"

Jamie decided that if no one was going to offer him a drink, he might as well get his own. The bar was sandalwood with gold leaf accents. He pulled back a heavy stool and settled in, nodding to the young woman behind the counter. She diligently poured him a gin and tonic.

He closed his eyes and took a long swallow, idly wondering how long he could work on a sponsorless campaign that couldn't pay him. Two months? Three? When his eyes opened, he was surprised to find Shelby had grabbed the stool next to his.

"I feel like I'm up for auction and nobody's bidding," she said.

"They'll come around. They just have to kick the tires a bit first. These people want to make sure they get a seat at the table if they buy you."

"Jamie, I thought this would be fun. I usually enjoy charming rich folks out of their wallets. There's a Robin Hood aspect that I've come to appreciate. Problem is, you can only take from the rich so many times before they tell you to fuck off."

"The media is calling you a populist. You should embrace it."

"Tough to be a populist around these folks. Besides, populism is cheap. Campaigns are not."

"Then bite your tongue a little bit. Smile through clenched teeth."

"Might as well tell a moose to hide his horns." She sighed, gave Jamie's hand a quick squeeze and stood up. "Back to it, I suppose. Maybe my speech will help." She looked at the bartender. "Stir 'em strong, sweetheart."

Jamie was about to get up and take a few wide angle pictures when a shorter gentleman came up to the bar, winching himself into Shelby's highchair. He ordered a whiskey double with ice and pointed to Jamie to see if he wanted to partake. Jamie shook his head, but with appreciation.

The short man tipped his hat to the bartender and slipped her a hundred. "Keep that bottle warm, darlin'." He turned in his seat to

Jamie. "Name's Sid Westing," he said. His Stetson was muted black leather and his beard resembled unpicked cotton, thick and long enough to shroud most of his bolo tie. "You're the video guy, right? The one I see following her all the time?"

Jamie nodded, slightly flushed.

"I'm 'fraid to say it, but things aren't looking good for your girl," Sid said. "You ask me, she's fishing in the wrong pond. These fellas might have money now, but they're in dire straits. Most're hoping that oil will get back on the map somehow, but it's long gone. The smart ones switched to water drilling, but there's only so much of that to go around."

"What would you recommend?"

"Getting away from these clowns, that's for sure."

Jamie waited for him to continue.

"Something that she had before. Something she could use again!"

Jamie looked puzzled and Sid bristled before stating what he saw as obvious.

"A rich-ass husband!" he said, brushing his beard. "Think I'm her type?"

"That's something you might want to broach with her yourself."

"Fair enough. But put in a good word for me, will ya? She likes you."

Jamie nodded, taking his own advice and smiling through clenched teeth. "I'll see what I can do. If you'll excuse me." Sid Westing held up his glass with a hopeful smile that bared several golden molars.

The clinking of a champagne flute silenced the club's patrons. Jamie saw Jack Skelton standing by the piano. Governor Monroe hovered at his side, both of them sharing a muted spotlight. Jack brought his pano to his chin and keyed on the microphone.

"Ladies and gentlemen, thank you so much for being here tonight. We greatly appreciate our honored guest, the esteemed Governor of Greater Texas, Shelby Monroe. Such a treat. And what a job she's doing for this wonderful state! Governor, the Petroleum Club and its members are all just thrilled to welcome you and your family tonight. Would you like to say a few words?"

Jack handed over the pano. Shelby playfully tapped its embedded mike with a forefinger – *Is this thing on?* The room remained hushed.

The governor began pacing around the room, the spotlight scrambling to stay with her. "Jack, my daughters and I are in your debt. This place gets more beautiful every time we come. Really, the honor is ours. To the members of the club that are here tonight, we couldn't be more grateful—"

The microphone went dead and Shelby's voice cut off as she examined the device, tapping it for real this time.

The universe of stars below their feet disappeared, the PanoScreen in the floor gone to empty black. Then it became an azure blue, showing the image of a bright sky. The image panned down to an American flag with its seventy-five stars grazing in the breeze. An audio track began to play, in the opening notes of the Star-Spangled Banner – but it wasn't the typical orchestral version, instead sounding like it came from kindergarten instruments, like a kazoo and a recorder. Shelby looked at the pano in her hand and saw its smaller screen playing the same clip as what was showing on the floor, the bizarre National Anthem sounding even tinnier through the device's speaker. The governor slapped the side of it, as if it were an old rabbit-eared television.

Some in the club looked at their own panos, all playing the video, but most kept their eyes to the screen at their feet. The flag took up more than half the floor as a burst of wind straightened it out. Then bolts of blue light started flashing, punching quarter-sized holes in the flag's stars. The video faded out with the national anthem's closing bars...

...and faded in, to an aerial long shot of Ellis Island. Liberty Island and the Statue of Liberty could be seen beyond it. Jamie noticed a cylindrical, blurred shape in the immediate foreground of the shot but couldn't tell what it was. It became clear, though, when the object started firing, the rifle-barrel showing no recoil as it discharged flashes of blue light into the crowd during last week's Open Borders Ceremony. The camera zoomed into Ellis like a high-powered telescope as it fired, the bodies so close and so real Jamie felt like he was stepping on them. He lurched back and out of their way before realizing how silly that was.

The governor trotted over to him. "Jamie, what's going on? Is this a hack?"

Jamie pointed to himself and shook his head.

"Well, I know it wasn't you!"

He showed her his own pano, also playing the video. His device was an older model than Skelton's. *If whoever's doing this has breached the parent network,* he thought, *this could be happening on every pano in the world.*

On the floor-screen, the first-person shot of Ellis faded to black...

...and faded back in, showing stock footage of Mount Rushmore. The video then cycled through other landmarks – Independence Hall, the St. Louis Arch, the Golden Gate Bridge – only to show them exploding in fountains of iridescent green, in a more dramatized manner than the Statue of Liberty's forearm. Jamie could tell these new explosions were CGI renderings, but the production values were decent enough to make him shudder.

A voice came through on the video, scrambled to sound like an old-timey robot from a black and white movie. The voice spoke in fits and starts, as if making calculations between each syllable that kept resulting in a different pitch.

"WE are THE light BRI-gade. AND we ARE com-ING."

As suddenly as it began, the PanoClip switched off. Around the room, handheld devices reverted to their home screens. The floor resumed its animation of a galactic spiral of stars, spinning in silence.

The only sound in the Greater Texas Petroleum Club came from jangling ice cubes in the base of a rocks glass and someone asking, "What the fuck is the Light Brigade?" to no answer.

Another man – Nathan Moore, it turned out – asked the governor if she had anything to say about this new threat of domestic terrorism.

Shelby Monroe kept the pano and its microphone at her side. "Yeah. What a bunch of dicks," she said, loud enough for all to hear.

CHAPTER THIRTEEN

Governor Granger: *Hey, big guy! Do they just grow adorable children in a lab around here?*

Audience member: *(Scratches head) Um, I'm not sure.*

Governor Granger: *I mean, seriously. Something's going on in this state, you're all too cute. What's your name?*

Audience member: *Rajesh.*

Governor Granger: *Well, Rajesh, I'm so happy you and your family could find a home in Iowa. That's really great.*

Audience member: *My grandparents moved here a long time ago.*

Governor Granger: *Good for them, it's great they got to stay. Did you have a question for me?*

Audience member: *(Reads from card) I am currently class president of my third grade. If I wanted to run for real office someday, what advice would you suggest?*

Governor Granger: *Oh! A future POTUS! Where are your parents? You guys, you're raising a helluva kid. To answer your question, Rajesh, the one quality I've noticed most grown-up politicians share is a healthy dose of self-importance.*

Audience: *(Laughter)*

Audience member: *(Scratches head)*

Governor Granger: *Or, if you're thinking about running for Congress, you might need the ability to willfully ignore reality. But seriously, Rajesh, grown-up politics is a rough business. If you'd rather be a doctor or an inventor or something, I would totally understand. Those careers usually add more good to the world than politicians can do. On the other hand, we could use smart and decent fellows*

like you, and should you commit yourself to public service, nothing is more rewarding. I've found if you have a deep sense of commitment the rest will work itself out. Commitment is what you need, when times are tough.
- Acton Granger town hall meeting in Council Bluffs, Iowa – November 3, 2059

"I can find the breach."

Ben Allen's old office had changed so much he barely recognized it, a jarring transition from his tasteful minimalism to whatever the opposite of minimalism was. A mishmash of paintings and murals clogged the walls and a multi-patterned carpet coated every inch of the floor. Sculptures – if you could call them sculptures – were stuffed in every corner. Ben knew Alicia Waters had eclectic tastes, but this was something beyond eclectic. Hating himself for it, he had to admit it kind of worked.

"Ben," Alicia said, "the FBI's gone through it. Our best programmers have gone through it. We've got indexing bots running through every line of code."

"Alicia, indulge me. Walk outside on that veranda and look to your left. You'll see a great big sign. Come back and tell me what it says."

"I know what it says on the building—"

"It says *AllenCo*, which is interesting because *Allen*, the first part, happens to be *my* name – *Co*, the second part, means *company*. My...company. The letters are quite large, and I specifically remember requesting a clear typeface. When I deemed you my successor—"

"You didn't deem me anything, the Board did."

"Yes, that's true." Ben frowned on the outside but thought to himself, *I'm glad she's the one to put that out there.* "When *the Board* deemed you my successor, they also advised you to seek my counsel if a crisis should occur. I would hope that terrorists hacking your global network might qualify. So, hello."

"You've been retired for a while now, Ben. You might not even recognize the code."

"I built the system. Even if you ruined my code, which given the bugs in your last release makes that apparent, there are channels buried within it that only I know about."

Alicia leaned across her desk of swirled marble, impressed with her own logic. "If only you know about them, then how could they have been breached?"

Touché, Ben thought. Alicia wasn't a programmer, but she was nobody's fool. "I don't know, but let me find out."

"Very well," Alicia said, pursing her lips. "We'll set you up on a programmer's console." She tapped her desk pano. "Jason, can you give Mr. Allen—"

Annoyed, Ben lifted his left index finger, swirled it in a circle, and then opened his palm in a stop sign.

The call dropped.

Alicia's exasperation was a familiar sight, even after a few years. "Why would you go ahead and do that?"

"I could make your pano stand up and dance if I wanted to."

"Benjamin, this is childish."

"You know full well I can't access everything I need to from a console. You should give me an intern's pass while you're at it. You need my help, Alicia. When the market opens tomorrow, this company's share price is going to tank, and when it does the Board will call me themselves. I don't think you want that."

Alicia said nothing, but let out a conciliatory sigh as she swiveled in her chair. For a moment, she pretended to contemplate an Escher piece on the wall – downward staircases going up, and vice versa. She turned back around to face him. "All right, what do you need?"

"I need to see Winston. I need to get into the ARCH."

"I suppose I knew you were going to say that."

"Come on, Alicia, you heard the voice on the recording. You know where it comes from. This hack could have been internal."

"You know what? Fine. But I'm setting you up with a guest account and read-only privileges. You can look all you want, but you can't touch a goddamn thing."

Ben held his hands up defensively. "That's all I'm asking," he said.

The private lift tube opened after a bio-scan confirmed Alicia's identity. Once they were inside, she selected the sub-basement floor with a voice command.

She reached out and gave Ben's hand a cautious but reassuring squeeze. "The service was beautiful," she said. "Everyone watched it in the auditorium."

"Thank you. I appreciated the flowers."

"I'm so sorry, Ben. We all loved Dylan very much. If there's anything I can do..." Alicia trailed off as Ben grimaced uncomfortably.

"You're doing it," Ben said. The lift tube pinged open and he strode out. Alicia hustled to keep up.

The sub-basement hallway was short and unremarkable except for its lofty ceiling, which sloped upward to over thirty feet above. A Vendomatic (still stocked with caffeinated beverages) stood to the right, perched next to the entrance of a rudimentary bathroom. In front of them at the hall's end was a door, the words *Augmented Reality Coding Hub* digitally etched into it, under a bright red sign that read *RESTRICTED ACCESS.*

Alicia stepped in front of Ben when they reached the door, addressing it directly. "Winston, good morning," she said. The door lit up in a warm green glow and an animated face appeared. Ben realized with a jolt how much the face resembled Dylan's – or more precisely, some younger mix of Dylan and himself, like the child they never had.

"God," Ben said. "I didn't realize I'd made it that obvious."

Alicia patted his back. "We always thought it was sweet. Maybe a little unnerving, but sweet."

On the screen, Winston's face smiled warmly. "a-LIC-ia, HELL-o. i TRUST you ARE do-ING well." Ben hadn't heard that voice in years, at least, not until he'd seen the hacked recording from whomever called themselves the Light Brigade. He'd seen the threatening video like everyone else with a pano, showing all the exploding landmarks – but he was one of the few to recognize the voice, and the only one who could call it his creation. Ben had always been a fan of old science fiction movies, the ones with robots made of cardboard torsos and rubber-tubing arms, and he'd put that voice in Winston as an homage.

Hearing Winston's voice in the Light Brigade's message gave it a creepier connotation.

Alicia smiled at the animated face on the screen. "Winston, I brought back an old friend. You remember Mr. Allen?"

The door pulsed from green to white. "OF course I re-MEM-ber!"

Ben smiled despite himself, studying Winston's digitized face. *There's so much Dylan in him, it's like looking at a ghost.* There was a slight break in his voice when he spoke. "Winston, how are you?"

"FA-ther, I am WELL. How ARE you?"

Father. Ben had forgotten how Winston was programmed to address him – Winston, it seemed, had not. Ben placed his palm on the door by where the animated face was smiling. "Winston, I could be better. But it's—it's nice to hear your voice again."

"FA-ther, I would SAY the SAME."

Alicia stepped forward. "Winston, Mr. Allen is here to look at you. Someone breached your operating system and interrupted your signal. You were hacked."

"a-LIC-ia, YES, that WAS why THOSE men CAME be-FORE."

"Winston, that's right, those people were from the FBI. But Ben is here to see if he can find something they could not."

"a-LIC-ia, that SOUNDS wise. FA-ther KNOWS best."

Alicia rolled her eyes at Ben. "At least someone thinks so," she said.

Ben found himself smiling.

"Winston," Alicia said, "create guest user account Allen-zero-zero-one, with universal read-access rights. Write-access will be denied. Vocal recognition on your mark."

Winston's face appeared thoughtful for a moment as he processed the command. When he spoke again, his voice had normalized into a stale, digital tone. "Alicia, account created. Allen-zero-zero-one, repeat the following words for vocal imprint and recognition. Salamander."

"Salamander," Ben repeated.

"Hot sauce."

"Hot sauce."

"Quartz."

"Quartz."

"Vocal imprint confirmed. Allen-zero-zero-one, account creation complete."

"Winston, thank you," Alicia said. She turned to Ben. "He's all yours."

"I really appreciate this."

"Soon as you find anything, you let me know. It's been pointed out that I have an anxious Board that is no doubt getting an earful from very anxious shareholders. If we could announce something before the market opens, it would be nice not to lose a trillion dollars before the opening bell stops ringing."

"I'll do what I can."

"Good luck, Ben. See you on the other side." Alicia turned and walked back into the lift tube, giving a hopeful wave as the doors closed and she was whisked away.

Ben took one more look around. He'd felt a whiff of nostalgia with Alicia here, but now that she'd gone it hit him fully. He was rarely not alone in this place; only alone did it feel like home again. He faced the door. "Winston, buddy, you gonna let me in?"

The door slid open. "Allen-zero-zero-one, entry granted. Welcome to the ARCH."

Ben stepped through. Despite its acronym, the ARCH was a cube of a room, and an immense one. It stretched a hundred feet to each side, empty but for a lifted platform in the middle. On the platform sat a cushioned reclining chair with a side table next to it.

A swirl of butterflies seemed to flutter through Ben's insides, filling him with warmth and energy. He practically sprinted over to the chair – which at his age, was more of an urgent lope – and plopped into it with abandon. He didn't remember his belly protruding quite as far out as it once did, but no matter. *I'll have to get in better shape if there's a campaign in my future*, he thought, but that was for another time.

The side table held a pair of gloves and wraparound, tinted glasses – the kind a baseball player might wear during day games, or so Ben was told. Ben set the glasses on his face and pulled the gloves on. They fit as perfectly as ever. He wondered if Alicia had known that it would likely come to this and ordered these tools placed here ahead of time, sized to his dimensions and waiting. She was often shrewder than he gave her credit.

He rubbed his hands together, questioning how many thousands of times he'd done this routine before. He used to spend days at a time in this place, only stopping to visit the toilet, grab a booster from the Vendomatic, and occasionally check on Dylan, usually at odd hours. Time stood still in the ARCH – it was a place removed from the outside world. Ben saw it as both his sanctuary and his church.

The recliner normally rocked back into a dentist's chair position, but Ben pulled the pin out and tilted it further until he was flat on his back. It felt like laying on a patch of grass and looking at the night sky. He inhaled and gazed into the empty space between himself and the ceiling.

"Winston, play Tchaikovsky, Third Suite please."

Winston appeared on the wall facing Ben's feet. "Allen-zero-zero-one, PLAY-ing TCHAI-kov-SKY, Third SUITE."

"Winston? Cut the robot voice for now."

The wall turned white in silent confirmation.

Silky, dulcet violin notes opened the concerto. After a few measures, the sporadic tones of a cello filled the violin's resting beats, a lullaby stirring to life. Ben let the music wash over him.

Ba-dum ba-dum ba-dump-bump-bum.

All right, let's roll, he thought.

"Winston, activate the ARCH."

"Allen-zero-zero-one, ARCH activating."

The Augmented Reality Coding Hub came to life just as Tchaikovsky brought in the flutes. Through his wraparound shades, Ben could see the virtual architecture of the operating system running every pano device in the world. A galaxy of floating, interconnected cells lit up above his head, comprising the entire room, awesome in its splendor and complexity.

In many ways, the ARCH was Ben's attempt at replicating the greatest OS the world had yet to know – the human brain. Instead of building his architecture with the typical programming framework of subsystem processes and microkernels, the ARCH was divided into lobes. The lobes broke down into Senses and Functions, such as the Sight Sense for processes like facial recognition, or the Language Function for processing speech.

Within each Sense or Function, the codebase consisted of multiple layers. The top layer was called the front end, the module an end-user would see and interact with. The back end comprised every layer behind it, all the hidden workings that told the user-facing front end to do all the things that it should.

Tchaikovsky's Third Suite was the first work its composer had actually been pleased with, and so it went with Ben and this iteration of the ARCH. The system had been rehashed and fine-tuned over the years, especially the service layer that pulled commands through the database, one of the many back-end components.

Ben tooled around the service layer to start, mainly curious to see what Alicia's programmers had done to his code. Using the gloves, his gestures worked through the ARCH's virtual lobes and flipped through the cells within them, like a speed-reader plowing through a book. He became more dismayed than even his cynicism expected. He found unbracketed endscripts that left commands open, negating whatever it was they were supposed to do. He traced through service calls that seemed to go nowhere – or worse, they went somewhere and never came back. The whole layout of the system had become spaghetti code, loose strings in an indecipherable tangle.

When Ben built the ARCH, it was something personal, a projection of his own mind. This meant organizing the system in a way that was natural and organic to himself, but inherently different from anyone whose brain might work differently than his own (which was almost everyone). It would appear as a foreign language to anyone else. Most programmers never realized how deeply personal an OS could be, the system's intelligence limited only by the imagination of its engineer. But no one else could understand his construct the way he could – however, this didn't prevent him from getting pissed off when he saw what had become of it.

He could only look for so long.

"Winston, go for command prompt."

"Allen-zero-zero-one, command prompt denied due to insufficient permissions."

Right, Alicia had limited his access – how quickly he'd forgotten! That was easy enough to circumvent. Ben worked the gloves to delve deeper into the codebase, finding a Function marked System Libraries. This housed common subroutines and configuration data, along with what he'd clearly labelled as the System Bible, the knowledge database set up for other ARCH coders to understand the programming structure (and basically see why things were the way they were). Given the state of things, Alicia's programmers had given the Bible short shrift.

Ben suppressed his annoyance and let Tchaikovsky's strings and flutes soothe him, fingers scrolling through cells. Then he saw what he was looking for – a floating, miniscule speck, tucked within a basic DLL cell. In the galaxy of folders and files and data, it was invisible unless you knew exactly where to look. Ben enlarged it by miming a swimmer doing the breaststroke – it took half-a-dozen gestures before the speck became large enough to read its label.

System library: n3cromanc3r.

Most hackers refer to themselves through an avatar, a codename they live by. In Ben's younger days, he wielded his avatar with immense pride – the Necromancer, a wizard whose spells used inert computer language to bring life to any interface. He'd been a prodigy then – the envy of every peer, the marvel of every teacher.

In Tchaikovsky's symphony, a movement began that always reminded Ben of a sunrise. In step with the rhythm, he activated the *n3cromanc3r* file.

"Welcome back, Ben." Winston's voice had taken on a third tone and was now smooth, human, and unmistakably Dylan's. It featured his jazzy vibrato front and center – his husband always sounded like a dive-club singer trading stories between sets.

"Hello, old friend," Ben said. *How I miss you*, he thought. "What's my user status?"

"Super-user status," Winston-Dylan said. "All privileges restored."

Ben looked at all the swirling lobes and Functions and Senses and cells and files with renewed vigor. It was an unparalleled sensation of creative power and control, how he imagined a god might feel molding the clay of the earth.

"Go for command prompt," Ben said.

A virtual keyboard appeared just above his gloves. "Command prompt active," Winston responded. "Awaiting command."

Ben started typing.

run: n3cromanc3r.diagnostic

As young children navigate the world at large, they learn about themselves. *Turns out I'm pretty good at that*, they'll discover, *not so good at this*. Ben Allen discovered at a very young age he possessed the social abilities of a houseplant. All children are told they're special at one time or another, which is usually not the case, and Ben's only specialty was the ability to appear mute. His classmates teased his reclusiveness in taunting phrases as unforgiving as kids can summon. Ben was an outcast, and not because of his sexuality, though that was already becoming apparent. Nevertheless, he retreated deeper into antisocial behavior as he grew, not understanding how he saw the world differently. That was, until his parents bought him a computer.

From the moment he'd turned his new machine on, Ben learned two more things about himself – he could make friends, albeit digital ones, and he *was* special.

How his life had changed from there.

Tchaikovsky's Third Suite quickened to a bouncy allegro. Running through his diagnostic, Ben's fingers flew through scripts and commands like a conducting maestro. He flipped past encapsulates and concatenates, implicit parallels and explicit obfuscations. The music erupted as he burrowed, the symphony's horn section on a thunderous rampage.

Then the cymbals came clashing in on the downbeats, and the ARCH was awash in a triumphant euphoria of sound.

He found the breach. He was shocked to discover it so quickly. What happened next shocked him even more.

By the time Ben returned to Alicia's office, it was well after midnight. The building would be vacant, aside from the graveyard shift helpdesk staff. *They're probably busy*, Ben thought.

Alicia was still at her desk at the late hour, pounding away at a keyboard. "About time you showed back up," she said. "I've written about thirty versions of this letter to the Board."

"Sorry to take so long. I got a little carried away and fixed a few bugs. I had Winston log them for you in the source control records. You can release a new patch once they're approved."

"I thought you only had read access?" Her tone was chiding, but unsurprised.

Ben shrugged.

"Well, what else did you find?"

"There was a file embedded in one of the background channels for the VMWare mapping service. Basically, we have everyone's pano types set as Virtual Machines, and the mapping service caters to their different parameters and screen sizes—"

"I know what the mapping service is."

"Right, of course you do. So, there was a file buried within it, and this file had an automated execution prompt that matched when the hack occurred. I could see it was a video file, but as soon as I tried to open it, the file deleted itself. I'm not sure if it was supposed to auto-delete after it ran and that failed, or if it wanted someone to see it first, like a taunt. But it's definitely gone now. I didn't get a chance to see it, but I have no doubt it was the Light Brigade PanoClip."

"See any other files like it?"

Ben shook his head.

"Well, that's some good news, I suppose. I trust Winston logged all your findings?"

Ben nodded.

"Good. How can we prevent it from happening again?"

"I'm not sure yet. But for now, go on a code freeze. Don't allow anyone near a programming console, let alone in the ARCH."

"Do you think it was internal?"

"I don't know. But you can't be too careful. You can get past this type of thing if it only happens once. If it happens again, there's going to be a lot worse than a dip in your stock price."

She registered this silently, swiveling again in her chair. Ben took this as a chance to leave.

He only made it a step.

"Ben? Have you heard this crazy rumor that you were running for president?"

He'd known this was coming, but thought for a moment he might get away before it did. He paused before turning, trying on his most enigmatic politician's smile. "What? Who told you such a thing?"

"If it's not true, that's a shame. I might've actually voted for you."

"You? You're one of the Freedom League's biggest Sponsors."

Alicia smirked. "Sitting this one out, so far. But if you are considering it, better do so quickly. Looks like Jordan Cromwell will be the first one in."

"Freedom Leaguers don't know what to do when they're not campaigning. They certainly don't govern."

Alicia refused to take the bait in his jab. "I think you should give it a shot. But if you don't, maybe we can find something around here for you to do. It might be good for both of us. You'd be able to keep yourself occupied, and it would send a message to both the Board and our billions of users all over the world."

"I'm not sure that's a good idea."

"I've missed that feeling I used to have when we worked together. It's like equal parts awe and exasperation."

"Goodnight, Alicia," Ben said, abruptly turning to leave.

"Maybe not equal parts," she muttered as he reached the main lift tube. He was about to step in when she called again. "Ben? Are you sure there isn't anything you're not telling me?"

He put on his politician's smile again, awkward as it felt. This needed practicing. "Course not," he said. "The ARCH logs captured every record of what I did down there."

Alicia met his smile with skepticism. "I'm choosing to believe you," she said.

"Much appreciated," Ben said, and he stepped into the lift tube. Once the doors were closed and he was descending to the lobby, he un-held his breath and thought back to the ARCH.

The breach – someone meant for him to find it. There was simply no other explanation. Which meant they knew an awful lot about his codebase and the channels where he might look but no one else would.

The video file he'd seen had his name on it – not *his* name, his avatar's.

n3cromanc3r.2064, it read.

The file was a PanoClip file, as he'd told Alicia, one without attributions or source designations. Ben checked the audit logs and no records of it existed – it was completely traceless, which for anyone but him should be impossible.

And contrary to what he'd told Alicia, he *was* able to open it, and able to view the playback. The hackers' message began just as it had across the world the night before, portraying the destruction of the various monuments and landmarks as it had originally shown.

But there was a difference in the sound, as if the track had been switched out for this private viewing. The goofy national anthem was still there, but instead of the threatening warning from the Light Brigade that everyone else heard in Winston's robot voice, it was Dylan's silky vibrato that echoed through the ARCH.

And Dylan's voice said three simple words, just at the end.

"Don't run, Ben."

Ben played the file a second time, to make sure his ears weren't deceiving him. He played it a third time, just to triple-check.

Don't run, Ben.

Without thinking twice, he deleted the file and overrode the logs accordingly.

CHAPTER FOURTEEN

"Above everything else, you have to be strong. Strength is not an attribute our candidates can merely claim to possess; if you're to be viable, you must demonstrate strength through action."
- *Victory in 2052*, Freedom League strategy memo

John Dolley blended into the crowd.

It was certainly easier to blend in now, compared to last week or any time before. He'd been told the dermal transplant was painful but necessary, and surveying the many faces he could see why. *Lily white, the lot of 'em.* The transplant had left him a shade or two darker than most, but it could pass for a midsummer suntan, and that was good enough.

But goddamn, the pain had been excruciating. The numbing baths helped, by now it was mainly his emotions that throbbed. Try as he might to shake the feeling, something roiled inside him each time he looked down at his hands, or checked his reflection in a mirror. He was now foreign to himself, so he could be native to others.

It rankled him, a feeling that only seemed to grow. After the transplant, he found himself unconsciously ducking from reflective surfaces – car windows, storefronts, puddles of water. Now he avoided them like the plague. Part of this new skin was freeing; he no longer felt like a magnet of suspicion, no longer sensed the heightening tensions in others sparked at his presence. But his sense of shame outweighed any freedoms. His momma had told him that God made him this color to contrast the brightness of his soul – if that was true, where did this new shade leave him?

And more than his skin had changed. Thankfully, they hadn't seen the need to alter his bone structure, but they did chop off his hair – hair uncut for years, in braids that reached his waist. His neck and back now felt cold and unprotected, a superhero without a cape. He missed the bounce on his shoulders when he walked.

They'd also shaved his face and his body – damn near head to toe – and he could feel the bare flesh of his chin for the first time since he'd sprouted adolescent peach fuzz. His cheeks itched relentlessly, tickled by the breeze, and he had to force himself not to scratch himself bloody – or worse, back to black, though he didn't know if that's how it worked.

The crowd was beginning to fill in, though the event wouldn't begin for another hour. The men who'd dropped him off made it very clear that he needed to get in early to be near the front – there would be scant room in the upper courtyard around the stage, and if he wasn't close enough, he couldn't accomplish his mission. This left a lot of time to kill, and he had no one to talk to. John didn't own one of those fancy devices everyone always carried around, playing games or holo-chatting friends, so waiting was a bore.

John had never been to this part of town. To put a finer point on it, he hadn't been much beyond his nesting grounds beneath the overpass, not for years. It wasn't a home as most would think of it – parallel lengths of concrete served as his roof, with no walls to speak of – but it was near the river and he could huddle in the shuttered train depot when it got cold.

As John waited for the event to begin, he sniffed the air. It smelled crisp and clean, quite unlike his home on the riverbank. Such a difference a few miles could make!

John looked out at the Kansas City skyline to the north – it was that perfect distance where you could see all the tall buildings in one place but still make out each one clearly. He gazed up, and had to admit the monument towering above him was impressive. Liberty Memorial was Kansas City's finest work of art – a circular spire over two hundred feet tall, built to honor the soldiers in the First World War. Red ridges ran up the length of the limestone tower – when the sun hit just right in late afternoon, they looked like vertical gulches of flame.

Four figurines were carved into the top of Liberty Memorial, massive gargoyles that faced north, south, east, west. As gargoyles went, they weren't grotesque – more like watchful angels, staring passively over the city's expanses, their expressions muted in everything but judgement. Above them at the tower's tip, a great billowing flame burned eternally, and the Liberty Memorial looked from a distance like the world's tallest Olympic torch. From John's perspective, standing at its base, it looked more like a bridge to heaven.

Someone bumped into him and John whirled around sharply, forgetting that he was in a crowd and these things happen. John Dolley wasn't used to masses of people. To the south, he could see folks waiting to come in through security, a line of them stretching beyond the ridge. They were already filling out the lengthy courtyard, clustered into herds between flanking rows of dogwood trees. Each person was handed a sign when they entered, most tucking it under an arm while they waited. A few of the faithful waved them in the air.

CROMWELL '64 – NOT JUST TALK!

According to the men who'd dropped him off, John was on a mission. His first mission in many years – since the war, when he ran messages to the front lines for the Underground. During the worst of Civ-2, the Majority was regularly blocking electronic communications, so it fell on John Dolley and his cohorts to sneak through barricaded city perimeters and run messages personally.

According to the men who'd dropped him off, this mission wasn't so different. As in the war, John had to find the gap in a defensive perimeter and somehow get through it to deliver a message. There were two exceptions. The first, they said, was the reward – he'd be richly paid upon delivery. The second, they said, was that he wanted to get captured, at least once the message was conveyed. He'd be arrested but, according to the men who'd dropped him off, the cops would let him go in a day or two.

But the reward! A million dollars didn't go as far as it used to, but he could be off the streets and in a decent apartment with the opportunity to start over. He could afford another dermal transplant and get his skin back.

And the real reward – according to the men who'd dropped him off, they could take his name off the List, the List that had caused his life such misery, the List that was the source of his pain.

After the war, something changed in John Dolley. He'd seen horrors that no man should see, and most of his friends were dead or locked up. He became so lonely that maybe he'd grabbed a woman inappropriately, once – okay, a couple of women a couple of times. He tried telling the judge he just wanted to hold someone close, to be part of them, to smell their spirit. It wasn't *really* sexual – he only wanted to connect, to feel and be felt. But the judge shook his lily white head and put his name on the List.

The List brought insufferable burden. It forced him to knock on every door within a thousand yards and explain to grim strangers – with as much self-loathing as he could muster – that he now lived in their midst. He wasn't dangerous, but he touched some people and they didn't like it. The repulsion of these grim strangers tore at his heart – they would spit on him, tell him to leave forever, and slam their doors in his face.

He made a bleak calculation: if he didn't live near anyone, he wouldn't have to knock on any doors. The List was a shadow that darkened his humanity; if he avoided its burdens, maybe he could shine again.

Before the war, John was studying to become an actor, playing Othello at the Metropolitan Community College. His drama professor said John had the voice Shakespeare dreamt of when writing the part. John had a gift – what the professor called *star quality*. But after the war, after he made the List, all he had was disgrace.

The event would begin soon. Feel-good country music played in the background, the kind where the only thing you loved more than your woman or your truck was the good ol' American flag. The crowd in the courtyard was nearly shoulder-to-shoulder, and the lawn below was really filling up, now one big herd instead of several smaller ones.

The floor plan of the Liberty Memorial grounds resembled an uppercase *T*, with the monument at the top and the lawn running down in a skinny line. The courtyard spanned across from left to right, intersecting the top of the lawn at a large stage platform, in the shadow of the tower. John tried to hide his discomfort around all these people, but held his ground in the courtyard, keeping close to the stage and fixing his eyes on its podium.

A woman brushed past and he felt a spasm of excitement. She wore a fuzzy white sweater, tight enough to broadcast her bosom in firm outlines. She smelled so nice that John lost all his focus, having to fight the urge to grab her.

The music stopped. The woman disappeared into the rows of people behind him. John brushed his nose nervously, the regular stench returning to his nostrils. In prepping for his dermal transplant, John's body was scrubbed in every crevice, but even then the stench didn't go away. He'd acquired it in the war, spending his nights slithering through sewers and Loop tunnels, delivering his messages. No matter what, the stench never left him. But maybe it would after this.

A million dollars. No more List. A new life.

John was practiced in smuggling small objects through supposedly secure places, and doing it again after all these years had been so easy, he couldn't help but smile during his pat-down as they let him in. He smiled now as he rocked side to side to loosen his stage prop. It was a simple plastic cylinder, like a stubby pen, easy enough to fit and unfit. All it took was a little tuck-and-turn to get it in, a little unclenching to get it out.

John reached into his pants, feigning a male adjustment, and coughed softly, releasing tension in his pelvic muscles. He retrieved the cylinder and tucked it in his pocket in one smooth motion. He wasn't quite sure what it did, but it reminded him of one of those holo remotes he'd seen once at the science museum.

Men in dark suits – different from those of the men who'd dropped him off, but not by much –fanned around the stage. To John, who'd spent a lot of time analyzing defensive positions, their arrangement was curious. Three stood at the stage's front and three others took the back – but they were concentrated in the middle, leaving the sides open.

Some others came out, these people working up the short stack of steps that opened onto the stage, lining up shoulder-to-shoulder behind the podium. They included two men and a woman, and the woman pulled along two girls in her tightly clasped hands. The men waved fervently in broad strokes. The woman gave the little girls a soft push forward, and they shyly clam-shelled their hands in the audience's general direction before retreating to the woman's hip. The crowd cooed at their cuteness.

The woman on the stage brushed back sun-reddened hair from her eyes, adjusting the bow at the front of her maroon dress. She was beautiful, if you were into the Midwestern-vanilla type – wearing a glamorous smile. But as John studied her, there was a vacancy to it, a shield she hid behind. John knew acting when he saw it. The woman huddled the girls close to her, like she was hoarding reinforcements.

John felt an uncontrollable yearning to know what she smelled like, maybe strawberries or grapefruit. He'd find out soon enough.

The crowd was really grooving now, chanting *"CROM-WELL! CROM-WELL!"* in zealous unison. Their passions boiled so avidly, nothing short of witnessing an exorcism would likely appease them.

A disembodied voice announced the Lieutenant Governor of West Missouri, Raymond something-or-other. One of the men on stage took the podium and started talking about a tragedy in New York and how we needed to be vigilant against our enemies and he went on and on. He introduced the other man on the stage, the East Kansas Attorney General. That man talked for quite a while about how what happened in New York was truly sad, but that perhaps some good might come of it, as it had put a pause on the scourge of immigration that would blight our beautiful countryside. John found the stage presence of both men lacking, strongly-worded performances sullied by thin voices and a lack of bravado.

The second man turned toward the woman on the stage, saying how she would make a tremendous first lady and weren't those kids adorable? The woman's name appeared to be Helen, and she smiled humbly at the acknowledgment, her skin blanching almost the same shade of red as her hair. She was clearly uncomfortable being around all these people. Then the speaking man said he was proud to introduce the next President of the United States, and John Dolley realized he'd been under an overpass for too long because he thought there'd just been a next president and now his head hurt from the confusion and he couldn't stop looking at Helen. He tried to lean forward to get a better view of her, but he was stuck in the fifth row and a dull thrum had begun to penetrate his ears, and it sounded like he was back in the tunnels and a Loop train was coming. His stench was getting stronger; he was surprised no one else had noticed it. Blinking, he could almost see the train's halcyon lights stretching toward him from down the Loop tracks.

Music blared some old-school rock ditty, and a new man emerged on the other side of the stage platform. Trying to get himself right, John's first impression of the man was that he had a little too much spit-shine, polished to the point of blinding fluorescence. John thought back to the cast during his run in *Othello* – this new man would've made a killer Iago.

John watched the man hunch over the two little girls, showering kisses on them as they tried to shrink away. Undaunted, he took Helen in an overtly long embrace before moving on to exchange hearty handshakes and brotherly hugs with the two other men,

Attorney General This and Lieutenant Governor That. Finally, he took the podium with his hands outstretched, basking in the exultant cheers from his audience. When the man asked for quiet and rolled up his shirtsleeves, John flexed his knees and tried to loosen his cramping legs. He blinked and saw the Loop train once more, coming at him from behind his eyelids.

The man – introducing himself as Jordan Cromwell, the Cromwell everyone was chanting about – waited for silence to fall, and then spoke in a vibrant tenor. What gravitas he had, so unlike the others!

"Thank you so much, everyone. My heart goes out to all of you, truly. I'd like to also thank the Attorney General and the Lieutenant Governor for being here, they are public servants of the highest order. And of course, I'd be remiss not to thank my incredible wife, Helen, and my two children, Abigail and Evelyn. They are my whole heart. Now, I'm sure some of you are wondering what a senator from East Kansas is doing in West Missouri. I would like to remind of you of this city's history. Two hundred years ago, a border that divided two states within this city, and the border raged in conflict. *Bleeding Kansas*, it came to be known. And it was a terrible time, but we got through it and the heartland was peaceful for generations. Then came another war, a Second Civil War. And during that terrible time, we fought together, Kansans and Missourians, for shared victory over the Underground. We showed that Kansas City isn't defined by borders, but by what's in our hearts!"

Pitched screams cascaded around John's ears. In the pits of his eardrums, the sound of the Loop train grew louder, and he realized he'd forgotten his cue.

What the hell was it? *Stronger together? United we're stronger? Together united?*

It was early spring but Midwestern afternoons were already sweltering. John felt knobs of sweat collecting at his temples. He cast his eyes to the top of Liberty Memorial's tower and asked its angels for inspiration.

Onstage, Jordan Cromwell went on, "I chose to announce my candidacy here, as this Liberty Memorial shares its name with the great statue in New York Harbor. Liberty – a truly American concept, one that runs from our coasts to right here in the heartland. We mourn for the damage that the Statue of Liberty took, for the needless lives lost. But I stand here to say that we will not give in to terror in these United States. We will find every symbol across this nation that goes by the name of Liberty and we will protect it from the cowardly animals that call themselves the Light Brigade!"

John didn't think he'd missed his cue yet, but the words of Cromwell's speech were running together. The Loop train roared in his eardrums, and the angels he beseeched did nothing to quiet it.

"I fought the immigration policy of our current president—" boos rained down around John, loud enough to drown out the Loop train momentarily, "but the rule of law must stand above all. We will hunt down these terrorists, and if this president can't find them, I will!"

Cheers now, but the train grew louder.

"The people of this country must come together, like the people of Kansas and Missouri. Because we're stronger when we're united!"

John rubbed his head and closed his eyes, the Loop train blaring its horn as it split his skull like a migraine. He'd lost countless nights in those tunnels, laying in his own filth as he waited out the sentries until it was time to move.

On the stage, Cromwell paused, but his face didn't crack as he scanned the crowd, a wistful smile teasing his lips. His expression reminded John of when Iago reveals his nefarious plan to Cassio in Othello's second act.

"Let me say that once again," Cromwell asserted, "because it's so vital to the spirit of our nation – we're stronger when we're united!"

John moved.

His first step was a faltering one, his knees not what they used to be. But as he got going, the old slither came back to him, and he slipped through the rows of onlookers like a wind gust. The men in dark suits weren't anywhere close enough to intercept, and a moment later John Dolley was back on a stage.

Two steps later and the woman, Helen, was in his arms.

John clasped her shoulder and her hair swung into his face, a fragrance of straw lilies filling his nose. The woman struggled against him, but John only held her tighter. As his hand wrapped around her waist, it slipped past her breast, and John shivered as he felt her pulse racing beneath it.

As with anyone in their last earthly moments, time slackened to a crawl, moving forward in inches instead of feet. John dug into his pocket and with bravado pulled out his stage prop, the stubby pen or holo remote or whatever it was. According to the men who'd dropped him off, he'd have to hurry to get his line out, but the men in dark suits around the stage kept their distance. John took an extra inhale to gather his voice. Waving the pen-thing in the air and feeling Helen's bosom against him, he felt disjointed enough to nearly forget the line, but the voice of Othello roared through.

"For the—FOR THE LIGHT BRIGADE!"

Whatever that meant. But he never fully understood Shakespeare, either, and that didn't affect his acting. As he'd been instructed, John shook his fist with the prop in his hand, careful not to push any buttons.

"Get away from my wife, you bastard!"

Jordan Cromwell was leaning into his microphone as he screamed at John. *What stage authority,* John marveled. *He's a better actor by far!* Helen continued to struggle in John's grip but he couldn't let her go; the straw lilies smelled too inviting.

Where are the men in dark suits? John's eyes swept around and saw they'd drawn weapons but still kept their distance. Why hadn't they tackled him already? He would go down without a fight; he'd done all that was asked to earn his reward.

Helen's eyes squeezed shut and she started hysterically convulsing, as if in the worst throes of a recurring nightmare. John saw her face, the pain in it, and his hand slowly un-bunched the side of her dress. He forgot what he was doing up here, the thousands of people watching, the million dollars coming his way. The play had gone all wrong, the unexpected depth of the woman's agony dashing any pleasure he might have expected – and what pleasure could he gain, other than a passing whiff of something he could never keep? Her pain revealed her to be as broken as himself – but maybe, just maybe, he could save her.

John let go of Helen and retreated a half-step. Then, he reached out to brush her cheek and show he posed no harm. "Come with me," he whispered.

"I warned you—" Jordan Cromwell reached into his jacket pocket and pulled out a stubby, pen-like cylinder, pointing it at John.

Hey, that looks just like mine—

A bright flash blinded John's vision and the air went out of his lungs. He smelled smoke and an acrid odor that reminded him of the dead catfish that occasionally washed up on his riverbank. He vaguely realized that he'd lost the ability to hear, as if the sounds around him were getting sucked up by a vacuum. Even the Loop train running through his eyelids had gone silent. His head bobbled forward and he was dully surprised to find a hole, roughly the size of a salad plate, boring straight through his abdomen. His intestines looked like mealworms in a muddy petri dish, tunneling around and over each other.

John's legs buckled, and he dropped clumsily into a sitting position, blood and bile sputtering out his mouth. Then his hollowed torso fell backward and he lay on the stage floor, arms twitching as the life ran out of him.

He could see a cloudless blue sky above, with the sun-drenched Liberty Memorial stretching towards it, thrusting into open air. Black edges began to narrow his vision, as if night was descending in the height of afternoon. The tower's angels dwindled away, receding to a darkening sky.

John's view of the tower became blocked as Jordan Cromwell knelt over him, taking his hand and invoking the Lord's Prayer. His tenor's voice was soft and melodic like a lullaby.

John Dolley's vision was nearly gone now – he could barely make out the outstretched hand reaching for his face until two long fingers settled on his forehead. They felt like feathers as they traced downward, gently pressing on his eyelids, and then the darkness became complete.

CHAPTER FIFTEEN

"Some years ago, one side of this country sought to destroy the other, and vice versa. That we could not avoid this conflict is a black mark on our government that we must confront ourselves with every day. But this failure of peaceful coexistence goes beyond our governance. We must examine our humanity at every hour, celebrate our freedom every minute, and glorify in our differences every second, if we are to move past this dark time and become the people we need to be. We must be better than what we were, all of us, if we are to move forward and prosper as a nation."
- Acton Granger, *A House Again Divided* campaign address – May 25, 2059

If Tess were forced to choose, the kitchen would be her second-favorite room in her father's house.

It certainly contained the most memories. She loved the study, it felt like a piece of her – but there wasn't much to do in there besides sit, sip coffee, and read. Those might be her favorite things in life, but they weren't the most memorable.

Her father, in the time before (as she now referred to it), was an amazing cook – to the point where he could look in the pantry, see only a handful of random ingredients, and somehow still whip out a gourmet meal. It was where her father was at his most vocal, his most animated, his most...himself. There would be a sizzle in the air from whatever was on the stovetop, with the conversation sizzling to match. The room was devoid of wall-sized holos or other intrusive technologies, save for the small PanoScreen in the refrigerator door.

Tess sat on her usual counter stool, but the room was quiet. She observed her father closely as he emptied the dishwasher, or tried to. Like watching him struggle through so many other mundane activities, it was dispiriting. He would pick up a dish, turn it over in his hands quizzically, and then scan the cabinets for where it belonged. His hands were trembling as each decision became more vexing.

But Tess was stuck. If she stood to help him, he would shy her away, often with unkind words. His irritability had increased of late, his mood oscillating from apathetic to agitated.

She tried helpful suggestions from her stool. "Dad, the bowls go in the cupboard next to the fridge."

Though he was over by the stove and looking in the opposite direction, he grumbled, "I know that, Tess," and threw her a nasty look. He put the bowl where it belonged, but now its placement came with a flare of annoyance.

Like she'd done with any policy proposal that came across her desk, Tess approached her father's affliction by studying the bejeezus out of it. Knowing the details of his illness, however, provided no comfort. Each degenerative stage normally was supposed to last a year or two, but her father was flying through them every few months, the pace accelerating.

As she watched him put a coffee mug in with the dinner plates, she wondered what would come next.

The fridge pano quietly cycled through the day's news. There were still no updates on the Light Brigade hack, nor many details on the Light Brigade itself – who they were or what they wanted, aside from being terrorists who murdered immigrants, hacked the pano network, and wanted to shoot up monuments. Senator Jordan Cromwell, the Freedom Leaguer from East Kansas, was expected to announce his campaign for president within the hour, becoming the first candidate to throw his hat in the ring. The market was down half a percent.

On Tess's mind was: doesn't he know the silverware goes in the left-hand drawer?

"Dad, there have been some break-ins around here recently. I think we need to put the razor wire back up."

Richard Larkin set a plate down with a grimace. "Come on, Tessa, it makes me feel like I'm living in a prison. I can't even look at the garden when it's surrounded by all that."

At least he remembers he has a garden, she thought, though she'd been the one to tend to it these past few months, and the water it needed was getting expensive. "It's to keep us safe. It'll just be around the outer fence. Most of the houses on our block have it. What if we're the only ones that don't?"

Her father murmured something that vaguely sounded like *Fine, whatever*. Tess gave up on following where the dishes went – she'd fix them later – and tried to focus on her reading materials, scribbling out notes to compile into a briefing book.

While Vice President Schroeder was still mustering the gumption to pitch the Convention Project to the president, he'd asked Tess to assist in refining his tax proposals. It was jarring to have a decorated economist request her help on a policy so in his wheelhouse, and Tess wondered whether this was a genuine appeal or a trial balloon to test her comprehension. Either way, she'd have to be extra-prepared. It was one more thing to study the bejeezus out of.

She'd always had a knack for learning something new. Tess regarded her brain like a sponge, dropped in a bucket of water. By kindergarten, she was reading three levels above her peers. The rest of school was a breeze – high school valedictorian, college graduate in three years, law school full honors.

Humility, Tessa. You'll be surprised by all the things you don't know.

Once again she was back to recalling her father's advice, but she had to keep reminding herself since he rarely uttered them anymore. Truisms like "The smartest person's sum of knowledge is just a sand pebble in the beach of the universe" no longer peppered the conversation. She used to hear them all day long, now almost never. Would that she could get them in a happy medium!

Richard finished putting away the last of the dishes, wherever they might be. He ambled over to the breakfast nook and sat down, flexing his fingers. He did that more often now, working through the joint pain that locked up his hands.

Tess got up, poured her father a juice, and brought it over to him along with a book he'd been reading, or re-reading. She ran into a tangible odor.

"You're a little ripe, dad. Didn't you wear that outfit yesterday?"

"Tessa, hell, I don't know."

"Did you shower this morning?"

"Ask your mother."

Tess knew this response would come, eventually – in the time before (way before), this was his reflexive answer any time his daughter asked too many questions. It would surely slip out, sooner or later. But now? It had to be now?

"Dad, mom's gone. Remember?"

Remember? She was asking this question a hundred times a day, sometimes out loud but mostly in her mind. Was it even worth it at this point? Of course he didn't remember, and there came a time when it was useless to pretend he did.

Part of her felt he was regressing so rapidly because he'd been so goddamn brilliant in the first place – the way a room, blindingly lit, makes the darkness more severe once the light extinguishes.

"Of course I remember she's gone," he said, trying to play it off as banter. But disappointment colored his look of fear. He shook his head and chuckled nervously, grabbing at the book. Tess retreated to her stool and they read quietly for a while.

Tess was starting to feel comfortable with the Hall-Rabushka tax model when the fridge pano started chirping, pawning the Cromwell announcement off as breaking news. Tess gestured to mute it.

"Hey, I was going to watch that!"

"Dad, you can't be serious."

"A lot of what he has to say makes sense."

Tess couldn't tell what surprised her more, that her father knew who this man was or that he was receptive to his words. Richard Larkin was a small-c conservative, a man whose distrust in government only exceeded his distrust in the people that attempted to run it. Jordan Cromwell was not the type of politician her father would look at with anything but disdain.

For Tess, this was worse than him thinking Mom was still around.

"He's a fear monger, Dad. You don't need to listen to that." She kept it on mute and went back to her reading.

Tess felt mostly good about the tax proposals she was putting together. The generation gap was the biggest hurdle in the country's finances, a widening discrepancy between the number of working-age citizens and those who no longer received an active income. Civ-2 had deprived the country of millions of able-bodied individuals, creating a void, and with the elderly living well into their hundreds, the balance between the generational populations skewed further. America's entitlement system hemorrhaged trillions of dollars a year, the contributing tax base far too small to make up the difference.

It was an open secret on Capitol Hill that any member of Congress recommending a raise in the retirement age was effecting their political suicide, but it was the only possible solution that Tess could see. Was that the recommendation that Elijah was looking for? Did he only want her to confirm what he already knew?

"Whoa! You see that?"

"Huh?" Tess looked up. On the pano, men who looked like security types were shuffling about hurriedly. In the middle of the scrum, Jordan Cromwell was kneeling next to what looked like a body.

"He shot a guy! With some sort of light gun! What the hell was that thing?"

Tess tried to look past the hard truth that her father had spent the last two weeks watching wall-to-wall coverage of Ellis Island, complete with programs exclusively detailing the technology of Weaponized Light, and un-muted the pano. The camera was darting in and out between hefty pairs of shoulders, trying to get a steady shot through the wall of security. Once it honed on Senator Cromwell, he looked up with tears in his eyes.

"I—I don't know what happened! I was only protecting my family!"

"Where did he get one of those things?"

"The Weaponized Light device? That's, well, classified."

"Oh, did my clearance not go through yet?"

Elijah smiled ruefully. As Tess was still not on the vice president's official payroll, a security clearance application had not been offered. "All we really know is what he said on the news afterward – that once he saw what happened in New York, the best way to protect his family was to find who made them and ask for one. Apparently he got a campaign Sponsor, too."

Tess studied Elijah from her seat across the conference table. He had opted to stand in the corner, looking out the window when he wasn't responding to her over his shoulder. Occasionally he'd pace, a step left then right, and his hands were fidgety, either scratching his chin or running through his hair. When his eyes were on the window, he looked like he was puzzling at an equation on a chalkboard, one he'd yet to crack. Tess wondered what he would've been like as a professor, whether he looked down on his students as elemental nimrods or if he took the time to bring them to his level.

They were deep in the catacombs of the Eisenhower Building, in the formal Offices of the Vice President. Constructed in the 1800s, the building was originally intended for the State, War, and Navy Departments, but as it was directly across from the White House it gradually became overtaken by the Executive Branch and its staff. The Eisenhower Building, as it was later named, was once the largest and most unique office structure in the United States. The Pentagon may have taken its title of largest office in 1943, but with its elaborate French facade, ornately-tiled floors, and great curving staircases, the Eisenhower Building would never be unseated as the most unique.

The conference room, first used by the Secretary of War almost two hundred years ago, certainly had its flourishes – the green-and-gold-patterned wallpaper clashed spectacularly with the red velvet drapes. Tess felt like she was in the Palace of Versailles.

"You buy that?" she asked. "That Cromwell just happened to get his hands on the same weapon used at Ellis?"

"Course not," Elijah said, finally turning her way. He took a step out from the corner, around the American flag nestled by the door. "But that's what investigations are for. For the Senate's part, the Homeland Security Committee has asked him to appear next week for an inquiry, so that should answer a few things."

"Appear? Or testify?"

"Depends on who you ask. But Mr. Cromwell has few friends in the Senate, I can assure you that."

"Isn't Cromwell *on* the Homeland Security committee?"

"He is, and I'm sure those that know him best have more reason to hate him than anyone."

I wonder if he's counting on that, Tess considered. "Their animosity won't play well on camera; if they go after him too harshly, it'll just bolster his base. But some are probably afraid of his base, and they'll go easy on him."

"Careful, you're starting to think like a politician."

"God help me," Tess said. Elijah smiled for the first time, though there was still the shape of a grimace in his lips. Most of the politicians Tess came across could have the world falling around them and still look camera ready, but Elijah Schroeder's sensitivities always permeated his persona. Perhaps that was part of his appeal, as voters identified with the tragedy that befell his family, and he felt more genuine than the others. His magnanimity in the face of grief had been his biggest asset.

He was probably the nicest professor ever, Tess thought.

"The concern I have," Elijah said, "is that thousands or even millions of people are asking where they can get a hold of one of those light weapons."

"As is their constitutional right."

"Yes, and no. There have always been limitations to the Second Amendment – you can't just order a grenade launcher or a tank through the PanoShop. Like any of our rights, it has the boundaries of reason – free speech doesn't mean you can say whatever you want without consequences."

"The question is, is this Weaponized Light a regular firearm or something beyond that? The one he had was basically the size of a pen."

"But you saw what it can do. Its size makes it more deadly, not less." Elijah was back at the window. He removed his glasses and swiped at his brow with a shirtsleeve. At first it seemed he hadn't heard Tess's question, but he began speaking after a long sigh. "It seems we're back to a pre-war stalemate of legislation. Anyone in the Conservative League that even thinks of curtailing firearm rights immediately finds themselves challenged in a primary. The Freedom League is worse – they'd skip the primary and just tar and feather you out of office. And the other side of the aisle is worried about sparking another Civil War, so they aren't exactly screaming about it, either."

"Do you think the president would come to you? This is one of those chances at a big compromise."

Elijah laughed – a soft, regretful chuckle. "We tried that once."

"I'm sure you have ideas on this. Don't you?"

"Absolutely. But it's doubtful that Granger would consult me. With his immigration policy in ruins, I'm not sure what he wants to do. I haven't talked to him since he got back from Ellis. I've heard there's a big speech coming, but that's about it."

"Why don't you go to him?"

He bristled at the notion, with a quick sigh of annoyance that reminded Tess of her father. "I doubt the president's handlers would want that right now," he said. "It's one thing to come at him with tax recommendations, another thing with national security proposals on weapons proliferation."

Then how the hell is he going to propose an idea for a new Constitution? But Tess decided to let it go. "Fine, then. But taxes get you in the door, then you should talk weapons." In the end, she couldn't help herself. "And, of course, that other thing we're working on."

"I haven't forgotten about the Convention Project, Tess."

"I hope not..."

"But let's talk taxes."

Butterflies started to make their presence felt in her stomach. "Right," she said with hesitance. "I've been going through your old research..."

Of all the topics they'd discussed, it took this one to bring him away from the window. He took a seat opposite her at the conference table, his demeanor freshly eager, and tapped his fingers expectantly on the dark wood. The table was so old it hadn't even been retrofitted with a pano embed.

Tess noted the dark circles around his eyes, but they now ringed a brightness within. "Well?" he asked. "Whatcha think?"

Tess unpacked her briefing book. "It's a puzzle, and one without a perfect solution."

"No silver bullets in economics. Everything's a trade-off."

"But there is something that I think could help."

Elijah leaned back in his chair, looking at the gilded ceiling. His fingers continued their tapping. "Go on."

"I read through your academic works – there are a lot of them, to say the least. You make many interesting arguments with no shortage of opinions."

"Tess, I didn't ask you for my opinion. I want your opinion, with maybe some hope that it reinforces mine."

"I noticed there's something missing in your work," she continued. "Something that you've never really touched on, but should have."

His eyes still on the ceiling, Elijah tilted his head slightly to the left. "Go on," he said again.

Tess wasn't sure if this was the tack to take, but at this point there was no retreating. "Well, you talk a lot about curtailing spending, healthy living incentives, and getting rid of the AMT. You wrote a dozen or so articles on reclassifying capital gains, which won you lots of favor on Wall Street but doesn't solve the annual deficit windfall. You also wrote about shrinking the disparity in progressive tax rates, which conservatives like because there are fewer free rides, and progressives could live with because the rich chipped in a little more. All of that helps, but still doesn't get you there."

Elijah's head tilted just a little more.

"Then there's entitlements," she continued. "But those have already been whittled to the bone, emptied on both sides for the war coffers. And yet, there's not even a mention of raising the retirement age."

Elijah dropped his eyes to hers. "You're right, there isn't," he said. "But there should have been."

"In hindsight, it's obvious," Tess said. "But why doesn't anyone talk about it?"

"Because they're politicians, and politicians are craven."

"Why didn't you write about it?"

"Because I knew I'd be a politician, and I was craven. I hate to say it, Tess, but if I had written a paper in favor of raising the retirement age, I wouldn't be where I am today. I wouldn't have been able to run for district comptroller."

"But it's the only feasible solution."

"It's not a winning issue. People vote their self-interests."

"To a point. It's not like they'll support someone that says they'll eliminate all taxes, or promises unlimited water for everyone. There's an expectation of responsibility behind proposed solutions, at least *now* there is, and in the case of balanced budgets, raising the retirement age is the only answer."

"The only responsible one, yes. If we're talking long-term budgets, I could always fudge the projection numbers, make otherworldly assumptions about long-term GDP growth. If I pretended the economy were to grow at five percent per year that would add ten trillion to the revenue side over a decade."

"Eli, we both know what a crock of shit that is." Then she wondered, *When did I start calling him Eli?*

If he noticed, it didn't show. "That we do," he said.

It was nice to hear a politician admit that much, at least. Pretending that GDP would rise by impossible amounts in the next decade was the oldest budget-balancing trick in the book, but many still fell for it.

Elijah brushed at his disheveled hair, looking back at the ceiling. Tess wondered if he was trying to hide the creases that were forming in his forehead. "Tess, I know it's the only way. And now that we've gotten here, in this office, we have a chance to make it happen.

Sometimes you have to promise the popular thing that gets you into office, even if you mean to do the unpopular thing."

"The right thing, you mean. Or, you could convince people it's the right thing in the first place. I think that's called campaigning?"

"You're right, of course. But the question remains, can we sell it to the president? Maybe, but I've found that he's not the tipping point. Can we sell it to his staff, just as they're laying the groundwork for reelection? That's a steeper hill to climb."

"All the more reason you should bring up the Convention Project. The system is paralyzed, and our problems just build and build. If the president truly understands, the way I think he does—"

"First things first, Tess. This, then that."

Something occurred to her. "If you're going to try to sell the president on the tax policy, wouldn't it help to have some polling? Speaker Cunningham used to do snap polls all the time. Of course, he'd always word the questions to get the response he wanted, but the numbers were effective in corralling his members."

The mention of his old mentor brought a wry smile to Elijah's face, but he still showed concern. "That's a good idea, but we can't afford a leak on this. If someone called a PanoNet reporter and said they'd just been asked about yanking up the retirement age, there would be a feeding frenzy. It would pull the proposal off the table before it was proposed."

"If we can't put some numbers behind it, you can't sell the policy in the first place. We need a way to gauge opinion. Is there some way we could guarantee privacy?"

Elijah's finger-tapping ended abruptly. His eyes strayed from the ceiling and came back to her, wide with revelation but tinged with worry, as if whatever door he was about to open could not be closed.

"There's someone I can talk to," he said.

CHAPTER SIXTEEN

"What spreads quicker than fear? Sadly, very little. That is why we must remain vigilant in guarding ourselves against it, for we should all know by now that fear is the iniquity that sets us to violence."
- Acton Granger's second State of the Union Address – January 23, 2063

"All right ladies, what do we wanna do about this?"

The Monroe sisters eyed each other warily from around the conference table. They sat in the same room where Shelby had announced her candidacy, though the current mood was less jubilant. Jamie sat in the corner, quietly filming while the team plotted their next course of action.

For intimate strategy meetings, he stuck to two cameras – one fixed on the governor, while he rotated the other to whomever was speaking. He kept the cameras at a distance and his gestures to a minimum, confining them to the upper corners and implementing a hefty zoom.

He typically shot staff meetings in black and white, to convey the seriousness of the setting. He tried to capture the sisters in no-nonsense poses, getting their best angles when they offered smart suggestions, and then capture the governor weighing her options with presidential solemnity. Much of what he shot would be used as b-roll, but he archived his footage in case the need arose to review it.

Shelby's eyes ping-ponged back and forth among each daughter, and she grew dismayed at their lack of response. "I know you're all excited to get to the fair, but our primary opponent just killed a person on live television. I'm pretty sure this is unprecedented, at least since the days of Hamilton and Burr, but they didn't have much polling back then. What should we do?"

Tracy was the first to speak. She chose her words deliberately, knowing how tightly wound her mom was in this moment, but the numbers had to be shared. "The overnights show Cromwell jumping twenty points among likely primary voters."

"Because of course," Shelby whistled.

"That's only Freedom Leaguers. The general electorate goes the other direction, but our target demographics are eating it up. They think he's a hero."

"A hero," Shelby muttered. "How the hell did he get one of them light things?"

"He said he felt he needed one after watching the New York attack. He said it was a premonition."

"Did he obtain it legally?"

"He's got a concealed carry permit for regular firearms, not sure if this applies. But his new Sponsor owns the company and gave him one."

"Sponsor, so I heard. Granger's going to be cautious about going after him with the election coming up. Everyone knows lefty presidents don't go after guns until their second term."

Jamie twisted his wrist to zoom in on Shelby as she chewed her lip in thought. He had the perfect angle to frame her squashed-beehive hair, the steely warmth of her eyes, the subtle curl of her mouth. There was a beauty in her that he'd come to appreciate after several months of seeing her through a camera lens, a dignity to her features.

"What about the dead guy?" Shelby asked.

"They just ID'ed him," Tammy said. "Homeless, been off the grid. Registered sex offender with two attempted assaults. Rumor is, he served in the Underground during the war."

"But his skin was so light," Shelby said.

"He'd had some sort of pigment alteration, presumably to blend in with Cromwell's crowd."

"Jesus," was all Shelby could say. Jamie tightened the shot further on the governor as she sat in contemplation. "So how does the Underground connect to this Light Brigade that he was shouting about? God, he sounded like an opera singer."

Silence around the table. The girls were out of their depth. Shelby banged her fist in frustration.

"That's twice those fucking terrorists have stepped on our campaign. And we're not even campaigning yet!"

"His name was John," Jamie said, from the back. The members of the Boot Squad all turned to him. "John Dolley, that was his name. Whatever you say about him, don't forget that he had a name."

"Yes, of course." Shelby cast a glance up at the camera fixated on her. "Jamie, what are your thoughts on this?"

"He was a patsy," Jamie said. "He was what my mom would've called a stumblebum. Wrong place, wrong time."

Shelby eyed him keenly. A couple of the Monroe sisters busied themselves with their panos. "What are you getting at?"

"To put it frankly, he was somebody's bitch. Poor bastard just couldn't help himself."

"How do you figure?"

"Look at some of the posts on *Snark!* There are people that have caught on to this."

"Jamie, we're not in the business of casting our lot with the tinfoil hats of social media."

"Then listen to me. He had a skin – whatever – treatment. How much does that cost? Can a *homeless guy* afford that? And just check the tape! Look at Cromwell, right before John runs on stage. He says something, hesitates, and then says almost the exact same thing a second time. Was that by accident?"

"Look at the terror on Helen Cromwell's face, Jamie. She was absolutely petrified."

"Maybe she was a patsy, too. The fewer people that have to sell it, the better."

Shelby sat back in thought. Jamie trained his other camera on Trudy, who was looking out the window in one of her trances.

"Girls, what do you think?" Shelby asked.

"I'm just not sure," Tammy said.

"Pretty far-fetched," Tawny said.

"I don't really see it," Tracy said.

Trixie didn't say anything, she just leaned forward to see if anyone needed more water.

But Trudy's face crinkled as she gazed into empty space. Jamie tightened his shot on her as she worked it out in her mind. "I think it's worth exploring," she finally said.

Shelby nodded. "Girls, I think it's about time we hired a few folks. We need lawyers and we need spooks."

"That's great, mom," Tawny said. "But our campaign has no money. You said it yourself – we're not even campaigning yet."

"Until we get a Sponsor, I'm gonna have to ask you gals to work pro bono. Just like old times, right?" The Monroe sisters grumbled a bit, but overall they seemed accepting. "And Jamie, I'm gonna have to default on our contract, but only for a little bit. You'll still get what you were promised, just later than promised."

"Yeah, fine."

"All right. We're going to need a friend in the Senate to do some of our work for us. Cromwell's been summoned to appear in front of the Homeland Security Committee, when is that?"

Tawny scrolled through her pano. "Looks like Tuesday at nine."

"Who do we know on that committee?"

The others scrambled on their own devices, pulling up names.

"There's Rollins from North Arkansas—"

"Nah, he's a prick."

"—Kirkpatrick from Colorado—"

"She's useless."

"—Young, out of Brigham—"

"It shouldn't come from a Conservative."

"What about Kinsler, West Missouri?"

Shelby stopped. "Hmm...female, freshman, she might be looking to make a name for herself, and the John Dolley incident was in her home state...*yes*. Trixie, reach out to her staff and set up a call. I want to talk with her myself."

"Sure thing."

"Great. Thanks everyone, as always. Jamie, if you share this video with anyone, I'll have your ass."

"I know the difference between artistic integrity and the need for confidentiality, ma'am."

"Goddamn right you do. All right, ladies, we have a fair to get to! Go on and get ready, we'll meet back here in an hour. And you'd better look good."

Jamie chuckled as the Boot Squad offered more protest at the scant window to look their best than at the news they were no longer getting paid.

* * *

The Greater Texas State Fair was – as with so many things in this part of the country – something larger than life.

Simply stated, there was nothing else like it. From the Auto Show to the Skyway, the Longhorn Labyrinth to the Tiltin' Texas GyroWheel, the fair attracted visitors from the Five Texases and beyond.

In front of the main entrance gate, Big Tex gave a hearty greeting to all the comers and goers. The fifty-foot holo had been a fair icon for more than a century. In his first incarnation, Big Tex was the world's largest papier mache sculpture, an enormous static cowboy figure that lorded over the fair. Over time, Big Tex was given some rudimentary animatronics to wave and say howdy, but he kept short-circuiting in the Texas heat, even catching fire once. Now fully digital, Big Tex had tremendous freedom of movement (without being a fire hazard), and could wave and lasso his lasso, among other tricks.

The girls only had an hour to ready themselves, but they still looked like ranch-hand beauty queens, their boots finely polished and their checkered shirts buttoned only where needed. Shelby went with a more modest get-up, a tasseled denim top and black jeans.

As the governor and her squad approached the fair's entrance, Big Tex adjusted his straw-colored cowboy hat and puffed out his chest with an exuberant, "Howdy, partners!"

"Hey Big Tex!" said the girls, and the holo leaned over to give them a low five, the tips of his digitally-projected fingers passing through their hands.

As the sun dipped into a faded burnt orange, the fair lights blinked on. A perfect setting for filming. Jamie fitted his gesture gloves and tossed up three cameras.

Tawny led them to a side entrance where several fair officials were waiting. They greeted the governor with fawning reverence and passed out VIP chips to everyone, Jamie included. The head official, whose holo tag read *William Brown*, held a passing resemblance to Big Tex himself – and wasn't shy about playing it up.

"Call me Big Willie," he said, his chest swelling like the fair's mascot. "Come on in, I'll take you around."

Jamie had a feeling the Monroes knew the fairgrounds as well as any tour guide, but the ladies gamely followed as Big Willie took them in through a side entrance. They came onto the Esplanade, one of the fair's main drags. Swarms of visitors immediately mobbed the governor and her kin, eager for PanoPics and autographs. Trixie always carried extra pens, passing them out dutifully.

Jamie squeezed his thumb and forefingers to bring his floating cameras down and in, capturing some of the interactions between Shelby and her people. He felt a sharp elbow sting his side.

"Now hold on there!" Big Willie said. "Whatcha think you're doing with them things?"

"It's alright, Big Willie," Shelby said with a smile. "Jamie here is filming our little campaign."

"Oh. Sorry 'bout that, fella." Willie clapped Jamie on the back, nearly taking the wind out of him. Willie muttered something about how you can't be too careful these days, what with terrorists and all, but he said it so innocently Jamie didn't take offense. Then his eyes swelled as wide as his chest. "Wait, did you say campaign? Does that mean you're really—"

Tammy rushed to whisper something in his ear.

"Oh, gotcha," he said, tipping his hat. "Secret's safe with me. But you've got my vote, no worries there. How 'bout we check out the Midway?"

They cut across First Avenue through the petting zoo. The smell of straw and some less savory farming odors pervaded the air. Children in neckerchiefs and plastic cowboy hats rushed back and forth amongst the goats, miniature horses, and pigs. The livestock regarded them with weary disdain.

Hollers and catcalls from ginned-up fairgoers followed the governor's scrum down the Midway – the atmosphere was as crackling as the kettle corn. A hundred feet overhead, transparent floating bubbles paraded along the Texas SkyWay, their occupants waving down to the earth-dwellers below.

Jamie took it all in, the scent of fry oil tickling his nose. What a place this was! His mouth began to water as he looked salaciously at the bank of food vendors to his right. He turned his cameras to get some footage of the fair-folk ordering up some grub, wading in closer to stay in range. A man was ordering for his family and turned to ask them a question, startled to find a camera hovering in his vicinity. He cast his eyes suspiciously at Jamie. Something metallic on the man's hip winked in the fading sunlight.

Big Willie caught up to Jamie and put an arm around him. The man turned away and put in for an order of fried pickles. "Don't you worry, little buddy. All these folks are just looking out for themselves. Ain't been an incident here in thirty years, there's not many fairs can say the same. Won't be no trouble."

Jamie wanted to believe it, but for a moment there he thought he was about to get shot. *Safest place in the world*, he remembered the governor saying. *Hope she's right.*

The enormous Cotton Bowl stadium stood in the middle of the fairgrounds, acting as its centerpiece and events hub. The Monroe clan tacked around its exterior in a meandering walk. Jamie could hear an enthusiastic announcer from inside, calling out a rough play-by-play of a lassoing contest.

"There's a rodeo goin' on," Shelby whispered in his ear. "Big one. We'll get to it soon, but for now we've got some rides to ride."

As they came upon the rides, Jamie pushed his cameras up and up, then swept them across for a flyover. It would make for a perfect transition shot.

Jamie felt a poke on his shoulder and turned to see Trudy, bright with curiosity. "Someday, you're going to have to teach me to do that," she said.

"You want to be a filmmaker?"

"I'm better with words, but yeah, maybe. I've seen all the dailies you upload and they're just wonderful. It's really inspiring to see mom at her best like that, you know?"

"I'll teach you anything you like, as long as you promise not to steal my job."

Jamie meant it as a joke, but with the way Shelby was cutting back on expenses, you never knew. Trudy shook her head playfully – *Well, I'd never!*

Big Willie turned around just short of the fair rides. "All right, ladies, which of these heart-stoppers do you want to hop on first?"

Some indecision followed, at which point Shelby said whatever's closest, as long as they got to ride them all. Big Willie said no problem, the lines weren't long this time of day. They barreled through canyons at impossible speeds in the Chuckwagon Chase, survived impossible drops on the Alamo Coaster, and spun at every possible angle on the GyroWheel, their stomachs pitching as the ride paused wickedly at its six-hundred-foot apex before plunging them sideways in inverted somersaults to the bottom.

Jamie felt a dizzied flood of relief when he stepped back onto stable pavement. The Monroes were all catching their breath and teasing their hair back to respectability when Big Willie clapped his hands.

"Time for the main event – y'all ready for a little rodeo?"

Big Willie was met with a middling response, everyone's enthusiasm tempered by a lingering queasiness from the GyroWheel, but he deemed it acceptable. He spun and walked briskly to the stadium, forcing his contingent to follow.

They entered the Cotton Bowl through the Northwest Employee Entrance. The stadium was a pre-millennium concrete relic, but it featured some new features – moveable bleachers, a new Holotron scoreboard, even a few Mr. Cocktails littered the concourse. It wasn't anywhere near as fancy as the ultra-modern TexaDome across town, but it served its purpose.

And when it was fair season, the Cotton Bowl put on a hell of a rodeo. The crowds on the main concourse were packed so tight that few realized the governor of their fair state walked among them. Besides, they had seats to find.

Big Willie pulled them away from the throng and into a private lift tube that went to the suites level. They passed through security on the way to a private box. A dinner feast had been set out for the occasion – barbecue ribs, baked beans, potato salad, and a fajita bar. Hungry after all the rides, the girls eagerly piled up their plates and sat down to watch the show, except for Trixie. Like Jamie, her full attention had to be on the governor at all times.

Shelby shook a few hands of the fair trustees that gathered around her and took a minute to thank the help as they milled about bussing dishes. *All votes count the same,* as she might say. Occasionally, her eyes would snap to the Holotron over someone's shoulder to catch a glimpse of the action, but for the most part she stayed focused on work.

The governor usually kept a couple sandwiches in her purse because she never got to eat at these events – a drink wasn't a problem if others were indulging, but eating and mingling always felt distasteful, especially when you were being asked about Important Things. Right now, it looked like a sandwich type of night, as the governor was cornered by some corporate types from the neighboring suite, interrogating her about commercial water prices. Jamie kept one camera hovering at a distance but pocketed the others.

A great uproar coursed through the stadium and Jamie sidestepped for a better vantage. A rider had just been thrown and tumbled through the dirt. His bull continued to buck and thrash about, as rodeo clowns popped out of open barrels and bounded about the arena floor. The bull gored through one of the clowns before realizing it was a holo and confusedly sulked away.

Had Trudy not told him the bull was mechanized, he would've taken it for the real thing. Its movements were lifelike enough, the applied skin and hair utterly convincing. *If the bulls are mechanical, why do they need the clowns?* Jamie thought, but guessed the rodeo operators wanted to maintain the illusion of untamed danger.

As the rider jogged off and hurtled himself over a paddock fence, the announcer chimed in. "Another great run by Austin Midland, give him a hand! While he waits for his scores, for our final ride tonight we've got Luke Hawkins. Luke will be riding Old Bess, and he's insisted that she be turned up to level eight!" An audible gasp went through the crowd. "Level eight, folks, you heard it right. Steam will be flying from that bull's nostrils, let me tell you."

The lights focused down on young Luke as he settled onto Old Bess in her paddock, wrapping one hand in her bridle and raising his other hand for balance – and maybe a little showmanship. The paddock flung open and Old Bess bucked and roared, thrashing to high heaven. She curled up and performed a series of twisting back flips like a champion gymnast doing a floor exercise, but Luke stayed with her. The monster broke into a full sprint with just two strides, zigzagging its back end wildly, but Luke stayed with her. Finally, the beast whirled into a series of impossibly violent spins before closing with a bucking jump-stop, a maneuver that finally proved too much for its rider, and Luke was thrown fifteen feet in the air before getting a face full of dirt.

The crowd squealed, then roared. Old Bess lorded over her fallen subjugator, the bull's remote operator playing up the moment. The mechanized beast pawed the ground and snorted in angry triumph.

"Holy hell," Jamie said to himself. "I'd hate to see level nine."

"You ain't kidding," Shelby responded, and Jamie realized with a start that she was standing directly next to him. He was supposed to be giving her his undivided attention, but she didn't seem to mind. "Come on, they're gonna take a break to set up the barrel racing, and I want to say a few words to these fine folks. Bring your gear. Trixie!"

Trixie was of course already waiting, and the three of them followed Big Willie toward a back stairwell angling down several flights. As they descended, hydraulic motors began to kick on around them – the bleacher seats rearranging themselves to allow more room for the barrel races.

Once at floor level, Big Willie threw open a set of double doors and they were in the rodeo's frenetic wings. They walked past a huddle of bull-riders, including brave Luke Hawkins, tipping their hats. A gaggle of horses neighed to their left. On their right, an engineer was tending to Old Bess, the bull's skin flaps pulled back to allow for inspection and minor repairs.

"Big Willie, is there a horse I can ride out on?" Shelby asked, and neither Jamie or Willie were sure if she was joking. She brushed it aside with a smile. "Eh, never mind. Would be neat, though."

They stopped before the main paddock gate that opened out to the floor. The re-fashioned bleachers clicked into place with a snap and the stadium announcer came back on over the loudspeakers.

"Ladies and gentlemen, we have a special treat here tonight. Let's give our best Greater Texas welcome for the governor of our beautiful state, Shelby Monroe!"

Shelby trotted out and was immediately bathed in intersecting spotlights. Tassels bouncing, she jaunted to the middle of the stadium floor – a lone figure in a fishbowl, surrounded by fifty thousand sets of watchful eyes.

Big Willie turned to Jamie. "Fella, instead of going out there, you might want to stay here with me."

Jamie didn't think much of it, but he obliged, sending two of his cameras out to follow the governor, and a third he floated up for a bird's eye of the audience.

Governor Monroe curtsied when she reached the middle of the floor and then waved her arms for everyone to pipe down already. As Jamie's cameras reached her, they began to flutter and wobble.

Jamie grunted with impatience. "Shit, she went out of range. I need to get a little closer."

"Kid, I'm not sure that's the best idea," Big Willie said, but Jamie was already jogging away. After just a few steps he was in plain view of the crowd, not hearing the troubled murmur infecting the stadium as he focused on his wobbly cameras. He stretched his arm out to help the signal reconnect.

The crowd's murmur rose to a feverous pitch.

"What's that guy doin'?"

"He's aiming something at the gov—"

"It's another one of them Light Brigade!"

"Somebody stop him—"

Jamie saw blood in his eyes before he ever heard the gunshot, like lightning before thunder. He began to fall.

CHAPTER SEVENTEEN

"When we took up arms against each other, both sides lost. Within each of us, a collective part of our humanity vanished. But some lost more than that – mothers, fathers, daughters, sons. What do we do with that? Can our losses spur us toward a better age, or will they confine us to the same destructive patterns?"
  - Acton Granger, Civ-2 Memorial Dedication Ceremony – November 11, 2061

My children.

Elijah had spent the last five years hiding from it, clothed in a sheath of denial. The holos weren't the real thing, of course – just stitched-together memories enlivened by modern programming – but they blunted his grief by giving him something to hold onto. They filled a hole – not the full hole, not by a long shot, but enough that he could continue living.

How could they be gone if he could see them every night, could talk to them and play with them?

But all that was over; by cutting the holos, Cassidy had ripped the bandage off a wound that had never healed. Elijah felt like a knife was stabbing him in the heart every second, *jab-jab-jab*. It took everything he had simply to keep his body from shutting down, to move himself out of static inertia. How could anyone go through this?

My children are gone.

Some memories began to return, like pieces of a shipwreck floating to the surface, bobbing into his consciousness in fragments. The first snippet he recalled was maybe a month or two after it happened – the time he and Cassidy initially revisited their bedrooms. They'd lived in the Governor's mansion then, the three bedroom doors lining the upstairs hall in a tidy row. He remembered the painful debates he had with Cassidy – which room to start in, whether to tackle them separately or together. They didn't know what to do with all their stuff, they just knew they couldn't bear to see it every day. They packed everything up and rented a storage locker.

Elijah looked at a piece of toast on his breakfast plate, ridges of teeth marks in the one corner he'd bitten off. The eggs, scrambled with a touch of pesto, went untouched. The bacon smelled inviting, but he couldn't bring himself to eat it.

Ellie, Charlotte, Nolan.

Cassidy sat down next to him, cradling a coffee mug in two hands. She blew on it softly, the steam dispersing into nothing.

"You know I'm here for you," Cassidy said. Elijah could hear the unspoken part of her words – I'm here for you, *in all the ways you weren't there for me.*

And he hadn't been there. He had a state to run. He went back to work as soon as he could, ignoring the sympathetic, almost pleading suggestions of his aides – that he should take a break, all the time he needed.

What he needed, he thought, was to do the state's business. And it was mercifully all-consuming. There was a war still going on, after all.

All three of them, gone.

Cassidy sipped her hot coffee delicately. A thought struck Elijah.

"All those times those agents barged in and took me to the bunker...how many of those were real?"

Cassidy rarely responded well when confronted – she could be evasive, or lash out. But she seemed beyond that here.

"The first one was real," she said. "After that...there were just times when I needed you. I couldn't think of another way."

This came as no surprise, Elijah supposed, but a suspected lie still stung when acknowledged.

"Elijah, I'm sorry. When we moved in here, and you said you wanted to set up their rooms again, I should have said no. When you brought in those holo things, I should have stopped you. But watching you after the campaign and with all the stress you were under with this new job, I thought it might have some benefit. And maybe it did, at first. In the end, it's just not healthy."

Elijah stared at his breakfast. When he closed his eyes, an image of falling leaves appeared. He wished it away.

"I have someone coming over," he said to Cassidy. "Tonight. I'll be up late."

She blinked a few times, but nodded. "There's a museum opening I can go to, or something," she said, making a note to call her social secretary.

Elijah tried another bite of toast.

They're never coming back.

The airpod touched down just after ten on the outskirts of the Naval Observatory.

It had been a long day. Elijah began it in the White House, for a parade of security briefings and updates. Intelligence officials were still trying to piece together the trail left by the Light Brigade. According to Alicia Waters, the CEO of AllenCo, the global hack had left no trace in the pano's operating system or anyplace else. Elijah's idea to examine the subatomic remnants from the Weaponized Light had yielded few dividends, turning up only nitrous oxide and carbon compounds that were all too common, along with bits of sulfur. As for the enhancement glasses angle, there were still thousands of transactions to sift through.

If all that wasn't frustrating enough, the afternoon had been stuffed with an endless succession of meetings at the Eisenhower Building – an assessment of water subsidies for farming, a policy discussion on drone aviation, a review of land grant requests for national parks, on and on and on. As issues went, these were trivial – he could not help believing that his schedule was reflecting the continued effort of the president's staff to push him deeper into the periphery.

Still, he had some relief the afternoon's business was less than vital. And part of him had a soft spot for the minute details of governing. But he felt absent, detached – like he'd pulled a transparent curtain around himself. He wondered if anyone would notice.

The airpod's bottom opened slowly and yawned downward, sliding Yannik Vogel forward like a babe in a rocker. The enhancement glasses he wore had a greenish tint for nighttime vision. A larger man slid in behind Vogel, and both men stood up.

Elijah pulled tight at the hood on his sweatshirt, looking around as Vogel approached.

"Mr. Vice President," he said, his Germanic accent still thick. "Thank you for inviting us. We came right away."

The only man Elijah knew who could match the sheer size of the young man next to Vogel was the president himself. He wore a lab coat but looked better suited for a professional wrestler's unitard.

"Thanks for being here on such short notice," Elijah said. He nodded at Vogel's companion inquisitively, who smiled back. Even in the dark, Elijah could see the white-blue of his eyes – the clear indicator of Waardenburg Syndrome. *Genetics is a hell of a thing*, Elijah thought. "Relative of yours?"

"Ours is a family business," Vogel said. "This is my grandson, Heinrich."

"Where's Dr. Meijer?"

"Ah...Dr. Meijer has gone back to work in hospital," Vogel said, his accent thicker than Elijah remembered. "Neurology is her true passion. Fortunately, Heinrich knows our...dealings as well as anyone."

Heinrich nodded stoically.

"I am surprised that your Secret Service would let us fly within the...perimeter," Vogel mused.

"They're not as concerned about objects coming over the fence as I thought," Elijah said wryly, thinking of Cassidy. "Actually, as the president's Sponsor, your security clearance might be as high as mine."

They reached the house and went inside. Elijah led them upstairs to Nolan's room – the only soundproof area in the house, reinforced so any late-night gaming wouldn't disturb Cassidy, though that was no longer an issue. Nolan's bedroom furniture had been emptied per Cassidy's orders, and Elijah had hastily replaced it with a simple office table and a chair on either side.

Elijah looked at Heinrich apologetically. "Sorry, didn't know you were coming."

"No matter," Vogel said. "My grandson can wait outside." He muttered something in German to Heinrich, who took two steps backward and closed the door. Vogel looked around at the light-blue wallpaper. "It's like the Round Office," he said. "Not quite the same as the Oval."

"It's just a spare bedroom that we don't use."

"Ah. Well, I am pleased to be here. I thought after our last meeting six months ago, I would not hear from you again."

Has it only been six months? Elijah thought. "I know it's late," he said. "But this should be quick."

"Please proceed, I am most curious why you asked me to fly here on such...short notice."

"Well. The president has asked me to come up with a new tax policy, and I wanted to put some feelers out about some parts to it that might be controversial."

"Sounds reasonable. But that required this level of...secrecy?"

"By controversial, I mean that if they leaked, any legislation would be dead before the ink was dry. We want to know if Americans will swallow a proposal to raise the retirement age."

"I see."

"A staffer of mine put together the particulars, it's all documented for you."

"And that is all?"

Vogel looked at him expectantly while Elijah tried to phrase it the best way possible. "No, there is something else. Simply put, I want to know how popular the Constitution is."

"You want to..." For the first time, Vogel could not locate his English. "I am sorry – I do not understand."

"I want your people—" Eli mimicked being immobilized in one of Endure's silos, "—to tell me how they'd feel if the United States were to adopt a new Constitution. Or specifically, if we proposed holding a convention that revised the existing one, top to bottom."

Vogel continued to be at a loss for words. "The...implications of that are..."

"I'm aware of the implications. Hear me out. Our government has been broken for a long time. We're a young country and we've had two civil wars. Both with millions dead. We've solved nothing since the last one. What's to say a third isn't around the corner?"

Vogel sat back in his flimsy chair. "Well, you have the president's grand olive branch – a Reformation League president, a Conservative vice president. A government built on unity."

"The last time we talked, you told me all that was bullshit. That my selection wasn't about governing, or unity – it was a way to win. Maybe it brought about some civility for a while, but it's built on a lie. Meanwhile, we've got this Light Brigade bent on God-knows-what and pocket-sized light guns that can kill by the hundreds. Our democracy is threatened, what can we do to stop it?"

He didn't get a response from Vogel, but didn't expect one. This was a rhetorical question.

"Look," Elijah said. "The president calls himself a Reformer. If you survey the Constitution question and the numbers are encouraging, I can take that to him, and maybe we have something. For him it could be the biggest reform in American history. You might as well start at the beginning, right?"

Vogel scratched his chin, reflecting. "It is an interesting...proposition."

"I was thinking about the best way to test it. Maybe read the words of the document while you're doing your scans? And while you're doing that, contrast it with images of how it's been abused in all the years since? Maybe—"

Vogel cut him off. "Leave that to us. We should be able to create some advertisements that try to sell your proposal and see how our clients react."

"I can't stress enough to you how this needs to be kept quiet. At least until I talk to the president."

"That is why I confine my business to within my family, Mr. Vice President. I must request, however, a payment for this service. How would you like to settle that?"

"Payment? I'm sorry, is there not an open contract through the president? You're his Sponsor and this affects his administration."

"It disappoints me to say that we have not been...retained by the Granger campaign for this next election."

"What? They fired you?"

Vogel nodded. "Our subjects have come to some conclusions that the campaign did not like."

"Oh?"

"We found the president would lose, with or without us."

Elijah tried to contain his surprise. "He would lose? How? To whom?"

"Jordan Cromwell, the senator from East Kansas."

"Cromwell? Are you kidding? He just shot someone!" Elijah laughed at the ridiculousness of it. "Last I heard, you don't win elections by killing a man in broad daylight. Besides, the Freedom League can never win a national race, everyone knows it. The numbers just aren't there. How could you even suggest—"

Vogel had a look that Elijah had seen on more than one occasion on his professors back in school. *Your emotions cloud your conclusions,* the look said, *don't ignore the data.*

"Reelections are more difficult for someone who ran as an...outsider. For someone who championed big change. You can only promise the world once – everything will be better, beautiful bright future, on and on and on. Maybe we are better off now, but a...relentless opponent will remind the people of all the promises not achieved at every turn. And President Granger will not be looked at as a...harbinger of change, he is the government now. He is no longer the solution to a problem, *he* is the problem."

Vogel might be making sense, but Granger was still popular. Ellis Island and the hack from the Light Brigade had hurt his polling, but not fatally. Not yet.

It seemed the German was reading his mind. "We have seen his numbers drop far more compared to any published polls. When he rolled away in that ball while regular Americans were dying around him – I could make an attack ad, and without testing on our subjects I would know it could be...disqualifying."

"But Cromwell? There's no way he could win, and that's if he doesn't spend the rest of his life in jail."

"You saw the tape. Millions have. As he says, he stood his ground. Maybe it is...fishy, but we know his audience. They liked him before; they would die for him now. Blind with devotion. He is their champion. After the primary, all he has to do is be...acceptable to a few million others to win."

"Jesus." Maybe it was possible. Could enough of the American electorate vote for Cromwell to put him over the top? He would only need thirty percent of the vote, and if there wasn't a strong Conservative to keep the base from the Freedom League, maybe it was possible. Elijah wondered at it, but became preoccupied thinking of the catastrophic repercussions a Cromwell presidency could mean. The senator was a shill, a charlatan, but he was crafty. And if he'd already killed a man in plain sight, it was obvious that he couldn't be underestimated.

Elijah knew Cromwell's type – he would rule the country, not preside over it. He would stir up the worst in the people, fear and loathing, hate and mistrust. He would sneer at the values the country was built on. Instead of being an example to other democratic nations, they'd shun America even further away. There'd probably be...

Not probably. If Elijah considered another war already possible, with Cromwell it would be all but guaranteed. America barely survived Civ-2. Could it survive Civ-3?

"Is there any way to stop him?"

Vogel shook his head. "As things are now? We ran all the scenarios." Then the German brightened, as if he'd gotten an idea as insightful as Mark the Pipefitter's to put Elijah on the ticket. "There was one special...circumstance. One candidate that could beat him, but on one condition – that is, if they could run as the incumbent president, and not as another challenger. Granger promised the world and has not delivered – thus, incumbency hurts him. But this other person, when they last campaigned, made smaller promises. Achievable promises. Judged on that, and the office of president giving them more...heft, incumbency is an asset. Indeed, if this person was already the president, they would beat Cromwell, and everyone else."

"Sounds great, but Granger won the election. He's the president. Who else could possibly run as the incumbent?" As soon as the words left Elijah's mouth, he realized he'd asked another rhetorical question. The answer was obvious.

The German's one-word response barely registered in his ears.

"You," Vogel said, with a grin.

Half an hour later, Elijah called Cassidy. "Come home," was all he said, "I need you." He was in bed when she arrived, staring at the ceiling. The soft light from her pano grew brighter as she navigated toward him in the dark.

Cassidy slid into bed and pulled herself close. "How was your meeting?"

"Hey Cass. Glad you're home."

"Yes, I'm thrilled to be back in my own house and my own bed," she said, with gentle sarcasm. "You didn't answer my question."

His eyes stayed fixed on the ceiling – there was a subtle pattern in the plaster he'd never noticed before.

"Elijah, look at me." He finally turned, faced her. Even in the dark, he could see her blinking furiously. "Is everything all right? Are you all right?"

Jab-jab-jab went his heart. "Yeah. I'm fine. Just needed you by my side."

Normally she'd say something reassuring – *You know I'm always by your side,* or, *Of course, darling, anytime.* But she didn't respond, instead giving him the time to say something, anything. When he didn't, she sighed to convey her dissatisfaction. But she wasn't blinking.

"I love you," she said, a note of pleading in her voice. "If you want to talk about it—"

"I love you, too. Goodnight."

He went to sleep and dreamt of falling leaves.

CHAPTER EIGHTEEN

Audience member: *Good Afternoon, Governor. I was wondering, can you tell us what a presidential campaign is like when you're on the road?*

Governor Granger: *Ha, absolutely. What's your name?*

Audience member: *Hayden Murphy.*

Governor Granger: *Well, Hayden – you look to be around college age, is that right?*

Audience member: *I'm a Sophomore at Cedar Rapids State.*

Governor Granger: *Hey, go Eagles! First off, Hayden, a campaign is a lot a mobile college, where you have an exam every day in a different city. My bus is basically a dorm room – and I hit my head on everything in that damn bus, if you can imagine that. There's a shower on it that I can't even fit into, so I couldn't live without my dry shampoo. Probably like you and your college friends, I survive off mac n' cheese and pocket sandwiches and other foods less healthy than that. But I suppose there are some differences. In college, you're free to be yourself – that's what college is all about, finding who you are. In a campaign, you've got twenty different people telling you who to be, and that's just your staff. If you screw something up, it's all anyone talks about for the next three days. All too often it's a humbling, if not humiliating, experience. But damn if it ain't worth it.*

  - Acton Granger town hall meeting in Iowa City, Iowa – October 12, 2059

Ben Allen watched the quadcopter approach, anticipation and dread hitting him in equal measure.

He finished his coffee and stepped down from the rooftop veranda of his home. The staircase wound around the back of the house and onto a landing, then down to the first deck level before leading to ground. He could still see the 'copter over Casco Bay before it turned to run up the island.

The islands on the southern coast of Maine formed in jagged vertical strips, as if clawed out of the sea by a jungle cat. Some of the smaller landmasses had slipped underwater in the last century, but the major ones remained – Bailey, Orr's, Georgetown, among others.

Whaleboat Island stood as the jewel of them all, and when he and Dylan first scouted it twenty years ago, they knew it had to be theirs – even if it wasn't technically for sale. At the time, Whaleboat was a wildlife preserve possessed by the state. Although Maine would only agree to part with it because most of their state legislature owed Ben various favors, he and Dylan volunteered to keep the majority of it cordoned off as natural habitat, preserving the local ecology. They installed several freshwater ponds, planted hundreds of new trees, and surrounded the island with inflatable levees to protect it from storm surge.

Now, Whaleboat was as beautiful as ever, teeming with eagles and ospreys. Ben used to find great joy in coming home after an arduous workweek, toasting a gin fizz with Dylan, and walking down the leeward beach. There was solace in the constant rush of waves, their soft crashes frothing over the rocks onto cobbled sand, wiping away their matching footprints as the tide came in and out. After Ellis, Ben still walked the beach and watched the tide, but an impenetrable sadness struck him every time a wave erased his lonely trail.

Eyeing the 'copter, Ben picked his way down a rocky path to the landing pad. Centuries before, Whaleboat was fleetingly occupied by settlers to the New World, and they'd built several rudimentary walkways that managed to stay intact. When they built their house, Ben and Dylan decided to keep the paths, reinforcing them where necessary with native stones.

As Ben reached the pad, the 'copter swooped past overhead before dropping into its vertical descent, touching down soft as a cotton ball. The rotors whirred to a stop and the side door pitched out to reveal a cascade of steps. Four figures descended from the craft. The pilot minded his passengers as they stepped down, looking to Ben to ask when he'd be needed again. Ben mimed, *I think they'll be here awhile*, and the pilot gave a thumbs up.

The landing party consisted of two men and two women. The first figure broke from the rest and stretched his hand toward Ben. Anthony Butterfield, of Butterfield+Associates, was widely regarded as the preeminent political consultant working in the Progressive League. Anthony's head was shaved to the quick and he wore thin, nearly frameless spectacles. He was sheathed in a crisp, dark suit and loafers – snakeskin? – that probably wouldn't hold up on island terrain.

"Mr. Allen," Anthony said, gripping Ben's hand firmly, "I'd always hoped this day would come. Of course, I wish it were under better circumstances."

"Thank you, Anthony. Glad to have you here."

"I brought some of my associates." Anthony gestured to the others – the two women were smartly dressed and smiled politely, the other man looked like he'd never been outside before and was busy gawking at the island. "I'll introduce them when we get inside."

"Of course. Follow me."

He turned back up to the house, and Anthony waved to the others. They followed but kept well behind.

"What a marvelous place you have. I'd seen pictures in a PanoMag feature, but they don't do it justice."

Ben nodded his appreciation. The house was indeed a marvel, the fruit of years of hard labor and bottomless expense. The overall aesthetic was meant to convey a natural evolution of the island's terrain, as if its rigid outcroppings had developed innately into a comfortable human habitat. Ben usually avoided disclosing that the house came not from a human design, but rather an algorithm. He took a 3D model of the island and fed it into a program he'd created – a program built to create the ideal living, breathing space.

He'd necromanced his own house.

The exterior was a foundation of dark spruce, reinforced with brushed metal and limestone that framed panoramic, muted glass. A natural curvature, built into the outer walls, furthered the organic feel and gave the house a sense of weathering, as if its surfaces had been tempered by countless seasons of Maine's wind and rain.

As for the interior, Dylan had insisted on the decorating, of course. The result grew into a combination of Ben's programmed balance and Dylan's human aesthetic, perfect natural order complimented with stylish verve.

Ben had always taken great pride in the admiration of his visitors.

Whaleboat was built for sharing – wonders of the world aren't meant to be kept hidden. After the tragedy at Ellis, he'd considered just holing up here, living out his days in solitude. Maybe he'd become a recluse, one whispered about by children around campfires – old Boo Allen, driven mad by solitude, known to lure wayward boys and girls with a gin fizz in his hand.

Ben snuck a quick glance over to Anthony, whose head swiveled in wonder at each appreciated detail. The others seemed equally awestruck; the shlubby guy was secretly snapping PanoPics. What must they think of the man who built this place, as a hermit in some distant castle?

They approached the front door, which noiselessly rolled aside at their proximity. Everything in the home was automated by presence, gesture, or vocal command. Ben led his guests into the foyer – what a true Mainer would call a dooryard – a vast lobby spilling over with light. Some of Dylan's favorite Dutch Master paintings ornamented the walls, a collection the sure envy of any museum.

"Er, welcome to my humble abode," Ben said awkwardly. "How would you suggest we begin?"

Anthony remained standing, as his associates settled into various furnishings around the room. The two women sat cautiously, legs crossed in regal posture, while the shlub slouched and drummed his fingers on an armrest.

"Ben," Anthony began formally, "first of all, thank you for inviting us. My team and I couldn't be more excited to be here." The two women nodded and the shlub chewed on a thumbnail. "You've been the Progressive League's most generous benefactor, to great ends. We control nearly all the northeast – aside from that little state of New York – and we're growing, especially on the west coast. We're a national power again, thanks to you."

Anthony's associates applauded at this – even the shlub clapped twice before returning his attention to the thumbnail.

"We have the finest political operation in the world," Anthony continued, "and the smartest people. Everything's coming full circle thanks to your investments, and we're here to help elect you the next President of the United States!"

More applause, which from three people didn't quite set the room on fire.

"This is my best team. I call them the Gauntlet." Anthony walked around the seat of his first associate, a woman who somehow looked like a down pillow stuffed with steel. "Hannah is our media liaison.

She knows every journalist and pundit in the country on a first-name basis. You've probably seen her on the Sunday shows, reducing her debate opponents to whining puddles by the first commercial break."

"Killing with kindness," Hannah said, as her easy-going face peeled back to reveal a sharpened smile. Anthony strode over to the other woman, younger than the first. "Madison here is our best strategist and sloganeer. She can outwit a fox and brand anything. Her ads consistently rated higher than anyone else's—"

"Except for the president's," Madison corrected.

"Right," Anthony said. "Except for Granger. But now he's running on a record, and that record now includes terrorism on our soil – ads won't cut it for him this time." Anthony's snakeskin shoes padded over to the last associate, the poor sod who looked like he'd never seen the sun. He leaned forward from his slouch, which somehow made him look slouchier. "And this is our data head, Jeremy. Pick any address out in the United States and he can tell you who they're voting for, how their parents have voted, and what could win them over." Anthony smiled at Jeremy's nervous wave, instantly taking a shine to him and his unkempt hair, lack of social awareness, and blotched skin. Having come across armies of introverted program engineers in his lifetime, he knew this type well. He was one of them; he just cleaned up better.

"Thank you for coming," Ben said, "but this is just a tentative first step, a toe dangling in your waters. Before I decide on anything, I want to know what I'd be getting into." He looked at Anthony. "I assume that's why you didn't bring any policy people?"

Anthony smiled reassuringly. "Tell you what, let's take a walk, just you and me."

They hiked along the embankment on the western ridge, heading south – Anthony surprised him by navigating the rocks with ease, even in his fancy loafers. The island was only about a hundred acres in area, but narrow enough that it stretched over a mile from top to bottom. It was less breezy on this side, the chop of the water slapping genially against the seawall.

"Forgive me for saying this, but you seem tepid," Anthony said.

"It's a lot to consider," Ben said.

"Ben, I ask this of any candidate that hires me, and you'd be amazed how few of them have a good answer, or any answer at all. Why do you want to be president?"

Ben looked out to the coastline across the bay, if only to disguise that the question sent him into a panic. Why indeed?

It was on this path that he and Dylan would begin their evening walks. Ben had bought them both a set of enhancement glasses to catalog the wildlife, and from this point they could see the whole island. The first night they spent here, Ben led Dylan along a ridge down the bluffs. A small jetty protruded into the surf, and that was where he proposed. The morning they got married, they'd planted an evergreen sapling in that very spot. Alone and surrounded by waves, it now stood fifteen feet high, with a slight rightward lean, having grown tilted in defiance of the constant leeward breeze.

Ben sorted his thoughts. Dylan had been gone a month, and already he felt ten years older. Why run? Was it an exercise in distraction, to keep him from fixating on his own loneliness?

Ben thought of the current president, a man he'd admired but could only now see skirting away in a protective bubble while death came like rain. Was it an exercise in revenge, to take down the man who'd disappeared while his husband and so many others lay dying?

Ben considered his long career, of the technology he'd brought life to before the world. He thought of the fortune he'd made, much of it donated for honorable causes but much of it splurged on trivialities, like paintings by Dutch Masters. Was it a way to make himself feel fulfilled?

And Ben thought of who he loved, and how some still saw that kind of love as abnormal, especially in a political leader. Was he ready to become the champion of the gay community?

He searched within himself, and to his surprise an answer was waiting inside. And the answer was, it was all of these things. But there was something else.

"Across the country, there are people that have gone through what I've gone through, lost what I've lost, feel what I feel. I can help them."

Anthony nodded. "Good enough for me."

"Before we go further, there's something you need to know. Someone is trying to sabotage my campaign, even though my campaign doesn't exist yet."

"That's nothing new in this game," Anthony said. "With your resources and intellect, and now your passion, people will be scared of you."

"I'm not sure you understand. That hacked message from those terrorists – the Light Brigade – they used my personal programming account to send it. And when I found it, I also found that they'd left a message, just for me. Not for the authorities – the FBI, CIA, whatever. *Me.*"

Anthony's expression changed more than Ben would have liked, melting into concern and a splash of fear. This was never a good look on a seasoned political operative. "Jesus," he said. "You tell anyone else about this?"

"No."

Anthony tried to recast his normal sense of assuredness. "Listen, every candidate has threats on their life. Hundreds of them, thousands – some more credible than others, but they're always there. We'll get you the finest security, whatever it takes."

Ben had the feeling that a few burly guys in trench coats wouldn't make a lick of difference to someone capable of penetrating his operating system. But whoever the Light Brigade was, capabilities what they were – they didn't know everything.

They didn't know that when it came down to it, Ben Allen was the stubbornest son of a bitch to walk the shores of Maine. If they did, they'd know that by telling him not to do something, he *had* to do it.

Don't run, Ben – did they think that was all it would take?

Down by the jetty, a break in the wind allowed his tilted evergreen tree to straighten itself, however briefly.

"Fuck it, I'm in," Ben said.

The three associates looked on stoically as he and Anthony returned to the house.

"Thanks for waiting, everyone," Anthony said casually. "I was just telling Mr. Allen that the Progressive League nomination is ripe for the taking, which has nothing to do with the fact that none of the major players want to take on this president."

The associates chuckled cooperatively, even Jeremy.

Anthony spied an open seat in the far corner – an oculus chair Dylan had brought back from Denmark. Ben remembered getting angry about dropping six figures on what amounted to some metal and a few cushions, but damn if it wasn't beautiful – and a drop in the bucket next to what he'd spent on the paintings.

Anthony looked at Ben – *Mind if I move this?* and then slid the oculus along the floor to position it across the associates.

"Mr. Allen, if you please."

Ben sat and faced the Gauntlet, as Anthony had dubbed them.

They looked nice enough, Hannah and Madison offering warm expressions. Jeremy picked at his ear.

"Now, who would like to start?" Anthony asked. "Hannah, how about you?"

"Right," Hannah said, and her look of warmth transformed into a posture that impressed and scared Ben all at once. She pulled out her pano and played a video that consisted of clips from various interviews Ben had given in the past – appearances on financial networks, tech sites, talk shows.

"I've been watching you," Hannah said, in a voice that made Ben's spine tickle. "First of all, your posture is terrible. Look here, you're not even crossing your legs, leaning back like you don't even want to connect. Just what is this? There's almost no eye contact. Look at you this time, leaning away – it's like you want to disappear into the chair."

In this moment, Ben did.

"Not good," Hannah chided. "Put your left leg over your right, like so. Clasp your hands, interlace your fingers. Eh, better. Arch your back, lift your chin just a little, slight lean forward. We'll work on it. Now, let's talk about your speech. I notice your r's sound like w's when you talk, and worse there's this o-uh sound you sometimes make randomly, that's no good. This New England accent won't win any votes in the rest of the country. You need to pronounce your consonants. You run your words together. You also use too many er's when you try to think of what to say—"

And on she went. Ben felt like he was in the makeover scene in some bizarro romantic comedy – prodded, pushed, and teased. Only instead of fake eyelashes and hair extensions, he was getting a crash course in speechifying.

After roughly an hour of this, Ben was worn out. It felt like he'd just spent a full day programming in the ARCH.

"I think that's a good first lesson," Anthony complimented. "Thank you, Hannah."

"Yeah, thanks," Ben said.

"Just remember, Ben," Hannah said. "The media will worship and demonize you, sometimes in the same breath. Your head will spin from all the hypocrisy. But that's when you smile!"

"Madison," Anthony said, "why don't you go next?"

"Thank you. Mr. Allen, so pleased to meet such a legend in the Progressive League. What would you say is your worst quality?"

"Excuse me?"

"I'm going to ask you a few questions to start mapping out a strategy. You've never run for office before, so we'll start out generic and then hone in on specifics. Okay?"

"I guess, yeah."

"Great! So what's your worst quality?"

"Sorry, I still don't see the—"

"What's the worst thing about you?"

"I don't understand why you'd ask me that."

Hannah exhaled impatiently. "The first thing we'll need to do is come up with your campaign slogan. Your slogan should be the antithesis of who you really are. If your worst quality is that you're a compulsive liar, your slogan would be *Trusted and Dependable Leadership*, or something to that extent. If you're boring, your slogan might be *Dynamic Leadership for a New Age*. I know it sounds strange, but it's the best way to deflect criticism from your opponents. If a rival tries to nail you for resorting to your worst quality in the campaign, you can just point to the sign and say that's not what you're about."

"The fuck? That's really a thing?"

"Absolutely. This is lesson one in political jujitsu."

"It's the dumbest thing I've ever heard."

Madison scrunched her nose in thought, scratching a note on her pano. "Let's go with *Optimism for America's Future*, for now."

She peppered Ben with questions for the next two hours – the worst thing he'd ever done, what all his bad habits were, his typical first thought when he woke up in the morning. All these would translate to planks in his platform, she said, and then she asked about his mother.

What's my platform? To Ben, it was simple. *Rage, unfettered and pure.*

By the time Madison wrapped up, Ben needed a break. He shuffled over to the kitchen like a punched-out boxer, Anthony at his heels.

"These guys are the absolute best," Anthony said.

"Yeah, but the best at what?"

"Winning, and damn the consequences."

Damn the consequences? Ben thought of the Secret Service falling on the president while Dylan was being murdered, the leader of the free world rolling out of danger in his little ball.

Yes, damn the consequences.

"One more session," Anthony said.

Jeremy was up next. He stopped chewing his thumbnail when Ben returned to the oculus chair.

He seems harmless enough, Ben thought. *I should be home free.*

"Mr. Allen," Jeremy said, "I just wanted to say it's awesome to be here. I've never ridden in a quadcopter before, so cool! And what an icon you are to people like me, I mean, I use my pano every day – we all do. And you built that! I'm honored."

Ben smiled at the fawning appreciation. This would be easy.

"Let's do a little role-playing, Mr. Allen. Let's pretend I'm a mother of two in the Philadelphia suburbs, average income. Junior is about to go to college, Junior Miss is taking dance lessons. What do you think my most important issue is?"

Ben leaned back and uncrossed his legs in thought – all the things Hannah told him not to do. It dawned on him that his worst quality was the inability to follow direction.

"Er, I dunno, a decent job?"

"No, goddammit!" Jeremy jumped from his seat, roaring loud enough to rattle the Dutch Masters. "I WANT SECURITY!"

The next three hours were torture.

CHAPTER NINETEEN

In all the years I've known him, my husband has been the kindest, most caring man. He reads bedtime stories to our two precious little girls, Evelyn and Abigail. Evelyn just took up soccer, and her father loves watching her practice. Abigail's only in First Grade, but she's a natural at the violin, and Jordan never misses a recital. He's a busy man and travels now more than ever, but he's always there when they need him the most.

I say that with conviction because he's done the same for me. I've never spoken of this publicly before, but the attack on me during my husband's campaign announcement has galvanized my resolve. Years ago, in a desolate shopping mall parking lot, I was viciously assaulted by a man in a mask. He snuck up from behind as I walked to my car, and before I even heard him coming a metal object took out my legs. I screamed as loud as I could, but the pain was so fierce that I don't know if any sound came out. Before I knew it, he was pulling me into the shadows, and then he was on top of me.

I'll never forget what he said – "Just hush now, baby." He kept saying it, over and over, as his hands were over my mouth, dampening my cries. "Just hush."

You've seen my husband save my life once, but the truth is, he's done it twice. After the first attack, I was in a dark, desolate place for the longest time – so long, I began to think I'd never get out. I couldn't sleep because I was so scared of my own dreams. I felt worthless, and hopeless, and alone. But through my husband, and through our shared faith in God, I found reason to hope, to dream, and to love.

I refuse stay hushed any longer. I join my voice to the millions of other women across this country – and all over the world – who have been scared into silence, and I stand beside them with a message to our perpetrators: we have emerged from the shadows you tried to keep us in, and we are coming for you.

- Helen Cromwell, *My Story* – PanoMag feature, first published April 2, 2063

Official Transcript, United States Senate Homeland Security Committee
April 4, 2063
BEGIN TRANSCRIPT

LIONEL CHISM, W. KENTUCKY, COMMITTEE CHAIR (C.L.): Order, Order. Let's have order. Thank you. Now, we'd like to open this inquiry into the events surrounding the presidential campaign announcement of Jordan Cromwell, first-term senator from East Kansas. We appreciate you being here, Senator Cromwell.

JORDAN CROMWELL, E. KANSAS (F.L.): Of course, Mr. Chairman.

CHISM: I'm sure that, as a member of this distinguished body, and indeed of the committee you appear before today, you're familiar with what's about to happen. Each of our members will have five minutes for initial inquiry, at which point we'll adjourn for recess, and afterward come back for an additional three-minute round in the afternoon. Do you understand the rules as I've laid them out?

CROMWELL: I do, sir. Yes.

CHISM: Very good. And I understand you've already been sworn in and are currently under oath?

CROMWELL: That's correct.

CHISM: Very good. Then I will remind the senator from East Kansas that his testimony must be deemed truthful or he faces the penalty of perjury according to our Senate bylaws and the full force of its prosecution. Does the senator from East Kansas understand?

CROMWELL: I do.

CHISM: Thank you. Now, the committee recognizes the written statement that you've submitted and respects the thoroughness with which it's been prepared. That should answer a few questions at the outset, and hopefully help us ask better ones in this inquiry. So, let's begin. The chairman recognizes Mr. Rollins of North Arkansas and I would like to yield the remainder of my time for some questions at the end. Mr. Rollins.

ROBERT ROLLINS, RANKING MEMBER (F.L.): Thank you, Mr. Chairman. Mr. Cromwell, thank you for appearing before us today, I know you must be busy. What can you tell us about your relationship with Landon Breaux?

CROMWELL: Mr. Breaux is a friend.

ROLLINS: He's sponsoring your presidential campaign, is he not?

CROMWELL: He is a Sponsor, that's correct.

ROLLINS: And Mr. Breaux's company makes the weapon in question that you used to defend yourself, is that correct?

CROMWELL: Yes, it was given to me personally. For some background as I understand it, Mr. Breaux's company made some of these weapons for the government around the time of the war, but then the war ended. Some government entities held onto those weapons and apparently they fell into the hands of this Light Brigade, or whatever they call themselves. Now, Mr. Breaux and Monochromatic Industries are making them so people like you and me can defend ourselves against these terrorists, the way the Constitution intended. It's been said the only person that can stop a bad person with a gun is a good person with a gun, and I think that's true in this situation as well.

ROLLINS: You're right, they did say that. It's true, however, that this technology is not technically classified as a gun, or firearm?

CROMWELL: That is my understanding, yes. It does not fire a projectile, according to the law, it simply emits light.

ROLLINS: Do you know why that's important?

CROMWELL: There are laws against firearms being created by 3D-printing, for example, but since these devices are not firearms, they are exempt from such laws. There are laws that force firearms to be made of metal, but these contraptions are constructed from plastic.

ROLLINS: Contraptions, is that what you call them? So they aren't liable under the Undetectable Firearms Act?

CROMWELL: Contraptions, or devices, sir – I believe that's the term Mr. Breaux uses.

ROLLINS: I see. Well, thank you for clearing all that up, Mr. Cromwell, and I would just like to say that I appreciate seeing a man stand his ground. I'm sure your wife appreciates it as well. I yield the remainder of my time back, Mr. Chairman.

CHISM: Duly noted. Next is the Reformation League senator from Oregon, Ms. Thompson.

TAMRA THOMPSON, MEMBER (R.L.): Thank you, Mr. Chairman. Mr. Cromwell, in your opinion, do you think lethal force was necessary to subjugate Mr. Dolley?

CROMWELL: Like I said in my statement, I acted out of instinct. I offered a verbal warning, and he continued the threat. All I know is that I was defending my family, as is every man's God-given right in this country.

THOMPSON: Indeed, that's correct. Did you ever consider, however, a warning shot? Or some other non-lethal method? What happened in Texas with the gentleman who worked for Ms. Monroe's campaign was of course a tragic misunderstanding, but at least he wasn't killed—

CROMWELL: It all happened so fast, you understand. This man had his arms around my wife, the security agents were too far away to do anything. I simply had to act.

THOMPSON: Of course. So you saw no other course of action?

CROMWELL: I was defending my family, as is every man's God-given right in this country.

BREAK TRANSCRIPT

CHISM: Thank you, Mr. Blankenship. Moving along, our last member before recess is Ms. Kinsler, from West Missouri. Ms. Kinsler, if you please.

JACQUELYN KINSLER, MEMBER (F.L.): Thank you, Mr. Chairman. Mr. Cromwell, what can you tell me about the man who assaulted your wife, John Dolley?

CROMWELL: That he was a terrorist. I don't know much beyond that.

KINSLER: Yes, I see. Mr. Dolley was a vagrant, a registered sex offender. He lived off the grid, apparently in a hovel beneath the 1670 bridge on the bank of the Kansas River. Incidentally, his home was about a hundred yards over the state line from my state to yours, just over in Wyandotte County.

CROMWELL: I'm not sure why that's important?

KINSLER: It's important in that he was one of my constituents. So, Mr. Dolley was a man living on the streets, who would sometimes venture into the city looking for odd jobs or begging for money. They've shown some closed-circuit footage of that on the news, showing him as recently as a few weeks ago, I think. In those shots, his skin is dark as midnight, his hair's down to his waist. How do you think he got a dermal transplant that would cost something north of a hundred thousand dollars?

CROMWELL: Well, personally, I have no idea...I would assume the terrorists recruited him and set all that up, but it's impossible to know. We shouldn't speculate—

KINSLER: Do you think he was recruited and trained within a couple of weeks?

CROMWELL: From what I've seen on the news reports, Mr. Dolley used to be a part of the Underground.

KINSLER: Yes. As a courier.

CROMWELL: So perhaps he's always been a terrorist.

KINSLER: There were no records of him owning or using a weapon in the war, Mr. Cromwell, but I'd rather we not go there just yet. I would like to introduce an exhibit, if I could. Item 337, could we put that on a PanoScreen somewhere? Very good. Please take a look at this picture, Mr. Cromwell. What do you see?

CROMWELL: It looks like a close-up of a man's hand.

KINSLER: That's correct. It's Mr. Dolley's hand. And what is it holding?

CROMWELL: The contraption that he would have killed my wife with, if I hadn't intervened.

KINSLER: The Weaponized Light device, yes. You said earlier that Mr. Breaux called it a device? I would just mention that we own lots of devices, these days. The pano is a device, it does all sorts of things. But it doesn't kill people. So I'm not sure that's the best term. Anyhow, please take a close look at how Mr. Dolley is holding it. I'd like to introduce Item 338, could someone hand this to Mr. Cromwell? Very good. Mr. Cromwell, this is a replica – no danger here, but it's a copy of Mr. Dolley's device, same as your own. Could you hold that up for us, please, like you were going to fire it? Again, it's not a live firearm – excuse me, device.

CROMWELL: (*demonstrates*) Like so?

KINSLER: Perfect. Now, would you compare your grip of the...device, with the grip of Mr. Dolley? Wouldn't you say that they're different? You see, for example, that your thumb is on the trigger – the activation button, you called it – whereas his thumb is around his fingers? It's almost like he's holding the handle of a baseball bat, wouldn't you say?

CROMWELL: I'm not really into baseball so I can't foster an opinion on that.

KINSLER: Really? East Kansas – don't you like the Royals? I've been a fan all my life. But what I'm getting at, Mr. Cromwell, is that, if you look at this picture closely – zoom in a little more, will you? – you can plainly see that Mr. Dolley has no idea how to use it, and he's merely holding it as a prop.

CROMWELL: I'm – Ms. Kinsler, are you sure you're a Freedomist?

KINSLER: I am one of the Free, yes.

CROMWELL: All I know is that I was defending my family, as is my God-given right.

KINSLER: Of course you were. Thank you, Mr. Cromwell. I look forward to the next session. I yield back the remainder of my time.

END TRANSCRIPT

Jordan scribbled in the margins of his briefing book.

The briefing detailed some conflict brewing in Azerbaijan, whatever that mattered. Those savages were always killing each other over something, like rival colonies quarreling over anthills. Jordan was more concerned with amending his Enemies List.

Jackie Kinsler, he wrote again and again, until his pen gashed the page. *Jackie Kinsler Jackie Kinsler.* How the fuck could she call herself a member of the Freedom League? What a total phony. She was a woman – which could mean she's secretly a surrogate for Shelby Monroe. Was that her angle?

Speaking of Monroe – and she'd been on the list since the beginning, but it helped to keep her fresh in his mind (*Shelby Monroe*, he wrote, and debated moving her name above Jackie's). Instead he added a little note: *Texas Gasbag Bitch.*

One nice turn of events – the errand boy always following her around had gotten his. According to Breaux, that little fucker was the one who'd pulled that video stunt at FACPAC and damn near cost him the straw poll. In a serendipitous turn, a freedom-loving patriot had mistaken him for a Light Brigade terrorist (and who's to say he wasn't one?), and removed him from commission. Greater Texas, indeed – a state that solved its own problems.

As for Shelby, she'd get hers soon enough. If only he could sneak up behind her in a darkened parking lot. Maybe he could go after one of the daughters instead; perhaps he could talk to Breaux about that.

Goddamn, his head hurt! The coffee wasn't helping. The Voice had taken over throughout those six hours of testimony, commanding him to dodge, to parry, to counter. It was all going so well until Jackie Fucking Kinsler. She didn't have much on him, but she took her shots and did some damage, if anyone was paying attention.

And she'd grilled him harder in the second round than the first. Headline-seeking whore. How could she even begin to argue that Dolley was a plant, a dupe? What did she even have to jump to that conclusion besides her lousy grip theory and some testimony from the other vagrants he associated with? So they claimed he'd never said anything political since they'd known him, or mentioned any Light Brigade – what did that prove?

Jordan would have to find a way to humiliate her. Maybe the Freedom League's Commissioner could excommunicate her traitorous ass for going after one of their own. He didn't want to have to wait until he was president. He'd talk to Breaux about a way to destroy her, too.

The Voice kept yammering, hours after the hearing was over, telling him to cool it. Exhausted, Jordan retreated far into his mind, flipping an imaginary switch to *Off*. *Go to sleep, little Voice*, he thought, and his mind was his own again. Finally, the headache began to subside.

He was back scribbling (*KINSLER MONROE MONROE KINSLER*) when Helen walked in from the kitchen, her right hand entrenched in an oven mitt.

"Mind watching the kids for a minute while I finish dinner?"

"They're fine where they are, Helen. It's been a long day."

She exhaled slowly, looking at her feet. "You're right, I'm sure you're tired. It's...fine."

She turned away. Jordan couldn't identify the smell coming from the kitchen, but it didn't smell like the steak he'd requested. He went back to his briefing book, debating whose name to add next, then put it down to check his pano for the latest headlines on his performance.

Cromwell Passionately Defends Self-Defense
Family First – Jordan Doubles Down

They were using his name in their headlines now – no more "East Kansas Senator" or "Freshman Lawmaker". Some publications even went with just his first name – as if he were a Brazilian soccer star, a famous rapper, or Jesus. It meant something to be him, and more each day.

A few articles mentioned the back-and-forth with Kinsler, one calling it 'fireworks', but most included her lines of inquiry as a bottom-paragraph footnote if at all. Some of the leftist rags tried to make some hay of it, but unconvincingly. Only Jordan really understood what she was trying to implicate.

Helen came back in the living room. She was looking frumpy. "Jordan? Just a little help, please?"

God, would she ever stop? He slammed his briefing book down on one knee, exasperated. "Just hush now, baby, alright? These documents are vital to our national security!"

Her body doubled over as if kicked in the stomach, if just for a moment, before stiffening up like a steel rod. She let out two quick, halting gasps through an open mouth – *heh, heh* – before turning briskly to leave the room, on legs both locked and quivering.

Jordan noticed none of this. He slurped his coffee and returned to the briefing book, mind solely on his growing list of his enemies, and the revenge he would exact on each of them.

CHAPTER TWENTY

"Our candidates must be infallible when it comes to scrutiny – always on offense, always charging. Admitting to a mistake, however large or small, invites defeat."
  - *Victory in 2056,* Freedom League strategy memo

The slamming of a car door took Jamie from his daydream.

One good thing about the paper-thin walls of his apartment building – you could hear everything outside so clearly, no one snuck up on you. Jamie guessed that for a lot of his neighbors this was a vital selling point.

He struggled to lift himself out of the couch serving as his home base for the past week. He took a few halting steps toward the window and his stomach lurched.

She was here.

He'd assumed she would come to see him sooner rather than later – a hospital visit, or an escort home when he'd been discharged – but as the days crept by, he grew less sure. He even sat around the hospital an extra two hours after they told him he could go home. There were calls from her office and visits from Trudy and Trixie, but no word from the governor. Until now.

It was a cloudy day, one where the threat of rain seemed perpetually imminent, but the storm had held off to this point. The motorcade included three large utility vehicles flanked by cop cars in front and in back, which was probably why Jamie started hearing a sudden clatter in the downstairs unit – someone saying *"Oh shit! Hide the shit!"* in a desperate, muffled tone, with the sounds of furniture being rearranged.

Jamie watched through the blinds as the Governor of Greater Texas appraised the apartment complex. A security agent nudged his way to Shelby's side and she pushed him away with a yip, her voice carrying through the apartment walls undiminished. "I'm fine, Robert! I *will* take that umbrella, though."

She started toward the stairs. Her hurried footsteps echoed up the staircase and onto the landing, the clacking of her heels building toward him. They stopped at the door, replaced by a *rap-rap-rap* of knocking.

"Jamie! Jamie!"

For half a year, he'd heard that voice almost constantly as he followed her everywhere. It was the kind of voice that bypassed your ears and hit you in the back of the head. Now it sent a spasm down his arm. The doctors had warned him about something called phantom pain, but they didn't mention the tremendous itch that followed and wouldn't go away. They'd told him the bullet entered where his deltoid muscle met the triceps, clipping what was called the radial nerve as it went through bone.

"Jamie, I know you're in there! Can you let me in?"

Jamie stood paralyzed, staring at the door. "Display outside front," he muttered aloud, and the apartment's security system formed a holo image of the stoop – another feature his fellow apartment residents likely found useful – and it showed Shelby knocking furiously. Jamie stepped towards the image of the holo, his mind a muddle.

"Jamie! Please, I'd like to talk to you."

He didn't want her here, he wanted to hide forever and never be seen by anyone again, but Jamie knew the governor wouldn't be leaving without doing whatever it was she came to do. "Hide outside front," he said, and the holo flipped off. "Open door."

Multiple locks whirred with faint clicking sounds and the door propped open an inch. After a beat, Shelby cautiously pushed on it and stepped inside.

Her expression of worry changed to relief when she first saw his face, then it shifted to dismay when she saw the rest of him. She closed the door behind her.

"Oh, look at you," she whispered.

Jamie glanced down at the prosthesis dangling limply below his shoulder, then looked away. It would be weeks before the grafting took hold and he could move the limb on its own.

At that moment, the machinations within it applied their hourly salve to the connection points, allowing microscopic needles to stitch nerve to wire cable, bone to carbon fiber. Jamie flinched, twisting to his left, trying to conceal the arm. She took a tentative step closer.

"I know how you must feel," she began.

Jamie chose not to respond, opting to let her flounder. The truth, they both knew, was she didn't have a fucking clue how he felt.

"I'm so sorry," she tried again. "And Jesus, I didn't know you were living in one of these places. We could've put you up somewhere decent or—"

She was trying not to look at the arm, but her eyes kept finding it. Jamie twisted further.

"Doesn't matter now," he said.

Her eyes were pleading, but he could see she couldn't argue with that – what happened, happened. The prosthesis was a modern marvel, and perhaps eventually it would look somewhat normal, once they applied the dermal transplants. Jamie thought back to the skin flaps on the mechanical bulls from the rodeo – that would be him now.

One other thing the doctors had told him – the subtle, precise gestures he made when operating his cameras wouldn't be possible with a prosthetic. It was hard to have muscle memory with no actual muscles, and he needed both his arms to film properly. Eventually, he'd be able to move the arm, and might someday open his hand to grip small objects, but his life as a videographer was over.

"The man who did this," Shelby said, "he didn't mean it. He was just some wannabe-deputy who thought he was doing the right thing, who thought he was protecting me. He didn't know, Jamie. He thought—"

"He thought I was a terrorist. All of them did. Because of *one thing*."

"They didn't know you, Jamie. They didn't know you."

Jamie wondered if the governor realized the emptiness of that excuse.

"I'm just happy you're alive," she added.

Even Jamie might admit that it took a hell of a shot to clip only his arm at fifty yards, but the fact that the sheriff-in-his-dreams only sought to maim rather than murder was an empty consolation. Or maybe he *was* aiming to kill, and he missed – with a pistol at that range, who knew.

Jamie glanced at the floor. "I'm alive," he muttered. He wasn't sure he was happy about it.

"How's your head? You had a nasty concussion when you fell. My heart just about stopped, you know."

"Head's fine." As if a lingering headache was the worst thing about his predicament.

"Don't worry about the expenses, they're all taken care of. The lawyers tell me this qualifies under workman's compensation, as if that ain't the damnedest thing about all this."

She'd meant it as a joke, to break the tension – or at least break his facade of distant resignation. He tried to offer nothing in response, but a little snort seeped out of him.

"Well," the governor said. "It won't happen again, believe me. Once you come back, everyone will know who you are, I can guarantee you that. Hell, you're more famous than I am."

For Jamie, who had always longed for fame (or more precisely, recognition) through his art, there was little comfort in attaining it in this manner. This was fame in the vein of, *You hear about* this *poor bastard?*

He felt like a dormant volcano – his insides boiling hot but with some vital component neutralized, circumventing eruption. So much of him wanted to explode, but couldn't.

Where the fuck have you been?

He looked out the window, if mostly to hide a grimace when the phantom pain returned. Outside, it began to rain after all.

"Well," Shelby said, nodding to her waiting caravan, "I have to, you know, scoot out of here – big announcement and all. To be honest, 'tween you and me, I think this campaign has been cursed from the start. Guess I'll have to actually toss my hat in the ring to know for sure."

Jamie's insides still boiled, but only a miniscule eruption escaped his throat.

"I quit," he said.

Shelby nodded, registering no hint of surprise. She stepped toward him, careful to keep her distance from the lifeless arm, and cradled his face in her palm, her thumb wiping away moisture that Jamie didn't realize was there.

"Take care of yourself, son."

She tilted up on her tiptoes to kiss his forehead before walking out, the echoes from her footsteps deadened by the rain.

* * *

He couldn't stop pacing. Back and forth, up and down, stomping on shoddy tile. Jamie wondered if the downstairs residents would come up and yell at him, or worse – but his feet kept marching.

As he paced, he eyed the clock, ticking ever forward.

To watch, or not to watch.

After his discharge from the hospital, he'd avoided the news. The first hours were the hardest, but it grew easier than expected – like a junkie finding their withdrawal surprisingly pleasant. He didn't have to obsess over every happening across the world, a detachment that felt freeing. Sometimes you needed to unplug.

That was, until Shelby just came and went. The outside world had crashed through his solitary sanctuary and would not be ignored. That world would go on, with or without him – he might as well keep up.

At a minute before noon, Jamie activated the wall pano and sat down.

He was surprised at the location – Shelby had wanted to make her announcement in the Texadome as a testament to the innovation and grandness of Greater Texas, but this backdrop was more rustic. An empty podium stood before an old, concrete building. The building's edifice had a curved recess with flat, wide pillars running up it, fashioned in the timeless art deco style. A bronze-and-gold statue stood in the recess, an archer with his bow pulled taut, facing skyward, but with no arrow nocked. Two enormous flags hung from the building – on the left, the five-starred sigil of Greater Texas; on the right, the flag of the United States of America. The two flags shared an edge at the tip of the archer's bow.

Jamie could hear a country song playing in the background – the same foot-stomper from the limo ride to the Petroleum Club. He wondered if Shelby and Boot Squad were having one last barn dance before the big moment. *Of course they are*, he thought.

It was a decent crowd of several thousand. It still rained, softer now, but most decided their cowboy hats served as suitable protection from the elements. The camera panned left and right as more onlookers approached, and the setting became familiar.

The fair.

Jamie didn't recognize the building, but when the shot pulled back and showed the Cotton Bowl in the background, he saw why – they never made it to the other side of the stadium on their tour; that was for after the rodeo, and they didn't quite make it that far.

The goddamn fair. Jamie fought the urge to turn the pano off. Then a voice thundered through the crowd.

"Let's give a Greater Texas welcome to the next President of the United States, Shelby Monroe!"

The governor emerged from the front door of the building, waving joyously to her people. A few rows of steps came between the podium and the crowd, and she skipped down them to shake several sets of hands, lingering generously. She went back up to stand before the dais.

This was typically when the HoloPrompTer activated, but Jamie didn't see it go up. For a speech of this magnitude, that was...unusual.

"Thank you," Shelby said, gesturing for everyone to sit. "Thank you, everyone. Please. Before I begin, I want to tell you about a friend of mine."

Jamie's stomach lurched for the second time that day.

"About six months ago, I watched some campaign videos made by someone I'd never heard of, for a candidate I've never met. And they moved me. I knew, in that moment, that I needed to hire that person – and I did just that, on a pano call the next day. Now, when I first met Jamie Richardson in person, I must admit I was surprised by what he looked like. But it took ten seconds of talking to him to know I'd made the right decision.

"Some of you may have seen his work at FACPAC or on the PanoTube, but in the time that he's been at my side he has become part of my family. And I want to tell anyone that has a problem with that – well, it's an outdoor venue, there are plenty of exits to choose from.

"I screwed up. After I hired him, I brought him everywhere with me, part and parcel – but I kept him in the background. I didn't introduce him to all of you, to let you know him as I've known him. And my mistake proved costly. My only hope is that once he gets better, he'll come back. Then you all could meet this extraordinary young man and know why he's so important to me."

Jamie shifted uncomfortably on his couch, the phantom pain throbbing. Shelby went on. "Instead of giving a big speech about myself, I'm going to tell you a little more about him. It might be a little clumsy, but here we go."

Shelby looked offstage, covering the microphone. Jamie could see her mouthing, *Trudy, roll the damn tape!*

A holo vid began to play above her, and Jamie knew by the too-quick fade that it wasn't one of his. The color balance was off but not bad, the perspective slightly high.

It showed Tammy, sitting down with a half-smile, facing the camera. He heard a voice, off-screen in the clip – Trudy, doing one of her interviews.

What can you tell us about Jamie? asked Trudy's disembodied voice.

Tammy's face broadened. "He's my brother," she said.

Next, it showed Tawny, then Trixie, then Tracy, offering similar assessments. Jamie's phantom pain was in stark contrast to the numbness he felt taking over the rest of his body.

Then Trudy sat in front of the camera, answering her own question, completing the montage. "He's the most brilliant artist I've ever seen," she said. "I can't wait to share his work with all of you."

A flurry of images followed – various shots of Jamie, surreptitiously taken over the last few months. He recalled the girls, always on their panos – *guess they weren't just chatting*, he thought. Pictures of him setting up his rig in the governor's conference room for the first time, weaving through the crowd at FACPAC, sitting at the bar at the Petroleum Club, and a dozen other places, both at work and in quiet moments.

Then, Shelby. "Jamie is my friend," she said on the video. "But he's more than that. Although I am running for president," – Jamie could hear the fairground crowd reveling at this bit of news — "my campaign would be empty without him. It's like he knew me before he met me, and he knew Texas before he got here. Only he can turn my clumsy orations, my broken prose, into some kind of poetry. Jamie, if you're listening, I'm gonna need you back."

The clip faded out and disappeared. Something happened in the crowd then, sparked by a few scattered shouts, but more voices picked it up, and more, until they all chanted as one.

"Come back! Come back!"

A giant holo lumbered into the frame – Big Tex, leaning over to pat Shelby on the head. He did a graceful jump-spin, flashing his signature double-barreled thumbs-up to the crowd, and they went crazy.

Before Shelby would speak again, Jamie turned off the pano, liquid with emotion.

He thought about the last time he saw his mom, the night before she bolted for the Underground. Another knockdown, drag-out fight in the Richardson household. His mother screaming, "Why can't you let *me* be *me!*" His father, trying to be quiet and calm but not succeeding, responding with, "Because it's too dangerous!" And though there was love in his heart, it wasn't enough.

Althea Richardson ran away in the dead of night, never to be heard from again. Jamie knew she'd wanted to take her son with her, but you didn't bring a twelve-year-old into a war. When it came to choosing between her fight versus her family, she chose the fight.

Jamie looked down at his arm, really inspecting it, something he'd avoided since the operation. There were heavy bandages and braces from the shoulder to the elbow, protecting the attachment points as they applied their salves and did their work. Down his forearm, the servos and motors were visible within the bionic framework and plastic casing that would eventually be covered by fake skin.

He wondered if they'd get his color right.

He used his other hand to turn the arm over, wincing with pain. It was an incredible piece of technology. Jamie turned it back, setting it against his hip, thinking.

He stared at his index finger, a multi-jointed set of metal and plastic tubes.

Move, he commanded it.

For several seconds – at least, it felt like seconds but may have been hours – nothing happened. A mechanical phalange, still and useless.

But then, a twitch. Barely perceptible, but there.

Any movement at all will take several months, the doctors had told him. Some might be faster than others, but don't hold your breath.

Jamie held his breath.

Move, he commanded again.

Another twitch. Up, then down.

He stood up, found his knapsack, and fished out his rig.

CHAPTER TWENTY-ONE

"My personal take? One side wanted to govern. The other, to rule.
War was unavoidable – and frankly, it was necessary."
  - Acton Granger, off-the-record interview – November 11, 2062

"Where are we, Tessa? What is this place?"

"It's home, possibly."

"Doesn't look like home," her father challenged.

"Well...it's a new home."

She held his hand escorting him through the door. A handful of comfortable chairs dotted the lobby, occupied by current residents – some meeting Tess with a smile, some with stares of vacancy. A man hunkered in a wheelchair in the corner, head bobbed downward, facing the wall at an odd angle. A woman walked by with a cane and looked at Tess questioningly, as if wondering whether she should know her.

"This looks nice," Tess said, setting down her father's duffel bag.

And it did. The walls were bright with dark wood accents, inviting but stately. Several poster-sized wall panos ran through slideshows of nostalgia – images from fifty, sixty, seventy years ago. Many were cityscapes with all the buildings still intact, and Tess found herself glancing over at each new image until she was enraptured by them. *Simpler times*, she thought.

"Good morning, can I help you?"

Tess snapped out of her reverie. "Oh, hi, yes. I'm Tess Larkin and this is my father, Richard. We have an appointment?"

The receptionist thumbed through the logs. "Ah, of course. If you'll give me just a moment, I'll run and grab Mr. Whitacre."

"Thanks."

As they waited, Tess turned to her father. "What do you think?"

Richard looked about, absorbing his surroundings. "Big," was all he said.

"Really? I think it's quite cozy."

Ernest Whitacre approached them from down the hall, hand extended toward Tess. When she shook it, he pulled her in for a half-hug, and then he gave Richard a handshake and a sentimental shoulder squeeze. "Ms. Larkin, Mr. Larkin. How wonderful to see you."

"We appreciate being here," Tess said.

"Mr. Schroeder spoke very highly of you. Trust me, you will be taken care of. If you don't mind me asking, how do you know the vice president?"

Tess was briefly at a loss. "I work for him, kind of."

If Whitacre found her response odd, his professionalism wouldn't reveal it. "I understand this is just a trial stay?"

"Yes, through the weekend," Tess said in a low voice. Her father had stepped away to look at one of the pano slideshows on the near wall. "I wanted to see how he does before committing to more."

"That's common," Whitacre whispered. "It usually takes a couple days to know if something's the right fit. Let's have a look around, shall we?"

Tess replayed the last hour in her mind as she walked home alone.

It hadn't been a full-on disaster, not quite. The tour was of course impressive. Each setting – the Activity Room, the Breakfast Room, the Movie Room – became more intimately luxurious than the last. Richard followed along with the detached indifference that had become his default temperament. Then they came to Richard's new bedroom, which was really more of a suite.

Tess had taken her father's hand. "Daddy, this is where you'll be staying for the weekend. I brought everything you need, your shaving kit, glasses, the works. Do you understand?"

"Wha...you want me to stay here? But I don't know these people."

"You will, after a while. You can make new friends."

His eyes darted to and fro with renewed scrutiny. "What is this place?" he asked.

"Think of it like a hotel. But listen. I need you to give it a chance, okay? You need help, and this is our best chance of getting it. Whitacre MemCare only accepts a few people each year. This is an incredible opportunity. It offers more than either of us could ever dream. It's close to home, we're just over in Georgetown. There's outdoor space. You can work in a garden. They have games and activities and trips. You could—" She stopped, seeing he was no longer paying attention.

Her had wandered to the window. It was overcast and muggy out, only a gray light coming in.

"It's a really nice place, daddy. It was recommended by the vice president himself."

"The vice president? Of what?"

It went downhill from there. Tess reminded him of who she worked for. Then, a spark of memory.

"Oh...Schroeder, the economist?"

"That's right."

He turned back at her from the window and back at her. The sudden appearance of lucidity was startling. "Never liked him," her father said.

"But you voted for him, remember?"

He shook his head. "No, Tess, I didn't. I picked the other one, the big guy. Just never told you."

Tess always figured her father would jump in front of a walking tank before he supported anyone but a conservative. But then again, he'd taken a shining to Jordan Cromwell, right before he killed a man. "What was wrong with Schroeder?" she pestered. "Are you too Boston to trust a New Yorker?"

He shook his head dismissively. "He reminded me of when you went through that depression phase after we lost mom. You would laugh at every goddamn thing you could, you know, this big, fake guffaw. You overcompensated. He's like that, but in a smaller way." He was going to say more, but the narrowing of his eyes relaxed, the furrow in his brow smoothed, and the blank expression returned. The balloon-string of thought had floated away from his grasp.

Whitacre coughed politely behind them. Tess looked back, nodded, and then turned to her father. "Well, daddy, this is gonna be goodbye for now. I'll see you in a couple of days, all right?"

A placid smile crossed his face as she hugged him close. He felt bony and frail in her arms. She pulled back and eyed the exit, thinking of a conversation from last summer with a colleague. Between commiserating about working for Archie Cunningham, the friend described how she dropped her toddler off at daycare. If she made a big goodbye, the toddler would scream and yell – so instead she'd just hand the kid over and try to slink away unnoticed. Tess always thought that sort of cruel, but she gave Mr. Whitacre a look as she stepped back. He seemed to read the signal perfectly and moved towards her father.

"Right! Well, Mr. Larkin, in a few minutes we'll be gathering for dinner, so let's get you set up…"

And Tess slinked out of the room.

Turning the corner on the last block of her walk home, she spotted an aerial delivery drone drifting over the fence and into her yard. She quickened her pace and reached the gate just as it dropped a package on the stoop. While the drone buzzed away, she picked up the box and turned it over in her hands. It was the size of a paperback novel.

She looked at the return address: One Observatory Circle. She took the package inside and set it on the island in the kitchen, grabbing a pair of scissors. The tape fell away and she pulled out a black box with green buttons down the side. She saw a note attached.

Tess, maybe this will help you cope. Eli

Turning it over in her hands, Tess saw a logo on the bottom above the serial number. *AllenCo*, finely etched in silver script, like on her pano. She pressed a green button and the device came to life with a barely-audible hum. Behind her, a holo appeared.

"Morning, Tessa! Got a crossword we can work on?"

She spun around to see her father – or, a version of her father. He wasn't in his peak years but they weren't a distant memory, either. The gray at his temples had yet to work its way around his head, the hunch in his back barely perceptible.

What the fuck is this? Tess thought. She blindly groped for her purse, rooting through its contents. When she found the pano that Elijah gave her, she clicked his link. He picked up on the first tone.

"Hi, Tess," he said hesitantly, as if expecting the call.

"You need to send a car."

When the Automated Vehicle approached the Naval Observatory

house, Elijah was standing on the porch. Late afternoon was slipping into dusk, clouds shrouding the last vestiges of sunlight.

Elijah started down the steps as the porch lights around him flickered on. Tess sprang from the AV before it had time to stop. "What the hell was that thing you sent me?"

He flinched at her intensity. "I thought you could appreciate...How 'bout you come inside?"

Tess looked into the house. "Where's Cassidy?"

"She's gone to tonight's state dinner, for the European Chancellor. Along with apparently half of Hollywood."

"You didn't go?"

"I haven't been feeling well, Tess. I know my absence will spark up the usual rumor machine, but I just didn't have it in me. Needless to say, my wife was displeased."

"What's wrong?"

He looked at his shoes, grimacing, and repeated his initial request. "How 'bout you come inside?"

She followed him in and cautiously took a seat at the kitchen table. He went over to the coffeemaker and poured her a cup.

"Have you ever heard of loss aversion?" he asked, handing over the coffee and sitting across from her.

Tess shook her head.

"It's a basic principle in economics. I'll give you two scenarios. Scenario one: you have no money, and I give you a hundred dollars. Scenario two: you already have a hundred dollars, and I take it away. Loss aversion states that the first scenario gives you less pleasure than the second scenario causes pain. The scenarios are equal opposites – gain a hundred, lose a hundred – but the emotional responses are not. It's nice to gain a hundred bucks, sure, whatever – but you're super-pissed when you lose the same amount."

"So the good things in life are never as good as the bad things are bad?"

"Essentially, yes. And the behavioral result is that people are more likely to cling to what they have rather than trying to gain something new. And as we go through life, every time we lose something and feel that pain, the scales tip further and further. The less we have left, the more desperate we become. It's the hoarding mentality."

Tess sipped her coffee. What was he trying to say?

He stood. "Come on, I want to show you something."

* * *

The circular room was empty except for a plain desk and two basic chairs. On the floor by the door, Tess saw a holo projector like the one she'd opened earlier, along with what looked like a gaming console.

Elijah gestured for her to sit as he picked up the projector.

"Cassidy tried to hide these from me, just not very well. Back in New York, we had this old attic where we'd put the kids' presents up before Christmas. We'd hang this big blanket over them, as if that wasn't a giveaway. The kids would sneak up there – Charlotte figured it out first, I remember – and usually they'd know everything they were getting by the first week of December. Well, this house has an attic, too, and a blanket to boot. Sometimes we're all just patterns of behavior, you know?"

Tess crossed her legs, trying to conceal her worry.

"Anyhow, I'd like you to meet my son." He activated the projector. "This is Nolan."

The holo illuminated and the image of Nolan appeared before her, all in an instant. The young man had his hands in his jean pockets, rocking back and forth on his heels as if waiting for the bus.

She turned to the vice president, who was regarding his son with similar degrees of pride and grief. "Elijah..." she said.

"I know it's not real, Tess. But when you look at him, goddamn if you don't try to make it real! When there's a gap between what you see and what you know, your eyes win out in the end." Elijah stepped closer to Nolan, reaching out. "I know what would happen when I try to touch him, but what about when I stop trying to touch him? When I ignore the fuzz in the edges of the holo? Despite yourself, you begin to believe."

Tess thought she understood loss – first her mother long ago, and now her father. But there was a natural order to losing your parents, a generational cycle. Most pain, horrific and awful as it might be, is digestible – capable of being understood, processed, worked through. But she took one look at Elijah, as he sat captivated by the projected likeness of Nolan, and knew that any digestion was impossible. It was like an ant trying to eat a whale – no dent could be made, not in a billion years.

Elijah Schroeder, with his logistical, quantitative mind, must see the loss of his children as an equation that did not compute. An irrationality – one plus one plus one doesn't equal zero.

She recalled a comment Elijah made the first time she came to the

Observatory with her father. *Maybe Nolan will want to play hologames with him, or Ellie will braid his hair.* She thought she'd misheard him, or possibly that his way of coping was through horribly misguided sense of humor.

"Elijah, you need to turn it off. Don't you see, every time you do this, you're hurting yourself? It's like your loss aversion in a loop. You're giving yourself something by turning it on, and you're taking it away when you turn it off, again and again!"

He was quiet for a minute, unable to take his eyes off Nolan. "I never thought about it like that," he admitted.

"You're repeating a losing transaction. It's not a rational behavior."

"Parenthood makes a person irrational. Maybe you wouldn't understand."

I'd like to, someday, she thought, *but not if this is what it might do to me.*

Elijah didn't say anything for a moment, and then: "They tell me I'm not in his league, like I need a daily reminder."

"What? Who tells you?"

"Granger's people."

"You're not in his League. You're a Conservative."

"That's not what they mean."

Elijah seemed to be spinning out of control, all his grievances flinging out at random. And he wanted her to witness it, as if she could track them and organize them into piles. It would be the only way to put this broken man back together again. At least he was admitting he needed fixing, if a cry for help was what this was.

"Why did you send me the projector?" Tess asked.

"You're a lot like me, Tess. Cassidy doesn't get it, but she and I are different. She's more emotional, though somehow that's made her stronger. You and I are numbers people, *quants*, but we dream. I needed to know how you'd respond, like similar conditions in an experiment."

"I'm not an experiment," Tess said, in the same tone she used when imploring Senator Duncan to kindly go fuck herself.

"You're right, of course. But I'm lost, Tess. I feel like I'm floating away. Cassidy's the tether, but you're the compass."

"I don't understand. Everything that happened with your family was brought up multiple times in the campaign. I remember a talk show host asking how you deal with your grief, you and Cassidy together, and you answered it so eloquently..."

"It's one thing to state a truth, another to acknowledge it. Isn't that the hallmark of any decent politician?" He frowned. "Maybe I have that backwards."

"You lost some votes because of it. People thought you were too damaged to really lead." She thought to what her father had said earlier at Whitacre MemCare. He was more right than he knew!

Elijah flashed a rueful, deprecating smirk. "Can you blame them?"

"And yet, more people voted *for* you when they otherwise wouldn't have, because it humanized you. You were relatable to every grieving family across the country that also lost people in the war. You shared their pain, but were an example in how to move on."

"That's the trick," Elijah said. "With this, I never had to."

Nolan's holo stared blankly into the distance, as if awaiting a command. Then he snapped to awareness, perhaps triggered by some internal timer. "Hey Dad, wanna hear what I'm planning for my next date with Allie?"

"Not now, buddy."

Tess looked at the holo and was stricken. So handsome like his father, but with Cassidy's lighter, more refined features. He'd win Class President at any high school in the country. Allie, if Tess was right to assume had been his girlfriend, surely was the prom queen or head cheerleader, or both.

"Well, there you have it," Elijah said, heaving a sigh, "the lengths we go to in maintaining delusion. It's funny, since Cassidy took these away, things are coming back to me in bits and pieces. I can remember the funeral now – and all so clearly, like it happened an hour ago. Three little caskets, side by side. Cassidy collapsed when she first saw them, I couldn't even hold her up. This horrible sound came out of her, I've never heard it before or since, just pure...*anguish*. She ran to them and tried to put her arms around all three at once, but couldn't reach. I'd say that was the worst day of my life, but..."

He shut down and cried in long, painful sobs. Tess didn't know what to say as she sat on the floor next to him, trying to help him solve the impossible. She kept staring at the holo – Nolan was tapping his foot impatiently, looking at his watch. "Hey Dad, wanna pop in a game?"

It's so goddamn lifelike, she thought, trying to console Elijah. *If I kept the holo of my father, is this what I'd become?*

She was pretty sure she knew the answer. Similar conditions, as

Elijah had said.

But her thoughts were interrupted by a tremor in the floor, faint at first but rustling harder like an approaching earthquake. She heard nothing, which was odd, but the feeling of it continued to build.

Where was it coming from?

Then she realized – footsteps, running up the stairs.

Elijah sensed it too, looking toward the door. "Cass can't be back yet, can she?"

The door exploded in on its hinges and five men in black suits piled inside. Tess recognized a couple as agents from the vice president's regular detail, but there were some new faces as well.

Four of the agents surrounded Elijah and the vice president ducked his head in what looked like a practiced ritual, though he didn't look pleased about it. The fifth stepped back and spoke into a device on his wrist. "Professor secure. Professor secure, over."

"Did my wife put you up to this?" Elijah asked, casting a wry expression at the lead agent. "I was only showing Ms. Larkin—"

From behind them, Nolan's holo asked, "Hey Dad, wanna hear what I'm going to do in the military?"

"Repeat, Professor secure. Heading to Rendezvous Bravo, over."

Elijah was pushed from behind but it didn't dim his sarcasm. "Did another drone jump the fence, guys? Fine, just finish the drill."

It looked nothing like a drill to Tess. "What is happening?" she asked, bewildered.

The four agents hurried Elijah out of the room, but the fifth hung back momentarily. "The president collapsed," he said, and then ran to join his team.

CHAPTER TWENTY-TWO

"What a country."
  - Acton Granger, general election victory speech – November 2, 2060

"I have to go to work," Elijah said.

"I know. At the *White House.*" Cassidy pronounced it with an unseemly pride. He didn't recall her so engrossed with the trappings of the presidency during the campaign, and this new attitude startled him. Maybe before, she always knew he'd lose, so she never got too worked up about it? But her private relishing of his new stature also emboldened him, like the first time a lover whispers naughty words in your ear.

And how they'd made love last night – not their typical, ritualized consummation, or even their occasional dalliance in the security bunker. This was drunken passion, like before the kids were born. Elijah had been so tired and the sun was already rising, but Cassidy insisted, her hands suddenly everywhere, and quickly he was more than game.

Who's the alpha now? he thought as he exploded into her, but a sense of shame lingered after. Now, barely an hour later and with no sleep, his new job beckoned.

Last night, when the agents had pulled him away from Tess Larkin and stuffed him in his state limo, he arrived at the White House just as the president was being carried away – a dozen vehicles, lights swirling, tearing for the nearest hospital. His detail took Elijah around the Rotunda and to a side entrance of the West Wing. Cassidy was waiting for him, still shimmering in her ball gown. She squeezed him tightly, only letting go when they reached the Map Room and someone handed her a Bible.

Elijah Schroeder repeated the Oath of Office with blurry detachment, the room crowded with the president's people all still in their finest formalwear. He felt silly as cameras flashed all around him – he hadn't even time to put a jacket on. But what was done was done.

You're the 55th President of the United States, Cassidy whispered, moments after. *Whether for an hour, a day, a week – no one can take that away from us.*

Immediately, Elijah was ushered this way and that, re-briefed on the protocols for the nuclear codes and updated on the state of the union as news of Granger's collapse blanketed the country like napalm. At this already late hour, chirping pano alerts were no doubt rousing millions from their beds, and groggy news anchors were steeling themselves for a marathon round of Breaking News.

Elijah recorded a hurried national address, doing his best to sound reassuring, even as he had no idea what was going on. Only after did he get some time with Cassidy to find out just what the hell had happened. There was no press pool at the state dinner and all guests were forced to turn their panos in at the door, so no visual recording of President Granger's collapse existed. However, every attendee would soon relay their version of the events to one PanoNet or another. Over time, their recollections would only get more fantastical.

But Cassidy was a reliable witness. She was sitting at the president's table, next to Susannah Granger. Dinner had just concluded, she said, which brought an exchange of gifts – the Chancellor offering some fancy new water cisterns from Switzerland, the president reciprocating with a desk made of wood from the deck of the USS Constitution. A musical act, the European Chancellor's rumored favorite, had taken the stage. People danced, movie stars intermingled with statesmen, all of them cutting loose with the diplomatic formalities concluded. And then, in the corner of Cassidy's eye, a burly shape dropped from view. She heard a hefty thud and a scream – Susannah's. The music stopped in mid-chorus, the dancing with it, replaced by the urgent choreography of the president's physician and the White House Medical Unit rushing for their man.   Dr. Granger huddled with them, prying open her husband's eyes and shining a PanoLight to check his pupils. And not thirty seconds later, they whisked him away, lumbering under the load, leaving the rest of the room stunned in their wake.

Elijah asked for a briefing on Granger's condition every hour, but so far there were no changes.

Now, as he scarfed the last bits of breakfast, an agent called for the president. It took Elijah two bites before realizing that meant him. He rose from his chair.

Cassidy wouldn't let him leave without a passionate kiss goodbye. "Strength," she said.

The sun was just a flat red sliver over the Naval Observatory telescope when he stepped out to his waiting motorcade.

So many calls.

It seemed like every elected official across the United States wanted a word with the new president – or Acting President, as the official title decreed. Most of these conversations happened in three stages: a note of sympathy, a probing question or two about Granger's status, and a request for a favor.

Exhibit A: The Speaker of the House, Archie Cunningham.   "I always knew you'd be president eventually," the Speaker began, "and I'm damn proud, although I wish it were in better circumstances. My condolences to the president and his family, truly. I recognize this is a precarious time in our government, but it's reassuring to know an orderly transition has been made. I trust he's still in the same condition, with no improvements? Awful. Still, we must recognize that Granger picked a Conservative to succeed him, and that was his choice alone. As Acting President, I hope you'll consider the House's agenda sooner rather than later. While the media's attention is transfixed on the president's health, we can get a lot done together."

"He could wake up at any time, Mr. Speaker."

"Oh? Rumor had it he was at death's door."

"You might want to reconsider your sources."

"Elijah, that's precisely why I called."

The truth was, no one had any idea what had befallen the president. A million theories and twice as many rumors, but no answers. His vitals appeared normal and there were no indications of a stroke, seizure, heart attack, or other catastrophic internal injury. As Cassidy had described watching the first lady check his pupils, it was as if the light in his eyes was simply switched to a holding pattern. He was catatonic, but the doctors weren't even sure if labeling it a coma was appropriate.

As Elijah daydreamed, Cunningham was still prattling on the other end of the line. "You know, if you're looking for a steady partner in all this, I wouldn't be against switching to the Executive Branch. You'll need a vice president sooner than later, if only to have someone watch your back."

Elijah hung up politely and looked around the egg-shaped room of the president's Oval Office. All the doors were open, with agents holding sentry at their frames. Everyone was still on high alert – if they still had color-coded emergency designations, this would be code black.

Granger's aides came and went, professionals all, conducting their business while finding it difficult to look Elijah in the eye. He found himself repeating the same trite words of comfort to each of them.

He's a fighter, he'll be back soon. Until then, I hope we can work together.

"Me too," they'd respond, without an ounce of intonation. When they left, he could feel their whispers through the walls.

Elijah looked left at the empty office adjacent to the Oval, reserved for the president's Chief of Staff. Brian Ricketts had chosen to stay with the president at the hospital. Elijah thought of calling him in – Ricketts knew how to keep the West Wing operating to its fullest, and that was needed today more than ever – but thought better of it, at least for now. Still, Elijah felt foolish any time he asked a staffer their name, like an understudy in a play who hadn't learned his lines.

Though he wanted to pay a visit as soon as possible, the Secret Service told Elijah that a hospital trip had to wait until the next morning – they needed time to ensure extra perimeter security for both the president and his stand-in.

The day stretched into a hazy whirlwind. By the end, Elijah was pretty sure he'd talked to every last member of the federal government and half the foreign leaders around the world. But as the day closed, he took one last call, and it didn't come through the president's desk but to his personal pano.

"Mr. President," Vogel said, his accent peanut-butter thick, "I have results from the survey you requested. When will you be home?"

* * *

Elijah ate a late dinner with Cassidy in the Naval Observatory dining room. Rather than keep their normal places across the table, Cassidy pulled her chair around to one side, and they ate shoulder-to-shoulder as if sharing a restaurant booth. She leaned into him when the staff took their plates away. It reminded him of the days when he first ran for office, and they lived on takeout in a closet for an apartment. Back then, all they'd had were their ambitions and each other. It seemed to have come full circle.

He was proud of his first full day of work – calming the nation, staying principled, keeping his head in a crisis. He had it in him to be a uniting figure, if he could hold himself together first. Ironically, the prospect of the nation tearing itself apart helped him do just that.

"Anything new on his condition?"

"No changes."

"What happens if he just stays like this for days, for weeks? Longer?"

"I don't know, Cass, we just have to take it hour by hour." But he knew, once the shock wore off in the public mood, it would give way to something meaner. They'd be back to their trenches, as Granger liked to say, and with fresh ammunition. If Elijah couldn't keep the people appeased, there could be riots, bloodshed.

"I invited a friend to come over tonight."

"Who?"

"Yannik Vogel."

"Acton's Sponsor?" She pulled her head off him, startled. "Why would you ever do that?"

"I asked him to poll something for me. Something that could be big. What Theresa Larkin and I have been working on."

"It has to be now? Don't you see that as completely callous? God, what if word gets out?"

"It's something that could bring the country together."

"Jesus, Elijah, sometimes you come off like a goddamn robot. You don't see it at all, do you?"

"This began long before what happened yesterday. Remember Chicago?"

"Back in October? I remember you saying you saw him, after you lied to me."

"I never lied, Cass. I just kept it to myself."

"Same fucking thing, asshole. Don't remember what we agreed on? No secrets!"

"That's why I'm talking to you now."

He was talking to her back by this point, however, and her back was already gone from the room.

Elijah watched from the porch as the airpod tilted toward him in the night sky and slowly descended at the edge of the yard, same as before. Several agents formed a makeshift receiving line around the craft, and escorted Vogel to the house.

"You've made some new friends," Vogel said, coming up the steps. He'd come alone, a folder in his hand.

"A few changes since you were here last," Elijah admitted. He thought the Secret Service had been an intrusive burden before, now they felt suffocating. Still, they were charged with protecting his life; it was on him to live with it.

A fair exchange, once he weighed the variables.

"You know, I have yet to meet your lovely wife," Vogel said. "Is she home?"

"She is, but she's asleep. We were up pretty late last night." Truth was, Cassidy was probably staying up just to yell at him some more after Vogel left.

"That is...understandable," the German said. "I do appreciate you making such time for me in these circumstances. Your schedule must be overwhelmed."

"Tomorrow will be worse, I'm sure."

"I understand you will be visiting the president."

Elijah nodded as he led him into the house, two agents flanking the front door.

"You have done a fine job handling this crisis, according to all the reports," Vogel said. "No less than I would expect."

Elijah thanked him as they took the stairs to Nolan's room. When he reached for the door, an agent intervened.

"Sir, I can't let you in there with someone else without one of us present."

"What? This man and I met in there last week."

"You weren't the president then. It's a soundproof room. I need either visual contact or audio on you at all times."

"Yannik was the president's Sponsor."

"Which is why he was allowed to land on the premises. But different protocols apply for you at this time."

Elijah swallowed his annoyance. He'd wanted the soundproof room for a reason – even the most professional agent might leak word of a new Constitution being bandied about. "Here, take my pano. We'll link it to Mr. Vogel's and you'll have video. If you lose the connection or see something happen, the door's unlocked."

The agent took the pano grudgingly, and two other agents flanked behind him. Elijah opened the door for Vogel, who activated his own pano and propped it against the wall.

"Good?" Elijah asked the agent, allowing a nod before closing the door on him. He took a seat opposite Vogel. "I assume you muted that."

"Of course," the German said.

"All right, what do you have?"

"Well," Vogel said, "make room on Mt. Rushmore."

He opened his folder and was about to pour out its contents when Elijah held up a hand.

"Hold on. Something's been bothering me. When I visited your facility last fall, you told me about that project you were working on. The one with the panos? Wouldn't that make just about any candidate's election a slam dunk?"

"It certainly would, but the president did not see it that way. He asked that we no longer pursue it. And then he terminated our contract."

"Why?"

Vogel shrugged. "The president is softer than I realized. The attack on Ellis, it...affected him. His leadership, his assuredness, weakened. He's lost the will to win. Or, the will to do what's necessary to win."

Vogel unfurled the folder's contents. Elijah picked up a few sheets of data and studied them. "Jesus, eighty-three percent approval? You don't see that kind of popularity for ice cream."

"That is only the beginning," Vogel said. "Eighty-three percent for you, just from watching the news today. No advertisements necessary." He pushed another set of pages toward Elijah. "Eighty-six percent for your Convention Project."

"Holy smokes."

"The people are starving, Mr. Schroeder, for a new age of governance – one that reflects the times we live in. And, it would appear you are the man to take us there."

Elijah chewed on his bottom lip as he went through the data. More than once he checked the pano against the wall.

"There's a catch in here, has to be." He looked back at Vogel. "It would save some time if you just told me."

"Last time we spoke, I mentioned a payment. Endure Technologies would put its full support toward your candidacy. With the unconstrained capabilities from the pano project you mentioned, you could serve the remainder of this term and win two more. You would lead this country for a decade. Think of all the good you could accomplish in that time. All the history you would make. Why, you would be among this country's greatest leaders, remembered forever."

"If the president doesn't get better."

"That leads me to one little thing," Vogel said.

The German reached an open hand into his breast pocket. When he pulled it out, the hand was closed. "I'm holding onto something we call heartsbalm. When you visited our facility, you remarked that the silos housing our clients were warm – heartsbalm is the reason why. Freezing someone like a popsicle is somewhat barbaric, no? All it takes is this tiny capsule, administered once a week. The money we've saved! Such a tiny capsule. And how well it works – a perfect hibernation, until the next dose is needed."

As Vogel spoke, Elijah heard a clarity in his voice not apparent before. He no longer searched for his words. *He's practiced this speech.*

Elijah thought of President Granger – unconscious, in stasis. "Yannik, what have you done?"

But Vogel ignored him and continued. "In a large enough amount, the heartsbalm is lethal. I must admit, we underestimated the president's ability to fight it off. Maybe he's not so weak as I thought. We gave him double what we felt was needed. He should have died before he hit the floor."

"How...?"

Vogel shook his head – *Tsk-tsk.* "Do not concern yourself with the how. We got to him before. We could get to him again. I could say the same for you, though I would rather consider ourselves partners. And this situation creates an opportunity. We spoke of payment before, for our research. You will see the president tomorrow, yes? To cement that partnership, it would only take a second. You're a man who balances costs and benefits, are you not? A decade of peace for a moment of your time. And your idea of a new Constitution, so popular – it would make you the second father of this country."

Elijah looked at the pano again. God, he hoped it was on mute.

"Or," Vogel said, "you can stand by as Granger revives in a week.

Then, in next year's election, you watch as he loses the country to this Senator Cromwell."

A fog of silence hung over the room. The agents hadn't kicked down the door to break up their conspiracy, so the pano was indeed muted. As an extra precaution, Elijah found himself favoring the far side of his mouth when he talked, to avoid any aspiring lip readers in the Secret Service.

"Loss aversion," he said.

"I am sorry?"

Elijah did the calculations in his head. *People want to keep what they have more than they want to gain something they don't.* Now that he was the commander in chief, the thought of going back to the vice presidency pained him. If hadn't spent the last day as president, would he even consider taking the capsule?

He thought of Cassidy and her newfound passion. He thought of Tess and the Convention Project. He thought of Jordan Cromwell – and of collapse. Ruin. War. The country couldn't go back to that.

"Loss aversion," he said again. With Civ-2's horrors in America's past and a new era of peace begun, wasn't that worth preserving beyond anything else? Were he to win the presidency, Cromwell could destroy it all.

Elijah looked at the pano against the wall once more, silently filming. Then he looked at Vogel. "I'm going to shake your hand," he said slowly. It sounded almost comical coming out one side of his mouth. "And you'll give me the capsule."

Vogel tried to hide the broad relief breaking across his face, but he'd been sweating. It's not every day you suggest treason. He reached out his hand.

"This nation needs leadership, Mr. President. You're the only man who can provide it."

The hospital hallway felt a mile long.

He walked with Cassidy at his side, a cavalry of agents and aides at their backs. The entire floor had been closed off for one patient, but dozens of hospital staff were required to attend to him. The president's inner circle orbited the waiting area – Elijah spotted Ricketts in the corner, glowering into a Styrofoam coffee cup as he listlessly paced.

The capsule felt heavy in his pocket – it was just a few grams in weight, but it seemed to throw his balance off. Still, he'd slept a dreamless sleep last night. No falling leaves or anything else.

A moment, versus a decade.

Or, Elijah considered – *One life, for millions.*

It was a classic example of the human behavior model. Altruism – the philosophy that individuals work toward a common good, their contributions continually bettering society. He was a spoke in a wheel – but right now, the only spoke that could keep the wheel from collapsing.

Several agents flanked the door at the end of the hall, along with two marines in full regalia. Elijah hadn't spotted Susannah Granger, figuring she must be in with her husband.

To his right, the hall opened into a nurse's station. A PanoScreen was mounted on the counter, a couple of doctors and an agent monitoring it. The screen showed the president in repose, holographic vitals projected over his chest. Susannah sat at his side, knitting. Elijah studied the angle and bent his ear toward the screen to check for sound. He didn't hear the jangling of her needles – muted, likely at the first lady's request.

Elijah was surprised that no one stepped forward to receive him or his party. He scanned around the room, spotting the president's physician. He approached him as the entourage behind him scattered, except for Cassidy. "Hey, Mark," Elijah said, shaking the physician's hand. "What's the latest?"

"Same, I'm afraid. He was fine through the night, vitals steady. Couple blips here and there, he's got a bit of a cough. I wish I could say more. It's *like* a coma, but who just goes into a coma for no reason? I can't figure it out."

Elijah shook his head solemnly. "Has anyone considered foul play?" he asked.

"We'd be remiss not to," the physician said. "If only we could find a sign. Forty years in the field, never seen a thing like it."

Next to him, Cassidy had already begun wiping away tears. She looked at Elijah in sorrow – he could sense the guilt she felt in her private exuberance at his promotion. She was heartbroken to see this up close. Her presidential dirty talk would end here.

"I'd like to see Susannah," Cassidy said to him.

"Let me go in first, I'll send her out."

His wife nodded in agreement. Elijah turned to the door. He looked appreciatively at the agents and saluted the two marines. The door was opened for him and he walked in.

Susannah Granger looked up at Elijah with a mournful smile. She set aside her needlework – the blanket she'd been working on looked nearly finished – and stood.

"Hello, Mr. President," she said.

"Don't say that, Suze. How is he?"

Her composure snapped like a matchstick and she immediately erupted into tears. "I wish I knew!" she sobbed. He took her hand and waited patiently for her to recover. She grabbed a tissue off the nightstand next to a stack of sympathy cards. "Elijah, listen to me. Officially, no one's dared to mention any kind of conspiracy, but I know this man better than anyone – not just as his wife but as his doctor. He is healthy as an ox. Somebody did something to him, I just know it." She started to pace around the room. "They think it might be neurological. They've been wanting to open his head up, get a look inside his brain. A craniotomy. I just don't know what could happen, Eli. I mean, it's risky, but..." she broke off in another fit of sobs, losing her breath.

Elijah knew what it was like to cry like that. Susannah inhaled deeply, and then she thrust an arm out to him, gripping his shoulder in a vise. She stared at him intently, blinking like Cassidy would when begging the truth out of him.

"Elijah, please – swear to me on all you hold dear, on your life, on Cassidy's." He reeled – *If she mentions the kids, I'm going to break.* Mercifully, she omitted them. "Swear to me that you know nothing about this."

"Susannah, I swear."

She appraised him thoroughly, as if taking mental x-rays of his body. "All right," she said at last. "I'm sorry to even think it, but with all the crazy theories flying around, I had to ask. The fact that you're in a different League..."

"It's fine. I understand."

"Some people still think there's a war going on, you know? And you can't always tell who."

"Some hatchets never bury," Elijah said, then felt stupid for saying it.

"Exactly," Susannah said, then was quiet. The ping of Acton's heart monitor became the room's only sound.

"Cassidy is here. She brought something she wanted to give you."

"That's sweet of her."

Ping, ping, ping, went the heart monitor. Elijah looked to the president, his own heart doing three beats to Granger's every one.

"Did you want a moment?" Susannah asked. "I could use a break."

"Thank you, if you don't mind."

Susannah turned and headed for the door.

"Wait," he said. She stopped, swiveling around expectantly in a neat pirouette. *Even now, she looks like a goddamn movie star*, he thought. "Back at the AllenCo Center, I kissed you and you kissed back. Why?"

She visibly cringed, as if he'd just told her he came from Pluto. "Elijah, what the fuck? You're asking this *now*?"

"Please, it's just something I need to know."

She shook her head in disbelief, then looked to Granger. "I did just ask if you tried to kill my husband, maybe you're entitled a completely bonkers question to even things out. But Jesus, Eli, I don't know. Pity? Loneliness? Curiosity? I mean, no marriage is perfect, but—"

"Okay, I'm sorry, it's fine. Enough."

"I'll be outside." Her eyes lingered on him in a way Elijah might interpret as accusatory, and he felt her x-ray scanning him again. But then she exited, closing the door behind her.

Elijah moved quickly, coming around the bed and situating himself at an angle to block the PanoCam. He sat in Susannah's chair, pulling it closer. He reached for the heartsbalm in his pocket, cupping it carefully – the capsule rolled around in his palm. He leaned forward, then back, indecisive. How small it was! All he had to do was set it on his lips and give it a slight push.

His breath grew heavy and he felt a sharp pain in his lungs. Perspiration beaded above his pores. He just needed to reach out his arm, why wouldn't it move?

Rocking back and forth, smelling his own sweat, a paralyzing thought occurred to him: *If the capsule dissolves in saliva, what about sweat?* He panicked, then, reaching for a tissue on the nightstand to wipe his hands. Clumsily, he knocked over the adjacent stack of cards.

Fucking hell.

Elijah reached down for the cards, using his capsule-free hand to push them into a pile before picking them up. Why did this feel familiar?

Suddenly, a spasm of electricity coursed through him, seizing his mind and body. His subconscious memory surged forward, like an incoming tide at midnight, and he experienced for a second time the worst day of his life.

* * *

"Let me out! Let me out!" Nolan banged fruitlessly against the window.

"You know the drill," Elijah said, looking up from his PanoPad in the third-row seat. "Wait for Dwight."

Dwight D'Amato rolled out of the driver's seat and came around to the passenger door.

"These safety locks are bullshit," Nolan said.

"Language!" Elijah chided. "It's a government vehicle – they have regulations that don't always make sense. But your sisters don't need to hear you cursing."

"Eh, they're not listening," Nolan said. He wasn't wrong. Next to Nolan in the second row, Charlotte was bopping her head, her earbuds endlessly repeating the latest Teen Dream song, and Ellie was absorbed in her pano game, feeding coins to some horrid-looking elephant creature. She sat next to her father in the back, but he could be a thousand miles away and she likely wouldn't notice.

Dwight pulled open the safety-locked door and let Nolan out.

"Have a great day at school, kiddo. Say hey to Allie for me."

"Sure thing, Dad," Nolan said reflexively. "Hey, maybe tonight we can talk to mom about that thing?"

Elijah pictured Cassidy's reaction. *My son, in the Marines? Have both of you LOST YOUR MINDS?* It wouldn't be pleasant, but maybe with the war winding down and a properly presented argument, she could be turned.

"Yeah, okay," Elijah said. "Maybe if we show her how good you are at *Civil Discord*, she'll come around."

"Dad, you know you can just borrow that sometime if you want to play it so bad."

Nolan wouldn't understand, but Elijah didn't care much for the *Civil* series, though the graphics and gameplay were admittedly incredible. He would play the most boring, derivative game out there if it meant time with his son. Especially as Nolan was about to leave home.

"See you after school," Elijah said.

"Almost forgot, we're getting out early for Remembrance Day. An assembly after lunch, and then we're done."

"Is that for your sisters, too?"

"Yep, all three schools."

"You tell Dwight?"

Nolan looked to Dwight, who shrugged. "Just did," Nolan said.

"All right, I'll catch you at home."

Nolan nodded back, shutting the door behind him. He shuffled quickly along the automated sidewalk to the front steps of his school, Allie waiting for him. They disappeared together inside.

Rensselaer High School wasn't the most renowned educational institution in Albany, but Elijah had insisted on public schooling for his children so they grew up as normally as possible. There was also some politicking involved – Cassidy would rather they attend something private, or at least on their side of the river, but Rensselaer was a blue-collar district that Elijah wanted seen as embracing. As a wonky economist, hardscrabble New Yorkers weren't his most reliable constituency, and he wanted to reach out.

Dwight returned behind the wheel and they rolled to the next drop-off. Rensselaer Middle was just down the street, but Elijah always wanted to get a word in with Charlie in the short commute. He nudged her shoulder.

She pulled out her earbuds mournfully. *So much angst in everything she does*, Elijah thought. *Who knew a life of privilege could be so difficult?*

"What?" Charlotte snapped, her impatience visible.

"I wanted to know what you've got going on in school."

"We're doing astronomy in science class. Planets and the solar system and all that."

"Ah. Sounds exciting."

"It's all right. We're really getting our asses kicked in the space race, did you know that?"

"Language!"

"But the Chinese are—"

Almost mercifully, Dwight parked and scuttled around to open the passenger door.

"Good luck in school, Charlie. Love you."

"Yeah, bye, Dad."

Charlotte disappeared into the mess of adolescent bodies, all enraptured by their panos as they stood on the automated causeway ushering them to the school's front door. Elijah found it an odd behavioral quirk that children in this rebellious phase were the most likely to conform with one another. They moved as part of a singular mass, like a centipede with pre-teens for legs.

Dwight pulled out of the drop-off. Rensselaer Elementary was the last stop, a little farther down the same road. The other advantage of having the kids in these schools was that they were all in a tidy row, like their bedrooms at the mansion.

Ellie nudged him in the side. "Help?" She dropped the pano in his lap.

"What's up? Who's this little guy?"

"That's Mookie the Coin Monster. I need to give him exactly six dollars and eighty-three cents."

"Okay. Well I think you need one of these," he said, dropping in a five-dollar coin. The elephant-thing wolfed it down and rubbed his belly. "It's best to start with the highest amount and work your way down." He fed Mookie a dollar coin, then three quarters. "Here you go, Bubbles. See if you can get the rest."

"Thanks, Dad!"

They pulled up to the school. Dwight came around a third time as he pressed a button on his pano, and the second-row seats tucked themselves into the floor. Dwight let Ellie out as she tugged on her oversized backpack, waved to her father once, then scurried over to a group of friends.

"Love you!" Elijah called, then moved forward as the second-row seats came back up.

"Ready, boss?" Dwight asked, settling back behind the wheel.

Elijah nodded. Dwight pulled out and then took the access road to get back onto Route 90, heading west. They ran into traffic the moment they reached the Patroon Island Bridge, which crossed the Hudson River and would take them to downtown Albany.

Cassidy took the kids to school most days, but Elijah insisted on accompanying them once or twice a week. That was a major reason why he'd left his seat in Congress and run for governor, even if it meant moving upstate. Long Island was too close to the war, anyway. And the kids seemed to like arriving in the governor's car – it impressed their friends, riding in a miniature tank.

Dwight inched them forward across the bridge, orange barrels forcing them to merge into a single lane.

"Traffic with this bridge construction is getting worse all the time," Elijah observed. A crane was loading girders to his left, taking up half the bridge.

"Someone should alert the governor," Dwight responded.

"Construction equals progress, so I've been told. Unless you're stuck in it."

"Want me to flip on the sirens?"

"Nah, it's fine. But turn on the news, will you?"

The top story this morning was the same as it always was, for as long as Elijah could remember – an update on the war. Now, though, a degree of optimism colored the reporter's voice, as if they were perhaps at the beginning of the end of this national nightmare.

The Majority Coalition appears to have the boroughs of New York City surrounded, and they are closing in. It could only be a matter of time before the Underground succumbs to pressure and lays down their arms, but they are well entrenched in this and several other major cities.

In his daily update from the feds, Elijah knew that the end might even be closer than that. Special forces were deploying in Chicago, Los Angeles, and most importantly San Francisco in a coordinated offensive. They were looking to flush out the resistance in all the major hotspots at once, effectively breaking their backs.

They reached the other side of the bridge, pulling to the first exit – 787 South, which would lead them straight through town and back to the Governor's Mansion.

It turned out to be a relatively uneventful morning at the office, with Elijah mostly keyed on news either from the PanoNets or his federal sources. He met with several Girl Scout troops, had lunch with a few State Legislators he was trying to lean on for local tax reform, and worked on a speech to the American Legion next week.

Then, just after noon, the door burst open. His assistant, in a panic.

"You need to take this call," she said.

Elijah picked up his desktop pano.

"Eli, it's Roger."

It was a voice Elijah immediately recognized. "Mr. President. What can I—"

"Goddamn media, somebody leaked our operation. The Underground knew we were coming. They're fighting back in the other cities, but in New York they didn't have the numbers. So they ditched."

"Ditched? Where?"

"They tried to go through the bay to the ocean, but the blockade turned them around. Now they're moving upriver. They're coming up the Hudson, Eli – maybe to get to Canada, or hide in the mountains, who knows. But they're headed your way."

"Holy Christ."

"They're moving fast, but we've got some National Guard units nearby. We'll have them positioned on opposite sides of the river. We might have time to set up another blockade."

"What do you need from me?"

"Call the local authorities, get them to clear out as many people as we can. We need police, fire, EMTs at the ready. At a safe distance, but ready."

"Yes, Mr. President."

"Do it quickly. When they get within twenty miles, we're going to drop a blackout. This time, they won't see us coming. You won't have any digital comms except on our encrypted military channels. Have someone tell the media so they don't freak out, but tell them it's a drill."

"Yes, Mr. President."

He heard a sigh over the phone. "It might really be over, Eli. God willing, this could be it. Someone will patch you in to your military liaison for the rest of the details."

The pano went silent.

Could it be true, the war at an end? Something that seemed so far away, that might never come, really here?

The liaison came on the line, Commander Gorsky, and relayed the necessary specifics. Afterward, Elijah made his calls – the Albany police chief, fire chief, the head of the State Reserves, directors of emergency personnel. He instructed his communications team to alert the local media, but to stress it was a drill.

In a blink, it was twenty past two. School would be letting out soon. He called Dwight.

"Hey, boss."

"Dwight? When you pick up the kids, head east. You hear me?"

"What's that?"

"Pick them up and go east! Get out of Albany! Understand?"

"Boss, we're already on the bridge. School's out early – Remembrance Day, remember? 'Cept everything is stopped for some reason. Some military trucks just passed me, dunno what's going on."

Elijah's heart jumped through his chest. "Dwight, get off the bridge! Get off the bridge!"

The line went dead. As did all the power. The military had dropped the blackout.

Elijah bolted from his office, screaming for a car. Driving up from the south, it took just three minutes to get to the access ramp leading onto the bridge. After that, there was nowhere to go. He jumped from the car and bolted up to the edge of the bridge. Two walking tanks were already positioning themselves in the construction area and multiple military trucks were mounting their guns. He heard hoverjets from somewhere, but didn't see them – they must be standing by in the clouds.

He looked down the river. He could see the water trails before anything else, jets of vapor spewing fifty feet in the air. Elijah counted about twenty skeeters, streaking toward them in a spear formation. They were easily recognizable by their sloping nosecones. Skeeters held about forty people each in their bullet-shaped fuselages, their noses stretching out and dipping into the water in front of them – they didn't hover so much as create a seam with the nose and plow through the opening.

As the skeeters came within range, an order was given and the shores on each side opened fire, assailing the river between them. Sure enough, the hoverjets dropped into view, showering missiles, great plumes of water erupting where they landed. But the boats kept coming, their nosecones spiraling like drill-bits, and they dove beneath the water like submarine torpedoes.

Elijah kept running up the gradient and onto the bridge. He spotted his governor's car some two hundred yards ahead, hemmed into a single line of traffic by the crane and an army of assault vehicles, with no room to maneuver. A mini-tank, he'd always thought of his state car, but how small it looked compared to the real thing.

The actual tanks on the bridge began to fire down-river as the skeeters kept coming. Civilians were streaming from their vehicles and started running Elijah's direction in panic. He saw Dwight hop out of the driver's door, bee-lining towards him.

No! The safety locks!

Dwight made it five steps before he seemed to hear him, turning back. Elijah could picture Nolan banging fruitlessly on the window, begging to be let out.

The skeeters were firing on the bridge; Elijah ducked as he ran. A shell ripped into the framework of the construction crane and it began to tip over, metal supports whining as they folded in half. The top of the crane fell onto the asphalt between Elijah and his children, but the bridge held.

The tanks went silent as the skeeters reached the bridge, trailing underwater like salmon on their summer run. Dwight had reached the passenger door, yanking it open. Charlotte came first, then Nolan, carrying Ellie.

Elijah continued racing toward them, the air becoming thick with grit and smoke from the artillery. His lungs were fire. As the skeeters swam underneath, the tanks swiveled their cannons full around in precise unison, training their aim upstream. Once the skeeters became visible on the other side, they resumed launching shells.

Elijah was now well out over the Hudson. The skeeters were to his left, weaving in evasive maneuvers as they darted away. Two took direct hits from the tanks, their wreckage spinning out from bank to bank. The others cleared their debris and tightened into a diamond.

One boat dropped back from the others, drawing fire to let the remainder escape.

Elijah kept running. Almost there. Almost there. "Come on! RUN!" he shouted, but couldn't hear his own voice.

A hatch opened from the back of the final skeeter. Three floating orbs emerged, glowing green like plasma bubbles. They bobbed in the air a moment, marking their surroundings. Once calibrated, they shot toward the Patroon Island Bridge.

Elijah saw them coming. His body seized up and froze, and he watched helplessly as the plasma grenades disappeared into the middle of the bridge in front of him.

The world became awash in green fire. A wall of expanding air pummeled against Elijah's chest and ran into his lungs. He was picked up and hurtled backward like a cannonball. Flying over a hundred feet, his legs collided with a concrete barrier and he tumbled over it, somersaulting blindly down an embankment, limbs flailing.

He came to a stop flat on his back at the bottom. It took a moment before he dared to open his eyes again, and the only thing he could see were trees, blocking out an orange sky. The trees were shaking as if they'd been pulled down, let go, and were just snapping back into place.

Cymbals clashed in his eardrums, making it impossible to hear. Above him, thousands of leaves fluttered everywhere, like feathers in a soundless wind. They fell toward him, collecting on his body. Already, they were browning and brittle, and smelled of ashes.

It hurt to blink, as if his eyeballs were fire. A leaf slid into his mouth, stuck in his throat, and he began coughing in violent silence. The convulsions brought forth pain.

He might have lain there for hours, or a minute, he didn't know. The leaves continued falling but he could not move, and gradually he became entombed in foliage.

Elijah tried shouting but only managed an inaudible croak. His hearing began to return, however, and it sounded like voices, but muffled and far away as if from the wrong end of a megaphone. Then out of nowhere, two pairs of muscular hands reached down and pulled him from his leafy shroud, sliding a stretcher underneath him.

He lost consciousness after that.

Elijah didn't wake until nearly midnight. Miraculously, he'd come away with minor injuries – if a handful of broken bones, bronchial damage, and a severe concussion can all be considered minor. But everything inside him had shattered.

A delivery drone swooped in and out, dropping off flowers, cards, other trinkets of compassion. Elijah refused to acknowledge them, as if they cemented the reality of what brought him here.

The drone was running out of room to put things. It swerved toward his nightstand and dropped down a teetering stack of cards. As the drone retreated, the top few to the floor. Elijah cursed as he leaned over the bed to pick them up, his body protesting.

The top card was half-open, as if beckoning to be read. Elijah saw a scribbled note from a hand he didn't recognize. He picked it up. It was only a few short, simple words.

Elijah, All my heart. I mourn with you, brother. – AG

AG? Who was that? He turned the card over and saw it postmarked with a North Dakota address, but nothing else.

The handwriting, of course, was all too familiar now. The little loop at the bottom of each *y*, the bit of slant in crossing the *t*'s. He'd gotten so many of these notes in the past two-and-a-half years, he could forge Granger's script from memory.

All my heart.

Elijah looked at the stack of cards he'd hastily piled on the nightstand. There were hundreds. He grabbed the top one and opened it carefully.

Mister President,
Please get well soon, you are the bestest president and I hope
you feel better right this minute! I was sick on my birthday

*and my mom gave me some medicine and it made everything
ok, maybe she can come over and help you feel better too.
– Love, Sarah Watkins
P.S. I'm ten now!*

Elijah read the card once, twice, a third time. *This is what my Ellie
would sound like at her age.*

He realized absently that his left hand was balled into a fist. The
heartsbalm! A moment of panic flushed through him – *Did it
dissolve?* – as he opened his hand. The capsule remained intact.

He stared at it. Such a little thing, the size of a bead. But how it
called to him.

The first time he'd met Acton Granger, the two men debated in
front of a hundred million people. There were other candidates on
the stage, as all the four major Leagues qualified, but by then it was
really a two-man race. Elijah had been encouraged by his aides to
lay into Granger, to question his sympathies during Civ-2, to paint
him as a tacit Underground sympathizer. He'd demurred and lost
any chance of winning the election.

Granger's gargantuan figure looked bigger lying down, somehow.
Elijah watched him breathe, his inhales slow and deliberate. His
eyes fluttered as if in the midst of a dream.

And as he regarded the man, peacefully dormant, Vogel's
predictions of an apocalyptic future dimmed.

Whatever happens, Elijah thought, *we can take down Cromwell
together.* He gave the capsule one last glance before tucking it back
in his pocket. He grabbed Sarah Watkins' card, silently apologizing
as he tore away a blank portion, and pulled out a pen.

*Acton,
All my heart. As your words once consoled me, I hope mine
might do the same. Honored to be considered your brother.
– ES*

He put it in the stack, just under Sarah's.
A brother I don't deserve, he thought.

Some minutes later, a knock rapped at the door. Susannah poked
her head in. "Elijah, are you all right? The press is waiting."

"Yes. My statement. I know. I was just reading..." he held up a
card. By now, he'd gone through several stacks and they surrounded
him on the floor in little mounds.

Susannah stepped into the room and closed the door behind her.

"He is so beloved," she said. "It constantly amazes me. I worry about our country all the time, but when I see all this..." She stopped herself from sobbing again.

Elijah struggled to get up, and they stood together, watching Granger.

"He'll pull through," Elijah said. "He's a bear, like you say. Or a lion."

"I wish I had your optimism. I just can't allow myself to hope at this point."

Elijah turned to her slightly, but tried to keep his tone casual. "Tell me something. Do you know anything about a company called Endure Technologies?"

Susannah scratched her head. "I've met Mr. Vogel as my husband's Sponsor, of course, but I don't know much about his company. Ad testing, polling, that sort of thing." Her eyes turned suspicious. "Why would you ask?"

"I heard they'd been let go."

Susannah bit her lip, as if thinking something but afraid to put it into words. Her eyes closed, reopened again. She risked it. "Yes. Mr. Vogel told Acton he wouldn't win if you stayed on the ticket. And my husband fired him."

What? Elijah was dumbstruck. He gaped at Susannah until he realized she was studying his reaction. How would she expect him to take this bit of news? Hurt? Shocked? Grateful?

Is she even telling me the truth? Vogel had to lie to one of us, but which one?

Susannah paced, thinking out loud. "Mr. Vogel did a lot for my husband. But if you think there's something there..."

"No, no, of course not. I just wanted to know why he'd gotten rid of Vogel if he was so useful the last time." He forced a self-deprecating laugh. "I guess I have my answer."

Elijah offered nothing further, worried that with any more words Susannah would see through him, catch his tell. But her eyes never left her husband. "He said he'd look after you, Eli. Acton keeps his word."

"Granger's a good one, Susannah. In our business, that's so goddamn rare."

"I know it."

"I'm just...so sorry. About everything."

She nodded, finally looking up, curiosity behind her eyes. Did she suspect him more than she was letting on?

But all she said was, "Thank you."

"It's going to be all right, really. He'll wake up in no time. And when he does, tell him I'll do anything he wants. I'll resign, whatever it takes. The important thing is he wins another term. Cromwell..."

He realized he was rambling. Susannah's attention had reverted to her husband, as it always seemed to do. "Of course," she said absently.

The room settled into silence. *Ping, ping, ping,* went the heart monitor. Elijah's heart seemed to be matching it now.

He checked the clock; he was an hour late for his statement. "Holy smokes, I've gotta go," he said.

Susannah snapped back to the moment, reached out and took his hand. "Let me come with you. Lend my support in public. With all these crazy theories going around, even the PanoNets are throwing crap at the wall. Let me do my part. If he doesn't get better..."

The heartsbalm felt so heavy he thought it might pull him through the floor. He patted his jacket coat without thinking.

"He'll get better. But that's very kind," he said.

She reached out and embraced him. Elijah shifted subtly to the side, making sure it wasn't too tight that she might feel the small protrusion in his coat pocket.

When he opened the door, he was struck by how bright everything was – such a contrast to the muted lighting in Granger's room. Incandescence blinded him from every angle, and he squinted like a newborn.

Two agents immediately flanked him, moving with each step he and Susannah took. Two others took their positions behind, to remain at Granger's door.

As he adjusted to the light, he spotted Cassidy talking to one of the president's senior aides. She came over and reached a sisterly hand to Susannah. Elijah wondered what they talked about while he'd been in with the president.

"Remember," Cassidy said to the first lady, "we're here for you, alright? Anything you need."

Susannah nodded. Elijah retreated a half-step, watching the two women interact. They regarded each other with hands interlaced, speaking in expressions instead of words. Elijah wished he understood their feminine vernacular.

An aide stepped forward. "Mr. President, everyone's waiting." Elijah felt himself both nodding and shaking his head in response.

"Um...yes, of course. Ladies?"

He took a few disjointed steps forward, vaguely realizing that about two dozen people were falling into step behind him. As a group, they moved down the hall, both women to his right, still clutching each other.

A row of doctors and nurses stood at attention ahead of them.

"One second, everyone," Elijah said, stopping. He met the first doctor and shook his hand. "Thanks for all your effort," he told him. "I know you're doing all you can."

The doctor nodded, grateful but businesslike. Elijah worked his way down the row like a rope line, thanking each in turn.

He came to a woman at the end. She wore a surgical mask, pulled down just below her chin, her hair balled up in a tight ballerina bun.

"Thanks for all—" As he saw her eyes, he nearly felt the heartsbalm capsule jump from his coat pocket, expelled by the force of his heart punching against his chest.

He froze, still gripping her hand. The irises of her eyes were whitish-blue like icicle spokes, brighter even in the hospital light.

"I'm...sorry, doctor, I didn't catch your name?"

"Meijer. Rebecca Meijer. I'm a surgeon here, Mr. President."

She offered a kindly smile, blinking once. Elijah let go of her. "Of course you are," he said. "Well. I know you're doing all you can."

She nodded sweetly, a stark contrast in her character from last fall.

Elijah vaguely realized that a throng of people were staring at him, hinging on his next move. How Vogel had outclassed him! He was boxed in, beaten, and yet he couldn't show it. In his breast pocket, the capsule tugged at him – he wanted shove it in Dr. Meijer's grinning mouth and hold his hand over it until she stopped breathing. A million calculations flashed through his economist's mind – actions and reactions, behaviors and consequences. All of them ended in the same result. What would it mean, to be convicted of treason? Would they hang him from the top of the Washington Monument? Would he face a firing squad, perhaps riddled to shreds by those new light weapons?

He took a shallow breath, turning to both Cassidy and Susannah. Cassidy shot him a look – *Coming?*

And what else could he do? It was the only behavior that didn't result in his arrest and execution. Meijer was Vogel's insurance; the

German had played his hand well. How long until she'd know that he hadn't performed as instructed? How long before she did what he couldn't?

He felt like a driver in an Automated Vehicle – the left lane was open ahead, and he had no control over the wheel.

All openings had to be filled, some way or another. That was how altruism worked.

Make room on Mt. Rushmore, he thought, and nearly choked.

Then: *No! You have to stop her!*

His thoughts rattled like cathedral bells, but he felt a leg lifting off the linoleum, taking a hesitant step toward his wife. The other leg followed. The pack of agents and aides surrounding him fell into step, a spear formation with he at its tip.

From behind, he dully heard Meijer speaking to a colleague. "Let's get another blood sample in an hour," she was saying. "I'd like to run some tests."

Still walking, Elijah swiveled his head back toward the doctor. Meijer was still facing him even as she talked. She smiled again – no sweetness in it, this time – tapping at her lab coat's breast pocket.

But on he walked, with momentum now, as if propelled by the rest of the spear behind him, pushing him to the waiting lift tube, to giving his statement, to being President of the United States.

He entered the lift tube and turned. Meijer's figure had dwindled to a point at the end of the hall, continuing to watch him.

Stop, he wanted to shout, as the doors began to close. In his narrowing vantage, Meijer pivoted, walking away to rejoin her medical team.

Stop!

STOP!

But the doors continued closing, until they sealed shut at last.

Book Two

Coming June 2018

Available for Pre-Order April 2018

ACKNOWLEDGMENTS

This story has been a long time coming, and wouldn't be possible without the love and support of a lot of people. Those who inspire aren't always aware of the spark they lit in someone else, so I'll try to spell them out here.

I'd like to thank my parents, all three of them, for their guidance and love. I wasn't the easiest child to raise, so above all I appreciate your patience with me – hopefully some good came out of all those times I didn't do my homework.

I'd like to thank my grandmother, June Merritt, for always sharing my old stories and encouraging me to put words to paper. Where you are I hope it's always Christmas.

I'd like to thank my uncle/twin brother, Randall Merritt (aka Big R, aka Ol' Rand-o), for his feedback and support on this project. To both you and Lori, I appreciate you letting me hang out in your basement all those years.

I'd like to thank all my early readers for their notes, especially Tom Crable.

I'd like to thank you, the reader, for taking a chance on this book by picking it up – I hope it was worth your while and that you'll stick around for the next installments, as there's much of this story yet to tell.

And finally, I'd like to thank my wife, Jenny, who amazes me every day. There was my life before I met you, and my life after, and one pales in comparison to the other. I don't know what else to say other than I love you and you're the best thing that ever happened to me.

Scott McDermott
2/16/16-2/12/17

ABOUT THE AUTHOR

Scott McDermott lives with his wife and two furballs in Virginia Beach. You can reach him on Twitter @DudeWhoWrites.

11793888R00177

Made in the USA
Lexington, KY
16 October 2018